PRAISE FOR
THE NOVELS OF WATERVALLEY

EACH SHINING HOUR

"Heartwarming, refreshing, and often amusing, this touching novel about a likable yet conflicted new doctor sent to a rural Tennessee town is a rare gem. A bustling medical practice, a budding romance, and a passel of small-town dramas make this a rich read, but a decades-old murder mystery adds the icing on the cake. The pristine setting and lovable characters will make readers search for Watervalley, Tennessee, on a map and plan a visit."

—Karen White, *New York Times* bestselling author of
A Long Time Gone

"A young doctor, marking time until he can leave a somnolent farm town for the bustle of a big city, finds more excitement in Watervalley than he bargained for—an alluring woman, or two; an unsolved murder, or two; a crafty banker who knows more than he's saying; and a cache of . . . well, I'll let you find that out. *Each Shining Hour* kept me reading far into the night hours!"

—Ann B. Ross, *New York Times* bestselling author of the
Miss Julia series and *Etta Mae's Worst Bad-Luck Day*

"Come back to Watervalley for another endearing tale of Dr. Luke Bradford and the good folks of this small Tennessee town. Heartwarming and tender, *Each Shining Hour* is a bright and lovely story."

—Lynne Branard, author of *The Art of Arranging Flowers*

continued . . .

MORE THINGS IN HEAVEN AND EARTH

"Told through the eyes of Dr. Luke Bradford, a newly minted MD, the story of the little town of Watervalley, Tennessee, and its inhabitants comes vividly to life. Jeff High's medical background gives him that cutting edge in the technical details of his tale, and his love of his native Tennessee and the human race shines from every page. Dr. Fingal Flahertie O'Reilly is delighted to welcome Luke, a transatlantic colleague to be fiercely proud of."

—Patrick Taylor, MD, *New York Times* bestselling author of
the Irish Country novels

"The best of small-town Americana and the eccentrics who live there is brought to life in *More Things in Heaven and Earth*. This story warmed me, made me laugh, and then kept a smile on my face. It's delightful, compassionate, humorous, tightly woven. If you're looking for a feel-good read, spend an afternoon with Jeff High's novel."

—Charles Martin, *New York Times* bestselling author of
Unwritten and *When Crickets Cry*

"A well-spun story of the mystery and microcosm that is small-town America. Jeff High skillfully captures the healing places, the hurting places, and the places where we so often find out who we are truly meant to be."

—Lisa Wingate, national bestselling author of
Tending Roses and *The Prayer Box*

Books in the Watervalley Series

More Things in Heaven and Earth

Each Shining Hour

EACH SHINING HOUR

A NOVEL OF WATERVALLEY

JEFF HIGH

 New American Library

New American Library
Published by the Penguin Group
Penguin Group (USA) LLC, 375 Hudson Street,
New York, New York 10014

USA | Canada | UK | Ireland | Australia | New Zealand | India | South Africa | China
penguin.com
A Penguin Random House Company

First published by New American Library,
a division of Penguin Group (USA) LLC

First Printing, October 2014

 REGISTERED TRADEMARK—MARCA REGISTRADA

LIBRARY OF CONGRESS CATALOGING-IN-PUBLICATION DATA:
High, Jeff, 1957–
Each shining hour: a novel of watervalley/Jeff High.
p. cm.
ISBN 978-0-451-41927-9
1. Physicians—Fiction. 2. Man-woman relationships—Fiction.
3. Small cities—fiction. I. Title.
PS3608.I368E23 2014
813'.6—dc23 2014017235

Printed in the United States of America
3 5 7 9 10 8 6 4 2

Set in Adobe Garamond
Designed by Spring Hoteling

This book is dedicated to my father-in-law,
Lloyd George Hartly Bardowell.

A gentle servant of God and man,
he never failed to give his best to each shining hour.

How doth the little busy Bee
Improve each shining Hour
And gather Honey all the day
From every opening Flower. . . .
In Books, or Work, or healthful Play,
Let my first Years be passed,
That I may give for every Day
Some good Account at last.

—"How Doth the Little Busy Bee" by Isaac Watts

And the floors shall be full of wheat,
And the vats shall overflow with new wine and oil.
I will restore to you the years that the locust hath eaten.

—Joel 2:24–25

EACH SHINING HOUR

PRELUDE

Watervalley, Tennessee

April 28, 1944

*T*he grass was taller here, moist and cool in the dark April night, only a few sloping steps away from the road. He would rest for a while, keeping his hand pressed firmly over the small bullet hole above his right hip. But the handkerchief . . . the handkerchief was getting soaked.

"It must have been a low-caliber pistol," he whispered. "Perhaps a twenty-two." It was only a small wound, barely penetrating the soft tissue.

He had been running. His suit was drenched with sweat. As he lay in the fresh, delicate grass, steam rose from him and drifted elusively into the soft air. He breathed in great heaving gasps, staring up into the vast, silent sky, an eternal canopy pulsing with a million radiant stars.

It was the telegram. He had come back for the telegram. He'd thought it was with everything else. But when he'd buried the box, he hadn't found it.

In his agony, he whispered softly: "Oh Elise; dear, precious Elise." He would tell her everything. Explain everything. His mind drifted.

His eyes wanted to close. Then, down the far reaches of the road toward town, he heard the long, slow wail of a police siren. He stiffened. His thoughts raced. They were coming. Someone at one of the farmhouses must have heard the gunshot. He flattened himself deeper into the tall grass.

The car blew past, flying headlong toward the lake and stopping in the distance, the headlights pouring across the bandstand. No one had seen him. He would have to wait before moving again.

Once more he stared briefly into the infinite heavens. But now the stars were fading. "Elise; darling, beloved Elise. I will . . . I will tell you . . ." His breathing slowed. His eyes were surrendering. They grew tired, heavy, and in his delirium, he spoke tenderly, sliding into the distant language of his childhood. "I will tell you . . . über die Diamanten."

I will tell you about the diamonds.

CHAPTER I
Estelle

As I approached, I could see that getting past her was going to be difficult. The woman, bless her heart, was large, blocking part of the grocery aisle. Her askew and drifting cart was barricading the rest of it.

She seemed lost to another world, intensely focused on a midshelf item. And there was something about the red spandex covering her lower half that was difficult to ignore. Even though her vibrant and oversized Christmas-themed sweater hung sloppily past her considerable hips, the spandex was clearly not the most complementary fashion choice, like memory foam that had lost its memory. For anywhere in the South, and especially for here in Watervalley, Tennessee, the outfit took unabashed flamboyance to a new level. Moreover, although the scent was pleasant, she had apparently chosen to marinate herself in perfume.

Absorbed in the moment, she was oblivious to my presence. I was about to utter a simple "excuse me" when suddenly the woman bolted upright. She jerked violently with a convulsion that seemed to start at her ankles and rippled viciously up through her entire body, ending with a fierce shuddering of her head and hands.

"Sweet Jesus," she exhorted, "that was a big one!" She took a deep breath, regaining herself. After a stunned moment, my doctor instincts kicked in.

"Ma'am, are you okay?"

I had startled her, if that was possible given what I had just witnessed, and she gasped lightly. Then just as quickly she responded with radiant animation.

"Oh, hi, sugar! I did not see you standing there."

"Ma'am, do you need to sit down?"

She smiled broadly and flipped her hand airily toward me. "No, no, no, I'm fine, sweetie. I was just having one of my moments." I gauged her to be about fifty and despite her robust size she had a lively, pretty face with near perfect chocolate brown skin. She wore no shortage of holiday-colored bracelets and beads and ornate earrings, all of which were adventurous by Watervalley standards but just short of gaudy. And despite her gushy delivery she spoke with a subtle articulation that wasn't the norm for around here. It had definitely been molded in an urban setting.

She reclaimed her wandering shopping cart and smiled warmly at me again, speaking with another quick gesture of her hand. "You have a nice day!" Then with an emphatic, cheery nod she proclaimed, "Happy holidays," and was off.

I returned the smile and nodded cautiously. "And you as well."

She continued at a leisurely pace down the aisle. I paused for a few moments to give her some distance. But after five or so steps, she once again halted and stood straight up at rigid attention with her entire body quaking and shuddering so violently that she rattled her grocery cart.

"Sweet heavens!" she announced in a loud voice.

I immediately left my own cart and dashed to her side. "Ma'am, something's definitely not right here. I'm a doctor. Are you having some kind of seizure?"

She regained possession of herself, and regarded me with the same engaged, bright face. "Goodness, sugar, are you Dr. Bradford? I have heard just so many wonderful things about you."

"Well, yes, I am Luke Bradford, but right now, ma'am, I'm more concerned about you. You seem to be having some kind of neurologic episode. By chance are you epileptic?"

She dipped her head, pursing her lips in an adoring smile. "Listen to you. Aren't you just the sweetest? No, honey, I'm not epileptic. It's just my silly pacemaker. Sometimes it gets a mind of its own and shocks me for no reason. It usually quits after two or three times. So I'm fine, just fine."

"Ma'am, if the ICD on your pacemaker is shocking you, it may mean that your heart is in a lethal rhythm. I think we need to get you over to the clinic." Numerous times in my brief medical career I had had to deal with patients in cardiac arrest. But the heroics needed to care for someone in remote Watervalley made this situation an absolute adrenaline shot. This lady needed critical medical attention, and fast.

"Oh, that's not necessary. I can tell when I'm tachycardic because my hair tingles." She gave a light pat to her head and increased the wattage of her smile.

"Well, you may be right, but I still think it best to get you over to the clinic immediately. We have a pacemaker programmer and I can analyze yours in a matter of minutes."

She studied me for a brief moment with no break in her effervescent smile. Then she shrugged her shoulders. "Dr. Bradford, it's really not necessary. But something tells me you're not giving up on this, are you?"

I grinned, shaking my head.

She exhaled in resignation. "Well, okay. If you insist. So look, I've got four more things on my list. Let me just grab those and I can follow you over there."

I stood dumbfounded. Given the gravity of what was happening to her, this suggestion left me incredulous. "Ma'am, I was actually considering calling the EMTs and having you taken to the clinic right away."

Once again she flipped her hand at me in dismissal. "Oh, sugar, it is not worth that much trouble. Just let me grab these few items and I'll meet you in the parking lot."

Despite what I considered to be a potential disaster, it was clear that I was not going to win this part of the argument. I sought compromise. "Okay, I'll help you round up what's left on your list and then you can ride with me over to the clinic."

She folded her arms, giving me a look of complete adoration. Her words began in a high pitch of inquiry and then descended lower. "Really? You're willing to do that? Well, darling, if that's the case, then you may need to pucker up 'cause I might be laying a little bit of heaven on you."

I paused, slightly taken aback. "Well, thanks. But I'm sure that won't be necessary." I wasn't certain what to make of that comment or of this incredibly colorful, unreserved woman. She was patently unconcerned and, admittedly, was showing no symptoms of cardiac distress. "So, tell me what things you need," I said.

I collected the last few items on her list and met up with her in the checkout line. Wanting to move quickly, I grabbed her bags and headed for the door. But the woman had other ideas. Her top pace was more of a saunter and her jovial manner was a clear indicator that she saw no urgency in the situation. With pained effort I bridled my steps to keep even with her. Meanwhile, she was talking nonstop about how happy she was to be back in Watervalley, and about the warm day, and about starting a new business, and occasionally injecting some adoring commentary about how kind I was being. Truthfully, I felt more duty-bound than kind. As the only doctor in Watervalley, I knew full well that this woman's ill health was mine to deal with, either now or later.

Impatiently I walked toward my old Corolla. But as we neared, she spoke up. "Oh, that's my car next to yours. Do you want to just take it?" Beside my shabby Corolla was parked a late-model BMW with a license plate that read "Bonbon1."

Driving her car threw too many variables in the mix, so I insisted that we take mine. I tossed her few bags of groceries into the backseat and opened the passenger door, only now realizing that my pocket-sized car might be an uncommonly awkward fit for a woman of her heft. To ease the process, I took her hand and arm to help her squeeze in. With some effort she maneuvered into the front seat and swung both feet inside.

I was just about to release her when a lightning bolt jolted me to attention and zipped up my arm. The world went black.

When I awoke, I was seeing double, lying with my back on the pavement and my face pointed skyward. The large woman was peering over me, but she had two faces. One was leering at me with scornful disdain while the other regarded me with a wide-eyed look of innocent anticipation. Then I realized I wasn't seeing double. Standing above me were none other than Connie Thompson, my devoted, critical, and—ironically—wealthy housekeeper, and beside her, the walking Christmas ornament lady from the grocery store. Against the clear blue midday December sky, they looked like twins.

I pushed myself to a sitting position and rubbed the back of my head where a considerable knot was rising.

Christmas ornament lady bent over and held my cheeks between her plump, fragrant hands. "Oh, sweetie, I am so sorry. My silly pacemaker went off while you were holding my arm. The car tires insulated me, but the jolt must have grounded through you. You fell back and bumped your head on my Beemer."

Connie, on the other hand, peered at me sternly through her gold inlay glasses. She spoke in her typical expressionless, no-nonsense manner. "Dr. Bradford, do you need medical attention?"

I sat there for a moment with my arms crossed over my knees and eventually looked up again at the two women, one with the face of an eager puppy, the other with that of a disapproving schoolteacher. I pondered Connie's question and responded impassively, "Yeah, looks like I have a lump on my head. What say you kiss it and make it better?"

Connie rolled her eyes and regarded me with placid disdain. Her voice was absolute deadpan. "Why am I not surprised that you would use even this situation to exhibit some foolishness?"

I rose to my feet, rubbing the tender bump. "How long was I out?"

Christmas ornament lady responded, "Only a couple of minutes. I called Connie immediately. Fortunately she was only a block away."

I stood for a moment, gazing back and forth at the two women. They were complete opposites in both manner and dress, but strangely, they looked similar.

"So, you two know each other?" I inquired.

This brought a shrug and giggle from the colorful one, while Connie tilted her head and regarded me with disbelief. "Dr. Bradford, have you two not met?" She exhaled with a tiresome frown. "Then by all means, let me introduce you. Dr. Bradford, this is my younger sister, Estelle Pillow. You two have something in common. She got her doctorate from Vanderbilt also."

CHAPTER 2
Sisters

Connie drove her sister over to the clinic while I followed close behind in my Corolla. It probably wasn't the brightest idea for me to drive after receiving the bump to my head, but then again, it was only four blocks.

Set in the remote hills of Middle Tennessee, Watervalley was a quiet farming community that seemed to breathe the air of a different century . . . a slower, more accommodating, more charitable time. I had arrived only six months earlier to serve as the town's new and only doctor. In return, Watervalley was paying off my med school debts, provided I set up practice for three years. Having grown up in Atlanta, I found that life here brought a whole new meaning to the concept of social adjustment. It had been a bumpy start, but the place had grown on me. And in return, well, I had grown on them. Watervalley had become home.

It was Thursday morning, two days after Christmas. Since the clinic staff was officially off for the holiday week, Connie unceremoniously offered assistance, speaking in a motherly blend of irritation and worry directed squarely at her sister. Seeing little harm

JEFF HIGH

in this, I had her follow along into the exam room in case help was needed. Besides, in the odd chance of an emergency, Clarence and Leonard, the Watervalley EMTs, were only a phone call away at the fire station. That is, if they hadn't become bored and slipped out to Fire Chief Ed Caswell's house to watch the Bowl games. Ed had a big screen.

With Estelle seated safely on the exam table I went about the methodic business of placing the leads and performing the pacemaker analysis. Connie hovered nearby, providing sharp-tongued commentary that escalated into a rapid-fire exchange between the two sisters, each strangely oblivious to the urgent medical matter at hand. Furthermore, they talked to each other in the third person, as if the other one was offstage in a soundproof booth.

"Dr. Bradford, I'm truly sorry about my sister. She ought to have better sense than to be out shopping in her condition." Connie spoke with great authority, clearly treating this as an opportunity for a teachable moment.

"Oh, pay no attention to my sister, Dr. Bradford. I was actually surprised that she was out and about. Usually she turns to stone if sunlight hits her."

Connie was unfazed. "You know, Dr. Bradford, I can't imagine anything sillier than someone coming to Watervalley to try to start a catering business, as if people can't cook for themselves."

"It's a bakery and catering business, Dr. Bradford. Everybody has a sweet tooth, including my sourpuss sister. Of course with her, it's just a working theory." Estelle was now wearing a subtle but superior smile.

Not missing a beat, Connie responded in a lilting, breezy voice, "Well, when we're done here, Dr. Bradford, I'll need to take my sister to the Dollar Store to buy her some marbles because it's clear she's lost all of hers."

"Dr. Bradford, my sister forgets that I have plenty of experience at running a business."

"Mmm-hmm. If I remember correctly, Dr. Bradford, the only business my sister ever started involved painting happy faces on people's toenails."

Despite the broadsides they were firing back and forth, there was no actual tension between the two. The conversation lacked any real sting of hostility. It seemed that such banter was the norm for them. Even still, all their comments were being directed at me, begging my engagement. I offered only some casual nods of understanding, doing my best to assert neutrality, and remained appropriately focused on the pacemaker analysis.

Connie finally forced my hand, speaking to me with a direct challenge. "So, Dr. Bradford. Are you going to sit there and play-act you don't hear any of this conversation?"

I kept my eyes centered on the monitor screen and responded in a low, undistracted voice, "That was my plan."

Estelle saw this comment as a small victory and her face lit up with smug and impish glee. She pressed her case.

"Dr. Bradford, you came from Nashville, where they had all those great shops and eateries down in the Village. I'd bet you'd love to have a bakery of that caliber right here in Watervalley."

Actually she had struck a nerve. I had just spent several years in Nashville doing my residency at Vanderbilt, and I'd grown up in urban Buckhead, north of Atlanta. I was no connoisseur, but the idea of fresh pastries and maybe even barista coffee sounded like a slice of heaven. The closest thing isolated Watervalley had to offer was the commercial-grade coffee and packaged fruit pies at Eddie's Quick Mart. Still, despite her stern exterior, Connie was a dear and beloved friend as well as my housekeeper. It would be unwise to take sides. I opted for evasive action.

"So, this bakery, or rather, this theoretical bakery. What are you wanting to call it?"

Estelle's face lit with delight and animation. "That's a good question! I've considered several possibilities: Scone Love, Nick of Thyme, the Pig and Pie, or maybe even Hot Buns Bakery."

She squinted her eyes in thoughtful, deep assessment and turned toward me. "Then again, this is Watervalley and you know, sugar, that last one might give people the wrong impression."

Connie responded immediately. "Dr. Bradford, given this foolishness, I think you should advise my sister to call it Half Baked. Or maybe since she'll have absolutely no business to speak of, she should call it Roll Over."

Estelle listened sourly to her sister's remark. Turning back toward me, she whispered in confidence, "Don't mind my older sister, Dr. Bradford. Bless her soul, she's always been a little jealous of my culinary skills."

This brought a prompt "humph" from Connie, who again spoke in a cadenced voice. "My, my, my, Dr. Bradford. Just know that if you're ever in the kitchen when my sister is frying anything, you might consider wearing a hazmat suit."

Fortunately Estelle's pacemaker analysis was now complete and I was able to exact an easy solution. The heart rate threshold on the implantable cardiac defibrillator, the ICD part of her pacemaker, was set too low and was shocking her at the slightest acceleration of her heartbeat. I adjusted it to an appropriate level, explained the problem to her, and just that quickly, I was done.

With her large, expressive brown eyes and an endearing smile, Estelle thanked me profusely, well past the point of making me feel awkward. I squeezed her outstretched hand as a gesture of acceptance, but she yanked me forward and wrapped me up in a lock-tight bear hug. After several embarrassingly long, self-conscious seconds I managed to disconnect gracefully and made immediate gestures of needing to do some work in my office. Connie seemed to sense my desire to retreat and spoke to Estelle with affectionate resignation.

"Come on, darlin'. Let's get you to your car." It was the first time she had addressed her sister directly.

As they were leaving, Connie turned back to me. "Dr. Bradford, I hope it's okay, but Estelle is joining us for dinner tonight."

"Sure. Fine by me. Should I bring a referee whistle?"

Connie lowered her head with a look of quiet reprimand. "Just bring an appetite, and leave your foolishness elsewhere. And don't worry about the groceries. We'll take care of that."

I folded my arms and leaned against the doorframe. "I shall look forward to every bite." Pausing for effect, I quickly added, "And snippet."

I watched them exit via the large front entry, arm in arm, talking in low but lively tones.

I adored Connie Thompson. She was a remarkable, brilliant woman. Sometimes I believed she still knew every fact from every book she had ever read and even a few she had only walked by. After her husband had passed away seven years ago, she'd taken his pension and focused her incredible intellect on the stock market. Now she was quite wealthy.

Soon after I had arrived in Watervalley the previous July, she had volunteered to come serve as my housekeeper and help me get started in my new life. Her deeply held convictions of faith and service had governed her offer when clearly she didn't need the money. She was not one to be swayed by fortune.

Yet in the previous months that I had known Connie, I had never seen anyone affect her so pointedly as her sister. I was not convinced that her opposition to the proposed bakery was as light as their banter suggested. It seemed, instead, to be rooted in something deeper. I shrugged. The sisters shared a strange bond of contention and connection.

Having a few hours to kill, I decided to tackle a project that had been nagging at me for several months. That was when I discovered the first incredible piece of paper.

CHAPTER 3

A Peculiar Discovery

In the 1930s, the town had purchased this stately antebellum home and converted it into the county medical clinic. The physician's office had previously been the mansion's library. With its high ceilings and wall-to-wall mahogany bookshelves, it was opulent almost to the point of embarrassment.

Except for the excitement of the last couple of hours with Estelle, the two days since Christmas had brought time to a standstill. Life in the town and surrounding hills had slumbered. Within their modest homes and farmhouses, the families of Watervalley had drawn inward, lazily embracing the small joys of the season. The clinic, courthouse, and downtown shops were all closed with only the drugstore, the bank, and the grocery store keeping regular hours. Seemingly, the people of Watervalley were the descendants of bears and had gone into hibernation.

So after Connie and Estelle left, I decided to begin the task of cleaning out the vast stacks of old journals and patient files left untouched for decades in the solemn confines of my office. It seemed that the staff had for years regarded this room as a kind of sanctuary, a holy of holies to be left undisturbed, in keeping with the reverence the small town placed on my profession. The languid pace of Watervalley life had so permeated me that this mundane endeavor filled me with a sense of anticipation and discovery. My threshold of thrill had dropped off the charts.

Normally a cacophony of life and sound, the clinic felt strangely asleep, a quiet stage of orderly rooms, sparse daylight, empty halls. It was an edgy, unfamiliar silence. And yet suddenly I felt an echoing presence, not of a chilling or ominous nature, but rather one of a sublime distant conversation. As I pushed open the door to my office, it seemed I was moving deeper into the curious and spellbound air of ancient whispers.

Three aged wooden filing cabinets filled the far corner of the imposing room. Having cautiously glanced into them a few months earlier, I knew that they contained patient medical records dating as far back as the 1930s.

To my delight, what I found was mesmerizing.

I discovered documents with familiar names, the ancestors of people I had come to know. Carefully handwritten narratives of visits, illnesses, and assessments were meticulously detailed on the faded paper: lists of medications, billing charges, summaries of small surgeries.

I had intended to place these ancient files in boxes for storage elsewhere. But I was captivated, engrossed in reading about these distant, forgotten lives, these ghosts of persons long past and buried in the numerous lowly cemeteries that dotted the community's frozen farms and fields.

And somehow, knowing the people of today's Watervalley, their voices, their faces, and their stories, made their ancestors in these dusty records come alive. Oddly, I found a subtle contentment in this exploration, a rich feeling of connection with the charitable, uncomplicated people in my small world.

Then, while working through the drawer labeled "1940," I came across a most unusual find. It was an oddly titled folder containing a single piece of yellowed paper, and it told a fascinating story—one that didn't fit this sleepy and isolated community. The file tab read simply: "Autopsy Report, Murdered German."

The document described a man in his midthirties who had died from blood loss sustained from multiple stab wounds. His body had been discovered near the old bandstand on the edge of Watervalley Lake. No wallet or identification had been found on him. While performing the autopsy, the doctor accidentally uncovered the only hint of who he was.

I read the words aloud, slowly. "Telegram written in German found in victim's suit lining believed to be indication of nationality." An inscription on the inside of his ring was also in German. Dr. Haslem Hinson, the county physician during the forties whose distinguished picture now hung in the long row down the main hallway, had signed the report.

I spoke in a low whisper. "Murder in Watervalley?" The words were at polar ends. The town was a quaint collection of homes, shops, and churches, a small island of life and commerce set inconspicuously in the middle of a broad, fertile plain of endless farms. The people here lived peaceful lives driven by the simple traditions of work and crops and family and faith. Threads of common values wove their world together and daily life was simple, routine, safe. Violent, grisly murder happened in faraway places, not here.

The minutes began to merge together. This fragile piece of paper pulled me deeper into a lost trance, prying at me with infinite questions. I read and reread the autopsy report several times, absorbing each word, hoping to satisfy my scant understanding of what had happened. But there were too many unanswered questions. What did the telegraph say? Who was this man? Who had stabbed him? Why? Most of all, how did this crime happen to occur here?

I stared vacantly, hypnotized. Steadily, the faint chatter from earlier became more pronounced. Low voices were humming in a muted overture from decades past. In a curious and enchanted way these forgotten files were brimming with the murmurings of long-ago lives, passions, hopes—with the unadorned chronicles of generations. The voices echoed with the hearty laughter, the robust energy, the symphony of rural life. And yet now, so it seemed, a singular tone of discord had blended in, hissing slyly of the gruesome business of murder.

In time I emerged from the spell of this peculiar discovery and looked at my watch. Two hours had drifted by and only part of one filing cabinet had been cleaned out. It was a poor showing. But the remaining drawers would have to wait until another day. I stared blankly at the folder for a few moments and decided to take it with me. I wanted to find answers, to know more, and immediately thought of one person who might be able to shed some light.

I grabbed my coat, locked up, and fired up the old Corolla. I was headed up to the high woods to see John Harris.

CHAPTER 4
Ancient Rumor

Turning off Fleming Street, I passed a multitude of downtown shops. Stacked side by side in something of a cereal box architecture, the decades-old buildings varied in style and color. Despite its years, Watervalley's downtown had a confidence, a sense of sureness about itself, a presence that was fresh and vibrant and welcoming. In the center square, the courthouse was framed by a broad lawn and tall maples that in summer would be lush with foliage. On this cool, bright December day the trees were bare and silent, serving as dormant sentries around the wide steps and limestone columns.

Despite the sleepy pace of the holidays, there was a delicate energy in the air of the idle downtown shops, a charming sense that life was still close at hand. Even when the townspeople were absent, their laughter and engaging kindness, which I had come to know, permeated my day. I was in high spirits.

After driving several miles deep into the hills, I pulled the old Corolla onto John's long brick driveway. The sweeping beauty of his incredible stone-, glass-, and wood-sided house never failed to impress. An architectural wonder with a breathtaking view of the entire valley, it enjoyed a splendor far beyond the simple frame houses that dotted the landscape below.

John Harris could be the most intimidating man I had ever met. Wealthy, retired, and in his late fifties, he held a doctorate in chemical engineering. He was tall, muscular for his age, and had a ruddy handsomeness that radiated sheer presence. In decades past he had been an icon of quiet strength and selfless leadership in town, but the tragic loss of his wife, Molly, to cancer two years earlier had left him a brooding and temperamental recluse.

In the months since my arrival we had struck up a tenuous but enjoyable friendship, full of shrewd exchanges and friendly banter. Although John was a master of wit and sarcasm, in the past weeks I had seen a softening of his hard facade. Even still, he was a man of little vulnerability.

Despite the cool of the mild December afternoon, I found John in his usual haunt, bundled in one of the Adirondack chairs around the back of the house.

I called out upon my approach and he stood and greeted me warmly with a mischievous, engaging smile and the usual glass in his hand.

"Hey, sawbones. What brings you up here?"

"Afternoon, John. Looks like you're in good spirits."

"Good spirits indeed. The fifteen-year-Scotch kind of spirits. Care for a shot?"

"I'll pass for now."

"Give it a try. It'll warm you up a little."

"You know, John, it seems I read somewhere that heavy consumption of alcohol is bad for your health."

John responded with a wry grin. "Humph. And what would you know about it?"

"Oh, it's not like I am a doctor or anything. Hold it. I just remembered. I am a doctor."

"Yeah, yeah. Suit yourself, smart-ass. Just remember, the odds are in my favor."

"How's that?"

"There are more old drunks than there are old doctors."

I shook my head. "Clever."

John laughed, extending his arm. "Come on, have a seat."

I eased into the twin Adirondack chair. The sun offered little warmth and I shuffled my back briskly against the frame to brush away the cold.

"Sawbones, you look like you have an agenda. What's on your mind?"

"Well, since you asked, here's the thing. I was cleaning out some old files in the office and came across something interesting. What do you know about the murder of some German that took place back in the forties?"

John thought for a moment. "You're talking about the old bandstand murder, during the war, Watervalley's only homicide. Most people don't remember it and hardly anyone talks about it anymore. Pretty interesting old story, though."

"What happened?"

He gazed into the distance, searching his memory. "A man came to town on the train carrying nothing but a briefcase. He went around to some of the shops and the bank showing a picture of a guy, wanting to know if anyone knew him, saying he was some lost cousin. The name didn't match up, but eventually someone noticed that the photo looked like the local bakeshop owner."

"And?"

"Well, this was a little before my time. But if I remember correctly, this mystery fellow went to the baker's shop and then to his house, but couldn't find him. That night there was a big dance down at the bandstand out on the lake to sell war bonds. The baker ran the concession, so this mystery guy caught up with him there. Apparently after everyone left, the two stayed behind to talk. But something went sour, because that's when the gunshot was heard."

"No, that can't be right. The autopsy indicated that the guy was killed by knife wounds."

"That's right, sawbones. Apparently, the baker stabbed the German multiple times and the stranger shot him in self-defense. After the police showed up, they found the German dead at the bandstand and later they discovered the baker by the road a couple of hundred feet away. Apparently he was trying to make it home. Odd thing was, they never found the gun, or the knife, or the German guy's wallet or briefcase. There was always a rumor that a third person was involved."

"So who was this baker?"

"His name was Oscar Fox. He was the great-grandfather of the little bandit whiz kid who lives next door to you on Fleming Street. In fact, Oscar lived in the same house."

"You're talking about Will Fox, my twelve-year-old neighbor?"

"That would be the one." John took another swallow of Scotch. His eyes grew sharp, penetrating. "You know, my father used to talk about all that. . . ." He hesitated.

I sensed that something was rolling through his memory. Some long-ago voice was whispering to John in the low breath of ancient rumor. In time he exhaled into the frigid air and turned toward me.

"Anyway, people always wondered if 'Oscar Fox' was an alias and he was actually German also. I think he came to town from North Carolina right after the start of the war. He had some kind of medical disability, although what I don't know. Anyway, he ended up marrying a local girl and started the bakery. If she knew anything more, she took it to her grave."

"Was his wife a suspect in all this?"

"No, if memory serves, she left the dance hours before the incident. She had taken the car. Oscar was trying to walk home."

"What became of her?"

"She stayed in Watervalley and ran the bakery. They had one son, who was just an infant at the time. His name was Wilhelm, not exactly a stout Southern name and another reason why people speculated about the German connection. The widow continued to run the bakery for years after that. We got fresh bread and baked goods there when I was a kid. I remember her as a small, pretty woman, always had a girlish face. Everybody called her Miss Elise."

He rubbed his chin. "You've probably seen the place. It's on the square, a corner storefront in part of the old Hatcher Building. I think the name Oscar's Bakery is still embedded in the sidewalk tile outside the front door."

"What's in the space now?"

"It's empty. Been closed up for years. Seems like the bank may own it."

"The bank? That's odd. Why wouldn't they have rented it out, put some kind of business in it?"

"Got me on that one, sport. You'll have to talk to Randall Simmons, the illustrious president of the Farmers Bank, to get that answer. Just be sure to wash your hands afterward."

"And why is that?"

"He's kind of a stuffed shirt. Randall could use a little less starch."

"I take it you don't like the guy?"

John's face thawed into a subtle, contented grin. Some memory of the banker was giving him great satisfaction. "Ahh, we go way back. It's a story for another time."

I left it at that. I was much more intrigued with this news of the bakery and Oscar Fox. What had begun as a one-sheet autopsy report had turned into a double murder. I sat for a moment absorbing everything that John had told me.

"Murder in Watervalley. That's quite a tale," I said.

"When I was a kid, the name Oscar Fox was synonymous with the boogeyman. We'd make up stories about Oscar's ghost roaming the night, looking for his next victim to slash. He kind of grew into local legend as a notorious killer. I think what really scared people about him was that before the murder, he was just a quiet, unassuming guy."

"And you say Oscar was Will Fox's great-grandfather?"

"Yeah. There's kind of a dark star over that bunch. Each of the men has died early, in their thirties or forties. People don't talk about it as much as they used to, but a lot of the old folks around here act skittish and superstitious if you bring Oscar Fox's name up. They'll tell you there's something dark and evil about that bloodline. It was a pretty horrific event and shocked everyone in the community for quite some time."

I knew that Will's father had been killed in a motorcycle accident about a year ago, several months before my arrival.

"Well, the whole business is intriguing," I said. "I'm thinking about visiting Sheriff Thurman and asking if he'll let me dig through the old police reports. They're bound to be tucked away somewhere."

"That may not be possible."

"Why is that?"

"There was a big fire at the jail in 1964. Pretty much burnt to the ground, long before anybody had computers. All the old records were destroyed. So, there's probably not much to go on."

I sank into my chair, deflated. This news put a damper on any real opportunity of pursuing the facts of this long-ago event. Still, the story captivated me.

John saw my obvious disappointment and spoke with characteristic resignation.

"The old bandstand murder is like most stories in Watervalley. It's gotten richer with age. There's a whole mythology around it about German spies and espionage, and even some wild rumors about lost diamonds. Not sure how that got into the mix. But it's Watervalley, sport. No need to let the facts get in the way of a good story. It's likely all bunk."

I nodded.

The sun was falling behind the distant horizon and suddenly the air had a biting chill. Far below, the wide valley plain spread to the faraway frozen hills. In the middle lay the small town, discernible by the small dots of white houses, the stalwart rise of church steeples, and the first frail glow of streetlights.

The people of Watervalley were huddled in the warmth of their homes, living out the peaceful routines and rituals of their daily lives. Yet buried in the distant past of this tranquil place was a raw chapter of violent murder, shrouded in obscurity and rumor. For me, it just didn't fit.

It was time to head back. But as I rose to leave, John stopped me. "Stick around, Doc. I'll fix some dinner. We can drink a little grog and get groggy."

"Rain check on that. Connie's expecting me."

John nodded. "Understood. You don't want to get on her icky list."

He walked with me up the short rise of yard to where my car was parked out front. All the while John was rubbing his chin, deep in thought with a face framed in curious inquiry. I guessed he was trying to recall more facts about the murder. To my surprise, he spoke of something quite unexpected.

CHAPTER 5
Heart of the Matter

John leaned against my car and folded his arms. "Well, sport, you were quite the celebrity the other night. Still warming in the afterglow?"

He was teasing me about my recent recognition at the community Christmas Eve service at the Episcopal church. Every year during this annual event, the town recognized someone who had given of themselves to the community. To my surprise and delight, I had been awarded the honor, despite what I believed had been a rather rocky start in my new job. It was a gratifying, humbling experience and had galvanized my determination to call Watervalley home and serve out my contract.

"Poke fun all you want, big guy," I said. "It won't change the fact that it was a wonderful moment." The earnestness of my response took some of the sting out of John's tone. He nodded diplomatically.

"And so it was. And I guess I would have to admit that it was well deserved."

"Thanks, John. Saying that had to be painful. Quick, drink some more Scotch."

John leered at me sharply, suppressing a grin.

"Besides, John, it wasn't such a bad thing that the two of us made an appearance in church. Might be a good idea to try it more often."

"Humph. You're probably right, Doc. The only problem with church is that it doesn't keep you from sinning—it just keeps you from enjoying it."

I, too, leaned against the Corolla. John continued to rub his chin, pondering another question.

"So, Doctor, now that you've had your lionization, your moment in the sun, as it were, I hear you've decided to stay here among us mere mortals. You sure you're not just going through a phase? You know, slumming to see what life in the sticks is like?"

"Wow, talk about cutting to the chase. You know, your veneer of Southern graciousness could stand a little polish, don't you think?"

"Huh! Don't try to outfox me by answering a question with a question. The last few weeks you had leaving written all over you. I could damn near smell it. Don't tell me a little bit of celebrity changed all that?"

"You sound like you're disappointed I'm staying."

"Nah, good to have you here, sawbones. On the odd chance I get sick again, you can throw some pills at me. I was just wondering, what changed your mind?"

"You do know I signed a three-year commitment with the town so it would pay off my college loans? Only six months have passed."

"Yeah, that's all noble sounding, but I'm not buying it. We

both know you've got inheritance money out there. I'm guessing something else lies behind your decision to stick around."

John was referring to a modest trust fund left to me by my guardian after my parents were killed in an accident when I was twelve. "The money from Aunt Grace does not come into play for several years and I'd like to eat between now and then."

"And what about the grants and research plans? You decided to give up those as well?"

I shrugged. "Sure, I still want to do medical research, but it doesn't look like that's in the cards right now." In truth, John was right. My tumultuous first six months had brought me to the brink of leaving Watervalley. But for multiple reasons I had decided to stay. Still, John's pushiness was odd.

"All right, Sherlock," I said. "You're just full of questions. What's this cross-examination all about?"

John persisted with this line of interrogation, but something was off-balance. Although his words had the sharp air of inquiry, he seemed hesitant to press for information about my personal affairs. This wasn't John. He was a man of wit and sarcasm who was normally blunt to the point of rudeness. Then it hit me.

"Oh. I think I get it. This inquisition wouldn't have anything to do with your niece, would it, Professor Harris?"

John's response was almost sheepish.

"Well, it might." He knew I had read his mind. His awkward mix of apprehension and obstinacy revealed that he had found this inquiry difficult, that it had cost him to pursue these questions.

An elementary school teacher, Christine Chambers was smart, athletic, and had cast something of a spell over me. After living in Atlanta for the past eight years, she had recently returned home to Watervalley. She was a beautiful brunette and I'd been attracted to her the instant we first met. But I had nicely botched our early encounters. So, although we had known each other for months, the dance of initial courtship had moved at a glacial pace. More than I wanted to admit to either John or myself, Christine probably had much to do with my newfound desire to stay in Watervalley. I responded evasively.

"John, I'm surprised you're asking," I said. "A few months ago you wouldn't even admit to me she was your niece."

"Let's just say the family and I have recently reconciled some past differences."

"That's good. So, are you the date police now?"

"Hardly, sport. Just curious, I guess."

I shrugged. "At this point there's not much to tell. We haven't even gone out, not that I haven't asked a time or two."

I paused. John offered no response.

"But, yeah, that could be changing. After the Christmas Eve service she mentioned I should call her sometime."

"So, what do you think?"

"About what?"

"About calling her, of course."

"John, pardon me for sounding like Obi-Wan Kenobi, but I just felt a great disturbance in the Force. Are you seriously asking me about my dating life?"

John held up his hand in resignation. "You're right, you're right. It's not my business. Must be the Scotch. I wasn't trying to pry."

"Ha! You'd need a crowbar to pry any harder. Look, I know that with her dad gone you're the closest thing to a father she has. So, I take it you don't object?"

"Object? To what? You going out with my niece?" John shrugged. "Don't misread me, sport. It's you I'm worried about. You're the one who's in over his head."

I was taken aback. "Oh, you think so, huh? Seems unlikely I can be in over my head when I haven't even jumped in the water yet."

He nodded and folded his arms. "Give it time. You'll see."

"So I'm guessing she's had a few callers in the past?"

John nodded. "Many have called. None have been chosen."

I shrugged. "Well, pretty girl like her, it's no surprise she's had a few suitors along the way."

"She has." John paused for a moment. "And none of them suited."

I grinned and we both stood silently. The odd conversation had played itself out. "Well, John, I'd love to stay here and listen to more of your clever responses, but I need to head back. As always, though, thanks for the heartwarming advice. I'm sure we'll both be fine."

John studied me for a moment, trying to read something deeper in my face, my words. "Just keep telling yourself that, Doc. I know you're a grown man and all, but that one will have you all heartbroken and crying like a little girl."

"Wow, John. You actually sound concerned. I'm not sure how to take this kinder, gentler you. I was just getting to like the crabby jackass version."

"Yeah, I know, I know. Kinda makes me sick to my stomach too."

I climbed in the car, shut the door, and rolled down the window. While starting the engine, I deliberated over John's unexpected advice. He had leaned forward with both hands on the frame of the open window, almost as if he wanted to hold on, to keep me around to continue the conversation. I put the car in gear and turned to him.

"Good to see you, John. And don't worry. I doubt love is in the air. But if it is, I'll be sure to keep my windows shut."

He grinned and stepped back, shaking his head as I drove away. As the car wound down the deep and desolate hills back to Fleming Street, my attention was drawn elsewhere. There beside me in the passenger seat sat the autopsy file, visible in the low glint of the dashboard lights.

Oddly, I had the sensation it was whispering to me, delicately casting its fragile voice into the air, pleading for me to draw closer and listen. Swelling curiosity was compelling me to know more, especially since the case involved my neighbor, the mischievous Will Fox.

I glanced at the file folder again, consumed with an unexplained desire to unravel this mystery, to bring light and understanding to the events of the past. I wanted to know more.

CHAPTER 6
Dinner

Will Fox filled my thoughts as I worked my way toward Fleming Street. Over the past months I had grown to like the little twelve-year-old boy who lived next door, despite his rather odd demeanor. He never seemed to play with any friends. He also had the unnerving habit of sitting on the metal fire escape attached to the side of his house and watching me anytime I was in my backyard. Still, my heart went out to him. I had lost my parents to a drunk driver at his age, so I understood something of his confusion and pain.

His father's death had left Will and his mother, Louise, in lean financial circumstances. But Will, with his brilliant mind, had figured out a way to hack into the computers of several Watervalley merchants and credit his mother's accounts as paid. In her grief over the loss of her husband, Louise Fox had spiraled into alcoholism and remained unaware of Will's clandestine activities.

Events in the weeks before Christmas had brought the family's problems and Will's thievery to light. I had taken a late-night soul-searching walk downtown and had accidentally witnessed

Will sneaking out of the alley next to the local drugstore. Earlier, Louise had apparently discovered him missing and, in her drunken state, had wandered into the backyard looking for him before passing out in the mud. Will had found her there and come pounding on my door for help. Later that night, through a flood of tears, he had confessed to the desperate measures he had secretly taken to help his grieving mother. From that moment forward, I was determined to do what I could to help them.

Now it seemed that Will was the last descendant of the man involved in Watervalley's most infamous crime. On top of all their other troubles, Will and his mother had to live with the stain of this terrible legacy. Perhaps John was right. It appeared that much about the Fox family tended to exist under a shadow of misfortune, as if for some families the universe could never quite find a happy ending.

I existed in a world of modest financial ease with all expectations for a prosperous future. Yet across the low rock wall of my side yard and in full view of my everyday life were an unemployed mother and her son living with the crippling daily worry about where they would get money for food, and gasoline, and heat.

As I pulled into my driveway, I noticed that next door Will was sitting on the steps to his front porch. In the thick darkness, the porch light weakly illuminated his small form against the night shadows. He sat with his chin in his hands, wearing a heavy coat, and his bike helmet . . . a true oddity given that Will didn't own a bike. I walked over to him.

"Hey, Willster, whatcha doing?"

"Just sitting."

"Um-hmm. A little cold to be sitting outside, don't you think?"

Will smiled. "Yeah, I guess so." He leaned forward and looked over at my driveway. "I see you're still driving that crappy car."

"Thanks for the reminder, I had almost forgotten." It wasn't the first time Will had taken delight in chiding me about my dilapidated Corolla.

"If you'd listened to me months ago, you'd have a girlfriend by now."

I nodded. "Solid dating advice, I'm sure. Even if it is coming from a twelve-year-old."

"The women in Watervalley aren't dumb, you know. They take one look at your car and think, 'Loser.'" He emphasized the last word by using his fingers to make an exclamation point.

"Okay, I get your drift."

"Hey, just trying to be a friend here, Dr. Bradford."

I had to laugh. Despite the weight placed on his small shoulders, Will was still a funny, fearless, and precocious boy. He had taken on the burden of protecting his despondent mother and remedying their bitter situation. I couldn't help warming to him.

"Hey, listen. I've got to get going. Don't stay out here too long. Otherwise, you know . . . cold, sniffles, frostbite, pneumonia . . . you get the idea."

"Sure."

Pausing on my porch steps, I gazed back over at him. He sat alone, brooding, and lost, I suspected, to an imaginary world. I exhaled into the cold air and went inside. Connie and Estelle were waiting.

The two sisters were in a flurry of activity in the kitchen, laughing and bickering and talking nonstop. As we sat down to dinner, I asked what they knew of the Oscar Fox murder story. They could shed little light beyond what John had already told me. Our conversation progressed to a discussion about Louise's predicament. Connie launched into an impassioned discourse.

"Her fool husband didn't have the sense God gave geese. Estelle, honey, pass the limas."

"Connie, dear, you know it's not right to talk of the dead that way. Besides, geese aren't so bad. Did you know they're monogamous for life?"

Connie offered a tired sideways glance, ignoring her sister's inquiry, and stayed on the attack. "I'd say it louder if I thought he could hear me. He always rode that motorcycle way too fast, and him a man in his forties. I know it was an accident, but he left Louise and that young boy without two nickels to press together. It's no wonder Will turned to thieving to make ends meet."

Estelle suspended her loaded fork in midair and turned to her sister. "Thieving? Will Fox? The little boy next door? What was he doing, pinching apples?"

"Hardly," Connie responded flatly. Using her knife for emphasis, she directed her gaze toward me. "You need to let the good doctor explain that one."

Barely paying attention, all I heard was the word "doctor." I was in casserole nirvana, floating in an ecstatic calorie coma brought on by all the dishes prepared by the two sisters. This wasn't just food; it was a love affair. I had become more emotionally involved with every bite. Connie's bayonet maneuver with her knife refocused me. I gulped and spoke.

"Estelle," I said, "it seems that Will kept the family finances afloat by hacking into the computer systems of local merchants and zeroing out his mother's accounts each month. I don't think she had the slightest notion what he was doing."

"My, my. That's just terrible, stealing like that. Think he could show me how to do it?"

"Estelle, girl, what are you thinking? You don't have any business hacking into people's computers." Connie leaned to one side, attempting to look into Estelle's ear, speaking sternly. "How many people are in there with you?"

"Oh, don't be silly. I want to make sure no one hacks into my little business."

Connie shrugged, returning to her food. "Emphasis on little."

"Constance, don't start all that again." Estelle turned to me. "So, is the boy going to have to do hard time in the big house?"

At first I thought Estelle was kidding, asking such a naive question. I hesitated, glancing briefly at Connie, who had closed her eyes and was shaking her head. "Well, no. I, um, I worked out a deal with Sheriff Thurman for Will to make compensation for what he stole."

"What Dr. Bradford means is that he paid off all the Foxes' bad debts," Connie injected.

I responded with reserved indignation. "Will is helping the stores out with their Internet and computer security. Anything beyond that is rumor, Mrs. Thompson." I had sworn Sheriff Thurman to secrecy on this matter. But somehow, as with all else in this town, Connie seemed to know everything.

"Actually, Estelle," I added, "it was your sister who marshaled volunteers from her church to help restore the Foxes' crumbling household and who are continuing to assist Louise in recovery from her alcohol addiction."

Connie spoke again. "Despite all the old rumors, the Foxes have been a generous, community-minded family, living here on Fleming Street for generations. But Louise's husband died with no insurance, leaving their home mortgaged to the hilt from some old business ventures that didn't work out. They're probably going to have to sell or face foreclosure."

We sat quietly, finishing the last of the incredible dinner with a dessert of chess pie. Connie broke the silence again, speaking in a reflective, empathetic voice.

"It's a sad business, is all I can say. They were a wonderful, happy little family. Then everything came unraveled. It just shows that life's a precious thing. You take it for granted. Then one morning you wake up and wonder, where did the time go?"

Estelle nodded in agreement, speaking with equal gravity. "And you know, not only that, but sometimes I wonder too, where did it come from?"

I stifled a laugh, but Connie's deadpan face never changed expression. She turned her head to the right and studied her sister's childlike face. After several painful seconds of absolute silence, Connie exclaimed, "Sometimes I just envy your brain."

In truth, I too marveled at Estelle. She possessed no ability to mask the depth or intensity of her heartfelt emotions, nor did she seem interested in doing so. She overflowed with an innocent exuberance, a tender, inexhaustible heartiness and enthusiasm. She was a grand contrast to her sister. While no less charitable, Connie saw the world through stern filters of order and reproach.

At first, the sullen looks Connie offered her sister gave the impression that she regarded Estelle as a simpleton, a difficult characterization given that she had a PhD in chemistry and had taught on the college level for twenty-five years. In truth, as the evening had progressed, it had become abundantly clear that Connie held a deep-rooted affection and admiration for her sibling. It occurred to me that perhaps her railings were driven more by a desire to protect, to keep her sister's seemingly innocent outlook on the world unspoiled. They were an odd pair.

Suddenly, Estelle slapped her hand down hard on the table, causing Rhett, my faithful but sometimes lethargic golden retriever, to sit up with a start. "I've got it!"

Connie responded in clutched alarm. "What's wrong with you, girl, slamming the table like you're killing a bug?"

Estelle giggled with a gesture of dismissal. "No, silly. I know what I can do. I can give Louise Fox a job at the bakery."

Connie closed her eyes and let her head drop in resignation. "Oh heavens, girl, I don't know where you think you are, but we need to book you a flight back to reality. You haven't even met the woman."

"Doesn't mean I won't like her."

"Doesn't mean she wants to work in a bakery either."

"I bet she'd be glad to work in a bakery and I'm sure she's likable. Do you like her, Dr. Bradford?"

Once again I was being sucked into the vortex of a Pillow sisters' argument. I enjoyed being a spectator, but not a participant. Diversion was the best tactic.

"So. I take it there is agreement to move forward with the bakery? Where are you thinking about putting it?"

Estelle responded, "I'm meeting with the bank tomorrow at ten about a property they own in the old Hatcher Building. It used to be a bakery years ago."

"Oh, wow! Are you talking about the place that was once called Oscar's Bakery?"

"I think so. I found out the bank owns it. The bank president didn't want to show it to me at first. When he realized I was Connie's sister, he got all down in the mouth about it and finally agreed."

To my surprise, Connie responded loudly, with a tinge of panic. "You didn't tell me about this. Why there?"

Clearly, Estelle had sensed the intensity of Connie's sudden apprehension.

"Well, dear, let's see. It's near all the downtown businesses. It has the right zoning. There's lots of parking. It's in that beautiful old Hatcher Building with all that stonework and glass and marble. Seems to be a perfect location."

Connie had regained her composure. She sat with folded arms, weighing each word. After what seemed an eternity, she pursed her lips and nodded.

"I guess you're right. It might be a good possibility."

But Estelle wasn't satisfied. "So what got into you just now? Why are you all in a state about that place?"

"It's nothing. I just had a silly notion in my head. It's not anything that matters anymore." Then, with noticeable effort, she inquired softly, "Why don't I come with you in the morning? If you're meeting with Randall Simmons, you might need some backup. He can be a little proud."

I spoke before Estelle could answer. "Why don't we all go? I wouldn't mind seeing the place myself. Not sure I'll be much help, but I'd like to tag along." There was a larger curiosity behind my interest, a desire to peek into the past regarding anything associated with Oscar Fox.

Estelle was ecstatic, almost giddy. Connie smiled lightly with a stoic resolve. The matter was settled. The two sisters rose from the table and began to clean up.

I, on the other hand, was now anxiously consumed with a completely different matter.

CHAPTER 7

The Windup

Connie and Estelle scurried around the kitchen keeping up a relentless chatter, much of it in a language I could barely discern. Apparently, over the years the sisters had developed cryptic idioms, catchphrases of one word that replaced a dozen, and even, on occasion, a casual injection of Latin. Even more intriguing, none of it seemed to involve the immediate task at hand of cleaning and putting away dishes. All of that happened with a synchronized flow and economy of motion that was second nature, a ritual they had obviously performed thousands of times.

The two sisters had insisted that I stay seated, or more accurately, stay out of the way. That was fine by me. I had another matter rolling around in the back of my mind. There was something I had to do, something that was causing me quite a bit of apprehension.

I needed to make a phone call.

Eventually Connie took notice of my brooding. Casually she inquired, "Dr. Bradford, what's that face all about? You look like someone just sold your prize cow for three magic beans."

I had been unwittingly drumming the fingers of my right hand on the kitchen table, staring vacantly. I looked over at the two of them, now paused in midwash at the kitchen sink.

"Connie. What is there to do in Watervalley on Saturday night? You know, with a date?"

Apparently, this comment caused a secret alarm bell to go off, one that was inaudible if you were carrying a Y chromosome. Instantly, Connie and Estelle gave each other a fixed look, one that demanded all hands on deck. Without either of them uttering a word, dishes were abandoned and aprons flew off. They scampered to the table, each grabbing a chair and scooting in close, forming a tight huddle around me. Even Rhett joined the circle, sitting obediently and regarding me with rapt focus.

What is it about women that makes them warm so quickly to the topic of matchmaking? Connie abandoned her normal reserve and, along with Estelle, started quizzing me. It felt like a scene right out of junior high. Connie launched the first volley.

"So, you're thinking about calling Christine?"

Before I could respond, Estelle flanked me. "She's awfully pretty, isn't she? I bet you two really hit it off."

"Do you need me to press your blue jeans?" Connie inquired. "I went by the cleaners yesterday, so clean shirts shouldn't be a problem."

Estelle countered, "I know she's really cute, but don't try to push things on the first date. She's a good girl and you'll need to be patient."

Connie added, "And I know you want to show her a good time, but this is Watervalley. Don't feel you have to flex your plastic a whole lot."

"But don't be cheap either," added Estelle. For good measure, she included, "And be sure to wear clean underwear." Then she looked at Connie as if a eureka moment had hit her. "Maybe he should record their conversation so we can critique it later."

I was drowning. Wave after wave of pent-up female advice was broadsiding me, counseling me in every detail of wooing, a subject in which I thought I had a respectable working knowledge. But apparently the Pillow sisters saw me as greatly lacking, even on the fundamentals. Following the volleys back and forth was like watching a tennis match. Except I was the ball getting smacked between the two of them.

Connie gave me a lengthy dissertation about being a godly man and the frailties of the flesh. Estelle executed the coup de grâce.

"And remember, there are three secrets to making a woman love you. Don't always talk about yourself, be sweet to her mother, and moisturize often. You should never underestimate the importance of good skin."

I held up my hands in surrender. "Ladies, thanks for all the input. I had no idea that a dating brain trust was so readily available. But all I really need is a suggestion about where to go in Watervalley to show a girl a nice time."

They immediately fell silent, shifting back against their chairs, offering me looks of mild pity, as if I were a second grader who couldn't figure out the answer to a basic math problem.

"Well, that one's easy," Connie said breezily.

"So very easy," Estelle echoed with sympathetic resignation.

I sat dumbfounded, still gazing back and forth at them. "Okay, then what?"

Estelle spoke first. "Go ahead, sweetie, you tell him."

"You sure?"

Estelle nodded confidently, almost conspiratorially. "Sure."

Connie took my hand. "Luke, darling, the simple answer is to ask Christine what she would like to do."

CHAPTER 8
The Phone Call

The sisters resumed cleaning up the kitchen. Meanwhile, I walked out to the back steps to clear my head and expel my foolish nervousness over one simple phone call. Rhett followed me. It was a clear, cold night and high above was a magnificent sky filled with crisp, radiant stars. After a few minutes, Connie stepped briefly onto the back porch with coat on and purse in hand. There was an uncommon tenderness to her otherwise stern voice. "Good night, Luke. I'll see you at ten in the morning, dear."

"Good night, Connie, drive carefully."

I followed her back into the kitchen. She exited down the hallway and out the front door. Estelle's departure was taking slightly longer. She would grab one or two items and then stop and stare ponderously, wanting to make sure she wasn't forgetting anything. Finally, she seemed satisfied that she was ready to go.

I walked her to the door and onto the front porch, where she gave me a gushing hug before heading off to her car. Arms folded, I leaned against a column, in the glow of the porch light, and watched as the taillights of Estelle's BMW turned off Fleming and vanished into the frozen, starlit night. Finally, I was alone and able to think.

I loved the cold. It sharpened the senses and centered me. I breathed in deeply, expectantly of the frozen air. Reaching for my phone, I dialed Christine's number.

On the fifth ring, she answered.

Except it wasn't Christine. The female voice on the other end was geriatric, raspy, blunt.

"Who is this?"

"This is Luke Bradford."

"Are you the doctor?"

"Well, yes. I'm sorry, but I was calling for Christine Chambers. Is she there?"

"Yeah, yeah, hold your horses, lover boy." What followed was something of a random mumbling, a running commentary spoken to the general air yet picked up by the phone. "You'd think they'd put a hold button on these fool devices." There were several painful squelch tones as the keypad was pressed. "Oh, the heck with it. Smartphone, my foot. There's nothing smart about these stupid things."

Then came the foghorn blast. "CHRISTINE!" Whatever elderly ailments this woman possessed, her lungs were notably in prime condition.

"Telephone! It's the doctor! What? Yeah, the doctor. He finally called." There was a long pause. "Okay, I'll tell him."

Although her previous words had been completely audible, the marked decibel increase indicated that she was again speaking intentionally into the phone. "Christine says she'll be right here."

"Okay. Thank you."

"Yeah, sure, sure." For several painful moments, I heard the annoying sound of forced, heavy breathing pouring directly into the receiver. I eventually held the phone at arm's length, looking at it in comic disbelief. Then I heard her speaking again.

"So, you went to Vanderbilt, huh? Did you like that place?"

"Um, yeah, sure. It was a good school."

"Did you play football there?"

"No, I went there for med school."

"Just as well. Their football team never seems to have much punkin'."

I wasn't sure what that term meant, but I politely went along. "They play in a pretty tough conference."

"Yeah, whatever. Guess that's as good an excuse as any. Oh, here's Christine." In a poorly muffled voice, she declared, "It's him."

Finally, Christine was on the phone.

"Hey. This is Luke. Did I catch you at a bad time?"

"No, not at all. Sorry to keep you waiting." Her voice was buoyant, sweet, accommodating. "I was in the shower and had to grab a towel to wrap around me."

Just that quickly, that one statement evoked images that sent me drowning in a sea of delightful, shameless thoughts. There's something undeniably sensuous about the idea of a pristine, freshly washed young woman, especially one wrapped only in a towel. That mental picture now coupled with Christine's yielding, engaging voice was hitting the primal bull's-eye. Fortunately, or come to think of it, perhaps unfortunately, this was immediately followed by the looming specter of Connie, and her stern comments on virtue delivered mere moments ago. I refocused and said, "That's quite an answering service. She screen all your calls?"

There was a slight giggle. "Yeah, sorry about that. That's Grandmother Chambers. She's visiting my mom and me from Florida for the holidays. She can be a little direct."

"I picked up on that."

"She'd like to meet you," Christine responded, although for a split second, I thought she said, "She'd like to beat you." It was my guilty subconscious thinking that her grandmother had telepathically read my wanton thoughts. I was still struggling to keep a controlled, casual focus.

"Sure. Send her right over." This brought an obliging laugh from Christine followed by an awkward pause. I searched for words.

"So, listen. I was calling about spending some time together Saturday. I looked in the paper and noticed that the Watervalley Line Dance and Bingo Club is throwing a blowout Saturday night. But I'm not sure if you're up for that much excitement on a first date. So, I thought I would ask what you'd like to do."

There was a moment's hesitation. "Are you by chance running in the fund-raiser this Saturday?"

"Fund-raiser?"

"Yeah. The Runs with Scissors 5K. They hold it every year on the Saturday before New Year's. All proceeds go to the elementary school fund."

A light came on. Nancy Orman, the clinic secretary, had asked me the previous week if I wanted to participate in the charity run, to which I had mumbled a distracted "Sure." I had given her a check to sign me up.

"Oh my gosh, I am so glad you mentioned that. As a matter of fact I am."

"Why don't we start with that and figure out the rest of the day as we go along?"

I liked this idea, probably because it so easily reflected Christine's unpretentious, confident nature, not to mention that there was the clear inference of possibly spending the entire day together.

"Sure. Sounds good. I'm glad you mentioned the 5K. I think I committed quite the social faux pas when I missed the annual 'Hog Jog' last September. Must be why Nancy signed me up this time. Anyway, what's the deal with the scissors?"

"Every contestant has to carry a pair of blunt-nose kindergarten scissors. It's kind of a conversation icebreaker when you're trying to get sponsors."

"I guess I missed that part. I haven't signed up a single supporter."

"Oh, don't let that bother you. The business sponsors give two hundred fifty dollars for first place in each category, and it's customary for the winner to donate that money to the fund."

"Sounds like I need to win to save face."

Christine laughed lightly. "Well, not exactly. I meant that the run is mostly for fun. The kids really love it, and the money is pretty much already raised before the event. But I guess it's possible you could win."

I was six foot two, had played college basketball, and considered myself pretty athletic. Since my arrival it had been my daily practice to take a morning jog, something that had made me the target of more than a few teasing but good-natured comments from the locals. For the past couple of months my usual route had taken me out Summerfield Road, right past the iconic picket fence and tree-filled yard surrounding the white clapboard farmhouse where Christine lived.

I responded playfully, "It's possible I could win? Gee, not a lot of conviction there."

"Well, I guess I have a confession to make. I've seen you out running in the distance. Not too impressive, Buckhead boy." Her voice carried a teasing, competitive tone. Even yet, it was combined with laughter, a sweet, subdued excitement.

"Oh, you think? Not impressive, huh? You know, it might just be that I slow my pace on Summerfield Road, hoping that a certain feisty but appealing schoolteacher might cross my path."

"Oh, wow, aren't you just the smooth one, Luke Bradford. How long have you been practicing that comeback?"

"About an hour or so. Why, did I rush it?"

"No, no. Timing was good. Then again, you might want to come up with a little stronger adjective. 'Appealing' just doesn't carry a lot of conviction, now, does it?"

"So noted. Any suggestions?"

"Give me a second. 'Gorgeous' is always good. 'Stunning,' 'dazzling,' 'sparkling,' 'radiant'—all those work too."

"Are we describing you or the Milky Way?"

"You're not helping yourself here." There was a slight change of tone.

"And there it is. You know, seems like earlier I mentioned the word 'feisty'?"

Delight was pouring through all of her words. "Okay, stop. You made your point." She paused for a moment. "Bradford, you are too funny. You should have asked me out a long time ago."

"All right, now you're the one losing style points." Over the past months, Christine had flatly turned down date offers on at least two occasions. But I sensed this was her way of telling me that now she regretted it, that my charm had finally won her over. Probably not, but I decided to go with that thought anyway.

When she spoke again, her voice was soft, deliberate, delightfully seductive. "Let's just say I'm really glad you're asking me out now. See you Saturday, down on the square. Bring your A game."

We said good-bye. I returned inside and walked to the back of the house in a slightly euphoric daze, oblivious to the numbing chill of the previous minutes in the December cold. I was exhilarated, staring vacantly at the warm and orderly kitchen around me. The remnant smells of cooking, the echoes of laughter and conversation from earlier in the evening, and now the charming, lilting resonance of Christine's voice filled the room. The air was electric. I was consumed, warmed with an enchanting, pure delight, and I knew that, at least for that moment, my small life in Watervalley was rich with magical possibilities. It now seemed that Saturday morning was all I could think about.

At least, that along with the towel.

CHAPTER 9
Sunflower Miller

I awoke early Friday morning, fed Rhett, showered, and decided to go over to the Depot Diner for a hot breakfast. I enjoyed being around the familiar faces down at the diner, but I usually sat at the counter reading the paper, content to eat alone. Yet when I arrived, the Depot was packed, a hubbub of clanging dishes, laughter, and animated conversations. Watervalley was slowly coming out of hibernation.

The counter was full, so I slid into one of the open booths that lined the front windows. I ordered coffee and breakfast and opened the Watervalley paper, blissfully enjoying what I considered a perfect world, privacy amidst a crowd of friendly faces. But my peace was short-lived. I soon had a visitor, one who brazenly decided to plop down across from me and invade my breakfast serenity.

It was Sunflower Miller.

John Harris had once told me that in this life some people need drama. As I recall, he was drinking Scotch at the time and I think he was generally referring to mothers-in-law. But for me, that person was Sunflower Miller. Sunflower was Watervalley's self-appointed hall monitor.

She was also the town's original and only remaining flower child, who still wore tie-dyed shirts and drove an old truck plastered with peace stickers. Although widely known and accepted, Sunflower had been relegated to the margins of mainstream Watervalley. Nevertheless, she was completely at home in her own skin, content to march through her days guided by some inner desire to change the present world order. And unfortunately for me, she had decided that my medical practice was the appropriate starting place. Sunflower had a disdain for the medical community and chided me because I was a doctor, although I suspect she would chide a nondoctor if I were not around, just to stay in practice.

Since my arrival the previous July, she had been to see me several times, trying to persuade me to integrate her brand of holistic and herbal medicine into the clinic's practice. Typically, by the end of a conversation with Sunflower, I would be hoping someone would shoot me with a tranquilizer gun.

She had placed her elbows on the table and was resting her chin on her coupled fists. I looked over the top of my paper and studied her for a moment before saying with mild sarcasm, "Hello, Sunflower. By all means, have a seat and join me."

"Your bedside manner needs some work."

I was doing my best to offer her a glazed, uninterested expression when the waitress brought my breakfast, the country ham special.

"Hang around five more minutes and you'll feel the same about my table manners," I said.

"Oh, by all means, Dr. Bradford, you go right ahead and enjoy your dead animal carcass. Don't let me interrupt." I took her advice and swallowed a huge bite of ham.

She was a tall, lean, athletic woman of striking Norwegian features and looked almost two decades younger than her sixty-five years. She was a marvel, actually. In her unadorned, organic way she was markedly beautiful. Even still, time had left streaks of gray within her blond hair, now neatly pulled back into a long ponytail. Despite her penchant for no makeup and sloppy clothes, she retained a weathered prettiness.

A silent minute passed and clearly she wasn't leaving. "Sunflower," I began, "why are you here at the diner? I thought you lived off a diet of tofu and dandelion fuzz."

"Even vegetarians like coffee, Doc. Besides, Lida buys all her eggs from me. So despite your misguided culinary ways, at least your scramble there comes from free-range chickens."

"You know, Sunflower, I make house calls. That sort of makes me a free-range doctor. Think I can get a little credit for that?"

She ignored this comment. "I've got something I want you to agree to."

I took a sip of coffee. "I'm open to agreement, Sunflower, provided agreement is all that's required of me."

"I understand the clinic is getting a new nurse. I want to team up with her and initiate some holistic health practices."

I swallowed a bite of ham and egg and wiped my chin with my napkin. Then I spoke in a confidential whisper. "Sunflower, listen." I paused for a moment, looked to the side, and then focused on her again. "Dear, I think your crazy is showing. You might want to go to the ladies' room and tuck it back in."

Sunflower rolled her eyes. "Come on, Doc, we're on the same side here. I'm just trying to get you to use your powers for good rather than evil. You know, break the spell."

I smiled and shook my head, continuing to eat. Despite her peculiarities, I liked Sunflower. She generated a kind of hypnotic fascination. She did macrobiotic gardening and lived alone on a small farm not far from Watervalley Lake. The flower child movement had long since died out, as had most of the flower children, but Sunflower seemed to be waiting for a comeback.

"I'm a little more comfortable using a stethoscope than a horoscope," I said. "Patient assessments are a complex business. It's not just a check sheet with the options of 'will be okay, might get better, and circling the drain.'"

"Just hear me out, Doc."

I exhaled a wearisome sigh. I might as well listen. Otherwise, she would keep up the verbal assault until only politeness prevented me from reaching across and smacking her. And probably more than she knew, I was actually in broad agreement with the concept of holistic care . . . that is, looking beyond just the sick or depleted body and equally considering the emotional, social, economic, and spiritual needs of the patient. The problem stemmed with the lack of boundaries with such an approach, a problem that quickly moved many holistic practices into the realm of quackery. I spoke with resignation.

"By all means, Sunflower, please do a tell-all of your sinister designs."

"I know you won't agree to any homeopathic medicines. That's because the corrupt medical education machine has brainwashed you into believing in synthetic pharmaceuticals and Mercurochrome."

"Not helping yourself here, Sunflower."

"I want to begin a series of community classes and initiatives on proactive health management."

"Such as?"

"Well, such as making lifestyle changes in diet, exercise, good mental health, proper sleep, stress management, maybe even teaching a little tai chi."

"Nothing wrong with any of that, except maybe the diet part. If you're thinking about convincing everyone to be a vegetarian, that's not going to fly in Watervalley. The people here think vegetarians are just lousy hunters."

"Okay, I get that. But proactive health is a good thing. I want to meet with the new nurse to come up with a plan of action."

I spent a moment considering her request. Watervalley could use more proactive thinking regarding healthy lifestyles, and rightfully, the clinic should be central to that effort. In my first six months I had focused on taking care of whatever came through the front door. But perhaps it was time to start thinking ahead.

"All right, Sunflower, here's the deal. Let's give the new nurse a couple of weeks to settle in. Then the three of us can put our heads together. As long as you don't start recommending some mélange of rosemary, mustard seed, and tree bark as a cure for arthritis, I'm generally okay with what you are recommending. Proactive medicine is a good idea, but I think it's going to be a tough sell here in the valley."

"Good. And don't be silly, Doc. Everybody knows that a garlic rub gets rid of arthritis."

"As well as anyone with a nose."

Sunflower placed her hand over mine, offering me a rich, engaging smile. "This is a good first step. I can already sense you moving away from the dark side." There was a seasoned cleverness to her delivery. Sunflower had an odd, appealing charm, a gift of smiling in an admiring, powerful way that would make any man think he was strong, audacious, attractive. Admittedly, myself included. She was such an odd quilt of eccentricities.

"Sunflower, sometime we need to sit and talk about you. And you can, you know, explain to me why you are the way you are."

She grinned mischievously and began sliding out of the booth. "You mean, explain all my mystical powers."

"Yes, and bring your magic wand for show-and-tell."

"It's in the shop. How about some fairy dust?"

"That works too." By now she was standing beside the table, preparing to depart.

"We'll talk in a few weeks," I said.

"Thanks, Doc."

As she exited, I couldn't help but notice a score of inquisitive glances and turning heads. No doubt, we were an odd pairing and those who had witnessed our brief conversation were curious to know more. So much for my private breakfast.

I finished eating and took my bill to the cash register. While she made change, Lida Wilkins, the owner, winked at me. "Looks like on the medical front, east just met west."

I grinned. Lida was more clever than many realized. I grabbed my coat off the rack and was preparing to leave when she came up beside me. With her back turned so no one could hear, Lida made a most curious request, one I was glad to accommodate later that day. But first, I had an appointment with Oscar Fox's past.

CHAPTER 10
The Old Bakery

I arrived at the Hatcher Building a little before ten. As I pulled my Corolla into one of the parking spaces that lined the wide downtown street, Estelle's BMW eased in beside me. Connie sat in the passenger seat.

From our discussion the previous evening, I had learned that the Hatcher Building was an Italianate structure built in the early 1920s by Hiram Hatcher, a local lumberman turned merchant. Constructed of white limestone, it consisted of five storefronts with large arched windows framed with Doric columns. Stairwells between the storefronts led to professional offices on the upper floor, a design that had allowed the structure to be divided into separate pieces of real estate.

From what John had told me, after Elise Fox closed the bakery in the midsixties, the Farmers Bank bought the corner unit with the thought of putting a small branch office there. But for some reason, that had never happened.

As Connie emerged from the BMW, the heavy scent of her sister's perfume permeated the air like an invisible cloud. Connie was fanning her face, wearing a sour frown and pinched nose. Estelle, on the other hand, was almost giddy with excitement. She nearly skipped around the front of the car, practically levitating as she headed toward the storefront. We all stood for a moment, peering in through the massive, dusty front windows. There was no sign of the banker, Randall Simmons. Connie looked at her watch and announced that she was going down the street to get something at Morrow's Drugs and would be right back.

Estelle and I stepped over to the entrance, where, just as John had noted, the words OSCAR'S BAKERY were laid beneath our feet in small mosaic tiles that filled the space four feet out from the door.

"My, that is such beautiful work. I would hate to tear it up," Estelle remarked.

"You could always change your name to Oscar."

Estelle studied me with great concentration and I realized that she might be seriously pondering the idea.

"I'm teasing, you know," I said.

Her animated smile returned and she flipped her hand at me. "Of course you are, sugar. It'd be much cheaper to replace the tile."

I was searching for a response when a grunted "ahem" came from behind us.

It was Randall Simmons.

In his late fifties, Randall was a man of modest height, neatly trimmed salt-and-pepper hair, and doleful eyes that gazed upon the world behind heavy, black-framed glasses. Sharply dressed in a conservative suit, he was the epitome of the emotionally detached banker. There was a clipped reserve about him, a smug politeness. He spoke with dry precision.

"Good morning, Miss Pillow. I see you've brought Dr. Bradford along."

He extended his hand to Estelle and we all exchanged

greetings. Afterward, there was an awkward silence. Estelle and I stood frozen, uncertain of what should happen next. Randall was looking back and forth between the two of us, assessing us coolly. Having satisfied himself, he spoke with great control.

"Why don't we have a look inside?"

There was a methodic formality and importance in the way he unhurriedly produced a key and placed it into the lock of the large stained-glass front door. When the lock finally clicked, he pushed the door open and stepped back, allowing Estelle to enter first.

Once we were inside, it took little imagination to envision what a grand place this had once been. It had an old-world feel to it, a store where Hansel and Gretel might stop by on their way home from school. Although a thick layer of ancient dust blanketed everything, the room was trimmed in intricately carved chestnut woodwork. Beautifully crafted rosettes and elaborate corbels decorated the wood-paneled walls. Broad, sturdy wood columns rose to the ceiling, shouldering the exposed and ornately trimmed structural beams. The room was the definition of enchantment.

Estelle and I absorbed everything in silence and I could tell she was on the verge of exploding with joy. About five steps in she raised both hands over her cheeks and left them there as she continued to walk around.

A collection of heavy wood tables and chairs had been pushed into a corner and stacked in a random, untidy manner. Down the center of the store ran a travertine marble walkway bordered on both sides by rich but well-worn mahogany flooring. This led to a line of ornate display cases made of thin, delicate glass. A swinging door behind the counters revealed a sizable kitchen with outdated ovens and old butcher-block worktables.

The place had an aged, enclosed smell to it. The floor was cluttered with paper trash and a few pieces of broken glass. The light fixtures had apparently been yanked from the plaster ceiling, with the remnants of old wires left dangling from the gaping holes. Other than the obvious wear and tear of age, the only other noticeable damage was five or six twelve-inch square holes that had been cut randomly in the walls and floors, without regard for the damage.

By now Estelle's eyes were like saucers, filled with pure inspiration and delight. I was beginning to wonder if I had set her pacemaker threshold high enough.

Randall had remained near the entry, standing as though carved from stone. He appeared to be consumed in some deep preoccupation and offered no commentary.

Estelle had stepped into the back room, no doubt assessing its potential as a revitalized kitchen. I stood in silence with Randall, who clearly felt no obligation to make small talk.

"I wonder what happened to the light fixtures and these holes," I inquired.

He moved slowly deeper into the room and answered with the same enthusiasm as if describing a head of cabbage. "Probably vandals over the years. It's hard to say."

"So, how did the bank come to acquire the property?"

"It, um, it was actually my father's idea. He was the bank president before me some years back. He wanted to put a branch office here. But, as you can see, that didn't happen." There was an air of discretion to his tone. He seemed to be choosing his words carefully.

I pressed him again. "What do you know about the history of this place?"

He inhaled a long breath and spoke dutifully. "I'm told that it was originally a men's clothing store, back in the twenties. I think the Depression almost did it in. When the Second World War started and all the men went off to fight, it closed up. Oscar Fox came to town in the summer of 1942. He bought this property in 1943 and spent quite a bit of money fixing it up."

"I heard some stories about Oscar Fox. What happened to him anyway?" I was fishing, wanting to see if Randall's version of the story added anything new.

"He was a murderer, you know, and apparently a rather gruesome fellow. He and some stranger did each other in. My father knew him. Mr. Fox did business with the bank." Randall's answer was oddly clipped. I wasn't sure what to make of it.

By now Estelle had returned from the back room looking so happy I thought she might start flying around the room like Peter Pan.

"It's perfect!" she declared. "I love it, love it, love it. When do you think the bank can get me a quote on what it might sell for?"

I could see Randall's neck stiffen. "We'll have to see. The bank hasn't actively tried to sell the property for some time, so I don't know what plans we have for it. Perhaps at the next quarterly meeting of the board we can get the real estate subcommittee to give a status report. I'm afraid it may take quite some time."

He spoke with unruffled aplomb, with a cool air of authority. And just that quickly I could see Estelle begin to deflate. That was, until a firm voice from behind Randall broke the silence.

"Oh, I think we can do much better than that."

It was Connie, standing calmly in the entryway, clasping her huge purse in front of her with both hands.

Noticeably alarmed, Randall turned toward her. It was the fastest he had moved all morning. In a single moment his superiority vanished and was replaced by a choking anxiety. He seemed at a loss for words. Connie's commanding voice and hard stare had melted him, had momentarily thrown him off-balance. Something more than her stern tone was at work here. She had something on Randall.

But he recovered quickly and responded in a diplomatic albeit slightly wilted voice, "Yes, certainly. Let me see what we can do to expedite an answer."

He glanced nervously at his watch. "Well, I really need to get back to the bank. Please feel free to take your time looking around. Just pull the door closed when you leave. I'll come by and lock up later."

His composure once more in place, he offered a rigid nod and departed quickly.

Estelle couldn't contain herself any longer. "Praise Jesus, this is the place! It's just what I was hoping for!"

Her elation was contagious enough to bring a slight smile to Connie's somber face. But she responded with a shake of her head. "I don't know, honey. It's going to take a lot of money to fix this place up, not to mention the cost of buying the property."

Estelle was undaunted. It was easy to see that she was all in: heart, soul, and retirement fund. "But it's perfect, dear. I know it, I just know it!"

Connie's smile was a blend of delight and resignation. "Well, okay, then. I guess if you're heading to the poorhouse, it's no big deal if you get there a day or two early."

Estelle grabbed Connie's arm with enthusiastic authority. "Come on, sugar, let me show you around."

Connie resisted. She spoke in a low, emotional voice, almost swallowing her words. "That's not necessary, honey. I know all about this place. I spent more hours here than I want to think about."

Estelle gave her a puzzled look. "How is that?"

Connie's words were mixed with anguish and confession. "It was before you were born, and I was told never to talk about it, but Momma used to work here."

CHAPTER II
Connie, Past and Present

"Constance, what are you talking about?"

"It was a long time ago. It's nothing that matters anymore."

"Well, sister, it matters now. All I remember was that Momma worked in the school cafeteria. You never talked about her working here."

"Like I said, it's water under the bridge."

Connie seemed resigned to the idea of not discussing this revelation, but as she spoke, I couldn't help but notice her reflective perusal of the room; she absorbed the elaborate details, scrutinized the dust and ruin, and breathed in the weighty air of ancient memories. It seemed she had returned to a place she had always known, one that had been burned deep within her life's story.

"Dear, you know Luke and I are not going to let this pass," Estelle persisted. "Maylene was my momma too. I want to know what you are talking about."

At first I didn't understand Estelle's comment about the need to assert her claim regarding their mother. But as Connie yielded to her request, I began to discern how the nine-year gap in their ages had created very different relationships with their departed parent.

As Connie began to speak, her face was transformed by the past. It was a face of wonder, of enchantment, of innocence. "Momma started working here at the bakery when it first opened in October of 1943. She was barely seventeen and had just finished high school. There were only eleven grades in those days. She continued working here after she married Daddy in 1950 and after I was born in 1954. By the time I was seven, most afternoons I would sit and do my homework in a tucked-away corner while Momma carried on lively conversations with Elise Fox. Elise was more than just a boss to Momma—she was her best friend. I have lots of memories of being here, some of the best . . . and some of the worst."

Connie took a few steps toward the display counters. Behind them and against the right side of the room was a short partition with a countertop and a large open cabinet space underneath. The counter had likely been a staging area for pans of baked goods from the back, a work space to place pastries into individual paper holders. She turned to me. "Luke, would you do something for me?"

"Sure."

"Look up under this counter. See if any thing is written there."

I squatted next to the cabinet opening and looked at the painted wooden boards underneath. There, penciled in beautiful cursive handwriting, was the name "Constance Grace Thompson." I looked up at her and smiled. "I'm guessing you put this here."

She nodded. "I probably read a hundred books in that little cubbyhole."

It was the perfect place for a little girl to hide herself away, to be lost in the imagination of a thousand adventures.

But when she spoke again, Connie's voice had lost its animation. "For some reason, in the fall of 1962, after nineteen years of working here, Elise pulled Momma aside one afternoon and through tears told her she was letting Momma go. No reason or explanation was given. Elise tried to give her six months' severance pay, but Momma refused. Her pride wouldn't allow it." Again, Connie paused and stared vacantly into the far reaches of the room.

She spoke distantly. "Momma was very hurt when all that happened. Crushed, really. It wasn't just the money—she felt like she had lost her best friend. I remember months later I would walk into the kitchen at home and Momma would be in tears. She never wanted to talk about it." Connie's voice had grown soft, reflective. She ran her finger across the glass of the counter, leaving a line in the dust.

I knew from previous conversations that Connie's mother had died of lung cancer in 1968. I did the math in my head. That would have happened when Connie was fourteen and Estelle was approximately four or five. No doubt, Connie's desire to protect her sibling became embedded during those years. Their father, whom Connie had described as a "quiet, hardworking, Christian man," passed away ten years later.

"It never made sense. A month before Momma died, she got a letter from Elise. At the time I assumed Elise wanted to come see her. But Momma refused to read it and returned the letter to sender. Momma said she knew that the bakery was having problems with its credit. Within a month after Momma was let go, Elise sold the bakery to the bank. Before Momma died, she made me promise to never talk about her working here. I'm sure she was hurt and embarrassed. That was just her way of handling things."

Connie's explanation revealed parts of herself she had never shown me. It was my first realization that she bore the scars of past wounds that she had neither revisited nor forgotten. I sensed that veiled within her words were age-old emotions that had stained her early years, events that had callously altered the direction of her early life. I felt for her. It seemed to have taken a toll on her to return to this place, to the silence and dust and confusion of these long-buried memories.

In that moment, the front door swung open, caught by the breeze. We had been standing in silence but now turned at the groan of the hinges. The fresh, cool air of December breathed into the room, washing past us, pushing aside the musty air of stagnant, locked-away years.

Connie gazed up at the high, arched ceiling, turning slowly to take in the entire room. She reached to wipe a large swath of grime from a glass display case, and for a brief moment, she studied the accumulated filth on her palm. Then she slapped one hand against the other in sweeping strokes, beating away the ancient dust. It seemed a defining moment for her. She turned and took Estelle's hand.

"Estelle, sweetie, you've got a great opportunity to do something really fine here. I think you should go for it."

She had spoken in a voice of unquestioned resolve. The two sisters hugged and then, just as they had done at the clinic, proceeded to walk arm in arm through the old bakery. There was a curious, secret bond between them, an intense affection. They were both talking loudly, robustly, and, of course, at the same time.

With the culinary brain trust now focused and in full session, I decided that there were no new insights about the Oscar Fox murder to be gained. I bid them good-bye and drove back home to Fleming Street. As I pulled into the driveway, a beautiful black late-model Mercedes turned in behind me. I knew of only one such car in the entire county, but I had never seen it in town. The driver emerged wearing a full-length black cashmere coat, a dark suit, and sunglasses.

"John Harris, just look at you. Power suit, power car, power glasses. No truck and work khakis like normal. You land a job with the Secret Service?"

"Yeah, yeah. Yuck it up, jackass."

We shook hands heartily, both of us wearing broad smiles.

"Well, come in for a while. I'll make some coffee."

"Sounds good," he returned crisply. "Lead the way."

Thankfully, my modest cottage home was generally tidy. Rhett greeted us warmly as we walked down the main hall toward the kitchen in the rear. John progressed slowly, casually observing each room with a bemused air. We had known each other for over six months, but this was the first time he had ever set foot in my home, despite numerous invitations.

"Quaint place here, Doc. Looks like Connie keeps it pretty orderly."

"And this is a surprise to you?"

John grinned. "Yeah, good point."

"You know, I've been meaning to ask you about Connie. What was she like years ago? You know, when you guys were both kids?"

John responded flatly, "Shorter."

John and Connie had grown up together, and while never close friends, they had shared an unspoken respect. Even though John had a PhD in chemical engineering, he readily acknowledged that Connie was the smarter of the two. She had, in fact, been valedictorian of their high school class, with John falling a distant second. But Connie had stayed in Watervalley, become a housewife and mother, and never studied at the college level.

While I made coffee, John stared out the back windows.

"Good-sized backyard, Doc. Come next spring, looks like plenty of room for a nice garden."

"Yeah, like that's going to happen. Growing up in Buckhead did not exactly provide opportunities to develop my gardening skills."

"Ah, don't sell it short, sport. There's something magical about getting your hands in the dirt, watching things grow. It's good therapy."

I laughed. "Well, I'll take that one under advisement." I was satisfied to let the topic pass, but John persisted.

"The Mayfields lived here when I was a kid and there was a huge garden in this backyard. Lovett Mayfield was retired from the post office. He and my dad were big friends and used to swap seeds."

I poured mugs of coffee and we settled at the kitchen table. "So, John, speaking of seeds, spill the beans here, fellow. What could possibly have motivated you to get all slicked up and come to town?"

"I had a meeting with the mayor."

"Mayor Hickman? Really? And the topic?"

"The bandstand."

"Seriously?"

"Yeah. He approached me after the Christmas Eve service and said he wanted to know if my offer to fund the renovation was still good. I said we should meet this week and talk through it. So, we met, we talked."

"And?"

"Can't be completely sure yet, but it looks promising."

"What did Walt say?"

"He's going to try and get it worked out. But you have to

remember, this is Walt talking and Walt's a politician. He's easy to like with all that backslapping and those big smiles. Unfortunately, Walt and his double chin are synonymous with double-talk."

John took a swallow of coffee. "Still, it seems a real possibility it could happen."

"So this is good news, right?"

John smiled broadly. "Oh yeah, this is very good news."

The renovation of the bandstand had become the singular mission of John's wife, Molly, in the months before she died of cancer. The bandstand had been boarded up for fifteen years and had fallen into dangerous disrepair. Despite John and Molly's efforts, the Board of Aldermen had voted down the motion for renovation, largely due to some misguided beliefs about the evils of dancing, which had always been the main activity in the bandstand. That defeat, along with Molly's death, had been the final straw for John and had left him with a festering resentment. Since then he'd isolated himself from life in town.

"Well, congratulations, fellow! I'm happy for you," I said.

"Yeah, thanks. So, enough about me. What have you been up to this morning? Anything happening at the clinic?"

I told John about the meeting at the old bakery and Connie's revelation about her mother having worked there.

John pondered for a moment. "I guess I had forgotten that. Interesting."

"Yeah, and get this irony. Once she gets the bakery started, Estelle wants to give Louise Fox a job there."

John chuckled. "Well, sport, that's what's known as Watervalley's version of the circle of life."

"Oh, I also met Randall Simmons. He's an awful queer duck. Connie sure put the fear of God in him, though."

"I told you he was a slimy one. His dad, Raymond, was a

honcho in the community years ago. Pretty hard-nosed and not very likable. I know my father-in-law didn't much care for him."

"Your father-in-law?"

"Yeah. Molly's dad, Sam Cavanaugh, was chairman of the board at the bank for many years. Good man. Loved this town. Raymond Simmons was the bank president. When Raymond retired in the early nineties, Randall stepped into his father's shoes. He hasn't quite measured up. Nevertheless, he has all the snobbery that second-generation money tends to breed."

"So what's the deal between you two?"

"There's no love lost, or found, between us. It goes way back."

"And?"

"I take it you really want to hear this story?"

"Sure, especially after what I saw of Randall this morning. Let's have it."

John drew in a deep breath, reflecting for a moment. "Elementary school, during the midsixties. I beat the crap out of him one day during recess."

"Seriously? Elementary school? This grudge goes back nearly fifty years? What happened, he try to cheat at marbles?"

John ran his finger around the rim of his coffee cup. "Nah, it was a little more complicated than that. It was the first year of school integration, which actually wasn't as big a deal as it sounds. Heck, it was a small town then just like now. We all knew each other, black and white. We played sandlot ball together; saw each other everywhere. So, finally being together in the same classroom seemed a natural development At least, that's the way I saw it. But Randall, he had a pretty smart mouth in those days. His dad had climbed the social ladder and I guess he thought he was somebody. Anyway, we were all playing a game at recess and he called one of the black girls a pretty lousy name."

"And you kicked his butt for that?"

"Well, it wasn't just the name-calling, although that was bad enough. After he did it, he laughed at her, humiliated her, and there was nothing she could do about it. So I proceeded to walk over and put my fist through his teeth. Then he did a second stupid thing."

"What was that?"

John's face eased into a bemused smile. "He tried to fight back."

No doubt, this was the memory John had been delightfully rolling around in his head the previous afternoon when we were discussing Randall Simmons.

"Okay, I just gotta ask. What did he call her?"

John turned and stared at me blankly, as if I had brought him back to reality. After a moment, he spoke in a detached voice. "He called her a fat, blue-gummed nigger."

"Huh. Sounds like he was asking for it. Whom was he talking to anyway?"

"Constance Grace Pillow, better known as Connie Thompson."

"So you're telling me you were sticking up for Connie? You've always said you didn't much like her in those days."

"That's true. I didn't like her. Even back then Connie was a bit of a tough personality. And I resented that she was smarter than me. She was always smarter than me."

He paused. "No. If I were being honest, even back then I admired her, but I didn't particularly like her. At any rate, she sure as hell didn't deserve that abuse. The funny thing is, she got all mad at me about it."

"Mad at you? For slugging Randall Simmons? Why?"

John exhaled a deep breath and shook his head. "That's Connie for you. Even back then she was bound by her convictions. All that turn-the-other-cheek crap."

"Really?"

"Oh, yeah. She felt that in time God would settle the score and I shouldn't have interfered."

I thought about John's comment. "Must be something to it. She sure had Randall acting like a frightened cat today."

John spoke with a breezy chuckle. "Uh, yeah. I think she got the last laugh on that one. She was reading the tea leaves long before the banking crisis struck a few years ago. When it did, it hit the Farmers Bank hard. Connie was sitting on a pile of cash and bought loads of their stock at a bargain price."

John turned to look me in the eyes, wanting to make sure I fully understood his next comment.

"She practically owns half the bank."

CHAPTER 12
The Winds of Change

John's words hung in the air, richly, elegantly floating like a pleasing aroma. There was something deeply satisfying for both of us in this knowledge. Not only did it fulfill some desire for justice in the order of things; it also amplified the awe and admiration we held for Connie Thompson. We sat quietly at the kitchen table, exchanging wry grins, awash in an unspoken mutual awareness of the long list of social and financial realities this little-known fact had no doubt exerted upon the old order in Watervalley.

"Half the bank, really?"

"Hmmm, I may have overstated that. Probably not half, but I do think she is the largest shareholder."

"Why doesn't she sit on the board of directors?"

"Doesn't want to. I think she's okay with Randall's ability to run the bank, but she's not interested in being in his company any more than she has to."

The blaring ring of the telephone broke the silence. I walked over and grabbed the receiver off the wall. It was Leonard, one of the EMTs, checking in. It was code. They never would admit it, but they did this when they were a little out of pocket for a while. No doubt, another Bowl game was on. It wasn't a problem. Dispatch could always find them if I needed them.

John spoke as I recradled the phone. "You need to go?"

"Nah. Nothing urgent. Although I am expecting an important phone call."

"Oh? Do tell."

"Mary Jo, the staff nurse at the clinic, suddenly gave her notice two weeks ago. She's taking a job in Nashville. Following a new boyfriend, I think. Anyway, we've got a travel nurse coming for six months to take her place. She's supposed to hit town today or tomorrow."

"Travel nurse?"

I rejoined John at the table. "Yeah, it's pretty common in the industry."

"And she's willing to come here?"

"Yeah. Said she has some old ties to Watervalley."

"Interesting. She say who?"

"Not really. All I know is she's well qualified and willing to come. I didn't press for details in our phone interview. Actually, I'm privately glad to be getting a new nurse. I liked Mary Jo, but she could be a handful."

Once I'd said this, it occurred to me that John's unusual curiosity the previous day about my dating life deserved some reprisal.

"You know, John, since lately you've been channeling your inner cupid, maybe you should meet this new nurse. Could be someone interesting for you."

John snorted. "In case you haven't noticed, I'm a little past the girl-crazy stage."

"I don't know, fellow. This new nurse could be a possibility."

His response brimmed with amused skepticism. "Oh really,

Doc. Some perky new graduate? A little young for me, don't you think?"

"I meant new to the clinic, not new to nursing. She's early fifties, I think; single, smart, and she knows CPR, always a benefit for a guy with your habits. Seems pretty independent minded too."

"Independent minded?"

"Yeah. Something about her. Seems like a woman who knows what she wants and how to take care of herself. Pretty low maintenance."

John looked at me sourly, not amused. "Wants to bait her own hook, huh? That's even better—some sharp-tongued broad-in-the-stern old gal? I don't think so."

"Like I said, I interviewed her over the phone, so I can't speak to the broadness of her stern, or any of her rigging, as it were. But she sounded pretty sharp. Might be good company; you know, someone you could tell your troubles to."

"What if she is the one causing me all the trouble?"

I chuckled. "Ah yes, always the optimist. Suit yourself. I just hate seeing all your charms going to waste."

John's focus never changed, but his face slid into a compressed and amused smirk. He was thinking about it. Maybe, just maybe, I had struck a nerve.

"So, you hired her over the phone?"

"Yeah, seems like a lovely gal. I'll give it a couple of weeks and introduce you. Don't want to scare her off too soon."

"Scare her off? What do you mean by that?"

"I don't know, John. It's not like your nickname is 'Bubbles.'"

"I'm crushed, sawbones, crushed. I mean, hey, look at me. What's not to love?"

"Right. What am I thinking? It's not like you're a cynical, foulmouthed heavy drinker or anything."

"Okay, smart-ass. Point taken. Anyway, you're wasting your time. I'm past my 'sell by' date."

I was about to respond when the sound of the front door opening caught our attention. Rhett perked up and began wagging his tail, driven by that innate telepathy that dogs have. He scampered toward the entrance hall to gleefully meet Connie, who had returned from her morning with Estelle.

As she entered the kitchen, it occurred to me that this was the first instance in which I was in the company of John and Connie at the same time. Individually, they were my best, if not only, friends. But it had never been just the three of us, John, Connie, and me. To my thinking, they were the defining individuals of their generation in Watervalley.

Having known each other all their lives, they shared an unspoken language, an intimate familiarity founded upon long years of mutual respect and, likely, a genuine bond of affection. This was revealed even in the way they greeted each other. John obediently rose from his chair and regarded her with a confidential, impish grin. He almost bowed when he spoke.

"Constance."

Connie responded in like form with a slight dip of her chin, something of a precursor to a curtsy. She was wrapped in an amused air. "Professor Harris."

For a brief moment we all stood and smiled warmly at one another, charged by an unexplained delight at this unexpected, long-overdue meeting of intimates. Finally, Connie broke the silence as she turned to put away her purse.

"My, my, my, John. Aren't you all dressed up? What brings you to the city proper?"

"A little business with our friend Walt. Anyway, I was just on my way back to the hills, to the city improper."

As always, Connie's tone was deadpan. "Wouldn't have anything to do with the rumor about renovating the bandstand, would it?"

I raised my hands in a gesture of low amazement. "How does she do that?"

John grinned. "Get used to it, sport. In Watervalley, God hears everything, and Connie's the first person he tells."

Connie offered a thoughtful nod, satisfied that she had attained her answer. "So, looks like I interrupted some important male bonding here. Can I fix you boys some lunch?"

John responded first. "Thanks, Connie, but I really am on my way out the door."

"Me too, actually," I said. "I need to go over to the clinic for a while. Oh, and Connie, I'm expecting a call from an Ann Patterson. Give her my cell phone number if you would?"

"Is she the new nurse?"

"Yeah. By the way, I thought I would pull together a little welcome gathering for her: you know, coffee or dinner or maybe something a little formal."

Connie lowered her chin and glared at me.

"You? Luke Bradford? Doing formal? Humph, I can already taste the frozen Sara Lee cake."

John folded his arms and exhaled a light chuckle.

I ignored him. "Well, yeah. I can do formal."

"Formal for you is putting basket holders under the Chinet."

I responded with mock offense. "I can't believe you're questioning the genteel refinement of my entertainment skills."

"Mmm-hmm. Genteel refinement, huh? John must have given you a thesaurus for Christmas."

At the mention of his name, John entered the fray. "Don't worry, Connie. I'm always available to give the good doctor a few pointers on the social graces."

Connie's neck stiffened as she regarded John skeptically. "John Harris, it might be a harbinger of the fall of Western civilization if you're the last word on charm and diplomacy."

John laughed and glanced in my direction. "Your turn, sport. I gave it my best shot."

I shook my head. "I got nothing."

We stood for a moment, snickering and exchanging amused shrugs. Both of us wanted to continue teasing Connie, but we also knew the duel was futile. She would eventually win. Finally, John spoke as if she were in the next room.

"Hey, you're just going to have to put up with it. She's a great cook."

I played along. "Yep. You're right. Great cook."

The two of us stood with our arms folded, shaking our heads in feigned resignation, and explosively smiling at each other.

A sly grin inched across Connie's face. "My, my. Aren't you two just the pair?" She turned and began to take off her coat. In a low, breezy voice her words lilted into the general air. "So many clowns, so few circuses."

She hung her coat over a chair and studied us for a brief moment. "Well, if you two will excuse me, since we are now doing formal, I must go fold the tea towels and check the polish on the silver." She walked away sporting an irrepressibly smug smile.

John and I left via the front door with him chortling at my expense the entire way.

"Thanks for stopping by, John. Glad to hear about the bandstand."

"I'm thinking I might start making a habit of dropping in. Watching you two is better than cable."

"Yeah, laugh it up. From now on there'll be a cover charge."

Within seconds, he was in his Mercedes and gone.

I walked to my ancient Corolla to drive over to the clinic for a private meeting with Lida Wilkins. When she had stopped me on the way out from breakfast earlier that morning, she had wanted to know if I could discreetly see her around noon. As I fumbled through my pockets for the keys, I had no idea that this next hour would add another layer of intrigue to the infamous murder mystery.

CHAPTER 13

Lida Wilkins

The bright midday sunlight was deceptive, offering an illusory promise of warmth against the cold air. As I started the Corolla, I reached into the inner pocket of my coat for my sunglasses. They were Dolce & Gabbana, one of my few claims to pretentiousness from my Buckhead days. I arrived at the clinic and drove around back to park. Lida was already waiting in her car.

In her late fifties, Lida Wilkins was trim and energetic with an infectious smile and a quick wit. I doubt she had ever been described as beautiful, but with her shining blue eyes that squinted whenever she laughed, her strawberry red hair, and her freckled face and arms, she had a tomboy prettiness about her. Underneath was a savvy business mind and a self-made woman who had started with nothing but now owned the Depot Diner and the Society Hill Bed and Breakfast. And while she was an astute entrepreneur, she was known for her tender devotion to family, church, and community. She was an uncanny combination of the saintly and the practical.

She approached me as I exited my car.

"Well, hey, Dr. Bradford. You're looking awfully stylish in those D and G's." There was a definite country twang in Lida's buoyant voice.

"Lida, aren't you just the fashion marm? I didn't know you had such a cultivated eye for style."

"Fortunately the turnip truck I rode in on had a copy of *Vogue* in the back."

I laughed. "Well, I always figured you for a quick study. Come on. Let's go in the back here."

I unlocked the clinic door and showed Lida to my office. I carried the autopsy file in with me, thinking there was little else it could tell me, and tossed it on my desk before sinking into my chair. Lida took a seat in one of the leather wingbacks across from me. We exchanged pleasantries for a few minutes, during which I couldn't help but notice that her smile seemed to slip into an expression that was pale with worry. It was time to ask questions.

"So, Lida. Tell me what I can do for you."

She exhaled a deep breath and looked down at the floor, signaling that her next words were likely ones she had repeated in her head. She spoke in a succinct, self-effacing tone.

"Doc, I think I'm falling apart."

I nodded, careful to maintain a calm concern. "Okay. Can you give me some details?"

"I feel anxious all the time. I'm eating my body weight in Tums, and lately I've been having some weird chest pains. And, well, there's something else. But we'll get to that in a minute."

"All right. Let's start with the stress. Any unusual events going on in your life?"

"Not much beyond the normal insanity. The diner and the B and B keep me hopping. My bonus baby, Leslie, just turned eighteen and is graduating from high school in the spring. So I still have a teenager at home."

"Well, that alone would explain the heavy need for antacids."

Lida's smile returned. She crinkled her nose and nodded. "Another one of my girls is getting married in July and Lindsey, my oldest, is expecting her first baby in August. They live over in Jackson."

"Sounds like you have enough stress for you and the next two people. So, tell me about these chest pains. When do you have them?"

"Mostly when I'm sitting still, like driving in the car, or when I'm watching TV, just, you know, thinking about things."

"What happens to the pain on exertion?"

"It goes away."

"Hmm. That's certainly atypical. Still, it may be a good idea for you to go over to Regional Medical and get a stress test."

"Doc, my whole life is a stress test."

"Lida, do you do any kind of regular cardio workout?"

"Only if you count running behind as exercise."

"You drink alcohol?"

"Glass of wine from time to time."

"Do you smoke?"

"Not unless I'm on fire."

I smiled and nodded. We talked for several minutes, discussing the frequency and severity of her chest pains and a range of other symptoms, none of which threw up any immediate red flags. I endeavored to assimilate the list of concerns she presented with, but could draw few conclusions. Ultimately, she pressed me.

"So, Doctor. What do you make of all this?"

"Lida, it's difficult to pinpoint anything without doing a physical exam, getting your vitals, and probably running some blood tests. Some of this could also be menopause related. At first brush, your chest pain doesn't appear to be cardiac in nature, but perhaps some kind of referred pain—that is, something originating elsewhere but manifesting in your chest. It might simply be caused by stress and anxiety. Still, we need to rule out cardiac."

She exhaled and nodded. "Anything else?"

"Isn't that enough?"

Lida studied me. She spoke in a confidential tone, wanting me to level with her.

"Doc, you're a sweetheart and I know you're being diplomatic. But I'm a pretty tough little country girl. Tell me what your gut says."

I smiled and leaned back in my chair, rested my hands on the back of my head, and reflected for a moment.

"My gut impression, Lida, is that you're overworked, stressed-out, and just spread too thin. There's more going on in your life than there is of you to go around."

She laughed. "Is there a pill for that?"

"Yes and no. The best thing to do is make some lifestyle changes."

"You're not talking about putting me on one of those diets where all you eat is spinach and flavored dirt, are you?"

I laughed. "Lifestyle changes involve more than diet, although clearly you're not overeating, Lida. You're the size of a Smurf. But all that acid reflux could stem from the types of food you're choosing. If I had to guess, I'd say that's what the chest pain is all about."

She nodded and exhaled deeply. "Well, I know we need to check it further, but generally speaking, it's a real relief to think that it's likely not a cardiac issue. I'll call Monday and set up an appointment, although I have to admit, I don't relish the idea of being poked and prodded."

"We'll try to keep the poking and prodding down to a minimum and focus on your heart. My job is to make sure you don't see that white light everyone talks about."

Lida nodded. "Thanks, Doc. Thanks for meeting with me like this."

I paused and looked at her curiously. "Lida, earlier you mentioned there was something else, some other concern. Did we miss that?"

She slumped back into her chair. "Oh, yeah, that."

I sat quietly, allowing her to fill in the silence.

"When all this chest pain started up, I was concerned it might have something to do with my past."

"As in . . ."

"Cocaine."

"Cocaine? Did you say cocaine?"

I sat for a moment, stunned. Then, spontaneously, I rose and rounded the desk, taking a seat in the leather chair beside her. Resting my arms on my knees, I spoke in an intimate whisper.

"Lida Wilkins, how does a salt-of-the-earth, solid-citizen Sunday school teacher such as yourself ever get involved with cocaine?"

"It was a long time ago. I'm not even sure it's necessary to talk about it."

I leaned back in the chair. "Lida, you do know that anything you tell me is protected under doctor-patient confidentiality laws."

"So if you ever breathed a word of this, I could have you publicly flogged and maybe even kick you a few times for good measure?"

"Not only that, the law says I'd have to pretend to enjoy it."

She grinned, crinkling her nose again. "Fair enough." After pausing a short moment, she proceeded. "So, here's the story. My dad was a deputy sheriff and my mom was an exceptionally strict Baptist. They were good people, but let's just say my home life was pretty rigid. That's why I ran off when I was sixteen."

"You ran off? Where'd you go?"

"Woodstock."

I could not hide my astonishment. "Woodstock! Really? As in the famous week of sex, drugs, and rock and roll?"

"Yep, I hitchhiked to the Catskills and was there at Woodstock for the three days of music, love, and peace, but mostly love. I was kind of a wild child. Anyway, I met some people and followed them back to Greenwich Village. In those days I smoked a lot of grass and along the way I did a little cocaine, the snorting kind. I worked in a French restaurant. That's where I learned to cook, really cook. Before I left New York, I had worked in French, Italian, even Moroccan places."

"Where did you go after that?"

"To rehab."

"Oh, wow." It was a lame response, but I was still amazed, unable to do little more than listen gawk-eyed to Lida's incredible description of her past.

"Yeah, I got myself dry-cleaned."

"Is that when you came back to Watervalley?"

"No, I spent a couple of years in a commune called the Farm. It's about fifty miles away over in Summertown, Tennessee. It was actually a good place for me. A lot of caring people."

"So what happened?"

She shrugged. "At the risk of sounding corny, I found my faith again. I moved back to Watervalley when I was twenty-four. Met Charlie, we got married, the rest is history."

"That's quite a story."

"So, I read somewhere that cocaine can cause heart damage. You think that's the case here?"

I grimaced. "It's possible, but I tend to think that any damage it might have done would have manifested itself long before now. Still, we can get all that checked out."

Lida absorbed this news for a few moments. Then, resolved, she looked over at me with her warm, girlish smile and patted my hand. "Thanks again, Luke, for meeting with me. I just wanted to discuss this privately."

"No worries. You can pay me in cheeseburgers. Although don't tell Sunflower."

"Yeah. You two were quite the curiosity this morning. Want to divulge any secrets about that conversation, Doc?"

"Ahh. The same old Sunflower. She has a few ideas about some community health initiatives she wants me to endorse. I told her we'd talk about it. She's such an odd duck. What was she like when she was younger?"

"Her name is Heidi, even though she's always gone by Sunflower. Anyway, she is about six or seven years older than me, although, darn her hide, she sure doesn't look it. And let me tell you, when she was a teenager, she was a looker. In those days, the school was all in one building, K through twelve. I was probably a fifth or sixth grader when she was a senior and I remember we all thought she was beautiful with her long blond hair and her peasant tops. She'd walk down the hall and it was like the parting of the Red Sea."

"Did she cheerlead or play sports?"

"Oh heavens, no. Sunflower has always had a nonconformist, antiestablishment way about her. Don't know where that came from, but that's always been her. She married some guy from

California and they tried to farm for a while. But they split up after a few years. Rumor's been that she was never able to have children, and that played in the mix. Anyway, she lives out there on her dad's place with her chickens, and goats, and three thousand cats and dogs. I wouldn't be surprised if she grows a little reefer. Gotta be some reason why she seems so peaceful all the time. Maybe I should go see her about my anxiety."

"Sure. Let me know how that works out for you."

Lida grinned at me, scrunching her nose in a way that made me feel we shared a clever and comic intimacy. I adored her. For all her country charm and inviting appeal, she just didn't take herself seriously.

She rose from the chair and was about to leave when her glance fell on the folder on my desk. With an expression of genuine curiosity, she reached for it.

"What is this?"

"It's an autopsy report from the forties. I was cleaning out some old files and came across it. Something about a murdered German. You know anything about it?"

"Yeah. Actually, I know a lot about it."

"Really, how so?"

"From my dad."

I tilted my head toward her, gesturing for her to continue.

"Remember I mentioned my dad was a deputy sheriff? He was the first one to arrive on the scene that night of the murders."

"Wow. Would it be possible to talk to him?"

Lida grinned. "Not unless you're clairvoyant. Daddy passed away in the early nineties."

"Oh, sorry."

"Anyway, my maiden name was Sanderson. My dad's name was Frank. He joined the army in 1941, signed up the Monday after Pearl Harbor. He was shot in the knee in North Africa, so he was discharged. He could still walk, but with a limp. Because of his military training, he got hired on as a deputy. So, he was on duty that night and answered the call about someone hearing a gunshot. He said there was a lot of blood, a pretty nasty affair."

"Well, I have to admit, since I came across the autopsy report, I've been fascinated by the whole business. I was wanting to go to the county archives to look at the police records, but I understand they were all burned up in the jail fire of 1964."

Lida spoke cautiously. "Yeah, well, that may not be completely accurate."

"How so?"

"My dad was obsessed by this case. No one ever really figured out what happened, so he kept digging into it over the years. He even bought a metal detector and spent countless hours between the bandstand and the place where Oscar Fox died, looking for the missing gun. I don't think he was supposed to, but I'm pretty sure he made a copy of all the paperwork so he could study it at home."

"What would be the problem with him continuing to look into it?"

"Daddy once told me that the two murders were ruled to be voluntary manslaughter. He explained that in Tennessee the statute of limitations on that crime is five years. It wasn't just a cold case—it was a dead case. So I always got the impression his boss didn't want him wasting any time on it. That's why Dad made copies and brought them home."

"But why? What about the case interested him?"

"Daddy used to say there was a lot more to the story than people realized. But all I know is that Oscar Fox must have been a bad hombre. The story has always been that he cut that guy to shreds. Anyway, If I'm not mistaken, those old files are in a box somewhere up in my attic."

I made no attempt to hide my excitement. "Do you think you could find the time to dig that out and let me take a look at it?"

She shrugged. "Sure."

"That'd be great. I would really appreciate it."

"Give me a few days. It's up there somewhere, but it may take some unearthing."

"Just call me. I'll be glad to come get it."

I thanked her, walked her to the back door, and watched her leave. Returning to my office, I was nagged by a burning question. If the mysterious German had an autopsy report, then there should be an autopsy report for Oscar Fox as well.

I spent an hour thumbing through all the files from the 1940s but found nothing. The conspicuous absence of his autopsy file along with Lida's comment by her father that there was "a lot more to the story than people realized" deepened my consuming curiosity.

I pushed the file drawer shut and rested my arm atop the ancient wooden cabinet. I half wished the old walls could talk, and offer some insight into the missing chapters. But there was not a whisper. The only voices to be heard were the ones in my head telling me that something about the Oscar Fox murder story felt terribly wrong.

I closed up and drove home. Tomorrow was the 5K race, and Christine.

CHAPTER 14
The 5K

The first invitations of daylight found me lost to the waking world, dreaming in a deep and forgotten sleep. Within the delicate chill of my upstairs room, I was snugly buried under my down comforter. The orange sun thinly crested the frozen rim of the far eastern hills, and inch by inch, the fresh new light reached across the bedroom floor, washing over my headboard, forcing my eyes open.

It was Saturday morning and the air was crisp, lively, charged with muted excitement. I placed my feet on the floor and stretched, extending my arms grandly overhead, squeezing out the stiffness of the previous night. I was consumed with a subtle and warming delight, an anticipation of what the day might bring—a day spent with Christine.

I had been unwilling to admit it even to myself, but ever since my conversation with her on Christmas Eve when she told me to give her a call sometime, my world had been infused with an un-voiced enchantment. In the quiet minutes of the day, Christine would drift divinely into my imagination, captivating me. I felt I was on the approaching side of a grand journey, aware that larger forces were carrying me toward a future ripe with possibility. In truth, I barely knew her, and sought to dismiss these idle daydreams.

But it seemed the spell was cast.

I slipped down the back stairs that led to the kitchen for some toast and coffee, fed Rhett, and returned to suit up in my sweats and running shoes. Grabbing my keys, I stepped onto the front porch. Despite the brilliant morning sunlight, a light frost covered the ground. The cold was tolerable, but still strong enough to leach through my clothes. I had thought about driving but chose instead to walk the eight blocks to Courthouse Square, hoping to warm up my stiff muscles. Besides, my beaten-up, dirty, and dented old Corolla sat frozen and pathetic looking, as if the whole point of the thing was to get a laugh.

As I made my way down Fleming Street, I began to hear music in the distance. As downtown drew near, the sounds thickened in volume and variety, spilling into the morning air. By the time I reached Main Street, a block away from the courthouse, I was awash in an ocean of people, roaring music, boisterous laughter, lively conversations, the rich smell of coffee, and the captivating aromas of breakfast being cooked on outdoor griddles. After a week of slumber, Watervalley had come alive.

It seemed that I had arrived late to a grand party, a riotous outpouring of community filled with energy and celebration. Runners in all shapes and sizes were stretching, jogging in place, clustered in groups. The whole downtown was alight with the myriad pastels of winter coats. The courthouse lawn was bursting with colored banners, grill smoke, cacophonous voices. Old farmers and townsfolk in Carhartt coats occupied the benches. Some amused themselves by whittling bits of wood, while others simply sat with smiles and folded arms, taking in the spectacle.

Beneath the surface chaos a diviner harmony was at work. Despite the cold and drab of winter, the people of Watervalley lived buoyantly. Their lives and livelihood were invariably modest, but they knew how to find joy among the mess and beauty of the common day.

Events like the 5K heightened their spirits. Smiles were everywhere. A salty wit and eager gossip permeated the air and excitement poured over everyone. These were people who welcomed one another with loud, uninhibited friendliness. As I made my way, they greeted me robustly, waving and shouting my name.

I found the sign-up table, had my number pinned to my sweats, and was handed a pair of purple plastic scissors in keeping with the "runs with scissors" theme of the race. I had been searching the crowd for Christine. I had to laugh. It seemed a rather unorthodox first date, one to which the entire town had been invited. But it was impossible not to enjoy the exhilaration and spontaneity. It wasn't long before I found her.

She stood in the middle of a throng of ecstatic, giggling schoolkids—probably from her sixth-grade class. They looked upon her with rapt attention. She was a rock star. She was laughing and teasing with them, smiling in pure delight. She talked to them in an easy voice of total acceptance, and I could tell they loved her for it. Her dark eyes and raven hair were made all the more radiant by the animation on her face. She was beautiful. I leaned against a nearby tree and watched.

She glanced up and saw me standing there taking in the drama of her adoring fans. Smiling sweetly, she sent me a nuanced look that asked me to give her a moment.

"Are you going to walk the race or run it, Ms. Chambers?" inquired one of the boys.

"I'm going to try and run the entire race, Edwin, but it's just fine to walk it. The important thing is to finish. There's nothing wrong with competition, but remember, our class goal is for everyone to complete the race. It's all for fun, okay?"

They nodded obediently. I think in reality she had them mesmerized. She could have told them to go rob the bank and they would have enthusiastically agreed.

"All right. Everyone go and have a good time. I'll see you at the starting line."

She began to make her way among them, stopping to straighten a couple of winter hats. As she approached me, we both smiled.

"Morning, brown eyes. Nice speech."

"They're great kids. So sweet. I love 'em."

"Well, the feeling appears to be mutual. You're quite the celebrity."

She seemed embarrassed by this. "Not really. I don't think it's me. It's just their age. They like having a young teacher. I bet you secretly adored one of your elementary school teachers."

I reflected for a moment. "Not really. My sixth-grade teacher was about a hundred and twenty years old and smelled like Vicks VapoRub."

She rolled her eyes at me without losing her warm smile.

"So," I said, "I have a confession to make. Ever since our conversation the other night, I've been feeling under pressure to win this thing. But after hearing you talk to the kids about how it's all for fun, looks like there's no worry about you showing me up." I was teasing her. I knew Christine had been an all-state basketball player and was no doubt athletic and competitive.

My comment invoked her rather cunning grin. She reached up with both hands to adjust the string on the hood of my sweatshirt. "Now, Doctor, surely you're not one of those guys who can't accept the idea of a woman beating him, are you?"

"No problem accepting that at all. I've known plenty of women who have wanted to beat me."

"You know what I mean."

I laughed. "So. Gloves off, then, huh? No holding back . . . mano a womano?"

Before she could respond, Mayor Hickman called over a bullhorn for all runners to assemble at the starting line. We had both turned to listen to the instructions. Now Christine looked mischievously back at me.

"Just don't be surprised if all you see at the finish line is my backside."

"If that's the case, at least I'll certainly be enjoying the view."

Again, she rolled her eyes. But her enticing smile lingered.

About one hundred runners assembled at the starting area in a somewhat orderly clump. There were four age brackets for the winners, ranging from eighteen to over sixty-five. Out of both courtesy and common sense, we instinctively organized ourselves with younger adults moving to the front. No one wanted to get run over.

Another one hundred or so kids, moms, dads, and others who were simply going to walk gathered behind us. Within this group were a number of colorful, whimsical, and intentionally tacky outfits. One woman carried a huge five-foot-long pair of scissors cut out of cardboard and wrapped in aluminum foil. Some of the high school girls wore brightly colored, striped socks under clunky Uggs. Even Hoot Wilson, a jovial and towering dairy farmer who had nearly died of cardiac arrest during my first week in Watervalley, lined up wearing cutoff overalls over bright yellow sweatpants.

I couldn't be sure if this was just for laughs or part of his normal attire.

Maylen Cook, the town barber, stood at the starting area holding a loaded twelve-gauge shotgun. Only in Watervalley. With his iconic hangdog face, Maylen counted off the start in his flat monotone.

"Runners, on your mark."

Everyone in the front group glanced around in puzzlement. There was not a mark to be on. Maylen picked up on this, frowned, and spoke again.

"Okay. Forget that. Is everybody ready?"

The entire group leaned forward, tensing into a release position.

"Get set." BOOM!

He fired the shotgun and we were off.

After two hundred yards a pack of about six of us moved ahead of the main group. Four of them were high school boys from the local track team who looked like they could run till February. Christine and I were the only ones in this lead group from our age bracket, twenty-one to thirty-five years. We settled into a steady pace and began the long loop around town. For me, it was time to think.

A 5K is three and one-tenth miles. An in-shape adult athlete will run at a pace of six to nine miles per hour, requiring somewhere between twenty to thirty minutes to finish the race. Some people in town knew I had played college basketball, but I had never revealed that in high school I had run track. Although it had been over a year ago, the last time I had run a 5K, my time was under seventeen minutes. I was a competitor on a completely different level. So, I had a decision to make.

I couldn't say I would enjoy losing, but winning this race was not a big deal to me. I had nothing to prove. I just wanted to be with Christine. At the same time, I didn't want to look like I was holding back, sandbagging. I rolled this dilemma over and over in my head for the first minutes of the race, but had no idea what to do. I decided to stay in the pack and let things work themselves out however they might.

We were running at a little over a six-minute-per-mile pace and Christine was having no trouble keeping up. In fact, she was making it look a little too easy. She even took the lead for a short while, picking up the pace. She was testing the group, watching to see who responded and how. She was crafty.

Two miles clicked by and the main pack was now far behind us. Two of the high school boys started a kick and accelerated ahead. We let them go. The other two began to drop behind, seemingly content to finish at a steady pace. That left Christine and me running together. Another half mile passed, leaving only a final half mile to go. Admittedly, I was amazed. Christine was still moving fluidly and had finished the first two and a half miles in less than seventeen minutes. I stayed with her.

Again, Christine accelerated slightly, slowly pulling ahead.

She knew that if we were even for a final sprint, she would probably not win. So she had to put some distance between us, enough so that my longer legs couldn't overtake her in a final dash. With less than a quarter mile to go, she made her move.

I was astounded. Without ever looking back, she found another gear and began quickly to widen the distance between us. I let her go.

We had turned on School Street and there was now less than fifteen hundred feet to the finish line, the length of five football fields. Christine had pulled ahead by some fifty yards. Then, for the first time since she had accelerated, she looked back.

It was just a glance, but I knew what it meant. She thought she had me.

That's when something primal kicked in, some raw competitive instinct that was indifferent to the subtle complexities of relationships. It was time to make it a real race.

I pushed hard off my right foot, practically launching from it. I did the same with the left. Putting power into each step, I accelerated my pace. I was gaining rapidly. Whoops and yells began rising from the bystanders along the sidewalk. Foot by foot I was reeling her in, closing the gap. She continued to move effortlessly, but I was in a rhythmic gallop, shortening the distance between us.

At about a hundred yards from the finish line, I caught her. I moved past her, pushing ahead about ten feet. I began to ease off, feeling well in charge, preparing to coast into the finish and a chorus of cheers.

But the next thing I heard was not the crowd, but the blaring ring of my phone in the back pocket of my sweats.

It was a call from dispatch down at the fire station. With the clinic closed, calls were forwarded there for screening. Despite the celebration, the fanfare, the intensity of the race, and the thrill of the moment, I was still the town doctor. And I was on call. If I waited till after the finish line, I would miss it. So, I did the only thing I could do. I stopped.

In ten seconds, Christine won the race. I was glad for her, and maybe a little bummed. But I had done the right thing. The timing was lousy, but the call was important. It was the one I had been expecting.

CHAPTER 15

From Morning to Eden

"Is this Dr. Bradford?"

I was fighting to catch my breath, making for a broken response. "Yes, yes, this is Luke Bradford."

"Hi. This is Ann Patterson, the agency RN. Did I call at a bad time?"

I lied. "No, no. It's fine. Just . . . hold on one second." I stepped across the sidewalk into a nearby front yard to escape the noise and arriving runners, and also to find a little oxygen. "So, are you in town yet?"

"Actually I arrived early yesterday afternoon. I thought I'd take a day to get my bearings and settle in before I called."

For some reason, I found this amusing. "You may have allotted too much time. You can see all of Watervalley in about thirty minutes."

"Oh, I drove out in the countryside also, to, you know, check out all the landmarks."

I let this comment pass, unsure what landmarks there were to see. "Okay, good. I guess you found the Society Hill Bed and Breakfast without any problem?"

"Yes. I'm there now. I walked downtown earlier to go by the library and stumbled into the big goings-on. Watervalley's quite a lively place."

I almost laughed out loud at this. "Well, not to worry. It'll calm down pretty quickly."

"Oh, and I met Lida Wilkins yesterday afternoon. She said she had just come from seeing you."

"Yes, that would be right. We met over at the clinic. She had a couple of questions for me." I knew Ann's comment was likely motivated by a desire to establish familiarity and find common ground, but I was quick to dismiss a conversation about Lida, given all that she had told me. "So, Ann. Do you need anything?"

"No, I'm good. I was just calling to see when we might get together and go over things at the clinic."

"How about tomorrow, say, one o'clock?"

"Perfect. I've got more exploring I want to do anyway. So that works fine." I wasn't sure what exploring she had in mind, whether it was antique stores or hiking trails, but it didn't matter. I was hoping to enjoy my day with Christine and was relieved that this timing worked for Ann as well. I gave her the address of the clinic. We ended the call and I headed toward the finish line to find that Christine was walking toward me with her hands on her hips, trying to catch her breath. She wore a flushed and worried face.

"Is everything okay?" she asked.

"Yeah. The call was one I needed to take, but not an emergency."

Her expression of concern melted away to one of resignation and frustration. "You had it. You had the race won."

I shrugged and smiled. "Maybe, maybe not. It's not a big deal."

We walked together back toward the finish line at the south end of Courthouse Square. After crossing under the banner, we stepped over to the side to avoid other runners who were newly arriving amidst rounds of cheers, whoops, and applause.

Christine turned and studied me for a moment, searching my face. Then she shook her head and shoved my right shoulder lightly with her hand. "Ugh! Don't be so nice about it." She was teasing me. Her elfin smile was warm, inviting.

"Hey, you ran a great race. You had every right to win. But if it will make you feel better, I guess I could tear up a little."

"Maybe. Let me think about it."

She stood shaking her head, mystified, as if she couldn't find words for her thoughts. Meanwhile, I was captured in the net of her adoring smile. For me, looking at her was far better than winning any race.

"Well, all I can say, Luke Bradford, is that you fooled me by jogging so slowly down Summerfield Road every morning."

I shrugged again. "Sometimes, it's all about taking in the view. Oh, speaking of which, that last shot at the end of the race was pretty fabulous."

"Stop while you're ahead, Doctor."

I grinned, holding up my hands in surrender. "Okay, just saying."

She smiled, reached over, and took my elbow. "C'mon, sand-bagger."

We walked back to the finish line to watch the rest of the competitors.

"Is it okay if I wait here for a while?" she asked. "A lot of my kids will be finishing soon and I want to cheer them on."

"Sure, of course."

One by one the children in her class crossed the finish line, their faces glowing. I walked over to grab a water bottle from the concession table and was soon engaged by several of the older citizens, who were only too happy to enlighten me with a litany of their ailments. Their complaints usually involved bodily functions, the kind I really didn't want to discuss openly. I kindly and diplomatically responded with as much discretion as one can have in the middle of a crowd. All the while I was glancing over at Christine.

To my delight, I noticed that she was doing the same, randomly turning and looking for me within the noise and throng. Eventually, the conversation around me drifted from health complaints to gossip about whose cow had died and whose tractor had broken down and who got what Christmas gift. I had long ago learned that in Watervalley a sympathetic ear was an essential medication.

Yet despite the clamor, the cheers, the wispy smoke, the cold, fragrant air, and all the chaos and celebration around me, it seemed I was caught in another world, one of coded glances and knowing smiles. From across the distance Christine and I maintained a patient, tender accounting of each other. Her eyes told me volumes. I could sense the affection in her gaze, the unvoiced apology for being so occupied by her students. I gazed back at her sympathetically. I understood. It seemed that as doctor and teacher we belonged, in part, to those around us. But the warmth of her delicate smile floated words into the air that only I could hear. The day had magic.

Eventually, all the runners and walkers completed the race. A short awards ceremony followed, in which the winners received plastic medals and were handed checks. In turn, each winner graciously offered the check to Cynthia Robbins, the Watervalley Elementary School principal. All of them, that is, except for the winner of the fifty-something bracket, who demanded a kiss from her first. I was somewhat taken aback until Christine whispered, "That's her husband."

The couple's quick and impromptu smooch was met with a grand round of applause along with a few whistles and light-hearted catcalls. Cynthia extended thanks to all those involved and with that, the event began to wrap up. A few people lingered, but soon most everyone headed to the warmth of their cars and homes.

It was almost noon. Now that we had the opportunity to talk, it seemed that Christine and I were at a loss for words. Silence ensued, and I was anxious to fill the void.

"So, any thoughts about what you would like to do with the rest of the day?"

Christine looked at me quizzically. "Gee, I don't know. What did you have in mind?"

"Hey, my mission is to fulfill your every whim."

"You sure? I can be pretty whimsical."

"Duly noted."

"Come on. Walk me to my car. I left my grandmother in it."

"What? Your grandmother's been sitting in the car this whole time?"

"Hey, it's okay. I left a window cracked."

Christine continued down the sidewalk, but I stopped, staring at her incredulously. She was grinning. She pivoted and began walking backward, facing me with an impish smile.

"I told you I could be whimsical."

I smiled and resumed walking. "Okay, Chambers. You got me on that one."

We leaned against her car and talked for several minutes, each of us awkwardly searching for a means to continue our time together. Nevertheless, our options on a cold December day in Watervalley seemed few.

"I have an idea, Luke. Why don't you come out to the house? I can show you around. It'll give you a chance to channel your inner farm boy."

"Okay. Sure. Don't know about the whole farm-boy-channeling thing, though. I'm not certain that frequency exists."

Christine smiled, again shaking her head. "I'll see you in a little while."

She drove off and I walked briskly back to Fleming Street, took care of Rhett, had a shower, and within an hour was pulling the old Corolla down the short farm lane that served as Christine's driveway. It seemed I had looked upon this place a thousand times, even memorized it, but always from afar. Now it was no longer a vision in the distant countryside. It was an inviting pathway opening grandly before me.

The broad yard was surrounded by a crisp, orderly picket fence. Decades-old boxwoods aproned the deep front porch. The white clapboard farmhouse was generous in scale, with massive brick chimneys bracketing either end. Toward the rear stood the garden, now fallow in the sleep of winter. Farther behind were several brightly painted red barns, a weathered gray silo, and neatly fenced-in lots. In the distance, Holsteins huddled tightly, standing on a thin veneer of frozen mud around a large round bale of hay.

The deep, sumptuous smell of woodsmoke hung in the air. As I shut the car door, Christine appeared on the front porch dressed in a flannel shirt and blue jeans. While her years in Atlanta had cultivated a well-scrubbed urbanity, below the surface was an earthy, sensuous woman who was at ease in the open fields, in the wooded hills, and with the work and rhythms of the farm. In my enchantment, she seemed to me to embody all that was resilient, strong, and good about rural life.

She leaned against one of the porch columns and waited for me with folded arms and a warm smile. I was sliding into my winter jacket as I approached the broad steps.

"Good. You wore your boots," she said.

"Can't very well see a farm in flip-flops."

"Mmm, you are a quick study. There may be a farm boy in there yet."

I climbed the steps and stood next to her, crowding slightly into her space, wanting to draw close to her. We were filled with subdued but spontaneous smiles for each other.

"Well, brown eyes . . . hello again."

She tilted her head, communicating something of a low censure. But the radiance of her smile sent a different message.

"Come on inside. I'll get my coat."

The spacious and graceful entry hall was paneled in rich mahogany with a high ceiling and a well-seasoned and handsome wood floor. To the right was a large entry into the dining room mirrored by a similar large entrance on the left to a sizable living area. Farther down the broad hallway on the left was a wide and well-crafted staircase that rose to a shoulder-high landing before turning to the right and ascending to the second floor. Christine gently grabbed my arm.

"Come this way."

We stepped into the large living room. With its immense fireplace and soaring ceiling the room had a stately feel to it. Yet it was also warmly filled with all the things of home . . . paintings and photos that covered the dark paneled walls, vases and lamps that were elegantly arrayed on small tables, and massive windows framed by thick, plush curtains. There were deep, leather sofas and side chairs in soft, colorful fabrics, baskets filled with magazines, and books stacked neatly on various ledges. The room had an understated formality yet felt graciously comfortable, rich with the fragrance of accumulated years and a whispered quality of enduring affluence.

Perhaps it was an extension of Christine's easygoing nature, but this home exuded a loving, breathing presence, a sublime, embracing warmth. Within these strong walls a relaxed and inviting welcome poured over me. I had been in Watervalley for nearly half a year, and yet at this moment, I felt I had finally arrived. After so many months of knowing Christine only from a distance, to now be so delightfully in her presence, to be so intimately brought into her private world, was nothing short of pure enchantment.

That was, until Christine's grandmother entered the room.

CHAPTER 16
Life on the Farm

In her midseventies, Mattie Laura Chambers was a small, rugged woman with a tight-lipped toughness about her. She was standing in the kitchen doorway with her hands on her hips and wearing a heavy farm coat, brown dungarees, and rubber boots. Despite a face that held the weathered lines of many seasons, she was staring at Christine with an absorbed adoration. The same look, I imagined, she had when she first saw the newborn Christine twenty-eight years ago.

But when she glimpsed me standing across the room, all that glowing adulation vanished. Instantly her expression turned to loathing, the kind of look you give someone who's about to testify against you in court. A moment earlier I had been in a trance, absorbing the captivating air of the living room, blissfully drifting in rural dreamland. Her glaring regard brought me back to reality. I wanted to speak, but her withering stare calcified the words in my throat.

"Oh, Grandmamma! There you are!"

Turning toward Christine, Mattie's hard face transformed again to ardent devotion. Christine put her arm around her grandmother and ushered her toward me.

"Grandmamma, this is Luke Bradford. He's the new town doctor. Luke, this is Mattie Laura Chambers, my grandmother on my dad's side."

"Good to meet you, Mrs. Chambers." I mustered all the courtesy I could but had the odd sense I was exchanging cordialities with a bobcat, an unhappy one.

Christine's grandmother looked at her, confused. "Isn't this that Jasper Smoot fellow?"

"No, Grandmamma. This is Luke. He's new to town."

Mrs. Chambers studied me again. Her neck stiffened and her mouth puckered, as if I were emanating a bad smell. "Humph, you sure? Could have fooled me."

Christine and I exchanged glances, but she seemed oblivious to the lethal flashes of dislike that her grandmother was shooting at me. I broke the silence.

"Well, again, it's good to meet you, Mrs. Chambers."

After a sullied stare, she finally spoke with a perfunctory nod. "Yeah, same here." She struck me as a woman of few words, someone you half expected to spit decidedly and with enthusiasm after each pronouncement. Given the way she was dressed, she looked like she'd just come in from the barn, where I could easily imagine she had been smacking the bulls around, for practice, just to remind them who was boss.

"Luke, I need to run upstairs and get my coat. I'll be right back." Before I could think of any plausible reason to follow her, Christine was gone. I smiled at her grandmother, who once again stared at me as if she wanted to debone me.

"So, I understand you're visiting from Florida?" I said.

Behind her thin lips she began to roll her tongue around in her mouth, contorting her face into a series of sharp, pinched grimaces. She ignored my question.

"Just what have you two got planned, Jasper?"

I disregarded the name. "Oh, I think we're just going to walk around the farm. Seems like a nice way to spend an afternoon. Um, by the way, the house is really lovely."

She folded her arms and continued the silent twisting gnarls of her mouth and tongue, chewing her cud, sizing me up.

"Mmm-hmm, well, just watch yourself."

"Excuse me?"

"Eh, you heard me. Just because you've become a doctor now, Jasper, don't try any funny business."

I opened my mouth to speak, then closed it, uncertain how to respond. "Mrs. Chambers, I'm not sure I understand what you mean."

She stepped toward me and assumed a conspiratorial tone. "Listen up, Jasper. I've got a rifle, a shovel, and a hundred acres out back. I'll drop you like a deer. Now do you get what I mean?"

I was frozen, unsure whether to agree, argue, or wrestle her to the floor. Fortunately, Christine's footfalls sounded on the stair-steps and in an instant she was in the room, smiling and glowing. We departed through the entry, but I remained visibly rattled. My exchange with Mattie Chambers had taken only a few minutes, including a couple to get over the shakes, but it left me subdued. As we began crossing the field toward a large barn, Christine took notice.

"You're awfully quiet all of a sudden. Are you okay?"

"Oh. Sure. Sorry." I walked a few more steps. "Your grandmother, she's, um, she's pretty interesting."

"Yeah, she's great, isn't she?"

This was a dicey moment. I was certain that the words "clueless" and "Christine" would not be a welcomed combination, but it was clear we were living in two distinctly different realities. In months past, I had accidentally insulted Christine's mother . . . an innocent but stupid mistake. I sure wasn't about to disparage her grandmother, whom she so clearly adored. I avoided the question.

"You're certainly the apple of her eye. She did seem a little confused, though. Who is or was Jasper Smoot?"

Christine glanced over to read my face. At that moment, jealousy was the last thing on my mind. But something in her look telegraphed that she might be wondering if that was behind my subdued mood.

"He was a friend back in elementary school. He had a little crush on me and rode his bike out here a few times when we were about twelve. I think he lives in Memphis now and has three kids. Anyway, Grandmamma never cared much for him."

"Yeah, I picked up on that."

This time it was Christine who filled in the silence. "You're right, though. She has a small touch of dementia and does seem to get confused easily. Mom's a little concerned about her going back to Florida alone."

"Speaking of which, where is your mom?"

"She ran into town to get a few things. She's doing so much better, thanks to you."

A month earlier, through a chance meeting at the local grocery, I had diagnosed Christine's mother, Madeline Chambers, with a vitamin B12 deficiency, something that her physician in Nashville had missed. After several months of poor health, she had made a remarkable recovery. She was a petite, handsome woman with the gracious refinement of a banker's daughter. I had never met Christine's deceased father, but given the grit and independence of her grandmother, I could easily discern the parental influences that had endowed Christine with the curious mix of graceful poise and farm girl toughness.

"Well, I'm glad. I like your mom." My answer was not motivated by some inclination to ingratiate myself, but from genuine experience. I had met Madeline Chambers only once, but she had engaged me with the reserved charm and delight that seemed imbued in Southern women of her generation. She had that rare gift of meeting you with authentic interest and you couldn't help but feel warmed by her presence.

"Well, she certainly likes you," Christine replied. "She'll hate that she missed you."

I didn't respond because I was still thinking about Grandmother Chambers and her gun, hoping she would miss me as well.

Soon, however, we had distanced ourselves from the house, out of range for even a crack shot. My mood lightened. "So, tell me about this place, farm girl. So far I've seen horses and cows. I know you ride one and milk the other, but I get confused which is which."

Christine smiled and stepped carefully through the dewy field grass. "It's a dairy farm, though not as big a production since Daddy died. The farm foreman, Mr. Pilkington, and his wife pretty much run the place now. They've been here as far back as I can remember. There's a white frame house on the back of the property where they live. He must be in his sixties by now, but spry as ever and tough as nails. We're not related, but he's always been like family."

We entered a large barn with a wide central hallway.

Towering thirty feet high to the ceiling were neatly stacked bales of hay, round ones on the left and square ones on the right. The frail warmth of the barn was thick with pungent aromas. Dank earth, manure, farm feed, salt blocks, old fertilizer, and diesel fuel permeated the air and mingled with the rich, honest aroma of hay. It was wonderful, sensuous, intoxicating. It enveloped me with a sense of drowsy calm.

We ambled to the far end of the barn, where there were several horse stalls and some open bays filled with tools, dusty stacks of wood, old sawhorses, and a large tangle of baling twine. A light was emanating through the chalky glass of a closed door toward the end of the hall. As we approached, I noticed a small sign plate that read TACK ROOM. Inside, someone was humming. Upon opening the door, we found a small man sitting on an overturned five-gallon bucket, meticulously working on a leather bridle. He rose and took off his cap, a vestige of old manners.

"Mr. Pilkington, hello. How are you this afternoon?" Christine asked.

"Fine, fine, Christine. And who's your gentleman friend?"

"This is Luke Bradford."

"Yes, yes, the doctor, no less." He greeted me with a toothy grin, vigorously pumping my extended hand. His delighted voice had a raspy, nasal quality.

"Good to meet you, Mr. Pilkington."

"Heavens, young man, call me Angus. Christine's never changed the habit from when she was a little girl."

I nodded. "Christine is showing me the farm. We didn't mean to interrupt."

"Not at all. Not at all. Just piddling with this bridle. One of the straps is coming undone. Needs some stitching. Anyway, just as well you found me. I've got to be getting the cows gathered for milking here directly."

The tack room wall was filled with tools for working harnesses and leather. Several saddles rested on neatly built railings and in the corner was a small wooden desk with various catalogs and medicine bottles lined up across the back. Above it, a long shelf was crammed with ribbons and trophies.

We talked for another few minutes. Angus was a clean, tidy little man with an alert, intelligent face. Like so many of the small-scale farmers I had come to know in the area, he seemed to desire little beyond his isolated fields and barns, living an orderly, well-scrubbed, and simple life. I would come to learn that Amelia, his wife of nearly forty years, sometimes worked alongside him in the milk parlor. They had no children, save for their "adopted" Christine, but seemed content to enjoy the animals, the gardens, and the ebb and flow of the farming seasons.

We were interrupted by a high-pitched whinny.

Angus grinned. "Sounds like Aragon knows you're here."

I looked at Christine. "Aragon?"

"My horse. He was given to me when I was thirteen, during my Tolkien phase."

"Okay. Good to know."

The three of us stepped down the hallway to the adjacent stall, where Christine opened the half door and walked fearlessly up to the massive animal. Her family had raised quarter horses for years and the sight of her delicate hands firmly holding the harness of this huge creature showed a different side of her. The soft, confident tone of her voice revealed an unabashed understanding and connection between the two of them. In that moment, as in so many others, she was unspeakably beautiful, an enchanting mix of reserve and refinement coupled with the bounding healthiness and open hardiness of the farm girl.

"I think he'd still give you a gallop around the farm if you wanted it," Angus remarked.

Christine continued to rub Aragon's long neck. "He probably would, the old dear." She looked affectionately into the horse's large, brooding eyes. "Those days are past, though, aren't they, big fellow?"

"Albert taught her to ride," Angus explained. "She was a natural. Won all them blue ribbons on the wall in there."

"Albert?"

"Albert, her father."

Angus stood admiring the two of them for a moment. He reached out and put his hand on my shoulder. "Young fellow, looks like you may be getting upstaged. Why don't you come and help me with the milking? That'll give you a real taste of life on the farm."

Christine peered around Aragon's head with a face of innocent inquiry, one that asked if I was interested in this offer. I was not a stranger to the outdoors, and being on the farm was delightful, but milking would push my comfort zone.

"I, um. I think I may have to pass on that. I don't really speak cow."

Angus laughed heartily, slapped me on the back again, and departed. I walked over and rubbed Aragon's neck, lightly patting him on his shoulder. He was a beautiful animal despite the slight protrusion of bones that revealed his advanced years. He turned and looked at me from the great depth of his brown eyes, assessing me. It seemed something I had grown accustomed to on this day.

"He's not near as rambunctious as he used to be," Christine offered.

"I'd say that's a good thing."

"It is. He almost trampled one of my previous boyfriends. But not to worry. It was years ago when I was in high school. He's calmed down a lot since then."

"The horse or the boyfriend?"

"Hmm . . . I'm guessing both." She rubbed Aragon's long neck for a few more moments. "Come on, Luke, I want you to meet someone."

We walked to the dairy barn, where the black-and-white Holsteins had been gathered into a narrow fenced area awaiting their turn in the milk parlor. All, that is, except for one. Standing in a small enclosure on a modest lot near the barn was a single Holstein whose straddled legs held up a bulbous, sagging frame. She stood munching on some dangling hay and for all practical purposes looked like a fixed statue, as if the apparatus of bones and muscle was no longer capable of movement.

"This is Princess Bess, the oldest milk cow on the farm. She's almost twenty years old now and produced milk for over eleven years. But she's no longer a milker."

"I'm not sure I understand. I thought being a milk cow was like being in the Mafia. You know, once you're in, you're always in."

"No, silly. Of course she's still a milk cow. I meant she no longer milks since she no longer has calves. Normally after they are not milking anymore, the best farming practice is to sell them. But we keep her around because she was my dad's favorite."

I nodded thoughtfully. We leaned against the wooden fence. Eventually, the old cow turned her head in our direction.

I spoke diplomatically. "She's kind of a tough read. Do you think she likes me?"

She whispered in return, "Too soon to tell."

"Well. It's understandable. I mean, after all, she is a princess. She has to be a little discerning."

"Give her time. She may come around."

Christine cut her eyes at me with a delighted smile half hidden behind the long dark hair that framed her face. After a short moment she bumped my shoulder with hers and laughed, shaking her head. "Has this been okay? Just, you know, walking around out here."

"Absolutely. I hope to be on a first-name basis with every single Holstein before spring."

Christine turned around, leaning her back against the fence. "When I lived in Atlanta, I really missed this place. Sometimes I wonder why I stayed away so long."

I also turned my back to the fence and gazed at the wide expanse of farm, absorbing all of it.

"Why wouldn't you miss it? It's beautiful," I said.

Christine turned and studied my face for a moment. "Do you really think so?"

At first I remained focused on the distant landscape. "Yes, beautiful." But then I turned and looked squarely at her. "Absolutely beautiful."

Christine's eyes seemed to be full of tenderness, of slow surprise as she absorbed the intended double meaning of my response. An embarrassed grin spread across her face. She gazed down toward the mud and grass.

"All right, Doctor. You're making me blush."

"I want you to blush."

But she said nothing more and simply continued to look down. My confidence wavered and I retreated to more familiar ground.

"Anyway, I guess I should be focusing my charms on Bess over there. After all, you're just a lowly farm girl. She's a princess. A guy's gotta maintain his standards, you know."

Christine looked up and smiled warmly at me. She rested her arms over the top fence rail, joining me in my casual admiration of Princess Bess. Then she closed her eyes, breathed in luxuriously of the crisp December day, and seemed deeply happy.

A cooler air began to tumble down from the high hills.

As we stood in the silence, I realized what had been happening all afternoon. Christine had been introducing me to the places and things she loved best. It was her way of showing me who she was.

It gave me an idea.

CHAPTER 17

An Evening with Old Friends

"Come with me," I said. "It will be getting dark soon and I want you to meet some friends of mine."

We walked back to the house, where we hopped in the Corolla and drove back to Fleming Street. Rhett met us at the door and I introduced him to Christine, beginning what would no doubt become a long-lasting love affair. I gave Christine a quick tour of the downstairs and put some food in a bowl for Rhett, who promptly ignored it in favor of Christine's adoring attention. I told her I was making some quick dinner plans but needed a minute to gather a few things. She shrugged and agreed without further question.

"Rhett, keep our guest company. I know she's pretty, but try not to drool."

Christine bent down, held his big shaggy face between her hands, and rubbed behind his ears. She looked into his brown eyes as she spoke.

"That's right, Rhett. Don't be like your big brother Luke, wagging his tongue all slobbery-like."

"You do know I'm still in the room, don't you?"

Christine winked at me. Rhett probably needed to go to the backyard and do his business, but now he seemed content to hold it till he popped. Meanwhile, I went outside to the firewood stacked alongside the house and loaded some split logs into the trunk of the Corolla. I phoned the Depot Diner and ordered a large pizza to go, then gathered some other items, including a couple of folding canvas chairs from the utility room, and returned to the kitchen.

Rhett was looking at Christine intently, making small whimpering sounds like he desperately wanted to speak.

"I've got some outdoor dinner plans in the works. Do you mind if he comes along?"

Christine's look told me it was a stupid question.

I snatched a few beers from the fridge and we loaded up the Corolla. On more than one occasion I had to remind Rhett that his place was in the backseat and not in Christine's lap. We stopped by the Depot, where I grabbed the pizza and placed it on the floor at Christine's feet, keeping it away from Rhett, who clearly had issues with impulse control.

The sun was beginning to fall below the western hills, setting the sky ablaze in deep hues of orange that fingered across the far reaches of the valley. After driving for several miles, I pulled off the highway onto a secondary road known as Gallivant's Crossing. Thus far, Christine had been a good sport, not asking any questions about where we were going. But as we headed farther into the countryside, her curiosity got the better of her.

"So, you mentioned earlier you wanted me to meet some of your friends. Can you give me a hint?"

"Patience is a virtue, you know."

"Oh, c'mon. At least narrow it down a little."

"Here's the deal. I've adopted a pack of wolves that love pizza. It's a Twilight thing."

"I'm going to go with a no on that one. Wolves don't eat pizza."

"Sure they do."

"And you know this how?"

"Hmm, I read it in an article somewhere."

"And would that be an article in *I Just Made This Up* magazine?"

"Rhett eats pizza."

"Rhett's not a wolf."

"Minor technicality."

"Quit stalling."

"Okay, okay, okay. Since you insist . . . we are going to Moon Lake."

Christine looked at me in disbelief. "No, we're not."

I hesitated, somewhat surprised by her answer. "Yeah, we really are."

"How did you manage that? I grew up here and I've never seen Moon Lake. The access road has been padlocked for years. Luther Whitmore has always owned it and he's never let anyone get near the place."

"Well, he gave me a key. Said I could go up anytime."

"Gee, Luke Bradford. I am impressed. Luther Whitmore is a pretty difficult character."

"You mean he's a horse's ass?"

"Yeah, something like that."

"I'll spare you the finer details, but several months ago he came to me with a chronic medical problem and I was able to cure him. Nancy Orman had always talked dreamily about seeing Moon Lake when she was a little girl. She said it was one of the most beautiful places she had ever seen. So, I asked him about it, and I guess in a moment of weakness he gave me a key."

"So, the lake, have you seen it? Have you been up to it before?"

"Yeah, several times actually. It's pretty incredible. We're almost there."

Moon Lake was a deep pool of about five acres that sat on a high, open grassy knoll. The lake got its name from the incredible way the moon reflected off the water because there were no trees to obscure the view. The surrounding land had belonged to the Whitmore family, who owned the local newspaper, with the idea that one day they would build a house here. But that had never happened and Luther had had the entire area closed off with a high fence and a heavy steel gate. Over the months I had occasionally come to the lake to clear my head, but I had never told anyone about it, partly out of respect for Luther's quixotic generosity.

We pulled onto a narrow lane and drove for half a mile. As I got out and unlocked the heavy gate, the sun's last rays were all but vanishing along the far hills. I drove the remaining hundred yards up the grassy lane to the lake and parked next to a small fire pit I had built on a previous visit. Christine got out and walked the few steps toward the shore, taking in the incredible beauty of the last glimmer of sunlight on the water. I let Rhett out and began to toss some of the firewood into the small stone ring.

"This is incredible!" Christine's voice rang crisp and clear against the vast silence of the broad sky and open hills. A three-quarter moon was already visible in the east. I finished unloading the wood and walked up beside her. She seemed quietly consumed, absorbed by the play of sunset and moonlight.

"I love this place," she said.

I smiled. It had been a good decision to come here. "I do too."

In the faint light of dusk Christine's face seemed transformed. She breathed in a deep draft of the fresh, cool air and exhaled slowly. Then she turned to me with a face full of sharp curiosity.

"You said you wanted me to meet some of your friends?"

"That I did."

By now the first flicker of stars was appearing in the large bowl of the night sky. I stepped behind Christine and conformed my body to hers. "This may seem a little corny, but just go with me on it."

Taking her right hand in mine, I lifted it toward the deep black of the northern sky, using her forefinger as a pointer. "See that? It's the North Star. And if you follow in this direction, these two stars always point to it. They're part of Ursa Major, also known as the Big Dipper."

Christine studied them for a moment. Then she leaned back against me, letting her head settle against my cheek.

"Show me more."

I moved her arm gently. "That's Ursa Minor, the Little Dipper. There's Orion. And there's Canis Major, the big dog. That's Rhett's favorite."

Christine brought my arm down, wrapping it tightly around herself. "So, these are your friends?"

"When I was a little boy living in north Georgia, there was a large field out behind our house. After sunset I would lie in the grass and look at the stars. When I moved to Atlanta, the city lights masked them. But out here there's not a light for miles. So the first night I came to Moon Lake, I saw all of those stars again. There they were, like old friends. Like I said, it's a little corny, but it's very real for me."

Christine slid around to face me. Still holding my hand, she pulled my arm around behind her. Her face was solemn in the spreading moonlight. We were only inches apart.

"Luke, I don't think there's anything corny about it."

Instinctively I reached up and began to slide my hand around the soft sweep of her face, pushing my fingers into her thick, glossy hair. She looked up at me with parted lips. I began to pull her closer.

Just then Rhett unleashed a ferocious bark. We both jumped back.

"Oh, my gosh," Christine exclaimed through a gasp of laughter. "That scared me to death."

I knelt and held Rhett's face in my hand, petting him affectionately. "Thanks, buddy. Great timing."

"I think someone wants pizza."

I continued rubbing Rhett's shaggy coat. "I think someone wants to be taken to the pound."

Christine reached over to where I was kneeling and lightly tousled my hair. "Come on, stargazer, let's get a fire going."

As I walked back to the fire pit, I responded in a low mumble, "That's what I thought I was doing."

We built a huge blaze that burned savagely, throwing bright folds of flames ten feet high into the night sky. It warmed us and cast a solitary light into the vast and solemn darkness of the open knoll. We devoured the pizza and sipped the beers. It seemed we talked for hours, about childhood years and college days; about family, and friendships, and favorite pets; about beautiful places, and travel, and about the chance moments of life. Christine talked and laughed, sometimes with a face of great animation and excitement, sometimes in a voice that was low and sweet and reflective.

Occasionally I would poke the coals with a shovel, making sparks fly toward the stars, giving new life to the flames. The glow of the firelight illuminated Christine's face, shadowed only by her long dark hair, which she would occasionally pull back with her hand. God, she was beautiful. But as the hours and the words flowed by, I saw in her much more. I saw a fascinating blend of a tender and confident woman mixed with a whimsical schoolgirl who could laugh, and listen, and fearlessly show her emotions, her vulnerability. I was falling deeper under her spell.

Late in the night the last of the firewood had smoldered down to ash and glowing coals. The cold was overtaking us again. The eternal night sky that had been a vast universe of brilliant stars had given way to a hazy cover of low clouds. Snow was whispering from beyond the hills. It was time to go home.

As we made the long drive back, I reached over and took Christine's hand, holding it gently in mine. Rhett must have thought this was a grand idea. He crawled slightly forward between the seats and placed his paw on top of our folded hands.

"Great, buddy. Thanks. I make my big move and you think it's time for some comic relief."

Soon we were within the faint glow of the downtown streetlights. As we circled Courthouse Square, we passed the old Hatcher Building, reminding me of the story of Oscar Fox. I told Christine about the autopsy report and asked what she knew about the whole business.

"It's always been a big mystery," she replied. "We used to tell ghost stories about it when we were kids. We tried to scare each other, saying that Oscar Fox would come get you in the night and stab you with a knife. When I had slumber parties, we would sneak out in the middle of the night and walk down to his grave. He's buried in a cemetery just down the road from the farm."

"Really?"

"Yeah. It's back off the road a bit, kind of hidden away. It's the old Taylor family cemetery. That's my grandmamma Chambers's people. She was a Taylor."

"And Oscar Fox is buried there?"

"Yeah, he was pretty good friends with my grandmother's

dad, Great-grandpapa Taylor. You should ask her about him. I think she knows a lot of stories."

I pondered this option in silence, not wanting to stir up any discord at the end of such a splendid day. But I was energized, fascinated by the relationship of Christine's family to this story. We arrived at the farm, got out of the car, and walked to the front porch.

"So, you're pretty consumed with this whole Oscar Fox mystery, aren't you?" she said.

I hadn't thought about the murder mystery all day, but now it seemed I was obsessed by it. I began talking about it nonstop. "Yeah, it's just . . . I don't know. There I was in my office cleaning out some old cabinets and I came across this file. And then something really strange happened."

Christine whispered softly, "Luke."

"There was a sudden chill in the air . . . not in a creepy way but in a strange, uplifting way . . . like one of those trances you go into when you hear an old song on the radio and in your head you're trying to remember what you were doing the first time you heard that song."

"Luke?"

"So I thought the whole thing was coming to a dead end and then Lida Wilkins told me she has this box of old evidence up in her attic that her dad, Frank Sanderson, compiled. So I'm thinking I should call Sheriff Thurman and—"

"Luke!"

"Oh, sorry. What is it?"

"Shut up and kiss me."

She didn't have to tell me twice.

CHAPTER 18

Fools Who Came to Scoff

I slept late Sunday morning—that is, if eight thirty can be considered late. I was in dreamland with only my hand exposed from under the covers, extending slightly off the bed. It was found by a big sloppy tongue and a very cold nose, not the sort of stuff that dreams are made of.

I took Rhett downstairs and let him outside while I made coffee. At nine o'clock, the first of the downtown church bells began to ring, the age-old call to Sunday worship. Since my arrival in town, I had not participated in the business of Sunday morning. I had wanted to keep my distance, not to engage in the larger life here. To their credit, despite how their faith permeated their lives in both word and deed, the people of Watervalley had not pressed me on this matter. Early on, polite invitations had been offered, but then the subject had been left alone. It spoke of a respect and perhaps a deeper understanding of what they believed. Their faith had patience.

This Sunday morning something stirred in me. I could honestly say it was a blend of motivations. I knew Christine would be in the choir, but that alone was not the draw. I had known of her presence there for months. There was something of the devout in the mix, as well as a desire to connect with others in my small world. It seemed the time had come.

I went upstairs, cleaned up, shaved, and dressed. My clothes could use pressing, but it wasn't a major concern. In Watervalley, you were considered a fashion aficionado if you didn't wear white socks with your Sunday suit. In time, the eleven o'clock hour approached and I grabbed my wool overcoat and drove over to Church Street.

Made from cut limestone, First Presbyterian of Watervalley was an impressive hundred-year-old building with Greek columns and elaborate stained-glass windows. Broad steps led up to the narthex, a stately room of deep-toned wood paneling and marble floor that solemnly brought you into an awareness of a subdued and sanctified presence. The sanctuary beyond was no less imposing.

After being handed a service bulletin, I shuffled into a full house save for an open area on the rear right pew. I landed just as the church bell rang for the eleventh time. Before I sat, however, my attention was held captive by a small well-worn brass plate on the end of the pew. It read DONATED BY OSCAR FOX, 1943. This struck me as rather odd given his notorious reputation. I knew that in the past John Harris had gone to church here. When I got a chance, I would ask him about it.

I had no sooner sat down than I recognized Will Fox and his mother, Louise, seated at the far end of the same pew. I smiled and nodded.

Will offered a slight wave and Louise returned a faint smile and I was again reminded of their desperate financial situation. She sat with her tattered coat beside her, staring forward with a shattered humility, doing her best to cling, at least in some out-ward way, to a lost standard of personal dignity. It seemed in that moment that, if for no other reason, the hound of heaven had drawn me to church that morning to convince me I must try to do something for them. What this was, I had no idea.

Nor did I have long to think about it.

I was abruptly shoved by someone wanting me to scoot over to make room. It was John Harris. As seemed to be his nature, he had arrived in a nasty way. Once again he wore his dark suit and coat, and looked polished and downright handsome.

As I moved over, he leaned toward me. "Don't say a damn word, sawbones. I'm here. So just shut up."

I looked down, repressing a roguish grin. When I glanced sideways toward John, he was doing the same. Even in church, it seemed we shared an effortless camaraderie. Admittedly, we were akin to two mischievous schoolboys full of mirthful exuberance. We knew where we were and were fully respectful of the moment, but we were not beyond being slightly irreverent.

The service began with Reverend Joe Dawson welcoming ev-eryone and reviewing the morning's announcements. Even though he had held the position for well over a year, he was still considered the new pastor. His predecessor had presided for thirty-three years. Standing in his black robe with an easy smile and great energy, Joe didn't fit the mold of the stoic Presbyterian minister. He read through the printed announcements and then grinned broadly.

"I do need to bring everyone's attention to a minor typograph-ical error in our bulletin this morning. Please note that our hymn of worship is actually 'There Is a Balm in Gilead' and not 'There Is a Bomb in Gilead.'" This brought a ripple of laughter from the congregation.

Joe continued, "This was my mistake. I texted it in to our church secretary and did not pay proper attention to the auto-spell feature. You would think I would have learned my lesson from my last church, where one Sunday the closing hymn was 'Just as I Am, Without One Flea.'"

More laughter ensued and with a grand smile, Joe implored us to stand and begin the service with the opening hymn. To my surprise, John had a rich baritone voice and only occasionally glanced at the printed words. He knew them by heart. I, on the other hand, struggled along. Singing had never been a long suit and I fumbled through miserably. When we finished, John leaned over and whispered, "The sheriff should record you singing and have it played to the state inmates. I can't imagine a crueler punishment."

He leaned back and folded his arms, quite pleased with himself.

With my chin low I turned slightly. "I hope you get very sick, and soon."

The service continued.

The familiar progression of responsive reading, asking forgiveness, receiving assurance, and singing centuries-old hymns followed. Curiously, I found the service amazingly comforting. Unlike other churches I had known, First Presbyterian of Watervalley had felt no compunction to reinvent itself. Here there was a high regard for traditional, liturgically informed worship. The church had not lost its ecclesiastical soul.

Faith in Watervalley was part of the common vernacular, far more than an occasional "Lord willing" thrown into the conversation. It seemed that God was automatically considered present in the room, participating in the conversation. I couldn't say that I always thought to operate under this mind-set, but I embraced it as genuine in those around me and had seen the transcendent goodness it fostered in their actions. Their lives were the outworking of their theology.

Joe Dawson proceeded to deliver his message. It was authentic and compelling.

His was not a sanitized gospel, watered down to accommodate behavior that inconveniently conflicted with scriptural absolutes. This was a gospel meant to be unapologetically accepted for what it was, not one in constant need of mending in order to incorporate the latest cultural trend. And yet the appeal was not premised on guilt and shame, but rather on being open to considering a gentle plea to a different worldview.

During the sermon John seemed to be absorbed in his own thoughts. Occasionally he would gaze at the ceiling with a collected stoicism. In time he began to survey the room, methodically and somberly pondering one individual and then the next. No doubt, he had a history with all of them. As John looked around at these people of Watervalley, at these souls in his small world, something in his countenance suggested that he still held a deep sympathy and affection for them. It hinted that his contempt toward them was changing, if only by inches.

The sermon drew to a close, leaving only the offering and closing hymn. While the organ played, several men and women discreetly moved the collection plates along the rows. John and I both made contributions and I couldn't help but hear the distinct clink of coins when the plate passed by Louise Fox. The sound stirred in me the voices of faith and charity. I didn't think poorly of prayer, but her situation called for deliverance on a more earthly level. Then an idea struck me. A good idea, but it would have to wait.

Suddenly, like all of those around me, I became an unintended listener to a loud conversation.

"How much you got there? Looks like a pretty good take today."

It was one of the ushers, Clyde Perkins, a rumpled little fellow in his early eighties who had probably performed this duty for decades. He wore hearing aids and was utterly incapable of talking in anything below a mild yell. He and another usher were standing at the back, waiting for the anthem to end.

"Nobody uses their offering envelopes anymore. I don't know why we print the darn things," Clyde said.

Grins erupted among those around me. There was an exchange of knowing glances, looks of tolerant amusement. Clyde's counterpart, a fellow in his thirties, held up a low hand to him, offering some quick nods and placing a nervous finger before his lips. It didn't help.

"Eh, what's that?"

Clyde's voice echoed down the long expanse of the church. In response, Lilith Warren, the church organist, began to play louder, no doubt in an effort to drown him out.

"Organ's awful loud, ain't it? How much longer do you think she's gonna play? I'm getting tired of standing here."

By now many were holding fisted hands over their lips, endeavoring not to laugh out loud. But one person did. It was the pastor, Joe Dawson.

Finally Lilith finished the anthem and began the processional music calling for the ushers to come forward. Clyde straightened his back as best he could and headed down the aisle, clearly wanting to lend sacrosanct dignity to his duties. The ushers placed their plates on the altar table and retreated to their seats.

When the organ stopped, Joe prayed. "Lord, we thank you for these tithes and offerings. May they be used wisely and prudently in the service of your kingdom." He paused for a long moment. Then, his voice tinged with humor, he added, "We also thank you,

Lord, because I believe Brother Clyde is right, it does look like a pretty good take. It is in your name we pray. Amen."

Joe looked up at the congregation, his face full to bursting with laughter. He wanted to speak, but couldn't keep himself from chuckling.

"Well . . ."

It was likely unintentional, but it seemed the perfect comic timing. The crowd erupted and Joe continued to snicker till his face turned red. Eventually he held up his hand and gave the closing benediction. The service had been inspiring on several levels. I had to admire the Watervalley Presbyterians. They might be God's frozen chosen, but they sure knew how to laugh at themselves.

The service concluded and Lilith played a lively piece as everyone began to leave. John and I spontaneously shook hands, grinning wryly at each other.

"Doctor, it's been a pleasure."

"That it has, Professor. That it has. We should try it again sometime."

John nodded with a slight shrug. "Sure, nothing wrong with a little pew aerobics from time to time. Come up later and we'll discuss it over a Scotch."

"Ah, that's the spirit."

John grinned and began to move among the crowd toward the narthex. He was immediately accosted with a slew of handshakes. I couldn't help but notice the engaging presence of the public John. He had the gracious capacity to look directly into the eyes of those who greeted him, energizing them, invoking a genuine feeling of connection. People flocked to him.

But I could also tell that John preferred to make a hasty retreat. I knew him well enough to discern the nuanced look in his eyes and the tightening of his lips that telegraphed his eagerness to depart back to his hilltop sanctuary. It seemed that coming to church, making this small step back into the life of Watervalley, had been an experiment for him. One, I suspected, he would not repeat anytime soon.

I turned to speak to Louise Fox, but she and Will had already gone. I moved to the outside aisle and worked against the crowd to make my way toward the choir and Christine. Apparently, she had been of a similar mind. When we met midway she was still in her choir robe.

"I hope you two behaved yourselves back there."

"Only barely."

"I figured as much." She turned her back toward me. "Here. Unzip me."

"May I just say that in my daydreams I've heard you speak those very words many times, but never in church or involving a choir robe?"

"You are so bad."

She let the robe drop from her shoulders and fall to her knees before she stepped out of it. As she stood in her blouse and skirt, I was once again reminded of the first day we'd met months ago at her school.

"I had a great time yesterday," I said. "Did I tell you that last night?"

"Yes, but you can tell me again."

"Okay. It was incredible."

"Which part?"

I considered for a second. "Why is it that the best moment that comes to mind seems inappropriate to discuss in church?"

Christine rolled her eyes in reproach. Yet all the while she smiled that wonderful, delightful, taunting smile that so automatically charmed me.

"Hey, why don't you come out to Sunday lunch? Mom would love to see you."

"Anyone besides your mom in that category?"

"Well, Princess Bess was asking about you. Apparently you made a real impression."

"Okay, last chance, Miss Chambers. I'm going to repeat the question. Is there anyone else who would love to see me?"

Christine's lips formed a small pout. Then she reached up with both hands to straighten my tie. She had an incredible, powerful talent for showing affection through small attentions.

"Well, maybe there are a few others who are wanting to see you," she teased.

"Hmmm, not good enough. I think some real groveling is called for here."

"Bradford, show up or shut up."

"Perfect. Sounded like groveling to me. I'm in." Then a simple reality hit me. "Oh, hold it. Crap. No, I'm not."

Christine's shoulders slumped. "Why not?"

"We're getting a new nurse at the clinic. I'm supposed to meet her at one o'clock."

"That's not a problem. Invite her to come along. Since she's new to town, it might make her feel more welcome."

"Actually, that's a wonderful idea, but it sounds like a real imposition."

Christine's smile returned. "Not at all. Grandmamma is frying up a big batch of chicken. There will be more than plenty. We always gather a crowd for Sunday lunch. Mr. Pilkington and his wife will be there and everyone pretty much just eats and laughs and eats some more till the last person falls unconscious."

"You're sure it's okay?"

"Absolutely."

"Fair enough. We'll be there shortly after one o'clock."

We parted and I grabbed my coat, shaking hands with Joe Dawson on the way out the door. I liked him. We were approximately the same age, although he had a wife and two children.

"Thanks for visiting with us today, Luke."

"Enjoyed it, Joe. Good to be here."

I departed down the steps, made my way to the Corolla, and headed home. I envisioned a delightful, lazy winter Sunday afternoon ahead of me. I couldn't have been more mistaken.

CHAPTER 19
Sunday Lunch

After stopping by the house to make a quick change into some jeans, I drove over to the clinic and arrived thirty minutes early. Fortunately, Ann Patterson was already there, waiting outside in her SUV.

I had worked with travel nurses before but only in large hospitals where they were part of a cast of thousands. This was quite a different matter. Other than the EMTs at the fire station, Ann Patterson and I would be the only medical professionals in Watervalley, working together day in and day out. If the chemistry was bad, it could make a misery of the daily routine. But we had seemed to click well over the phone, and my gut feeling was that we would get along fine.

She exited her car and walked toward me. A neatly attractive woman in her early fifties, she had dark brown hair and brown eyes under wire-rim glasses. Her skin had an olive complexion, almost Middle Eastern. She was of average size and carried herself in an attentive and assured manner. When she spoke, her voice was a blend of cordial and matter-of-fact.

"Luke Bradford?"

"Yes, you must be Ann?"

"Good to meet you, Dr. Bradford."

" 'Luke' is fine."

"Fair enough." She studied me for a moment. "You look younger than I imagined."

At first I wasn't sure how to respond. Ann stood there with a polite smile, but it was clear she was sizing me up. It occurred to me that a seasoned RN like her had probably worked in hospitals with dozens of residents fumbling through their rounds, trying their best to put on a dignified and knowledgeable air of authority. No doubt she had seen plenty of the likes of me. But there was a flip side; I had seen plenty of the likes of her.

I smiled and responded, "Should I show you some ID?"

"No, no. I'm sorry. That probably didn't come out right."

Her response was genuine, but lacked that effusive and accommodating cordiality that I had grown accustomed to in Watervalley.

"I guess it's not very fair, is it?" I said. "The travel nurse interview process tells me everything about you and your background, but you get to know very little about me."

"Actually, that's not completely true. I did some checking. I understand you finished first in your med school class."

"Well, that would be true. But I cheated a lot."

Ann laughed. "For some reason I don't believe that."

I nodded. "Come on, let's get out of the cold so I can give you the grand tour."

In a matter of minutes we went over the clinic's facilities, taking in the exam rooms, the supplies, and the medical equipment—or, rather, the lack thereof. Ann absorbed all of this attentively, offering only a few brief comments. She was a pleasant woman, somewhat reserved and undoubtedly very professional. She was not only an RN but also a nurse-practitioner who could do assessments and prescribe medications within some limitations. As well, she was certified in midwifery. Watervalley and I were getting a real deal.

We finished and sat in my office, where I briefly discussed the logistics of her work. I did my best to assure her that while there was no formal orientation, I would do my best to help her adjust to the rhythm and rituals of small-town clinic practice. This seemed to set her at ease. Even still, I had to admit, despite her amiable manner, she was something of a difficult read.

She was definitely an old-school RN, the kind who had endured the earlier decades of demigod doctors who lorded their rarefied knowledge straight down their noses to lowly nurses—nurses who had developed thick skins without losing their soft touch. In the short vernacular, she was a smart angel of mercy who had been taught not to take crap off anybody.

I glanced at my watch. It was almost one o'clock.

"Listen, we've been invited to Sunday lunch with one of the local families. I know it's kind of sudden, but it would be a wonderful way for you to get to know a little bit about Watervalley. Since tomorrow is New Year's Eve, it's only a half day of work and should be slow. We can continue with your orientation in the morning and you can meet the staff."

Ann considered this a moment and then responded with a brief shrug. "Sure."

I locked up and Ann followed me in her SUV out to Summerfield Road.

She was a short distance behind me as I was about to make the right-hand turn onto Christine's driveway. That's when I noticed a familiar truck barreling straight at me.

It was John.

After I made my turn, he whipped the truck abruptly in behind me, cutting off Ann and causing her to slam on the brakes. The three of us convoyed down the long drive and parked in the front yard. John tumbled out of the truck and walked toward me, offering only a disgruntled glance toward Ann's SUV. He was dressed in khakis and a flannel shirt.

"Well, sawbones. Looks like you made the lunch invite list also."

"Hi, John. How did you score a ticket for a free meal?"

"Hey, I'm still the brother-in-law. Madeline caught me on the church steps."

"See, being Mr. Nice Guy is starting to pay dividends."

"It's a meal, not a lottery win. Who's that in the Chevy?"

By now Ann was approaching us and regarding John sternly.

"Ann, I want you to meet a friend of mine. This is Dr. John Harris. He's a retired chemical engineer. John, this is Ann Patterson, nurse-practitioner. She is the new nurse at the clinic."

While I spoke, John was studying Ann, collecting the details with a mild indifference. "Oh, yeah. The traveler. Well, welcome to Watervalley."

Ann looked small, diminutive even, standing next to John's imposing six-foot-plus frame and commanding presence. That was, until she spoke.

"Hello, Dr. Harris. Do you always drive like an idiot?"

John's neck stiffened. He stared at her, flat faced, obviously taken aback by her directness. Then his eyes grew soft and calculating. He looked at me with a wry grin and then back at Ann.

"Charmed." With that, he gave a slight nod and turned to walk away. "See you inside, sport."

Ann and I stood there for an awkward moment, watching John depart toward the steps.

"He's an acquired taste," I said.

She grinned lightly and looked to the side. "Yeah, I know the type. I can already envision the duct tape over his mouth."

We proceeded to the porch, where Christine's mother met us at the door. Madeline was a small, attractive, and gracious woman who embodied the genteel nature found in Southerners who came from generational money. Yet, with Madeline there was none of the haughty exclusivity so often packaged in the mix. She clasped my hand between both of hers.

"Luke, it's wonderful to see you again. I am so glad you are joining us."

I introduced Ann, and in much the same way, Madeline greeted her warmly.

We moved into the large living room, where further introductions were made: Angus and Amelia Pilkington, and Mattie Chambers. John had poured himself a cup of coffee and stood on the periphery, reserved and distant, still stinging apparently from his sharp encounter with Ann.

Despite John's remoteness, there seemed to be no limit to the good spirits of this small gathering. Everyone welcomed Ann enthusiastically, even Christine's grandmother, who was outfitted in blue jeans, gumshoes, and an orange UT sweatshirt. Conversely, she still regarded me with a withering glare, as if I were lowbred, dirty, and had bad teeth.

Eventually I maneuvered over to John. "Beautiful place, isn't it?"

"Yeah, my brother-in-law, Al, built it."

"What was he like, anyway?" I had wanted to know more

about Christine's deceased father, but had thought it an awkward topic to pursue on our first day together.

"Albert was a class act. We were always friends, but not tight. He was a little older than me. Got his master's in agriculture from Tennessee and then came right back to Watervalley and took over the family dairy farm. He was smart, progressive, real down-to-earth. You'd have liked him."

I nodded, absorbing John's words. After a brief moment, he spoke again.

"So, that's the new nurse, huh?" He was staring across the room at Ann, who was engaged in conversation with Christine and Madeline.

"Yes. That would be her." Given their first encounter, I was unsure of what else to say.

"Well. She's certainly a piece of work. Did she bring her flying monkeys with her?"

"Not sure. Should I ask?"

John sipped his coffee. "Eh, probably best to play wait and see on that one."

"Yeah. Smart call."

"Humph. Well, it could be worse, I guess."

"How's that?"

"She could be ugly, too."

I nodded, making no further comment, but John's words told a story. My entire focus toward Ann was professional, and while I would easily describe her as attractive, it appeared that her small frame and schoolgirl figure had clearly sparked something in John. Apparently, his blood still had some warmth in it.

I spoke briefly with Angus and Amelia, struck by their polite friendliness. Angus's twinkling eyes said he was glad to see me back at the farm.

Eventually, we all took seats at the long dining room table. While I greatly preferred to sit next to Christine, I had no sooner taken a chair than Ann arrived to my right and John corralled the chair to my left. Christine was down and across the way, with her grandmother sitting directly across from me, firing sharp looks of disapproval in my direction.

Madeline asked Angus to say the blessing, and afterward, the group erupted into a hubbub of conversation and plate passing. The ritual of Sunday lunch was in full swing.

Christine spoke across the table. "So, Ann. Where were you before taking this assignment?"

"I was in Asheville for several years, where I worked and went back to school. I was able to get my master's and my certification in midwifery."

"That's good to know, Miss Ann," Angus interjected. "I can give you a call if one of the cows is having a rough delivery."

Ann responded with a good-natured grin. "Actually, that wouldn't be a problem. I grew up on a dairy farm in Pennsylvania."

John immediately responded in a detached voice, "So, you're an advanced-practice nurse . . . meaning, you can run a Code Blue?"

"Yes, that's correct," responded Ann.

It was the setup John was looking for. "Well, Angus. Looks like she can also give mouth-to-snout resuscitation to a dying cow if need be."

The group chuckled lightly and John resumed his slightly smug demeanor.

Ann chewed quietly for a moment. Then she responded lightly, "I'm better suited to doing CPR on humans. Of course, in your case, John, I'd probably just opt for declaring time of death."

This evoked a wave of laughter, including a restrained chuckle from John. But I could see him sullenly contemplating a return volley. Fortunately, Angus jumped in first.

"You see there, Dr. Bradford. Even your new assistant has milked cows. Matter of fact, John here milked some during his high school days."

I turned an inquiring eye toward John, who didn't look up from his food. "Guilty as charged. As I remember, though, it had more to do with a certain brunette who lived here rather than the pay."

This enlisted a series of comments, during which Ann leaned over to me and said, "Divorced?"

"Widowed," I whispered.

Angus implored me again. "So, Doctor. The invitation still stands to come help with the milking this afternoon."

I swallowed hard and looked around the table at the curious faces awaiting my response. "Thanks, Angus, but I think I'll continue to enjoy my status as the token nonfarmhand in the group."

A round of cajoling and laughter followed.

Madeline came to my rescue. "Luke, it was delightful to see you in church today. How did you like the service?"

"Very much. I really like Joe Dawson. Choir didn't sound too bad either."

I shot a wry grin toward Christine, who smiled discreetly at me.

"I did notice something curious, however. There was a small brass plaque dated 1943 on the pew with Oscar Fox's name on it. That seemed odd given his nefarious reputation."

Christine's grandmother responded, "It was during the war, Jasper." She paused for a moment, collecting her thoughts. Meanwhile, Ann spoke to me from behind her napkin.

"Jasper?" she whispered.

"Don't ask."

Mattie Chambers continued. "The church was doing anything it could to raise money for the Red Cross, so it auctioned off church pews. They didn't replace them, mind you. It was just a way to encourage people to fork over some cash, which there wasn't much of in those days. It was a throwback to an earlier year when the church raised money to buy new pews by putting up brass nameplates honoring the donors."

It amazed me how Mattie's mild dementia gave free passage to seventy-year-old memories, but brought recent ones to a grinding halt. She continued in her raspy, unvarnished voice, "Oscar Fox has always gotten a bad rap. He was a generous man. He had money, although you'd never know it by the way he lived. Things were tight during the war. He loaned my dad money so he could plant wheat and tobacco. Didn't demand a cent till after the harvest was in. They were good friends. Everyone thought Oscar was buried in the family cemetery because Daddy was an elder in the Presbyterian church. They thought it was a kind gesture, and, well, I guess it was. But Daddy told me in later years that Oscar saved the farm."

"Grandmamma, I never knew this," Christine said. "You've never told this story about Oscar Fox."

"Oscar was considered a pretty evil character after that bloody murder. It just wasn't the sort of thing Daddy wanted to talk about. Nobody really knows what happened or why, and probably nobody ever will."

Madeline followed her mother-in-law's comments, speaking in her kind, elegant way. "It is a real shame. There's always been a stigma in the community around the Fox family. It seems such an unfair burden for something that happened decades and generations ago."

With this, everyone became stewed into the conversation about Oscar Fox and all the old stories, and as well about the plight of Louise and Will Fox.

I leaned toward John. "I've got an idea regarding the Foxes I want to run by you sometime."

John responded drily, "Sure."

The discussion regarding the old bandstand murders lasted quite a while. So much so that I became concerned that Ann was being left out of the conversation. Conversely, however, she sat quietly and listened to every word with great interest. I was glad. I was still trying to figure her out. But her patience demonstrated a quiet intelligence and a low-maintenance personality.

In time we had all finished dessert and were lolling back in our chairs, swollen from our indulgence. Angus and Amelia invited Ann to walk over the farm with them, an offer she readily accepted.

She turned to me. "If it's all right, I will see you at the clinic in the morning, Luke. I don't want to monopolize your whole afternoon."

She departed and I focused my attention on John, who had grabbed his coat and was making overtures of thanks and departure. I walked him to his truck.

"John, I want to get you and Connie together to discuss this idea I have about the Fox family. I'll call you in the morning."

"Hmm, holding a summit, huh? Well, let me know."

As he opened the door to his truck, I couldn't help but prod him a little.

"You've been sort of quiet this afternoon. I expected you to have a little more comeback with our new nurse. She got your tongue tied?"

By now John had climbed inside, leaving the door open, and

had started the engine. He stared forward with a vacant expression, mulling over my chiding remarks. A slow, wry grin surfaced.

"Nah, sport. I just make it a policy not to negotiate with terrorists."

I laughed and stepped away, shaking my head. Christine stood on the front porch waiting for me.

"I want to go do something," she said.

"Sure," I responded. "Whatcha got in mind?"

"Let's drive over to the old cemetery."

"As in the old Taylor family cemetery, where Oscar Fox is buried?"

"Sure, why not?"

I shrugged. "Nothing spells romance like tombstones."

"Let me go grab my coat."

We headed inside and Christine went upstairs for a moment. I was still holding my now empty iced-tea glass and needed to return it to the kitchen. As I passed through the dining room, I was thinking about what a creepy, eerie thing it was that we were about to do—go to the graveyard of a gruesome killer. Stepping into the kitchen proved to be much more frightening.

CHAPTER 20
The Cemetery

I was three steps past the door when I realized that Mattie Chambers was leaning against the counter, holding a cup of coffee and staring at me with a quiet, brooding intensity. Madeline had apparently disappeared to some far corner of the house. Once again, I was Daniel caught in the lion's den.

I endeavored to place the glass on the nearest counter and beat a hasty retreat. But I wasn't hasty enough.

"Where are you two heading now, Jasper?"

I took a deep breath. "Mrs. Chambers, I feel the need to clarify something. My name is Luke, Luke Bradford. I'm not this Jasper person you seem to have me confused with."

"Don't get smart with me, Jasper. When's the last time you had a good butt kicking? Keep it up and I'll give you a real slobber knocker. So what if you changed your name? You watch yourself."

Dumbfounded, I folded my arms and stood my ground. What was I to do about this woman? Telling Christine that her 110-pound grandmother was a scowling tyrant would be relationship suicide, and I didn't know Madeline well enough to talk to her about the matter. I was stuck. My only consolation was that if push came to shove, I had eighty pounds on the old gal.

I tried to blow all this off and think of her in a clinical manner. That is, attempt to recognize the dementia for what it was and not take it personally. But this was difficult, especially in a room with so many knives. I began to nod and back toward the door when, fortunately, Christine arrived.

"You ready to go?"

"Yeah. Very ready."

Christine turned to leave and I glanced back at Mattie Chambers, only to catch her pointing two fingers at her eyes and then at me in rapid succession. She would be watching. It occurred to me that John had it wrong. Mattie Chambers was the one with the flying monkeys.

We got into the Corolla and before I could buckle up, Christine leaned over and grabbed my coat, pulled me toward her, and proceeded to plant a delightful, lingering kiss on me. After a delicious moment she released me, pushed me back, and began to buckle herself in.

"Okay, drive. Do you know where it is?"

"Gee. Give me a moment to reenter orbit. Not that I'm complaining, but what brought that on?"

"That's for encouraging my uncle to go to church and for being sweet to my grandmother. What were you two talking about in the kitchen?"

"Oh, just, you know. Stuff, things."

"Well, I think she really likes you."

I pondered this for an anxious moment. "Okay, good to know. And, well, as far as John goes, I probably dared him more than encouraged him."

"Either way, I was glad to see him there."

"Mmm, I wouldn't get my hopes up too high on that one. I

don't think he'll be putting a fish bumper sticker on the Mercedes anytime soon."

I started the car and headed down her driveway. "Boy, and here I was thinking you planted one on me because I'm a great kisser."

Christine looked out her window, wearing a coy smile. She let a few moments pass before she responded. "Oh, you're not too bad."

By now we had arrived at Summerfield Road.

"I assume I take a right toward Hoot Wilson's place?"

"Yeah, the cemetery backs up to his farm."

I turned in that direction. The countryside had the cold and barren look of winter, a sleepy world of tired fencerows and frozen grass. A solitary hush lay over the open fields, and even though the clock was only approaching four, the first shadows of dusk were beginning to spread across the chilly landscape. Within a mile we turned down a rough chert lane that availed only a small opening into a dense woods. It was a dark, sunken road shouldered tightly by an impenetrable stand of trees. Their thickly intertwined limbs overhung the narrow passage in an ominous canopy.

Moments ago, my only thought had been to escape for time alone with Christine. Now an awareness of where we were heading gained my full attention and a strange unease crept over me. "You know, not to spoil the magic or anything, but this feels a little creepy."

"We're going to see the grave of a knife murderer. It's supposed to feel a little creepy."

"Well, okay. But shouldn't we be wearing garlic around our necks or something?"

"This is Watervalley, not Transylvania."

"So, then, no ghouls, no Ring wraiths, no hounds of hell that you know of make a habit of hanging out here?"

"Not unless somebody tore down the 'No Demons Allowed' sign."

"Mmm, funny. And when you were a little girl and all those times you came over here with your friends, nothing ever happened, huh?"

"Oh, crud yes. Something always happened. We ran back down this road squealing more times than I can remember."

"You're not helping here."

I had pulled up to a small clearing where a crippled wrought iron fence overgrown with vegetation surrounded an area just large enough for some fifty-odd tombstones. Time and nature had slowly worked to reclaim this despondent plot with its dozens of stilled souls. Large maples and oaks had shouldered against the fence, bending and pushing it to their will. Over to one side were the remnants of an old brick foundation, now with several good-sized trees springing up within its broken walls.

"There used to be a small chapel here, dating back from the eighteen hundreds," Christine said. "I'm told my great-great-grandfather Taylor and his brothers built it. Quite a few of the Taylor ancestors are interred here, although I think Oscar Fox was the last person to be buried in the cemetery."

We made our way through the tall grass and approached the dilapidated gate that was shrouded on either side by a tall, dense thicket. The overcast sky offered only a bleak light. Wisps of our breath vanished into the moist air. As we stepped closer, a soft, moaning wind poured through the nearby trees. Nearing the gate, I heard a distinct rustling from among the bushes. I froze. My eyes caught a split second of some phantom movement. The attack began before I could utter a single word.

A snarling beast surged toward us in a blur of black eyes and large teeth. Both of us pushed back on our heels, stumbling over the grass and underbrush, falling on our backsides. It leaped closer, spewing forth a rapid succession of vicious, deep-throated barks.

The animal had the shape and form of a dog, but this was something more than a dog. Rhett was a dog. This was something you could ride into battle.

I instinctively held out my hand and yelled at the creature, accomplishing little more than to halt his approach and doing nothing to stop the barrage of bloodcurdling barks. It was Christine who got his attention.

"Rufus, stop. Stop that right now, Rufus."

Her voice was like magic. Immediately the huge creature sank back on all fours, staring up at Christine with watchful, cautious eyes. We both rose to our feet, and Christine put a hand over her heart and gasped while I kept a close eye on this massive dog, unsure of this uneasy truce.

Christine was wide-eyed and laughing. "Oh, my gosh. That scared the daylights out of me."

"Didn't do a lot for me either. So, you know this fellow."

"This is Rufus. He belongs to Hoot Wilson."

"Is he some cross between a wolf and a horse?"

"No, he's a mastiff hound. They're pretty rare. Hoot keeps him for protection."

"From what? This guy wouldn't just fight a bear—he'd try to date his sister."

"Well, he's not real good with strangers. Let me walk him back up to Hoot's place. It's only a hundred yards down that fencerow."

"You sure about that?"

"Oh, he's a big baby once you know him, but it's probably best if you keep your distance." She walked over and spoke to the enormous animal, gently grabbing him by the collar. They disappeared down a narrow dirt path and I was left to stand guard over the cemetery and, hopefully, get over the willies.

While I was trying to open the iron gate, another blaring

sound startled me. It was a cell phone ringing in the weeds a few feet behind me. Instinctively I patted my chest coat pocket, thinking it was mine. But it must have fallen from Christine's coat when we took the tumble. I scrabbled for a moment, trying to find the phone in the tall grass. When I finally did, I hastily answered it.

"Hello, hello."

"Where's Christine?"

I moaned. I knew that gruff, geriatric voice only too well. "Um, she's not here right this moment."

"What do you mean she's not there? What have you done with her?"

"Well, nothing. She's just not where she can talk right now."

"I don't believe you. Take a picture with your phone and send it as proof of life or I'm calling the cops."

"Mrs. Chambers, she'll be back in a minute. So just sit tight and I'll have her call you."

"Better yet, take a picture of yourself and send it. You better have all your clothes on."

"Mrs. Chambers, I'm hanging up now. Christine will call you in a couple of minutes."

I ended the call and stared at the phone, shaking my head.

After a few seconds of wrestling with the rusty latch, I was finally able to push the old gate open enough to squeeze in. Despite the cold weather, an undergrowth of green vines covered much of the graveyard. Time and weather had tilted some of the larger obelisks. Along with the headstones, some of the graves were also marked with thin, moss-covered concrete slabs. Most were old and cracked and likely not very heavy. A garden-variety ghost in decent shape could easily slide one aside and take a leisurely stroll in the moonlight.

I was reading the inscriptions on the various markers when

Christine called out and squeezed through the iron gate behind me. I walked toward her with her phone.

"Here, you must have dropped this when we fell. Your grandmother called. I think she's worried about you."

Christine smiled, shrugged, and proceeded to dial. I wandered back into the graveyard, taking notice of the names and dates that extended back almost two centuries.

I turned and watched Christine talking with great animation to her grandmother. The delightful lilt of her voice cut against the still and stark tranquillity of this modest place. I envied Christine and her deep well of family. For her, these humble markers were more than cold stone. They were the book covers of distant lives whose labor and laughter and love had transcended the years and were infused into her. Because she knew their stories, she never walked alone. I was only beginning to understand how this defined her.

She finished and headed toward me. "Everything okay?" I asked.

"Yeah. Grandmamma just wants to know if we can pick up a couple of things at the grocery since we're out."

"And . . . that's it?

"Yeah, is that not okay?"

"No, no, it's fine. It's just, well, never mind."

Christine shrugged. "So, find anything interesting?"

"Yeah, amazing really. There are some very old grave markers here. One of the inscriptions over there is pretty thought provoking."

"What does it say?"

"It says, 'I told you I was sick.'"

Christine pushed my shoulder. "Stop it."

"Hey, it's every doctor's nightmare."

She laughed again and grabbed my arm. "Come on. If I remember correctly, Oscar Fox's grave is toward the back."

Twilight and the soft tides of cooler air began to seep around our hands and faces. We made our way through the low thick vines and lonely markers. With each passing second, the gathering darkness seemed to be moving upon us at an accelerated pace. It occurred to me that in reality there was nothing to be gained by finding Oscar Fox's grave. But it had become something of a challenge to locate him before night blinded us. We hastily began to check the various tombstones. Many were covered with a light film of black grime and reading the names required rubbing with our fingers.

Finally, I came across a small marker with a cross mounted on top, standing in the back right corner of the cemetery. Although the stone was almost seventy years old, there was a noticeable difference in the weathering. I knelt down and read the inscription. "Oscar Fox. Born November 17, 1913. Died April 28, 1944. Rest in Peace."

I stood quickly and took a step back. "Dang. Now that's just a little weird."

"What's wrong? What is it?"

"I realize it's only a fluke happenstance, but Oscar Fox and I have the same birthday. What's more, I'm thirty years old. He was thirty when he died."

Christine exhaled a ghostly, shuddering laugh. "Oooh. That is kind of creepy."

I shrugged. "Well, it's a coincidence, that's all. No need to start going all *X-Files* about it."

We stood there for a frozen moment, staring at Oscar's modest grave site. Then in the remaining light, I noticed something wrapped around the marble cross on top of the headstone. It was a chain looped around the front and hanging toward the back. Someone had clearly placed it there. I lifted the chain and for a speechless moment, Christine and I stared at it in disbelief.

It was a Star of David.

CHAPTER 21
Open for Business

"What in the world do you make of this?"

Christine shook her head. "I have no idea." We were both equally dumbfounded.

The star was old and tarnished, with no way of telling how long it had been there. I knew of only one or two Jewish families in the area, and being so small, Watervalley didn't have a synagogue. As well, I was fairly certain that the Hebrew families I knew of had come to Watervalley within the last few years and would not have known Oscar Fox. The whole business was odd.

I returned the chain and star to its place on the headstone and we clumsily worked our way through the tangled vines and darkness to the car. We made a quick stop in town at the grocery, yet all the while, both of us were awash in uneasiness, wrestling with the same unanswered questions.

I pulled up to Christine's house and killed the engine. We sat for a moment, staring at each other, consumed in a fog of uncertainty. I realized that we each knew what the other was thinking.

Christine shook her head. "Yeah, that was all just . . . I don't know, weird, wasn't it?"

Preoccupied, I simply nodded. I didn't want to admit it, but Oscar Fox and I having the same birthday and being the same age invoked a haunting stir of thoughts. I generally didn't consider myself superstitious. I was a doctor, for heaven's sake, and by practice and training approached the world pragmatically. Even still, the similarities were peculiar and unsettling.

"Luke?"

"Oh, sorry. I was lost in thought for a moment there."

"Call me tomorrow."

"Sure. I mean . . . is that okay? Because the last two days have been, well, wonderful. But I don't want to crowd out all your time."

"I didn't say I was going to answer."

"Right, okay, fair enough."

"Brrrrr. It is so cold. Listen, you don't have to walk me to the porch."

"Are you kidding? I'd be missing out on the best part of the day."

Christine's smile turned delightfully elfin. She leaned over and once again, just as earlier in the day, grabbed the open sides of my coat. She spoke carefully in a low, hushed voice. "Okay, then. Why don't we say good-bye right here?"

I whispered in return, "Why don't we say good-bye both places?"

I drove back to Fleming Street, took care of Rhett, and was in bed early that night. Tomorrow the clinic would be open for business, and despite my casual prediction to Ann, I feared it might be a busy day.

Monday morning the weather turned uncharitable. A harsh, cold wind complained outside as I made coffee and toast. At my insistence, Connie was taking some time off, but candidly, I was looking forward to the holidays being over and getting back to our joint routine. I had grown to depend on her to keep me focused.

I arrived at the clinic at seven thirty, and just as on the day before, Ann was early, waiting for me in her SUV.

We went inside together and I introduced her to the clinic's small staff, including Nancy Orman, the office manager and receptionist, and Cindy and Camilla, the two middle-aged sisters who acted as the lab tech and phlebotomist respectively. They greeted Ann warmly, told her how glad they were to have her join the staff, and politely inquired about where she was from. Ann engaged them with courteous reserve. As kind as she was, I could sense that she still kept her distance. Admittedly, I understood this, given that she was an RN traveler and not expected to put down roots.

There was already a small crowd of walk-in patients, most of whom had winter colds, along with one or two of my geriatric patients, who had minor complaints or needed prescriptions refilled. Ann and I worked through these quickly, and to my delight, she easily caught on to the routine of meeting patients, taking their vitals, and asking the right questions. By ten thirty we had finished the last one and had retreated to my office to discuss a few details.

Moments later, Nancy simultaneously knocked and stepped through the doorway. "Dr. Bradford, Lester Caruthers is here."

"Is he bleeding?"

"Don't think so."

After a short deliberation, I asked her to put him in exam room two.

Lester worked on the loading dock at the Farmers' Co-op and had a hard, bony face that only a dog could love, a nearsighted one at that. In his forties, he had a lanky build and a mop of hair that was usually covered by a faded John Deere hat. His large discolored buckteeth protruded prominently from a mouth that was perpetually in a casual gape. I had come to know Lester over the past months as a likable soul with a mind that was happily not burdened by pondering any of life's complex dilemmas. His goal was just to get by.

On his previous visits I had stitched up some small cuts and scrapes. For farmers and laborers in Watervalley, it wasn't uncommon to acquire a few scars and even lose a digit or two along the way. But Lester's injuries were invariably self-inflicted and usually preceded by the comment, "Hey, hold my beer and watch this."

"Ann, no need to take vitals on this one," I said.

Her gaze sharpened under her wire-rim glasses.

"Lester is something of a special case. Just um, follow my lead."

We found Lester sitting on the exam table wearing blue jeans and his best Bud Light T-shirt. I introduced Ann and proceeded to ask him what seemed to be the problem.

"I'm feeling rough, Doc, really rough. I can't concentrate worth a flip. I think I need some more of them pills."

I rubbed my chin and nodded thoughtfully. "I see. And when do you notice this lack of concentration the most?"

"Mostly at work. But sometimes, you know, just all the time. It's rough, I'm telling you."

I responded with a low hum, again pondering his response with great deliberation. "Well, Lester, let me check a few things."

I proceeded to examine his ears and his eyes, and listened to his chest, careful to avoid the pungent waft of his rather noxious breath. All the while, Ann stood by, discreetly observing our exchange. I finished and once again stood rubbing my chin and deliberating.

"Gee, Doc. What do you think? I mean, it ain't like it's rocket surgery." Lester had a prodigious capacity for mixing figures of speech.

"Lester, you may be right. Hold on and I'll get you some of those pills. Ann, go ahead and take Lester's temperature and blood pressure just for good measure. I'll be right back."

She nodded. I returned shortly with a small, yellow plastic pill bottle on which I had taped a written label. Ann volunteered that his temperature and pressure were normal.

"Lester, take one, and only one, of these every morning. You should be fine."

Lester readily agreed. I patted him on the back, telling him to take care. He departed and Ann and I returned to my office.

"What in the world was that all about?" she asked.

"Oh, that's just Lester. He's an okay guy, just a little high maintenance."

"And the pills?"

"Lester came in a few months back wanting me to write a prescription for those 'special pills.' I looked in his file and noticed that several years back someone had prescribed Adderall, thinking he might have ADD. Adderall is amphetamine salts, so I'm sure Lester got a delightful buzz off of them."

"So you're aiding his addiction?"

"Hardly. The only thing Lester is addicted to is the path of least resistance. I hear he has a rich uncle somewhere, so probably the two most important words in his future are 'estate sale.' Besides, he doesn't have ADD, he has LOA."

"LOA?"

"Lack of ambition."

"I don't understand. You're giving him a Schedule II drug because he's lazy?"

I laughed. "No, of course not. I gave him a prescription bottle full of Tic Tacs."

"Tic Tacs? That's not going to cure anything."

"Apparently you didn't smell his breath." I leaned back in my chair. "Anyway, Lester seems happy, I'm happy, the Tic Tac company is happy. It's a win-win."

Ann lowered her chin, folded her arms, and stared at me incredulously. After a moment she shook her head and laughed out loud. "Wow, and I thought I'd seen everything."

I answered drily, "Welcome to Watervalley."

We talked casually for the next half hour. Ann's mood grew lighter. She seemed more relaxed. I suspected she was deciding Watervalley might be a good fit for her. I was thrilled. She also began to volunteer a little about her past, revealing a rather salty wit.

"Yeah, I was married for thirteen years. Been divorced for about the same number. No children, thank heavens. The world doesn't need any more like him."

"So how did you meet?"

"Through a mutual friend who I never speak to anymore. Anyway, my ex drove a beer truck."

"Hmm, well. At least he had that going for him."

Ann laughed at herself. "Yeah, he smoked, he drank, and he made funny noises under his arm. Who wouldn't fall in love with him?"

Our exchange was interrupted by a knock on the door.

"Come in."

The door swung open and the visitor stood grandly in the doorway. To my delight and surprise, it was John Harris. Again, this was a first. Over the months I had known John, I had never seen him at the clinic. Now he had breached the city limits for the fourth time in a week.

"Hey, sawbones." As soon as he spoke, he noticed Ann sitting in the chair opposite my desk. "Hmm. Looks like I'm interrupting. I'll come back another time."

"Don't run off on my account, Dr. Harris," injected Ann.

At first John stood quietly. Then he took a few steps into the room, assessing Ann with a collected reserve. It was clear he took her comment as something of a challenge. "Good to see you in your nursing uniform, Ms. Patterson. It changes you, makes you look so civilized."

Despite this understated jab, Ann didn't miss a beat. "Thank you. I'm thinking a muzzle would do the same for you."

John grinned. He seemed to enjoy the retort. He walked over and leaned his backside against the front edge of my desk so that he might face her directly and tower over her. For a brief moment, they glared at each other. But the air between them was more of a smirking tartness than a boiling animosity.

"Tell me, Ms. Patterson, does your parole officer know about your hostile tendencies?"

Ann coolly assessed John. She was straight-faced, but subtle lines of amusement were forming around her eyes. "You don't have a whole lot of friends, do you, Dr. Harris?"

"Not particularly, no."

"Wow. Shocker."

It was time to intervene. "Ahem. Okay, kids. If this keeps up, I'm going to have to put both of you in time-out."

Ann smiled at me and stood, squaring herself in front of John. She pulled back her small shoulders and stared at him, her intelligent and crafty brown eyes radiant behind her glasses. "No need, Dr. Bradford. I've got some things I need to tend to. Just let me know when you want him to leave and I'll throw a stick out the front door."

She lifted her left eyebrow, offering John a superior glance. Then she turned and walked out, closing the door behind her. Meanwhile, I couldn't help but notice John's intense focus. He tilted his head down as she departed, clearly admiring the movement of her modestly rounded backside.

With his arms still folded, he turned to me, shrugged, and took a seat in Ann's vacated chair.

"What in the world is with you two?" I asked.

John leaned back, locked his hands behind his head, and stretched out his legs, crossing them at the ankle. "Ahhh. Hard to say. I think the woman's crazy about me. Keeps her from acting in a normal way."

"John, I think we need to find you someone with the same mental disorder you have. That might work better."

He laughed, dismissing the subject. "Sawbones, I had to run into town and I recall you said something yesterday about the Fox family. What's on your mind?"

"Oh, good, glad you asked. Let me make a quick phone call. If it's okay, I want to discuss this with you and Connie together."

I dialed Connie's cell phone and she agreed to meet at the house in a few minutes. John said that was fine and departed, noting that he would see us there shortly.

Before leaving, I touched base with Ann to make sure she was okay. She was engaged in a lively conversation with the staff in the break room, acting right at home. Oddly, I noticed that the conversation dropped off the second I entered their company. She and Nancy assured me they had everything under control and would soon be closing for the day. It was, in fact, New Year's Eve. I nodded and returned to my office to grab my coat. As I walked out the back door, I was certain I heard John Harris's name spoken by one of the animated voices echoing down the hallway.

I drove to Fleming Street hoping John and Connie would be open to my little scheme.

CHAPTER 22
A Good Idea

As I pulled into my driveway, I noticed Will Fox bundled up and sitting on the bottom step of the metal fire escape on the side of his house just across the low stone wall that ran beside my driveway. Judging from its weathering, the metal stairwell had been there for many years. It led to Will's upstairs bedroom window and its presence struck me as oddly symbolic. Escape seemed to be a recurring desire of Will's life. Despite the cold, he had a large notepad in his lap and was holding a pen with a gloved hand. He was an odd kid.

"Hey, Will. Whatcha doing?"

He looked up at me slowly with discreet, probing eyes. "Writing a comic book story about a superhero."

"Sounds fun."

Will returned to his pad, slowly etching words on the page.

"Comic books have lots of pictures. You going to draw those too?"

He remained focused on the pen and paper. "Wendy Wilson said she would draw the pictures if I write the story." Wendy was

Hoot Wilson's daughter, a bright and cherublike girl. Both of them were in Christine's sixth-grade class.

I spoke in a haughty voice. "Sounds like an equitable collaboration for this artistic enterprise."

He grinned without looking up. My choice of high-flown words was intentional. With his imaginative and clever intellect, Will seemed to enjoy being regarded as something more than a guileless child.

"We'll see," he said.

"What's the name of your superhero?"

"Captain Blue Jeans."

"So, he goes around fighting evil with denim?" I couldn't help noticing the new pair of jeans that Will was wearing. It was likely the prize gift of what had been a meager Christmas for them.

Will peered up and regarded me with muted annoyance. "No, that's just what he wears. His brain has special powers. He uses it to help people."

"What kind of special powers?"

"Not sure. It's a work in progress."

"I see. Well, don't get too cold out here. Is your mom home? I notice the car is gone."

"No, she went out. She didn't tell me, but I think she went to the cabinet factory to apply for a job."

I nodded and exhaled, my breath visible in the cold air. "Good for her. Maybe something will work out." I was thinking of Estelle's offer about working at the bakery and made a note to remind her to consider talking to Louise. "I'm home for the day, so if you need anything, come get me."

I walked to my porch. Will sat in the cold, silently lost to everything around him, carefully writing words that I suspected were driven by a desire to be transported to a world without the loss, the fear, the uncertainty of the one he and his mother shared; one in which he was Captain Blue Jeans with the ability to make their lives whole again. Will wasn't guileless, but he was still just a boy.

I made coffee and within minutes both John and Connie arrived, bringing with them an electric, mischievous mood that banished my brooding over Will. They shared the teasing banter of two people who had been rivals and friends for many years. It seemed that my presence had served as a needed common denominator between them, the link through which decades of unspoken respect and understanding could find a voice.

I poured coffee and we gathered at the kitchen table.

"Constance, I see you're still driving your old Impala," John said. "Don't you think it's time to turn that 2001 in for a 2002?"

Connie cut her eyes at him and responded in her standard detached, breezy voice. "My little blue baby runs just fine, John Horatio Harris. Apparently, some of us are more interested in substance than show."

"Wow. You know, Connie, a lesser man might be hurt by such an insinuation."

Connie stirred her coffee. "Mmm-hmm. Well, I doubt you'll be tearing up, since I'm pretty sure there's not a drop of water in you."

John grinned and winked at me. He continued with the attack. "Luke, did you know that when we were in high school, Connie was a great dancer? She could do them all: the Frug, the Freddie, the Loco-Motion, and whoa baby, could she ever do that deep shoulder shimmy."

A tight-lipped grin inched across Connie's face. "Just keep it up, John. I'm about to put more doo-wop on you than the Del-Vikings."

John sat back and folded his arms, snickering.

I looked at Connie incredulously. "Is this true, Connie? You were a big dancer? How long ago was this?"

Connie responded dolefully, "Never mind. It's ancient history."

"Define ancient."

Connie was unfazed by my enthusiasm. "Long before your time. You know, back when we used to chase the great herds across the plain."

I was fascinated. "I'd love to see that. Could you show me some of your old moves?"

"Hmmm. Let me think of a good time for that. How about never? Is never good for you?"

"You're not denying it, though? You used to be a great dancer?"

John blurted out, "Absolutely, she was. She was practically a Rockette." He leaned forward in his chair and took Connie's hand, assuming a voice of feigned concern. "Constance, I think it's time to have a little confessional here. Go ahead. Just get it out. You'll feel better."

Connie leered at John for a brief moment; then she gushed a sly laugh and shook her head. She again stirred her coffee, gazing at it impassively as she spoke.

"Well, there may be some truth that back in the day I might have been known to have a little rumble and rhythm. But unlike Peter Pan here, there came a time to grow up. I don't do much dancing anymore."

I looked back and forth between the two of them.

John held up his hands. "What can I say? She was the dancing queen." He sat there with a grin of smug triumph, a grin that didn't go unnoticed by Connie.

"John Harris, you might want to think about wiping that look off your face, 'cause I'm fixing to bring down the thunder."

John's snickering erupted into outright laughter. It was contagious. Connie put her hand over her mouth and laughed so hard her shoulders began to shudder. I thought she might cry.

Eventually they calmed down. They were generally aware of the Foxes' financial situation, so I filled them in on some specifics I had learned.

"After everything came out about the break-ins, I met with Louise, Will, and Sheriff Thurman about making restitution. Louise let slip that they were three months behind on their mortgage and facing foreclosure. So here's what I want to do. I want to buy them some time. If each of us covers two months of the mortgage, that will get them caught up and give them three months to maybe get the place sold. I want to do this discreetly, because I don't think Louise will allow it if she knows."

"Why is that?" John inquired.

"I don't think she's too proud, but I'm guessing she doesn't want anyone to take on their burden. It'll be easier if it's done before she knows about it. So, that's my plan. What do you guys think?"

Connie and John glanced at each other. They responded simultaneously, "Sure."

"Okay. Good. Here's the other thing. I've got a rough idea about the amount, but I won't know exactly until I meet with Randall Simmons. I'll catch him later this week and give him a check and will let each of you know after that."

John nodded. "Humph. Good luck talking with that stuffed shirt. It's not a given he'll cooperate with this idea."

I shrugged. "I don't think he'll have a choice or will care so long as the bank gets its money. But I guess we'll see."

Connie interjected, "John, not everybody dispenses charm as astringently as you do."

"That's not true. Once people see things my way, I'm quite easy to get along with." He sat for a moment longer, reflecting. "Well, sawbones, I guess you're as good a man as any to talk with Simmons. I'm sure you can impress him with your dandyism."

Connie's neck stiffened. "Dandyism? Good heavens, man. Who talks like that?"

Connie's quick jab put John off-balance. "Hey, I'm just trying to be part of doing the right thing here."

"Well, I'm glad to hear it. I realize that when it comes to doing the right thing, you're certainly out of practice." Connie grinned. She had wasted no time resuming the offensive. Before John could respond, she turned to me.

"Luke, I think this is a fine thing to do. But on your salary, are you certain you can handle it? I'm sure John and I can cover if need be."

"Oh, I might have to take in laundry to make a little extra money, but yeah, I'm good."

John weighed in. "Connie, the man's a doctor."

"Mmm-hmm. And he works hard these days, which is more than I can say for some."

"Well, now listen, hard work and more hard work got me where I am today."

"That's true, John. Of course, in your case I presume you're referring to someone else's hard work."

He grinned. "That's just a technicality."

Connie returned her focus to me. "Again, Luke. I think it's a fine thing to buy the Foxes some time. God is many things, but punctual usually isn't one of them. So he stirs our hearts to do his work. Granted, when it comes to finding hearts he had to put on his bifocals to find John's."

John absorbed this for a moment. "Hmm. I was going to come back with a crushing metaphor, but suddenly nothing comes to mind."

I shook my head and smiled at the two of them. They were an

endearing yet contentious pair. There was between them an odd standing of affection and competition. I thanked them, filled with the conviction that what we were doing could be a huge help to Louise and Will.

John pushed away from the table. "Well, boys and girls, I need to get back to the house." He paused and directed his comments toward Connie. "I have work, real work, that needs to be done."

"My, my, my," she responded. "Must be time to organize your sock drawer again. Be sure to put on your hernia belt." She grinned at me, nearly winking.

John stood and stretched, smiling from ear to ear. "Luke, just let me know. I'll get you a check." He smiled warmly at Connie, who was still seated. "Constance, always a pleasure."

She spoke in a voice of genuine affection. "You drive carefully, John."

After he departed through the front door, Connie turned to me. I detected a slight darkening in her mood.

"Luke, I'd like to ask you a favor."

"Sure. What's on your mind?

"The bank board is meeting on Thursday to discuss selling the old bakery to Estelle and me. She's going to be out of town, so I'm meeting with them myself. I don't think it's going to be a problem, but I haven't told her about it. I know I should and I'm not sure why I haven't. But I want you to come with me. I guess I can handle my own with that bunch, but it might be nice to have a little moral support."

"Sure, absolutely." I was more than willing to go with her. But the nature and tone of her request spoke volumes. John had told me that Connie was the bank's largest stockholder, so I expected she had some sway. But something suggested that she had doubts.

Even though Randall Simmons had cowered before her at the bakery, the bank boardroom was his home court, a place far less predictable. Her anxious face communicated as much.

"So, the plan is to move forward with the bakery?" I asked.

"Lord willing."

She still had reservations but was resolved to help her sister. It seemed a good time to draw her out.

"You've never talked much about Estelle. Tell me about her."

Gradually, her face eased into an expression of muted pride. "Estelle's always been kind of a wonder to me. She's got this un-vanquished spirit about her, always fascinated with whatever the day brings. That girl could enjoy the scenery on a detour."

"So, what was it like when you were kids?"

"Estelle was only four when Momma passed away. With al-most ten years between Estelle and me, I was more mother to her than sister. Anyway, we were pretty poor, so we had to find ways to entertain ourselves." Connie's face grew soft, transformed by her memories.

"Seems like we spent all our free time either playing hopscotch or reading books down at the library. We didn't have a lot of things and you learned that what you didn't have, you did without. Es-telle was smart, smart, smart. But she couldn't stay focused on anything for more than five minutes. She could have been the poster child for ADD if we had known about it then."

"Has she ever run a business before?"

Connie smiled warily. "Oh, yeah. I wasn't kidding when I told you she once had a business painting happy faces on people's toe-nails. Poor Daddy. I think he was her biggest customer." She paused for a moment.

"Anyway, she went to Vanderbilt on a full academic scholar-ship, studied chemistry because it was the only thing that halfway challenged her, and stayed on and eventually got a full professorship. She taught there for over twenty-five years."

"So, she never married?"

"No. I guess Estelle was pretty much married to her work. She's diabetic and always had that heart condition, which I guess is why she's the way she is . . . wanting each day to count for something."

Connie stared out the window into the crisp midday light. She sighed and spoke with a cautious resolve. "Anyway, looks like the Pillow women are back working in the bakery business."

I knew Connie was referring to her mother and I wanted to ask her more. But I had seen the pain on her face the other day when she had told her mother's story. It was best left alone.

She rose from the table to take her coffee cup to the sink. "You sure you don't want me to make you some dinner for later?" she asked.

"No, I'm good. I'll probably get a pizza, watch some football, and call Christine a little later. She took her mom and grandmother to Nashville today, some kind of girls' shopping fling."

At the mention of Christine's name, Connie perked up sharply.

"Umm-hmm. Do tell. I heard you two were quite the item Saturday at the 5K. I assume things are going well?"

"Quite the item? Seriously? We weren't around each other publicly for more than thirty minutes. How does that equate to 'quite the item'?"

"The point is, you were around each other, period. People know how to fill in the blanks."

"Yeah, I guess you're right. Anyway, yes, it is true. We have been seeing each other, and yes, so far things are going nicely."

"Hmm, really? Define nicely."

I stared at her in disbelief. Connie and I were pretty tight, but I couldn't believe she was being so bluntly inquisitive.

"Who wants to know?"

Connie giggled. "Better get used to it, sweetie. A little romance between the new doctor and a town sweetheart like Christine . . . mmm, mmm, mmm. That's front-page stuff."

"Should I put out a newsletter?"

"It would help."

"Well, don't count on it." I rose from my chair. "You'd think a fellow could keep his private life private."

Still smiling, Connie gathered her things to leave. She spoke in a teasing lecture. "Mmm. I don't know, Doctor. It might be better if you kept me informed. People are going to be asking. And if I don't know the details, I'll just have to make them up."

"Show up in a cupid's outfit and we'll talk." I walked her to the front door. Before exiting, Connie turned to me wearing her familiar expression of reprimand.

"Just be sure you're a gentleman at all times around her, Luke Bradford. She is a fine young woman and deserves your best."

"Wow. First it's wash behind my ears and now this. I just don't know if I can live up to these high standards."

Connie opened her mouth to speak. With a puckered face she turned her chin to the side, cutting her eyes sharply at me. She grunted an exasperated "humph" and was out the door.

I turned to find Rhett sitting in the hallway behind me. He was looking at me with an awestruck, adoring face, as if my clever rebuttal to Connie had been the bravest thing he had ever heard. Either that, or he wanted something to eat.

CHAPTER 23
An Uneasy Feeling

The next morning I was awakened by the moist, smelly pant of dog breath. Not exactly the ideal start to the first day of a new year.

"Rhett, we need to have a serious discussion about oral hygiene." Undaunted, he proceeded to hop up on the bed and began the circling dance he always did before settling down for a cozy snooze.

"Away, you beast." My words went unheeded as he plopped down, forcing me to move. I crawled out the other side, stretched, and put on some jeans. It was nine o'clock. Even though this was a holiday, we were opening the clinic at ten for a couple of hours. When you are the only game in town, you have to make concessions.

I fed Rhett and ate a quick bite of toast before departing in the frost and cold. When I turned the key, the Corolla squealed in defiance before finally roaring to life. Actually, it was more of a moan. Even when I reached the clinic parking lot, there was nothing remotely resembling warm air coming out of the heater vent.

First, dog breath and now a frigid car. Yep, in this New Year I was living large.

The staff was already there and had my first patient waiting in exam room one. It was Margie Reynolds.

A housewife in her early forties, Margie was tall and big-boned with bold, expressive facial features. With her booming voice, sloppy smile, and unchecked gift for gab, she could do nothing in a small and quiet way. She would tell a perfect stranger in the grocery how much she loved their shoes or their purse and proceed to have an impassioned conversation for the next twenty minutes. Despite her spontaneous and clownish nature, you sensed that she wanted to present herself as possessing some modicum of style and refinement. But it seemed rarely to happen and no one laughed more about her efforts than she did. She was fun to be around.

Over the holidays, Margie had discovered a lump in her breast, and despite an understandable reluctance, she had come to the clinic for an exam. Even though I was her doctor, she and her husband, Larry, were also friends who had included me in a few social gatherings. Although breast exams came with the job, sometimes these situations made for some awkwardness.

Ann had already introduced herself and was taking Margie's vitals when I entered the room. She was dressed in a fitted blouse and pearls.

"Hi, Margie. You're looking smart today."

"It's early, Doc, and I'm holding a pose, trying to look skinny. Thank God you're here. I didn't think I could suck my stomach in for a second longer." She winked at Ann and grinned. But her words were spoken through a thin veil of worry.

"So, how are you?"

"Oh, I'm peachy, Doc. Other than, you know, thinking I might die."

I smiled warmly and tried to allay her fears. "Now, Margie, don't start panicking and having morbid thoughts about cancer before we've even done an exam."

"Forget cancer. It's the exam I'm going to die from. You don't by chance have X-ray vision, do you?"

"No, Margie, I'm afraid not. We're going to have to do this the old-fashioned way."

"Wonderful. Can we at least dim the lights and you buy me dinner first?"

I laughed. "I know, I know. It's no fun, is it? But it's best we figure this out sooner rather than later."

"Jeez, okay. Let's get it over with."

I asked several questions about the location of the lump, about any pain or tenderness, how she had discovered it, and when she'd had her last mammogram. She answered each inquiry along with a running commentary about the cold weather, her kids' braces, her husband's dieting woes, and anything else that popped in her head. It seemed this was her way of coping with her nervousness. Finally, I told her I would step out while Ann helped her disrobe and covered her with a sheet.

"Do I need to take my pearls off too, Doc? I mean, heck, you'll be seeing the rest of my jewels, might as well catch everything in one shot."

"Whatever you're more comfortable with."

Margie snickered and rolled her eyes at me. "Well, when my mother told me that in the South pearls go with everything, I'm pretty sure she didn't have this in mind. Anyway, I don't think the word 'comfortable' fits this situation. I'd rather wake up on fire."

I could only shake my head. "I'll be back in a few minutes."

Performing physical exams came with being a doctor. After you've seen hundreds of people in their birthday suits, it's easy to remain clinically detached. No doubt, the human body can be a beautiful thing. But in reality almost everyone falls short of a Venus de Milo or a statue of David. Many times I peeked at territory I really wished I hadn't.

I knocked on the door and found Margie and Ann in an amiable conversation. Ann removed the sheet and I began the exam. My heart went out to Margie. She seemed to be mortified. A blush started in her face and just kept going. Looking away, she did her best to hide her embarrassment, unable to hide much else.

Unfortunately, her suspicions proved valid. There was a palpable lump in her right breast. When I confirmed this to her, Margie melted into a face of pallid worry and a spontaneous welling of muted sobs. Ann wrapped the sheet back around her as I pulled up a chair and positioned myself squarely in front of Margie, who was seated on the exam table. I reached up and held her hand. "Margie, you're a smart woman and you did the right thing getting this checked out immediately. Whatever this is, my gut tells me that you caught it early. Now, we're going to do some blood tests and I'm going to refer you to an oncologist in Gunther County, a Dr. Kate Churchill. She'll do an ultrasound and probably a needle biopsy. This thing could be no big deal, a cyst or something benign, or it could be something more. Either way, we will get to the bottom of it."

With these words, I squeezed her hand. Margie pursed her lips and nodded, doing her best to act brave. "You really think so?"

"Yep, I do. It's a small lump and we need to get it checked out. But either way, I think you will get through this fine." I spoke optimistically for one simple reason. I knew that fear was the greatest enemy to the mind and spirit. Fear was a cancer of its own. The Watervalley Clinic was short on equipment and technology, but I was determined it wouldn't be short on hope. A weak smile poured across Margie's face as she absorbed my words. She sighed and the faint glow of resolve shone in her eyes.

"Thanks, Doc. If I wasn't half-naked, I'd hug you."

I stood, looping my stethoscope around my neck. "Well, shucks. Where's the fun in that?"

A smirking twinkle returned to Margie's expression. "Just tell me that you don't have a photographic memory and I may be able to avoid therapy."

I laughed. "Margie, I've already hit the delete button."

"You do realize that from now on every time I see you at church or at the grocery store, the first thought to cross my mind will be 'He's seen me naked.'"

I thought about this for an awkward moment. "Margie, I can't seem to think of a safe response to that comment."

"Oh, just scat. Go find another patient while I find my dignity. Pearls and a bedsheet don't keep a girl as warm as you'd think." She turned to Ann and winked.

"I'll be in touch." As I closed the door behind me, I was confident that Margie would be all right . . . on all levels.

I saw a few more patients and was home by one o'clock. I spent the rest of New Year's Day enjoying football, taking Rhett for a walk, and talking briefly with Christine on the phone. I was in bed early. The holiday break had been good, but the clinic would start regular hours in the morning. Candidly, I was ready to go back to work.

Wednesday morning I arrived early, made coffee, and was enjoying a few moments in my office before the start of the workday. But less than a minute later, Nancy Orman came bustling through the door. "You know, Nancy," I said, "I could be wrong, but it seems to me that when it comes to doors, God invented this thing called knocking."

She ignored me and we briefly discussed the caseload for the day. Soon after eight o'clock I called the bank to talk with Randall Simmons. His assistant said he wasn't available and asked my reason for calling. I told her that some friends and I wanted to help the Fox family with their overdue mortgage payments and explained our desire to deposit six months' worth of payments in Louise's account. I asked what that amount should be. She said she would get back to me. An hour later I received a return call from the assistant. In a detached voice she told me that the bank could not divulge this information and that I should discuss the matter with Louise Fox. I had known all along that this would likely be the bank's response, but had hoped that a spirit of kindness and accommodation would prevail. Evidently not so with Randall.

The clinic was busy, and the hours passed quickly. The day had the pristine orderliness that comes with the focus and resolve of a brand-new year. I found myself delighted to reengage with my life as a doctor, to once again care for those in my small but busy practice.

My last patient of the day was my friend and mechanic, Chick McKissick. I was surprised to find this normally happy and lively soul hunched up in a pitiful, sniveling huddle. It was clear he had a bad cold, the kind you carry in your bones. His voice sounded like he had sand on his vocal cords.

"Doc, I think standing on the street corner playing Santa Claus before Christmas put me under the weather."

A brief examination confirmed the diagnosis. "Chick, you're running a temperature and you look lousy. I'll write you a couple of prescriptions to help with the symptoms, but you need to go to bed and stay there."

"I hear you, Doc, but that's going to be tough. I'm really backed up at the shop."

"Well, Santa, I don't think there's a lot of choice here. Besides, you really need to be isolated. Otherwise, you'll be giving the gift that keeps on giving."

He reluctantly agreed and I retrieved my Rx pad. As I began to write, Chick said, "Hey, Doc. I saw a new Beemer in town the other day. Someone said it belonged to Connie's sister, Estelle. I figure she's just visiting for the holidays, but I also heard she's thinking about moving back here. Is that so?"

"Yeah, I think she is. She's living with Connie for now, but it looks like she's moving back to open up a bakery in the old Hatcher Building, the place where Oscar's Bakery used to be."

"Is that right? Hmm." Chick had a puzzled look on his face. "You know, Doc, I heard . . . or actually, I guess I overheard something about that earlier today."

"How so?"

"Banker Simmons was in my shop getting his oil changed. Man, he sure is a tight one. Anyway, he got a phone call about the old bakery and was handing out some pretty stiff instructions to whoever had called him. He didn't seem too happy about it. I heard Estelle's name mentioned."

"What kind of instructions?"

"Something about a vote. He stepped away, so I didn't get all the details. You know, Doc, I don't like to talk down about people, but banker Simmons, he's a squirrelly one."

I thought about what Chick had said while I finished writing his prescriptions. I wasn't sure what to make of his news, but it didn't sound good.

When I arrived home that evening, Connie had dinner waiting.

We talked briefly, but she left shortly after my arrival to attend to some business at Wednesday night church.

"Remember, you'll be on your own in the morning, Dr. Bradford. Estelle is out of town and there are some things I need to take care of for her."

"Did you tell me this already?"

"Umm-hmm. The other day. But you weren't listening because the sentence didn't have your name in it."

I nodded penitently.

"And you're still meeting me at the bank tomorrow at four o'clock, you know, for the board meeting?"

"Yes. I'll be in the lobby."

Connie was pensive, as if there was more she wanted to say on the matter. She stared at me for a lost moment. Something was troubling her, something she seemed unable to press into words. I chose not to mention what Chick had told me, thinking it might needlessly worry her even more.

I endeavored to be positive to try to allay her concerns. "I'm sure everything will be fine."

"Yes, I hope so." But it was clear that this was not what she thought. She turned and walked to her car.

I brooded for the next hour on what Chick McKissick had told me earlier in the day. Along with Connie's anxiety, there was an unsettled air to the whole business. I decided to make a phone call.

John Harris answered in a tone of unconcealed irritation. He was somewhat more accommodating once he recognized my voice.

"John, what are you doing tomorrow afternoon?"

"Ah, the usual. Work in the yard, make some dinner, drinky drinky."

"I've got something I want you to do." I went on to explain the situation with Connie and the board meeting and my concern that something seemed wrong. I told John I wanted him to come to the meeting. He didn't like the idea.

"Why would I waste my time watching another episode of moron versus moron? Connie will be fine. She can handle that bunch."

"I'm not so sure, John. She seems pretty uptight about it. I think it would be a good thing if you were there."

"Oh, crap. Don't tell me I have to go before the Sanhedrin too. I'd rather baptize a cat."

"Nice analogy. But I'm dead serious about this."

We talked for another few minutes and John reluctantly agreed that he would try to be there. I could tell he saw this as an unfair request and quite possibly an overreach of our friendship. He had made only a frail commitment and I could sense him withdrawing. He ended the call soon after.

I began to second-guess my decision to involve him. I wouldn't be surprised if he didn't show, but I was truly hoping he would.

CHAPTER 24
Fearfully and Wonderfully Made

The clinic wasn't busy on Thursday, making for a slow drag of the hours. I was unsettled, worried about the board meeting and thinking I would be glad when it was over. At a quarter of four I found Connie waiting in the bank lobby as planned. We shared tense and brooding faces, exchanging only a few words. With its dark paneled walls, cold marble floors, and gaudy chandeliers, the old bank building had an oppressive heaviness, an indifferent and stifling air that was stiff and ominous. One of the bank assistants escorted us upstairs and directed us down a long hallway to the boardroom.

There was a noticeable hush among the small groups as we entered. We sat in chairs lining the wall, across from the long side of the huge oval table. Nine board members were present, including some lawyers and local accountants. Curiously, even though it was the Farmers Bank, there wasn't a farmer in the bunch. Nor were there any women. Randall Simmons served as the tenth member and chairman. Other than the mayor, Walt Hickman, I was largely unacquainted with the men.

It was nearing four o'clock and there was still no sign of John. About two minutes before the hour, Randall Simmons entered through a side door. He gazed around the room with a placid reserve, showing no change of expression upon seeing that I was there with Connie. The directors ended their conversations and took their seats. As Simmons seated himself at the head of the table, the hallway door swung open abruptly.

John Harris walked in.

His arrival produced no small stir of whispers and mumbles. Body language stiffened, and inquisitive glances shot around the room. They all knew him.

John stood for a brief moment, deadpan, quietly surveying those assembled before him, taking note of faces and names. Satisfied, he walked over and seated himself next to me. Randall intently followed his movements and I could detect a slight twitch in his otherwise dour countenance.

The meeting was called to order. Within the confines of the lamplight and dark paneling, this group took on an august air, a cavalier attitude of detached importance. I was easily twenty-five years younger than anyone in the room and that alone elicited in me a certain unease.

Everything in Connie's demeanor told me that she was nothing short of intimidated. I had never seen her so cowed. Apparently, years of nuanced social cues had conditioned her, had made her uncertain. Since Connie was the largest stockholder, it was natural to assume the board would readily favor her request to buy the property. But she did not own a controlling majority, and now that thought nagged at me.

John was another matter. I couldn't imagine him to be any more relaxed. In his khakis, farm coat, and work boots, he sat slumped in his chair with his outstretched legs crossed at the ankles. He was cleaning his fingernails with a pocketknife, casually wearing a face of detached boredom.

During those awkward seconds before the meeting started, I realized that John's aloofness came naturally. In decades past, he had likely dominated the men in this room in sports, outshone them in the classroom, and perhaps even lifted half of them up by their underwear. Their unnerved regard of him communicated as much. I began to be truly glad I had troubled him to come.

The meeting was called to order and Randall Simmons wasted no time addressing the issue of the old bakery. He turned to Connie.

"Mrs. Thompson, I believe the board generally understands that you and your sister have an interest in buying the Hatcher Building property. If you would, please explain your proposal."

Connie stood, nervously clutching her purse tightly in front of her. At first she seemed frozen, unable to speak, her lips in an anxious, rounded pucker. Some ancient mix of voices was fighting within her, fretting with her to say her piece quickly and sit down. I smiled to encourage her. I found myself silently rooting for her, willing her to say the words.

"Gentlemen, I . . . um . . . my sister and I would like to buy the Hatcher Building property, the old bakery, that is, because she would like to reopen it as a pastry and coffee shop and a catering business. As, um, as all of you know, the bank has owned the property for many years and to my knowledge has no immediate plan for it. So we would like to buy it. It's listed as an asset on the bank's financial statement and we would like to offer ten percent above that amount. This seems a fair and equitable arrangement, and we would, um, we would like the board to consider this offer and move on this request as soon as possible. Thank you."

Connie half swallowed the last words and sat down stiffly. She had gotten through it, but it was clear that standing before these men had cost her something. Seeing her flustered and distraught served as an awakening for me. I saw the toll taken, and the stain left, by previous decades of subtle but persistent bigotry. Despite Connie's strength of character, towering intellect, and unquestioned courage, voices in her past had taught her that the color of her skin changed the rules against her.

By and large, it was a new and, in many ways, a better South than the one she had known in her youth. I felt strongly that the Watervalley of today had moved past the shameful mind-set of discrimination. Yet something about Randall Simmons and the stiff silence of those around him had churned up those deep memories of fear and exclusion. We awaited the board's response.

Simmons spoke impassively. "Thank you, Mrs. Thompson. Gentlemen, I think we all understand the nature of this request. Is there any discussion on the matter?"

I expected some general inquiries about the purchase price, or confirmation about the bank having no plans for the property, or perhaps even a question or two about the proposed business, if only from curiosity. But there was only tight-lipped silence.

Something was amiss here.

The board members sat pug faced, staring blankly at the table in front of them. Then I noticed a slight gesture, a tightening of the eyes and a subtle nod, from Randall Simmons to Rayburn Fulcher, the executive vice president.

Fulcher, a tall, rigid man with a permanently sour face, cleared his throat and spoke on cue. "Gentlemen, with all due respect, I see no need to rush into anything. It has always been our thinking that the Hatcher Building property might serve as a good location for a small branch office. I think it is time we revisit that idea. It seems appropriate to commission a research firm to evaluate this possibility and then get back with us. After such time, if a branch office does not seem feasible, then we can consider Mrs. Thompson's request."

Before another comment could be made, Simmons quickly added, "Would you like to put that in the form of a motion?"

Fulcher did so. The motion was immediately seconded. "We have a motion on the floor to table Mrs. Thompson's request and commission a branch office feasibility study. All in favor say 'aye.'" Parliamentary procedure called for a discussion at this point, but Simmons had moved straight to a vote.

The response was low and mumbled, but definitive. All save one voted for the motion. The only nay came from Walt Hickman, who spoke his rejection of the idea in a stern, defiant voice.

It had taken only seconds for Connie's request and Estelle's dream to be dashed. Knowing glances shot around the room. An almost imperceptible smugness crept across the face of Randall Simmons. "It would appear the ayes have it," he said.

Connie sat stunned, speechless. It had been a well-orchestrated charade, a short demonstration of power and politics with Randall Simmons wielding his influence over this roomful of invertebrates in business suits. For whatever reason, he didn't want the bank to lose possession of the old bakery, and he had effectively used his lackey Rayburn Fulcher to ramrod his will over the proceedings.

Connie clutched her purse even tighter. Her hands were visibly shaking. She turned to me, her face frozen and speechless. Despite her strengths, the situation was overwhelming her.

Incensed, I rose to my feet. "Gentlemen, this seems rather hastily done. Selling that property is a win-win for the bank and for the community. On Mrs. Thompson's behalf, I would ask that you reconsider her request."

Walt Hickman echoed the sentiment. "I agree with Dr.

Bradford. We're just wasting time and money delaying the sale of the Hatcher property."

Rayburn Fulcher ignored Walt and responded to me, his words imbued with subtle condescension. "As I noted earlier, Dr. Bradford, we will reconsider the request, but only after we thoroughly investigate the bank's best interest."

"And how long will that take?"

Fulcher regarded me down the length of his long nose. "Difficult to say. Probably months. If Mrs. Thompson and her sister's plans are time sensitive, perhaps they should consider some other property."

Small conversations began to erupt around the room. Walt was continuing to express his disgust. The others mumbled a spineless commentary. The hubbub grew until Randall Simmons loudly tapped a small gavel on the table, bringing the group back to order. He turned to Connie.

"Mrs. Thompson, thank you for coming. I understand your hope to revive the old bakery, but it appears that today is not that day."

There was nothing Connie could do or say. It was a crushing moment. She began to rise to leave when the heavy stillness was broken by a booming, penetrating, and unexpectedly jovial voice.

"Well, well, well. Isn't this just pretty?" The board members froze as John Harris's cool, taunting words poured over them. He remained focused on his pocketknife and fingernails as if he were talking to no one in particular. His deep, gruff, baritone voice filled the room.

"Just look at you boys. Five years ago Mrs. Thompson here poured her life's earnings into this bank and helped save it, along with this community. She's never asked for a thing, not even a seat on the board. Now she comes to you with a simple request and suddenly you fellows are short on memory."

John admired his nails briefly, folded his pocketknife, and looked up at the men in the room. "What say we talk about it?"

He stood, coolly engaging them. With his broad shoulders and powerful arms, he rose like an awakening giant. The directors began recoiling in their chairs. Even the walls seemed to expand away from him. This was the John Harris I had only heard about. It wasn't just his brawn and stature that held sway. The hard contours of his face conveyed a volatile, smouldering intensity. He had a raw, powerful presence and a brilliant, penetrating gaze capable of complete intimidation. He was a lion among them and they withered fearfully under his glare.

His amused words were crisp with confidence.

"Let me afford you boys a little history lesson. My departed wife and my very alive sister-in-law were Cavanaughs, the daughters of Sam Cavanaugh. He's the gentleman whose picture hangs on the wall over there. The Cavanaugh estate still owns a tidy share of the bank's stock. Coincidentally, I happen to be the executor of Sam Cavanaugh's estate, including the bank shares. Now, along with Mrs. Thompson's stock . . . well, you're all smart boys and I'm sure you can do a little basic math. I think the proper term is 'majority ownership.' "

John let this sink in as he began to walk slowly around the table, carefully placing his hands on the backs of chairs and looking into the eyes of all the suited men, who were now displaying the collective testosterone of beached jellyfish. They began to glance at one another with taut, worried faces, telegraphing their understanding of John's words. His lighthearted banter continued.

"Now, I know some of you fellows think you're clever, winking around the table and playing your little game of footsie with Chairman Simmons. Well, boys, that's today's news. Let's talk about tomorrow. Tomorrow's news will prove to be much more interesting. A few months from now, three board member seats come up for renewal, three more next year, and three more after that. So, here's what's going to happen."

Just that quickly, John's cajoling manner disappeared. Now his words were cool, hard, toxic. "By exercising both Sam Cavanaugh's and Mrs. Thompson's shares, I am going to personally castrate each one of you sum' bitches right out of here."

I knew John was in complete control. Even still, there was an intensity, a consuming fire just below the surface that even I found unnerving. The men on the receiving end of his chastening scorn were petrified.

His next declaration oozed out slowly, deliberately. "One by one by one I am going to replace each of you with living, breathing human beings." He paused again and began to shake his head. "Shame on you boys. What could you possibly be thinking, trying to pull a bullying stunt like this?"

A smothering, dreadful silence ensued and all the men sat paralyzed. John's words hung fat in the air, pushing out the oxygen.

Soon, however, his broad smile returned. "So, fellows, by damn, wink and think on that a little bit."

Now he turned his full attention to Randall Simmons, stepping slowly toward him. His tone remained low and calm. "Randall, old friend, you are correct about one thing. Today is not Connie's day. Today belongs to you and your little band of bobbleheads."

Then John stopped and did the most fascinating thing. With his eyes locked on Randall, he raised his hand and pointed toward Connie. "But take a good look at that incredible lady sitting in the chair over there, Randall, because I want you to remember something. Tomorrow is going to belong to her. Tomorrow will belong to Constance Grace Thompson. Bet your ass on it, sport. I'm going to see to it personally."

John wasn't done. He moved boldly up beside Randall and hovered over him. He put one hand on the back of the banker's chair and the other on the table. As John leaned in, Randall shifted to the side, pulling away as best he could, and looking straight ahead with a wincing, indignant face. Within inches of the banker's ear, John spoke in a low but audible whisper.

"Write this down, Randall. Dear Diary: Today, I pissed off the wrong guy."

His point made, John straightened and surveyed the room. The men around the table huddled with downcast faces, their guilt easily read. Their small scheme of stagecraft had gone terrible awry. No one said a word. No one dared to offer a challenge.

John smiled and spoke in an almost kind, instructive manner. "Well, looks like we're done here, boys. Now, I'm going to leave and give you fellows an opportunity for some important personal reflection, during which time I recommend you rethink *your* agenda. Otherwise, rest assured, in due time, each of you will be on *my* agenda." He looked at me, nodded, and then departed out the large door. Connie and I followed.

She was visibly shaken, her steps plodding as she progressed down the hallway, lost in hurt and confusion. John stopped her.

"Connie, I'm sorry. I had no idea Simmons would try to pull this stunt."

"It's okay, John. I should have seen it coming. I appreciate what you did in there, but part of me wants to get away from this whole ugly business. Maybe it's the Lord's will that the bakery not happen."

John's eyes tightened. "Connie, it's the Lord's will that a slimeball like Randall Simmons not get away with his shenanigans. I don't know what his motivation is, and frankly, I don't care. Just sit tight. The bank pays those clowns a goodly sum to sit on the board, not to mention the prestige they think it gives their tender egos. I felt it my duty to let them know that's all going away if things don't change. I'm betting the dollar bill will trump whatever loyalty they have to Simmons."

Connie stood silently with a downcast and ashen face. John, however, was hardened with resolve. It was only now, away from the tension and drama of the boardroom, that I realized I had witnessed something rather wonderful.

Days earlier, John had taken great delight in chiding and pestering Connie, teasing her in a game of one-upmanship. It was a match they had replayed over the years and a contest in which she invariably won.

But he stood before her now as a watchtower of strength, a champion against the petty injustices served upon her. Despite his cynical and brooding nature, John Harris had come down out of the hills, out of his self-imposed exile, and stood in the gap for Connie's sake. I had witnessed the return of the king. He was both fearfully and wonderfully made . . . but mostly, fearfully.

Connie shook her head. "I just don't know, John. I just don't know."

His eyes grew soft and a confident smile emerged. "Don't worry, Connie. I do."

Two hours later, I received a phone call at home from Walt Hickman. In a vote of eight to two the board had reconsidered Connie's request and had approved the immediate sale of the old bakery at the presently assessed value, no additional ten percent needed. Connie and Estelle could close on the property within the month.

CHAPTER 25

The Getaway Car

On the following Tuesday I received an unexpected package. Oddly, it had been delivered to the clinic rather than to my home. The large yellow envelope had been sent certified mail from a law firm in Nashville. It concerned the estate of Mildred Strum.

Mildred had owned low-rent shanties and dilapidated trailer parks in some of the meaner corners of the county. She had died in December after a lifelong love affair with booze and tobacco. Known as a scornful old harpy, she'd had a hard, angry face that was invariably adorned with a dangling cigarette. When people talked to her, she regarded them with a rude contempt, as if they were a waste of her time. Everyone who did business with her eventually found some reason to loathe her, usually sooner rather than later.

When Mildred came to see me in October of last year, she was already dying of cancer and had defiantly accepted her imminent demise. She simply wanted something for the pain. She was my last patient of the day, and before writing a prescription, I told her to follow me to my office. Once there, I pulled out a bottle of unopened Scotch that had been given to me and poured her a glass. She looked at me warily.

"What's this?" she asked.

"You said you wanted something for the pain."

She chortled a throaty laugh and drank it.

I studied her for a moment. "Tell me about your pain, Mildred. When did it start?"

She poured herself another Scotch, drank it, and released a grunted smirk. "Fifty years ago."

During the next hour, Mildred told me about her life.

"I never was very pretty and had a rough time of it in high school."

She went on to tell me that her mother had left her dad when Mildred was little. Even still, her dad had done well and owned a lot of property. After she graduated from high school in 1965, he took her to Nashville and bought her a sports car as a graduation gift.

"It was going to be my getaway car. I was going to leave Watervalley for good and go get a job on the West Coast and live there forever. But two days after we bought the car, my dad had a stroke. I ended up staying here and taking care of him. I took over the business and the years began to roll by. When my dad died, I was almost forty. So I thought, 'To hell with it,' and just stayed on."

Mildred told me she had parked the car in their barn a month after they bought it and it had sat there ever since.

At my insistence, I followed her home that night to make sure she arrived safely. We walked to the barn and she showed me the car. I guess she saw the captivated look on my face, because the envelope I received on Tuesday morning contained a letter of explanation from the estate attorney, a handwritten note from Mildred, and the title to the car along with the keys. Mildred was giving it to me as a gift. I was ecstatic.

I called Chick McKissick, who agreed to meet me with the wrecker out at the Strum place later that afternoon. I asked him to wait for my call because there was something I needed to do first. Chick said that was fine.

I had arranged a meeting with Louise Fox to discuss the offer that Connie, John, and I wanted to make. At three o'clock I knocked on her front door. She greeted me with a frail smile.

"Hello, Dr. Bradford. Please come in."

Louise Fox was a small, somewhat timid woman with a sweet face. She was in her early forties and the strain of her years had already placed fine wrinkles at the corners of her eyes. Still, she smiled warmly and did her best to engage me graciously with what I suspected was a slender supply of strength.

"Thanks, Louise. I'm guessing Will's not home from school yet?"

"No. He'll be home in about thirty minutes."

"That's good, actually. I wanted to speak to you privately."

We sat in her modest living room and I described our proposed plan of assistance. At first, she refused, not wanting anyone to take on her burdens, but I persisted.

"Louise, we all go through rough patches. This is just to buy you some time so you can get this property sold."

"I'm afraid I may owe more on it than it's worth."

"Well, we can try. How's the job search coming?"

"A little slow. I've been working part-time at some of the shops and cleaning a few houses. Connie has been wonderful. She and her sister have offered me a position at the bakery when it opens, but that's still a few months away."

The mention of the bakery stirred my curiosity. "Louise, can I ask you a personal question?"

"Sure."

"I've only recently learned about Oscar Fox and the old

murder story. Has that been difficult? I mean, has his reputation been something of a cross to bear?"

"Sometimes. Maybe not so much for me because I married into the family. But I think it haunted my late husband. His family always insisted that Oscar was a righteous man and didn't deserve the blackening of his good name. Why do you ask?"

I smiled. "Oh, no reason. Just curious, I guess. So, do you and Will have a place to go from here?"

"We're trying to figure that out. My husband was an only child and his parents are deceased. My mother lives in Nashville, but she has only a one-bedroom apartment. There are some places here I might can afford. They're kind of shabby, but Will and I will make the best of it."

My heart went out to Louise. She seemed so fragile and so poorly equipped to take on the hard challenges in front of her. Eventually, she agreed to our charity on the condition that she would pay us back when the house sold. Our conversation was cut short by the sound of Will's boots as he tromped through the front door.

"Hey, Dr. Bradford. What are you doing here?"

"Oh, just talking to your mom."

"About what?"

Will was a clever, perceptive fellow and I didn't want to divulge the truth about our conversation. I had to think fast.

"Well, I was asking your mom if you could go on a little adventure with Chick McKissick and me." Louise's face was a question mark. Out of a love of cars, Will had often spent his afternoons hanging out at Chick's garage and the two of them were steady friends.

"It seems that I have been given a car, an old convertible that needs restoration. Chick is going to meet me with the tow truck to bring it back to his shop. Want to ride along?"

Will's eyes lit up with excitement and Louise readily agreed to my proposition. I called Chick, who said he would meet us at the Strum property, and we hopped in the Corolla and headed out there.

"So, what kind of car is it?" Will inquired.

"A 1962 Austin-Healey 3000 Mark II convertible. It has less than three thousand miles on it and I believe it is blue and white. I saw it once, but it was covered in dust." I went on to explain to Will the story about Mildred Strum and how the gift had come to me.

"Yeah, she died not long ago, didn't she?"

"Yes. She has gone on to her reward, as they say."

"From what I hear, I don't think she's finding it very rewarding."

I looked over at Will and grinned. "Oh, and how is that?"

"Chick was talking about her down at the garage. He said she was as mean as a snake."

I endeavored to be diplomatic. "I think she may have had that reputation. But looks like she wasn't all that bad. She left me this car."

"Hmm, I guess. Anyway, from what I hear, she's moved on to a much warmer climate, if you catch my drift."

I exhaled a short laugh. "Yeah, I get it." Will stared out the passenger window and we rode for the next minute in silence. Then he turned to me.

"So, I hear you're dating my teacher, Miss Chambers."

"That's the rumor."

"That's amazing."

"Oh, and why is that?"

"With this old Corolla I figured you had a better chance of getting abducted by aliens than getting a date with her, or anyone for that matter."

"Clearly you've underestimated my charm with the ladies. I can explain it if you'd like."

Will stared out the passenger window again. "That'd be pretty good at generating a yawn."

"Mighty big talk for a guy who still has footies on his pj's."

Will snickered, enjoying this opportunity to rib me a little. He kept up the assault.

"So, is she a good kisser?"

"Will, you're being a little too chatty. Are you familiar with the concept known as the cone of silence?"

"Hmm. I'm gonna take that as a yes to my question."

I ignored this. "Okay, buddy. Time for a subject change. You play any kind of sports, Will? You know, like basketball?"

"Basketball? Are you kidding? Do I look like I'm athletic? I've got about a three-inch vertical leap, and that's only if I lift one foot at a time."

"I could teach you. I used to play a lot of basketball."

"Maybe. Sports really aren't my thing."

"So what is your thing?"

"Cars, computers. I like to write stories too."

"Oh yeah, like the comic book about Captain Blue Jeans."

"That, and other stories."

"Really? What other kind of stories?"

"Stories about doctors who drive ugly cars and have girlfriends who are really good kissers."

I pondered this for a moment. "Kinda walked into that one, didn't I?"

Will continued looking out the side window. "Surrrrrrre did."

By now we had turned onto the long driveway of the Strum property. Already waiting on us, Chick was talking with an older man who was the caretaker. He showed us to the barn and unlocked the latch to the large wooden door.

As he walked around the Austin-Healey, Chick blew out a long, sharp whistle.

"Mmm, mmm, Dr. B. This is one fine-looking piece of machinery."

With its spoke wheels, chrome grille, leather interior, wood dash, and sleek racing lines, the car was definitely a classic beauty. I wiped away a thick layer of dust from the fender to reveal a swath of the original powder blue paint.

Chick spoke admiringly. "I looked up this model before coming out here, Dr. B. This baby has a top speed of a hundred and fifteen miles per hour and can accelerate from zero to sixty in eleven point seven seconds."

"So what do you think, Chick? Can you get her running again?"

"I think so. But it's going to take some time. Lot of detail work."

"Well, how about this. What say you put Will here on the clock in the afternoons to help you restore her and put it on my tab?"

Chick smiled broadly at Will. "What do you say to that, Will my man?"

"Sure." During the brief time I had known Will, he had always been one to mask his emotions. Given our similar histories of losing loved ones, I understood this desire. But the look on his face was one of pure elation.

Amazingly, we were able to inflate the tires long enough for Chick to get the car safely loaded onto the flatbed of the tow truck. Will talked nonstop on the ride home, bursting with delight at his new project.

Mildred Strum had been a miserable old woman, but the gift of this car had brought a timely delight to Will's troubled life. The thought also occurred to me that come springtime a snazzy car like this along with a beautiful girl like Christine would provide me with some timely delight as well.

Truth be known, she *was* a good kisser.

CHAPTER 26
Pandora's Box

The short days of January continued. Some were bright and brilliant, with skies of pristine blue that spread a soft optimism over the daytime hours. But most were overcast, wrapping the distant hills in a hood of gray vapor, encouraging the townsfolk to stay inside, to sleep, to dream of warmer days.

Despite the freezing temperatures, I often walked to work for the daily exercise. Daylight had already arrived by the time I made my morning trek, but usually I returned home on the cusp of darkness. The windows of Fleming Street radiated a cozy glow, and as I passed them, I breathed deeply of the winter air, now laced with the intoxicating smell of woodsmoke. An awareness of these small delights was slowly defining me.

During the colder months the Farmers' Co-op served as little more than a gathering place for coffee and card games. Across the valley the fields lay frozen and the farm lanes became black ribbons of endless mud. Livestock huddled around hay bales and silage bins. The tall gray silos that dotted the landscape were the cathedrals of the rural architecture, standing sentinel against the severity of winter.

Christine and I continued to see each other, usually texting or talking on the phone on a daily basis. We went out on weekends, and as the days passed, from within the initial fog of intoxicating attraction, there emerged between us an enduring and easy friendship. Here was a finer harmony than I had known in previous relationships. When we were together, I sensed a gentle choreography to our thoughts, our choices, our actions. It seemed that a charmed ease had mellowed between the two of us. For my cautious heart, she was brave new territory.

By late January, Connie and Estelle had closed on the old bakery, but their plans for renovation were still on the drawing board. Conversely, a for-sale sign had gone up next door to me, a hope-filled step forward. My only regret was that the financial assistance we'd provided seemed to further Louise's humiliation. On the chance encounters between us, she kindly waved and looked away, regarding me with an unspoken yet embarrassed gratitude.

My pursuit of the murder mystery had gone cold and Lida had yet to find her father's old file box. Meanwhile, I was haunted by the Star of David that Christine and I had seen on Oscar Fox's grave. I found it difficult to reconcile the conflicting accounts of Oscar's apparent charity in light of his reputation as a vicious murderer. But my curiosity would have to wait. The tug of daily responsibilities had taken center stage. Still, I kept the autopsy report on my desk, mentally placing it under unfinished business.

The gray, sleepy days of January ended. February arrived and with it came the first faint breath of warmer air, the first frail stirring in the quiet fertility of the open fields. The second week brought a short string of warmer sunny days and the daffodils, the vanguards of spring, began to peek through in small golden clusters along the county roads. The nights were cold and winter continued to hold sway, but the expanding daylight hours and temperate days foretold the inevitable changing of the season.

The fourteenth of February, Valentine's Day, was a Friday. Every female who knew my name had reminded me of this fact, twice. It seemed that my budding relationship with Christine was broadly endorsed and they wanted to ensure that no doofus act of omission on my part should derail it. During the preceding week, Christine and I had talked about the day but made no definite plans. Getting together was naturally assumed, but in Watervalley, it didn't take long to exhaust the options for diversion. We had decided to touch base at the end of the workday and go from there.

Early that Friday morning I was sleeping soundly, undisturbed even by Rhett's incredible capacity for snoring, when a clamoring downstairs woke me abruptly. Connie was being unusually noisy, banging the pots and pans. The explosive sound I heard next made me sit straight up in bed. Booming up from the kitchen came the deafening, deep-lunged voice of a woman singing.

Even Rhett had an alarmed look on his face. I immediately grabbed my robe and tumbled down the stairs to the kitchen, where I halted, wide-eyed. The singer was Estelle, dressed in a sequined jogging suit.

With one hand raised above her head and the other one holding a wooden spoon as a microphone, she was belting out a song at the top of her lungs. Her eyes were closed and she was dancing, not with just a modest shimmy, but with her whole body rhythmically gyrating, including every appendage, her considerable hips, and her large, contralto bosom. She was caught up in her own hinterland of unabashed expression and dark creative freedom.

I considered retreating quietly back upstairs, but I was mesmerized by the spectacle, locked in a state of semishock.

She was dubbing her own words into the song "Lady Marmalade" and finished with an earsplitting "I made homemade marmalaaaaaaade!"

She held the last note in a long finale, stretching both hands skyward and ending at a volume approaching that of a tornado siren.

Upon finishing, she clenched her fist in a notable expression of satisfied glee. Only then did she notice me sitting at the bottom of the steps with a frozen and bug-eyed face.

"Mmm, mmm. I am in fine voice this morning. Good morning, sweetie! Did I wake you up?"

"Estelle, I think it's safe to say you woke up the entire zip code."

"Everybody should be up. It's Valentine's Day!"

My initial shock had passed. Despite Estelle's energy, I was returning to the half fog of sleep that I had been so delightfully immersed in only minutes prior. "And so it is. Estelle, where is Connie?"

"She had some things to do this morning, so I volunteered to come help get your day going."

"Well. Mission accomplished."

"I brought some of the pastries that will be in the bakery along with some homemade marmalade. I want to try them out on you."

"Sure."

"I have a few vol-au-vents and some chouquettes."

From some distant memory I knew these were French treats made from puff pastry. I poured a cup of coffee and moved to the table, where Estelle brought me a plate. The pastries were heavenly, and while I ate them, I could only wonder what Watervalley would think of having such unique culinary options. They also brought to mind another matter.

"Estelle, are you going to try and serve anything besides bread and pastries?"

"I'm thinking I might need to have some lunch options, maybe some sandwiches. I've been hearing a rumor that Lida Wilkins over at the Depot Diner is going to start selling fried pies and baked goods."

"Yeah, I've heard as much. Seems kind of a shame for you two to be in competition."

"Seems tacky to me. But if she wants to cut in on my pastry business, I'll just have to cut in on her lunch business."

I nodded, knowing this was just the way things had to be. Still, I really liked both women and wanted each of them to succeed.

"Here, Dr. B., try some of my orange marmalade. That's what got me going. It just seemed a cue for a song."

"I can see that."

"Oh, come on now, Dr. B. Don't you ever catch yourself doing something and just getting a song in your head?"

"You know, Estelle, I don't think I'm wired that way."

"Are you telling me you never sing to that pretty girlfriend of yours?"

"I'd say the fact that we are still dating is proof of that."

"Well, what about dancing? You take her dancing, don't you?"

"Mmm, can't say that's happened either."

She stood over me with her hands on her hips, shaking her head.

"Mmm, mmm, mmm. Dr. B., you need to loosen up, boy. You are just way too white and uptight."

She walked back to the stove, robustly giggling, amused to the point of giddiness. I finished eating, thanked her, and walked back upstairs to get ready for work. What was it about the Pillow sisters? One was stern and the other was silly. Both had a way of putting me in my place.

When I arrived at the clinic that morning, Clovis Benefield and his wife, Edith, were waiting on the front steps.

"Hey, Clovis. You're here bright and early. Are you okay?"

"I've swallowed poison, Doc. I need to get my stomach pumped."

His words alarmed me, but nothing about his appearance did. He was placidly calm, albeit clearly worried. It was like someone yawning while telling you he was choking. I unlocked the door and told them to come inside.

Clovis was a timid little fellow in his seventies who long ago had taken on the role of designated worrier. With his frazzled hair and stubbly chin he always wore a racked and anxious face. He would be constantly muttering to himself, adrift in some sea of interior monologue. He barely spoke above a whisper and sometimes it seemed he was drifting out of consciousness in midsentence. Edith was a lot more levelheaded and sociable, but had become legally blind in recent years. They made an interesting pair.

I was alarmed about the poisoning until Clovis explained the source. During the night he had reached for his glass of water and taken a huge gulp only to realize that he had grabbed Edith's denture cup by mistake.

"Clovis, you might feel a little icky, but I don't think we'll need to pump your stomach."

"You sure, Doc?" he replied. "I don't want to take any chances."

"Quite sure. Not to worry."

He nodded with a mix of reluctance and resignation. "Come on, Edith. Let's go back home." He took several steps away, but Edith remained, looking in my direction with a quaint grandmotherly smile. She was clearly amused by the whole affair. After Clovis was out of earshot, she spoke confidentially.

"Thanks for talking some sense into him, Dr. Bradford." She turned to leave and then stopped and added wryly, "Somebody has to."

At two o'clock Ann and I met with Sunflower Miller. After she'd spent weeks reminding me of our agreement, I had finally arranged to discuss her plan to implement some community health programs. To her credit, Ann was very much in favor of the idea, despite knowing that Sunflower would do everything she could to give the programs a holistic flavor. I was less enthusiastic and blamed myself for knuckling under in a weak moment of distracted hunger.

When she entered my office, Sunflower walked directly toward Ann.

"Hi, I'm Sunflower Miller. I hope Dr. Bradford here hasn't already tainted your thinking about good nursing practice."

"Good to see you too, Sunflower," I replied.

She smiled at me in her clever, taunting way. I was left thinking she was just teasing, but I couldn't be sure. No doubt, that was exactly what she intended.

Thankfully, the two women hit it off, allowing me and my ever-contracting attention span to be present in body only. I found myself wondering about Sunflower. In every conversation she found a way to throw out snippets of wisdom regarding the human condition. She could make any discussion take a somber turn by suddenly assuming a serious face, her way of telegraphing that it was time for a teachable moment. Unlike anyone else I knew in Watervalley, she saw life here as a complex construct of human affairs with undercurrents of conspiracy and oppression.

"Dr. Bradford?"

"Hmm?"

"Dr. Bradford? Did you hear what I said?" It was Sunflower. Apparently I had become oblivious to the discussion.

"I'm sorry, no. I guess I lost focus for a minute there. Would you repeat the question?"

She glanced at Ann, who was now regarding me without expression.

"Don't you agree that part of our Seniors Wellness program should include how to do a really effective herbal colon cleanse?"

Where had I been? How had the conversation progressed to this nonsense? "You know, Sunflower, for Watervalley that might be a bit of an overshare."

Her gaze turned withering. "I'm sure the pharmaceutical companies have some sanctioned torture we could teach instead."

Luckily, before I could answer, Nancy Orman opened the office door to tell me I had a visitor. I took this opportunity to escape.

"You two talk amongst yourselves," I said jokingly.

As I exited, my immediate thought was that John had stopped by to see me, something he had begun to make a habit of whenever he was in town. He always had a pertinent item to discuss, but I also noticed that he looked for a glimpse of Ann. Conversely, she always managed to appear with some pressing question for me during John's visits. They rarely spoke, but I noticed an unmistakable lift in her mood and a wry smile on her lips after he had stopped by.

But this time my visitor wasn't John. It was Lida Wilkins. I was surprised to see her, since weeks earlier the results of her stress test and blood work had come back normal.

"Doc, come out to the car. I've got something for you."

Her SUV was parked outside the rear door. She lifted the tailgate and brought out an ancient brown file box.

"It took a little while, but I finally found it underneath some old dresses."

It was her father's work on Oscar Fox. She handed the box to me.

I was beaming. "Lida, if you weren't a married woman, I'd kiss you."

She winked at me. "Crap, Doc. You're a good-looking young man. Not only would I let you kiss me, I'd insist on drawing a crowd to witness it."

I laughed. "When do you need this back?"

"That would be whenever you're tired of looking at it."

"Fair enough. Thanks so much."

"Hey, Doc. Not to change the subject, but is it true that Connie and her sister are starting a bakery?"

"Well, I don't guess it's a big secret or anything, but yeah. At least that's the plan."

Lida's face shriveled to a hard frown. "That's just great. Nothing like competition to raise my anxiety. I've been telling folks we're going to start making pastries so I can recoup some of the lost business."

"I see. Seems to me there should be plenty of business for both of you. I think she's shooting more for a coffeehouse along with sweets and some special catering."

Lida's frown remained unchanged. She looked away for a second, and then spoke with resignation. "Competition is competition, Doc." For a despondent moment she seemed lost in thoughts of what this news meant. I felt stuck in the middle with little to offer her.

Then in characteristic Lida fashion, she grinned at me, and spoke with a sparkling playfulness. "Hey, I noticed Sunflower's truck parked out front. Maybe I need to rethink asking her for some reefer?"

"These days, Sunflower's medical focus seems to have shifted more toward output than intake."

"I'm not following you there, Doc."

I shook my head. "Never mind, it was a dumb statement. Anyway, thanks again for bringing this over."

We said good-bye, but I could tell that the new bakery was still troubling her. Even in Watervalley, change had consequences.

CHAPTER 27

Unbridled Passion

The workday finished.

Arriving home shortly after four, I fed Rhett, took a quick shower, and called Christine. Her animated voice poured through the phone.

"So, any ideas about tonight?" she asked.

"I'm guessing I won't be needing a pub crawl wristband?"

"Not hardly. Why don't you grab a pizza and come over and we'll watch a movie?"

"Sure. What kind of movies do you like?"

"Adventure, romance, intrigue . . . no blood and guts. I'm kind of a PG girl."

"How about *The Little Mermaid*?"

"Hey, don't poke fun. I love that movie."

"Okay, and now you're going to tell me that you used to have a *Little Mermaid* bedcover and matching pillowcases."

"Have you been reading my journal?"

"Why does this not surprise me?"

"Oh, admit it," she teased. "I bet you know all the songs by heart."

"Hmm, possibly."

"Fess up, Bradford. How many times have you seen it?"

"Well, it's been a few years . . . but maybe four or five. And that was only because Ariel was a babe."

"Ha! I knew it."

"Hey, I was at an impressionable age and just starting to notice girls."

"And what about this has changed?"

"Point taken. But you know, the whole movie thing . . . let me think about that for a second."

When I lived in the city, doing it up big for Valentine's was part of the deal whether you liked it or not. But Watervalley was different. The men here had a difficult time with romantic expression. Despite the chidings of Connie and Nancy and a host of other women, I had gotten the impression from the guys down at the Co-op to tread carefully regarding Valentine's gifts. If you went too over-the-top and mushy for Valentine's Day, you were seen as a bad example, someone their wives or girlfriends could use against them. The next time you went into the Co-op, you were liable to be met with cold silence, contemptuous leers, and subtle inferences that you had betrayed the gender and should turn in your man card.

"What would you think about pizza and something other than a movie?" I inquired.

"I don't know. Define *other*."

"Lida Wilkins finally found the file box about the Oscar Fox murder that her dad had compiled. I'm thinking it would be interesting to look through it. You know, just to see what it reveals."

"You're still pretty taken with this whole business, aren't you?"

"Yeah, guess I am. Maybe this is my substitute for doing medical research. Is that a problem?"

"Not at all. You want me to come there?"

"Nah, I'll come out to your place. I guess I'm a little old-school, but one of us will have to drive back late. Might as well be me."

"And I thought chivalry was dead."

"It is if I have to ride a horse."

"Ooooh, that gives me an idea."

"Okay, now you're scaring me."

"What time will you be out here?"

"About an hour. I'll pick up the pizza and head that way."

"Perfect. I'll see you then."

I stared at my cell phone for a moment, wondering what was on her mind.

As I made my way out to Christine's, twilight was fading and the vast tent of darkness was spreading across the countryside. In Watervalley, when this time of day approached, time slowed to an amble. There was something in the unpeopled desolation, in the quiet lull of the raw and frozen fields, that filled me with a subdued tranquillity, a deep, intoxicating awareness of the symphony of rural life. I rolled down my window, breathing in the stimulating cold of the moist air. I absentmindedly followed the faded white lines of the country lane. My mind drifted.

A year ago today I had been steeped in the noise and revelry of a few beers shared with friends at a Nashville bar. Tonight I was driving down a dark and lonely country road, toting a file box regarding an old murder. My life and plans had so dramatically changed. It was a sobering realization. As much as I enjoyed the serenity of Watervalley, and as certain as I was about my decision to complete my three-year commitment, I knew that what my life would be afterward was a big question.

Watervalley was now part of me. Even still, I had not completely shed my love of the city and my hope of doing medical research. But as the weathered sign indicating Summerplace Farm appeared in the headlights, I was brought back to the delightful reality of Christine. I smiled warmly. She was the best thought of my day.

As the wheels of the Corolla crunched down her long driveway, I emerged from my mental fog to an alarming thought. My dreadometer began to ping off the charts. Christine had mentioned earlier in the week that her grandmother was back again, visiting from Florida. I had no doubt that Mattie Chambers, with her ability to summon the ghouls of hell, would likely be hovering over us the entire evening. My desire to be with Christine had clouded my brain. I should have thought through this plan more carefully.

As I pulled up to the house, Christine was standing on the front porch in her heavy coat holding a couple of small bags. I stopped the car and she walked over and got in on the passenger side.

"Hey. What's up?" I asked.

"Hi. Follow that dirt road beside the house."

"Okay. Where are we going?"

"I thought we'd go spread everything out on the table in the tack room of the big barn. It's a little more private."

"Works for me." I acted nonchalant, but inwardly I was ecstatic. This was an unexpected blessing from the universe. As I began edging down the farm road, Christine remained silent, focused on the dark path in front of us. I reached over and grabbed her hand.

"You okay?"

She looked at me blankly. "Yeah, sure. Why do you ask?"

"I don't know. You're just kind of quiet, and, in my experience, when a woman is quiet, she's usually mad."

She released a short laugh and squeezed my hand. "No, silly. It's just . . . Is this okay? I mean, Valentine's Day in a barn?"

"Actually, I was going to ask you that question. I haven't made a very big deal of it."

"No. It's fine. But the barn, are you sure it's okay?"

"Only if I can make really stupid jokes about taking a roll in the hay and horsing around."

"We keep pitchforks in there, you know."

"Ouch. Not very subtle, farm girl."

"Oh, it'll be fun. I love that old barn."

I thought about her comment as we rocked along in silence. "Lots of great memories, huh?"

"Yeah, the best."

We pulled up to the massive structure, where a solitary light from the high overhang of the extended roof stood sentry over the solemn, quiet barnyard. It cast the world in shades of gray and only faintly illuminated the large wooden doors. I retrieved the file box and pizza, shutting the door of the Corolla with my foot. Christine leaned against the car and we stood there for a moment in the still shadows. The open countryside was vast and soundless. She gazed into the night sky, searching the distant particles of light.

Closing her eyes, she breathed in deeply, lavishly of the frozen air, lost in some distant memory. It seemed she was listening, absorbing the rich silence of the darkness.

I stood patiently, realizing that for the moment part of Christine was given to a remote world: some faraway memory buried deep within that was sweet and happy. She opened her eyes and smiled delicately at me. I drew close beside her, leaned against the car, and, as well, gazed into the night sky. She pressed her shoulder next to me with a yielding tenderness and exhaled, her warm breath condensing into a visible cloud in the night air.

"I love the stars at this time of year," she said. "They seem brighter, more perfect."

I stared up. "Gravity."

"Gravity?"

"Yeah." I paused. "I always wondered how the stars stay in place, in perfect harmony. Each has its own energy, its own orbit, its own gravity. And somehow, all that force and attraction keeps everything in balance."

"Luke Bradford, look at you. If I didn't know better, I'd say there's something almost romantic sounding about that."

"Well, not to spoil the moment, but I was more or less quoting Isaac Newton."

"Well, okay, then. At least you didn't try to dork it up completely by making some stupid reference to 'heavenly bodies being drawn to one another.'"

"Thanks for the tip. I was going to use that as the setup line for my big move. But hey, forget it now."

"Hmm. Sorry to put you off your game. What's plan B?"

"Oh, I don't know. Maybe break into song."

"And has that worked in the past?"

"No, but it usually gets the coyotes pretty stirred up. That always impresses the ladies."

"Wow, you do make it hard for a girl to keep her principles."

"Ahh, not to worry. I'm an honorable fellow. I'll hold all my passionate maneuvers in check. That is, up to a point."

"Oh, and what point is that?"

"The point where I think they might actually work."

Christine's laugh echoed into the dark reaches of the cool and tender night. She turned to face me, stepping in close and snug. I put the boxes on the hood of the car and she slid her arms loosely around my waist.

"Okay, Bradford, let's hear what you got."

"As in?"

Christine drew in closer. She spoke slowly, deliberately . . . her voice soft and sweet and intimate.

"Well, it's Valentine's Day and it's just the two of us standing here under the stars. So, here's your chance at a romantic moment. What do you say to a girl to sweep her off her feet?"

The pale light of the barn illuminated the delicate lines of her face. To me, she was so marvelously beautiful. And she was right. It was a romantic moment—the two of us all alone, so passionately close together, pooling our warmth under the vast dark bowl of distant, brilliant stars.

But truthfully, I was freezing and the pizza was getting cold. And there was something about standing next to a box of gruesome murder details that pulled the enchantment right out of the equation. So when I spoke, I don't think it was the dreamy response she was hoping for.

"Mind grabbing the beer?"

CHAPTER 28
Ghosts

We moved inside the dark, massive hallway. On blind instinct, Christine found the light switch. A half dozen dusty bulbs in the high rafters came to life. With hay stacked high on either side, the barn had the same rich, fermented, earthy smell from two months before; a smell it had likely had for decades. I began to understand the comfort in this, to know with firmly tethered assurance that there were small constants in one's daily life that the roll of years could not change. I breathed in deeply of the strangely sweet and musky air.

We carried our things down to the tack room. Christine stopped briefly to rub Aragon's head and to pat one of the other horses. Once inside the small office, she started a propane gas heater that readily thawed the chilled air. We set the pizza nearby to keep it warm and stowed the beer in the small fridge.

On the way in I'd noticed something I'd missed on my prior visit. Hanging at the far end of the main hallway was a basketball hoop with a well-worn net. I was curious.

"Okay, question. I heard a rumor that you were a pretty good basketball player back in the day. Is that hoop out there in the hallway where you learned the game?"

"Yeah. Actually, it's one of several my dad put up for me. But I mostly practiced here because his office was in the tack room. He was my biggest fan."

"As it should be. So, how about it, Chambers? Are you any good?"

She gave a slight dip of her chin. "You know, Bradford. Considering the shame and humiliation I'm sure you must be feeling after losing the 5K, I can't imagine you want to add insult to injury."

"Now, there's a good example of selective memory. As I recall, you were in the rearview mirror when my phone rang."

"Hey, I'm not conceding anything. It would have been a dog-fight to the finish."

"Hmm, so that's how it is? Well, I guess if you're up to it, I'm game for a little one-on-one."

"Sure."

I lifted my arms above me in a long stretch. "Okay. But be sure to bring your books along because I'll be taking you to school."

"And would you listen to the trash talk, already?"

"Hey, just saying. I think we've got time for a little basketball clinic."

I was intentionally provoking Christine's competitive nature, something I had grown to adore about her. I had dated girls who were sweet and funny and interesting, but none of them had the sparring fire, the determination to win, that Christine had. There was something beautiful about it, something alluring, sensuous, primal. As a guy I found this wildly attractive, something I wanted to challenge, to subdue, to conquer.

Christine spoke with a relaxed ease. "Bradford, you are so in over your head. When we're done, you'll be crying like a little girl."

By now I was laughing, which I was certain riled her all the more.

Christine retrieved a ball from a storage cabinet. The last thirty feet of the barn hallway were paved concrete, making for a somewhat narrow but workable court. She took off her coat, tied back her hair, and put on her game face. Her intensity was incredible. "That's right, Bradford. Just keep wearing that silly grin. I love it when the opposition starts out overconfident."

I pursed my lips and studied her for a moment, completely disregarding her taunting words. "You're really cute when you get like this."

"I think we need to put a wager on the table, make this interesting."

"What you got in mind?"

Christine thought for a moment. "If I win, you help Mr. Pilkington milk the cows one afternoon."

"Oh, that's a bad call. I was going to take it easy on you. But now, no way."

"That's the deal. You started this."

I snickered and began to take off my coat.

Christine continued. "So, on the slim chance that you win, what's my poison going to be?"

"Hmm, the first three or four on the list are probably not appropriate, even though, you know, I am a doctor."

"Switch the dial to adult mode."

"Boy, you're no fun. Okay, how about this? What say you cook dinner for me, menu of your choice?"

"That's incredibly boring. I'd probably do that for you anyway."

"Yeah, but there's a catch. You have to wear the outfit of a saucy French chambermaid."

Christine scowled and shoved the basketball right at my chest. I caught it and cackled at her.

"Bradford, you're such a guy."

I dribbled the ball a few times, still laughing. "Guilty as charged."

"But that's okay. In twenty-one points you're going to be a little girl. You ready?"

I bounced the ball back to her. "Ladies first."

"You're going to regret that decision."

I shrugged. "You're probably right."

But in reality, I knew she wasn't.

There had been a time when basketball had been my whole world. But I had moved on. Basketball was a game, and games come to an end. Even still, what I knew and what I could do with a basketball hadn't changed. It wasn't that I was smug. I was just sure of the outcome of our game the same way I knew the etiology of over a hundred different diseases, and how to suture a wound, and what to look for on an X-ray. I had devoted my life to acquiring these skills, and there was a time when I had pursued basketball with the same passion. So, yeah, I just knew.

In no time I could easily see why Christine was the stuff of basketball legend in Watervalley lore. She was quick, smart, and skilled. Moreover she was a tough, calculated competitor. I watched as she tried to sniff out my weaknesses, looking for flaws in the way I guarded her, in the way I moved. She took a quick and early lead. In no time she was up eight to three. But I was deliberately keeping my game at a low ebb, waiting. When the score became seventeen to eight, it was time. I anticipated her next move and lightly tapped the ball away from her. She recovered quickly and went on defense. But after a couple of quick moves and a head fake, I dribbled past her and slammed the ball home.

I proceeded to score the next twelve points straight. Most of them were dunks as well. To her credit, somewhere about the eighth or ninth point in a row, Christine began to laugh and abandoned her previous intensity. She playfully shoved me or held on to my belt. I knew she wanted to win, but she had the class of a seasoned player. Instead of getting angry, you sometimes had to realize that the other guy could do things you couldn't. I should know. I had experienced it plenty of times while playing college basketball.

I made the final bucket to win the game, took a few steps, and bent over, placing my hands on my knees to catch my breath. I had won, but Christine had made me work for it. She gathered the basketball, walked over, and sat on a hay bale, also endeavoring to get her breath. I finally straightened and glanced her way, not at all expecting what I saw.

Christine sat with her head leaning back against the wall, still lightly gasping for air. But she was sweetly, radiantly smiling at me . . . a smile full of welling pride, as if she was gratified to have met her match. Between heaves of breath, I smiled in return, trying to figure what in the world she was thinking.

"Bradford, you're incredible. Where did you learn to play basketball like that?"

I plopped down beside her. "Prep school in Atlanta, and then four years at Mercer."

"You played at Mercer? Why didn't I know this?"

"I don't know. It's in the brochure."

"Oh, stop. What years did you play there?"

"From 2003 through 2006."

"You're kidding."

"Mmm, no."

"Oh, my gosh. I've seen you play!"

"Really? When?"

"In February of 2006. One of my friends at Agnes Scott was dating a guy from Mercer and she invited me to come along and see the game."

"Do you remember which game?"

"I don't remember who Mercer was playing, but it was the last home game and they won by one point."

I knew the game Christine was talking about. I knew it well. It wasn't just my last home game as a senior; it was a game that had much more meaning for me. I folded my arms, leaned back against the wall, and looked down toward my outstretched legs. My response was subdued.

"Yeah. I know that game. I scored thirty-one points. It was my career high."

Christine turned toward me, gape-jawed. Then she spontaneously rose from where she was sitting and stood before me, her face frozen in surprise and disbelief.

"I remember you! You put on a show that night. Why haven't I recognized you?"

"Well, I had a buzz cut, more muscle, and definitely better lungs."

"Luke Bradford, I cannot believe I saw you play basketball all those years ago and I'm just now figuring it out."

"Yeah. Shame on you."

She stared at me quizzically, paralyzed in a moment of astonishment. Finally, she sat down again, gazing straight ahead.

"That's just wild."

I responded with a shrug. This didn't go unnoticed. There was a wounded quality to her voice.

"Well, I think it's a big deal even if you don't."

"No, it's a good memory."

"But?"

"But, you know, nothing."

Christine spoke in a low voice of casual inquiry. "What are you hiding, Bradford?" She paused to bounce the ball a few times. "I bet you were trying to impress a girl."

"I guess you could say that."

"Humph. I knew it." Christine nudged me with her shoulder and regarded me with a bemused but wary smile. "Must have been somebody pretty special."

"Oh, yeah. She was."

"Okay. I don't think I'm liking you right now."

I had been looking down during this entire conversation. I smiled and turned toward her.

"Actually, I'm not being fair. The girl I wanted to impress was Aunt Grace. It was her last time seeing me play. She had just been diagnosed with lung cancer and was going to start chemo the next week. She died that summer."

Christine's playfulness vanished. "Luke, I'm sorry. I had no idea."

"No, no, no. It's okay. You had no way of knowing. And like I said, it's a good memory."

We sat silently, each absorbing the mix of remembrance and revelation. After a moment, I said, "Besides, looks like ultimately I did impress a girl."

Christine smiled with a slow nod of her head. "Yes. I'd say you did."

"Kind of makes you have a deeper respect for me, doesn't it?"

"Well, let's don't go crazy here."

I laughed and looked upward, taking in the details of the barn hallway: the massive poles, the high beams, the hooks and ropes and chains, the heavy wood of the corn bin, the sacks of grain, the smell of the horse-warmed stalls.

"So, you love this old place, huh. Why is that?" I said.

Christine's voice was warm, reflective. "Because of my dad."

"Tell me about him."

As Christine talked about her father, her voice had music in it. I began to realize that this huge, airy barn with its high rafters and dirt-floored hallway had been a sanctuary during Christine's childhood. Beneath the stalwart beams she had gathered a lifetime of memories, half-captured images of some magic country she had known.

"I probably spent thousands of hours here, shooting basketball, grooming the horses, just being with my dad. We'd talk about farming, and basketball, and life, and, I don't know, everything, I guess."

"Hmm, including boys."

"Especially boys."

"Any pointers I should make note of?"

"You're doing okay so far."

"Glad to hear it."

"When Daddy died in the accident, it crushed me and it took me a long time to get past it. I thought I had a lot more years with him. I think that's why I stayed in Atlanta so long. It was just too hard to come here when everywhere I went, everything I saw, reminded me of him."

She paused and my silence seemed to encourage her.

"But now, since I've been back . . . I don't know. It's just different. Now I feel closer to him. There's something reassuring and comfortable about being back here among all the things that are so familiar. Perhaps it's silly, but even now, his words are with me, alive in the stones of this old barn. I still miss him, but now everything I see that reminds me of him is a good thing, a good memory."

I reached over to hold her hand and she leaned her head against my shoulder. Her words deeply resonated with me, revealed to me the source of her depth and strength. All her life she had breathed in the familiar air of Watervalley, had lived out her life within the contours of these native fields and unchanging hills. The enduring love and the endearing words of well-known voices had filled her days.

I had no such wellspring of stability from which to draw upon. I had been loved by family but had had to say untimely good-byes to them; they were losses that still haunted my fragile heart and made me step cautiously, keeping my emotions in check.

Christine broke the silence. "He would have liked you, Luke. He would have liked you a lot."

"I'm sorry I didn't have the chance to know him."

We sat for the longest time, delightfully close to each other, wrapped in warm memories of lost loved ones, ghosts of our past. The silence was sweet, comfortable, enchanting. It seemed our lives were beginning to knit together in unexpected ways.

Eventually, Christine broke the silence. "What are you thinking about? Oh, and it better not be a saucy French chambermaid outfit."

I laughed as we both stood. "Hmm, so you're going to welsh on that one, huh?"

Christine lifted an eyebrow and stepped in close to me, while she carefully placed a finger over my lips. There was a flirtatious, bewitching quality to her voice. "Mmm, give it a little time, Bradford. We'll see."

I'm quite certain that my gape-jawed expression easily communicated how much her sultry response had thrown me. Christine was a deeply principled, wholesome, no-nonsense gal. I had known this from day one and was fine with it, even admired it. So when she occasionally broke character and spoke in this sensuous, taunting way, it had the immediate effect of turning my brains to tapioca. I had the same sloppy, euphoric look that Rhett got when he heard the scoops of dog food hitting his bowl, only with slightly less drool.

"Well, if I wasn't thinking about it before, I sure am now."

Christine rolled her eyes, never losing her sly grin. "Let's eat some pizza."

CHAPTER 29

Conspiracy

We moved into the warmth of the tack room. Christine cleaned off a worktable while I grabbed the pizza and retrieved a couple of beers. While we ate, I surveyed the ribbons and trophies lining the shelf above her father's old desk and discovered a dusty framed photograph of her that was tucked behind a stack of ancient equestrian magazines. She was mounted on Aragon and was completely decked in riding gear, including boots, riding pants, a buttoned coat, and a traditional British skullcap.

"Well, Your Highness. Was this taken before you were off to follow the hounds?"

"Very funny. Put that away. I had no idea it was still hanging around."

"Nah, I love it. How old are you in this picture?"

"Mmm, sixteen, I think."

"And why no smile?"

"Braces."

"You look very regal."

Christine swallowed a bite of pizza. "Yeah, I'm sure that's the look I was going for."

I smiled and returned the photograph to her father's desk.

"Okay, Hardy Boy," she said. "Let's have a look at what's in those old murder files."

"You sure you're okay with this? I mean, so far our Valentine's Day has included a sweaty game of basketball, lukewarm pizza, and now digging into an old murder. I don't want you dying of dream date overdose."

"You have an alternative activity in mind?"

"Wow, like that's not a loaded question. Let's think, you're a healthy farm girl. It's just the two of us in a hay barn. . . . Hmmm?"

Christine smiled and shook her head. "Shut up and get the box, Bradford."

"Right."

I laid out the thick manila folders on the table. We began with the one labeled "Crime Scene."

Inside were photocopies of the original black and whites taken at the bandstand. Even though they were faded and brown, they did little to hide the gruesome nature of the bloody death of the man infamously known as the "murdered German." Oddly, the man was still in his suit coat and the only visible wound was a huge gash across the left side of his neck. I found a photocopy of his autopsy report, the same one I had found in the clinic filing cabinet. Curiously, it clearly noted stabs to the chest, yet there were no bloodstains visible on the man's buttoned suit coat. It was a peculiar inconsistency.

We moved on, sifting through the file of the official police report. The findings stated that Oscar had attacked the man, who had shot him in self-defense. Oscar had bled out while trying to run from the crime scene. Oddly, there were no pictures of him.

Just as Lida had mentioned to me in weeks past, the report stated that Oscar's actions were ruled as voluntary manslaughter because there appeared to be no premeditated intent. Crawford Lewis, the sheriff at the time, had signed the document.

There was also a photocopy of the telegram found in the suit lining of the German. I held it up to the light to see it as clearly as possible.

"What does it say, Luke?"

I clumsily tried to articulate the words. *"Oscar geglaubt in Watervalley Tennessee pro Postadresse sein. Suchen und erholen."*

"Any idea what that means?"

"Not a clue. After *guten Tag* I've pretty much exhausted my German vocabulary."

In a matter of seconds, Christine had typed the words into her cell phone. "Looks like it means 'Oscar believed to be in Watervalley, Tennessee, from postal address. Find and recover.'" She stared at me blankly. "Find and recover what?"

"I don't know. Oscar, I guess."

"Hmm, looks like he didn't want to go along."

"No, you're right. That doesn't make sense, does it? It probably wasn't Oscar. And I'll tell you what else doesn't make sense. I haven't found a copy of his autopsy report. There's not one at the clinic, and I'm not finding one here either."

"What does that tell you?"

"No idea. But it should be part of the file." I studied the document a moment longer. "You know, this is odd. This is a Teletype message and not a true telegram."

"What do you mean?"

"It's not like a Western Union telegram. There is no letterhead and no name to which the message was addressed. It looks like it came from a personal Teletype machine. That means that whoever this German fellow was, he was getting these messages directly, not from an agency like Western Union."

"Who would have one of these?"

"I'm not sure. Businesses, I guess. Private individuals. Spies, maybe."

Christine shrugged. "Leaves a lot of room for speculation, doesn't it?"

"Yeah, I'm afraid so."

We worked through the balance of the interviews of people who had attended the dance on the night of the murders, including Elise Fox and a farmer by the name of Otto Miller, the man who had reported hearing the gunshot. These revealed nothing beyond what we already knew. As well, the interview with Elise Fox vindicated her, asserting that she knew nothing about the murder victim or the events surrounding the murder.

The file of newspaper clippings included copies of the front page from the local paper, the *Village Voice*. The accounts were general in nature and simply noted that the police investigation was continuing. Subsequent articles confirmed that the official investigation had been ruled a double homicide and voluntary manslaughter.

Frank Sanderson had also included a newspaper clipping from February 1945, nearly a year after the event. It was a microfiche picture of the clinic doctor, Haslem Hinson, shaking hands with Raymond Simmons, who was listed in the caption as vice president of the Farmers Bank. Hinson had just been installed as the newest bank board member. Right below the picture, a large question mark had been written in red ink.

Christine spoke first. "This is strange. Why did Sanderson include this photo? It has nothing to do with the murder."

I'd been thinking the same question. "I don't know. Apparently he thought it did."

"Maybe it just got in this file by mistake."

"Hmmm, doesn't seem likely." I read on through the details of the newspaper clipping. "It says here that Chairman Cavanaugh was not pictured. Wasn't he your grandfather?"

"Yeah, Sam Cavanaugh, my mom's dad."

"He was chairman in 1945? How old was he?"

Christine thought for a moment. "I know he was born in 1900, so he would have been midforties."

"Seriously, 1900?"

"Yeah, we used to hear stories that he was Watervalley's most eligible bachelor. He was always a trim, fit, handsome man. He married my grandmother when he was in his early fifties and she was barely twenty-nine. Kind of scandalous at the time, but I think the community got over it. Anyway, they stayed married till he passed away in 'seventy-nine, a number of years before I was born. Grandmother Cavanaugh died in 1999."

"John Harris told me that Raymond Simmons was president of the bank."

"My grandfather Cavanaugh retired somewhere in the early sixties and stayed on as chairman emeritus till his death. Simmons took over running everything around that time. I don't think they ever got along that well."

I set this folder aside and began thumbing through the file labeled "Oscar Fox." Frank Sanderson had detailed a timeline of Oscar Fox's life. Yellowed photocopies of deeds, land transfers, and newspaper clippings, all with handwritten notes scribbled at the bottom or on attached note cards, had been methodically arranged in chronological order. The document also included a list of benevolences and community charities in which Oscar was involved. At the end were several pages of handwritten notes, including a notation that Oscar traveled out of town often. It was the final page that caught my attention.

Written in print were the following items, each with a dash in front of them.

—All transactions paid in cash
—No driver's license
—No voter card
—No draft card or enlistment status
—No previous medical records
—No known previous address in North Carolina
—No North Carolina birth certificate

I looked wide-eyed at Christine. "No wonder Frank Sanderson was so curious about Oscar Fox. He apparently had significant wealth and yet no documented history prior to coming to Watervalley."

"Okay, Bradford. This just got really interesting."

"Didn't it, though? I've talked with a lot of people about Oscar Fox. Nobody has mentioned these details. For some reason Frank Sanderson kept this to himself."

Christine exhaled deeply. "Well, whoever Oscar Fox was, he had a lot of secrets and left a lot of unanswered questions."

"You know what else? Everything we have read here about Oscar Fox and everything that your grandmother said portrays him as a class A good guy, not a vicious murderer."

"That's true. But those pictures were pretty grisly."

"Something's not right."

"What are you thinking?"

"I'm thinking I wish I could find Oscar's autopsy report."

We proceeded to sift through all the files again to see if by chance the report had been misfiled or become stuck to another document. But after thirty minutes of searching, we had nothing. It simply wasn't there.

We had been poring over file documents for a couple of hours and weariness was setting in. I glanced at my watch.

"Wow. It's working on midnight."

"Really? Hey, stay there. I've got a little surprise. I left it in the car. I'll be right back."

Christine grabbed her coat and exited, pulling the door shut behind her. I stared at the stack of papers heaped in front of me, trying to understand all that we had read.

I grabbed the last unexplored item, Frank Sanderson's spiral-bound notebook. It contained mostly random names and dates, summaries of meetings, and details from interviews. Half of the notebook was blank. I skipped ahead to the last entry.

The word written at the top of the page caught my attention: "Autopsy." What followed were the notes from a meeting with Elise Fox, dated June 3, 1962, a full eighteen years after the murder.

The narrative was scribbled in his rough cursive hand.

"E. Fox finally agreed to meet. I asked her about her husband's suit. She stated that Dr. Hinson had given the suit to her after the autopsy. It was covered in dried blood and she threw it away immediately. Dr. Hinson had told her that Oscar had been shot in the hip and that the bullet had nicked his renal artery. I asked if she remembered a bullet hole in the coat. She said she recalled seeing a hole in the back right side. She assumed the coat had been twisted around him in the struggle. I asked her if she had seen the shirt. She had not. Dr. Hinson had discarded it. I told Elise that I never saw Oscar's body up close. The sheriff and Dr. Hinson had loaded his corpse into the back

*of Dr. Hinson's pickup truck and taken it to the clinic for autopsy. I
also told Elise that it was Sheriff Lewis who had instructed me to go
get her and take her to the clinic and stay there with her. The sheriff
handled the murder scene at the bandstand. 6/3/62."*

I read the document again. Questions poured through my
head. Why was there no bullet hole in the front of Oscar's coat?
Why would Frank Sanderson tell Elise that he never saw Oscar's
body up close? And why was he interviewing her again after all
those years? Something here was definitely wrong.

Christine returned carrying a pie with an unlit sparkler in the
center. I rose swiftly and hurried toward her, my voice full of excitement.

"Nice! You made a pie. What kind is it?"

"After that shellacking in basketball, I'm going to say humble."

"It looks great. But can I ask you to do something first?"

"Sure."

"I want you to read this."

She read through the words.

"What do you think it means?"

"It means that Oscar Fox was shot in the back. It means he
killed the guy in self-defense, not the other way around. Think
about it. The guy's throat was cut. There's no way he could pull a
gun and shoot Oscar after that. Oscar was walking away from the
guy and was shot in the back. After that, Oscar came back at him
and took him out with the knife."

"But all my life Oscar has been known as the one who initi-
ated the attack. Even the police report we just read states that."

"I don't understand it either. But the absence of Oscar's autopsy report sure makes that whole business look suspicious. For
some reason, someone wanted to frame Oscar Fox as the bad guy."

As soon as I spoke these words, the clock on the tack room

wall bonged midnight. We stood silently until the final chime. Christine looked up at me.

"Valentine's Day is almost over and I think I'm tired of playing Nancy Drew for one night." She reached for my hand and looked at me. In her gaze was a subtle request. No further clue was needed.

I tossed the notebook on the floor and pulled her toward me, slipping my arms around her. She drew her body delightfully against me. The embrace was effortless, natural.

Christine whispered softly, "Happy Valentine's."

"Yes. Happy Valentine's."

After a long, intoxicating kiss, Christine buried her face against my chest. It was a moment in heaven.

Then her whole body stiffened and she pushed me lightly from her. "Luke, I think you're going to want to see this."

She bent down and picked up the spiral notebook. When I had tossed it to the floor, it had randomly opened to the very last page next to the cardboard backing. In bold ink, three names were written in the corners of a large triangle: Haslem Hinson, Crawford Lewis, and Randall Simmons. In the middle of the triangle was a single word followed by a question mark.

Diamonds.

CHAPTER 30
The Calm Before

I flipped back through the pages of the notebook, scanning to see if there was any other mention of these three men or of diamonds, but there was nothing.

"I don't know what to make of this," I said.

Christine shrugged. "There's always been a rumor that diamonds were tied up in the Oscar Fox story."

"But these three men . . . the way he's written their names sure points to a conspiracy." I placed the notebook back on the table. "Okay, look," I said. "Here's what we know. After seeing the inside of the old bakery, it's pretty clear that a lot of money was spent renovating it. And based on what your grandmother said about him loaning funds to her father, Oscar seemed to have a lot of cash. But I get the impression that it was not money that his wife, Elise, knew about. Secondly, from the scant evidence and from Elise's testimony, it appears that Oscar acted in self-defense. But for some reason this has been twisted around. The dead German's briefcase, ID, and the gun were never found. We have three elements here: money, a body, and a crime scene. That means that any kind of cover-up of the truth would have to involve a banker, a doctor, and a sheriff. For some reason, Frank smelled some kind of conspiracy and thought these three men were in cahoots."

"Why wouldn't he let this be known?"

"Crawford Lewis was his boss, probably his friend too. Maybe he didn't feel like he had enough to support a conspiracy and start pointing fingers."

Christine sighed deeply. "I'm at a loss. There's just not much to go on."

I nodded reluctantly. "Yeah. I guess you're right. But I hate not being able to figure it out."

We were both exhausted, drained by the late hour and the evening's revelations. Despite our unspoken delight in each other's company and the wanton intimacy of moments earlier, we both knew it was time to go home.

I drove us back to Christine's house, where I walked her to the door and held her in the numbing cold.

"Call me," she said.

I nodded and headed home.

The cold days of February continued, providing no further revelation regarding the odd findings in the old file box. One morning at the diner I pulled Lida aside to ask if she had ever read the contents of the box or remembered anything her father might have said about it. Her response was a simple no.

"I'm kind of ashamed to admit it, but Daddy and I were never close. The whole running-away-to-Woodstock thing wasn't ever completely forgotten."

For now, it seemed, the Oscar Fox story had once again reached a dead end, leaving me with more questions and conjecture than before.

Ann continued to be a wonder at the clinic, demonstrating an incredible capacity for connecting with the variety of patients who came under our care. As well, she proved to have a substantial depth of clinical knowledge, making my job of assessments all the easier. She and Sunflower had developed a plan to schedule some community seminars on diabetes, prevention of cardiovascular disease, and, yes, proper exercise and diet. Ann had cleverly developed panels of community leaders to help promote these efforts. Admittedly, the two of them had brilliantly executed the program and attendance was overwhelming.

I also began to notice that Ann had a rather marked curiosity about two people and often mentioned them in conversation: John Harris and Oscar Fox. Ordinarily, I would have thought nothing of this. John, despite his crusty nature, was in fact a handsome, wealthy, and eligible bachelor. As well, my own fascination with Oscar Fox could easily invoke some polite inquiries just to make conversation.

Even still, conversations about both men created a certain stilted stiffness in her countenance, as if she desired to hide the depth of her interest. It puzzled me, but not enough to prompt me to ask her openly. We all had private concerns and the constant inquiries and teasing from the staff about my dating life made me sensitive to her desire to leave some topics alone.

On the last day of February, John came by the clinic in the early afternoon, walking on air. He had become a regular fixture in town, appearing at the diner or down at city hall on a regular basis. He entered my office with a large roll of blueprints tucked under his arm.

"Hey, Professor Harris," I greeted him. "Whatcha got there?"

John was beaming. "Take a look at this."

He unrolled the large sheets onto my desk. Before me were the details of a majestic bandstand.

"Hey, this is impressive. So, what's the scoop?"

"It's all been approved. We're going to partially rebuild and partially renovate the old bandstand. This is what it will look like . . . somewhat smaller than the original but still with a lot of classic details."

"Well, good deal. When does construction start?"

"Monday."

"Seriously? That soon?"

"Yep. Since it's being done with my money, the city agreed to provide the permits and inspections but let me oversee the work. The weather is fair enough, and I've had a work crew ready to go."

John flashed an irrepressible ear-to-ear smile. I had never seen him so happy. Then, as if on cue, Ann came in carrying some patient files. Normally she would feign some level of surprise that John was here. Apparently, she had moved past this. She spoke indifferently.

"Hello, Dr. Harris. Who let you off your leash?"

John cut his eyes at me with a wry grin. "Ah, Nurse Patterson. By all means, call me John. I mean, we're not old friends, but at least we're old enemies. Besides, today is a grand day. It's almost a delight to see even you . . . almost, that is."

"You know, John, I'm tired, which means I don't have the energy to pretend I like you."

John chuckled. "Well, that's not fair at all. You don't know me well enough to know you don't like me."

"Let's just say it's a working theory."

"I have a better idea. Go out with me. Then at least you can be certain you don't like me."

Ann was thrown off-balance by this offer. She hesitated. I

could see John's eyes tighten. He was a clever old fox. Her pause had told him everything. He already had his answer. To use a crude analogy, the hook was set. Now he simply had to be patient and slowly wind the reel. Ann gathered herself and did her best to pretend indifference.

"Gee, let's think about this. You're rude, insulting, and self-consumed. I can't imagine why I'm not jumping at the chance."

"I know, I know. You're just a mere mortal and I'm sure the thought of a date with me is a little overwhelming. But do it anyway. Go out with me."

Ann studied him for another moment. John's euphoria had increased the full weight of his good looks and surprising charm. She nodded cautiously.

"Okay, but only on the condition that you spend lots of money on me, continuously compliment me, and let me talk about myself all evening."

John shrugged. "Works for me."

"I'm only agreeing to the idea of a date in principle. I need time to mull it over, you know, think through all the downsides."

"Sure. Pick you up at the B and B at seven?"

"Make it seven thirty." By now Ann had a delightful, mischievous grin firmly in place. There was a crackling electricity between them: sly, furtive, expectant. I now realized that both of them had been casting their nets, and admittedly, I wasn't sure who had caught whom. Ann turned to me with a raised eyebrow, discreetly signaling a suppressed delight. With that, she turned and departed. All the while John, as had become his habit, was admiring her backside.

"Jeez. That was a pretty thick display of hormones," I said.

"Yeah, seems to be my lucky day."

"Well, Casanova, spare me any further details about how lucky your day gets, if you catch my drift."

John laughed. "Yeah, I understand. Anyway, it's been a good day on another front too."

"How so?"

"Because of another piece of business I've been discussing with Walt."

"And what would you and our good mayor be talking about?"

"Randall Simmons. After that stunt he almost pulled in January regarding the bakery, I intend to make good on my promise."

"Which is?"

"To can his ass. Walt and I have been privately talking with several of the board members and I think they will go along with a no-confidence vote at the stockholders' meeting in a couple of months."

"That's pretty strong medicine."

"Yeah, and I plan on being the pharmacist."

I nodded, noting his determined stance on the matter, and had nothing to add to this announcement.

"Well, John, enjoy your evening. And remember, whatever happens between you and Ann . . . I don't want to know about it."

John's gaze sharpened on me. "Speaking of which, how are things going with my niece?"

"Wow. What part of the 'don't ask, don't tell' policy are you failing to understand here?"

"Oh, get over yourself, sawbones. I'm just looking for the headlines."

"Fair enough. I guess the answer would be good. We seem to be enjoying each other's company." This was, of course, a major understatement.

"Well, watch yourself. Like I said before, that one will have you crying like a little girl."

I laughed and brushed him off. "Yeah, so noted."

John soon departed. My work was done, but I sat in my office for quite some time staring out my windows at the blustery day. Tomorrow would be the first of March and more things than just the season were getting ready to change.

CHAPTER 31
The Ides of March

Winter gave a final performance in the first days of March, spitefully blowing a bitter wind that leached into your bones. This was followed by a few gray days of cold rain that teemed upon the saturated earth. But by the second week, milder air began to pour over the valley and spring began to arrive. On my morning runs out Summerfield Road, the low hum of tractors could be heard in the distance. The countryside was beginning to come alive with the clamor of chirping birds, the drowsy smell of flowers, and patches of green clover conquering their old domains.

Despite John's determination and enthusiasm, the renovation work on the bandstand had made only modest progress. Rot had been found in a few of the piers, requiring delays until they could be properly inspected and replaced. Connie and Estelle finally had all the permits needed for the remodeling of the bakery, although no actual work had begun.

Estelle was still living at Connie's house, an arrangement that seemed agreeable to both sisters. The three of us would often have dinner together several nights a week. Watching the two of them spar over everything from renovation plans to recipes to disagreements about long-ago events, dates, marriages, and children's names proved to be wildly entertaining.

Altogether, though, I was seeing less and less of Connie. Her sister and the bakery project were steadily consuming more of her time. I was able to manage fine on my own and magically, the house remained orderly and spotless, proving she was still tidying up during the hours when I wasn't there, but I missed our conversations. Little had been said between us about the Randall Simmons incident and I wondered if she was aware of John's plans regarding his fate. Yet, given our limited time together, I chose not to broach the subject and churn up the deep well of hurt surrounding the incident.

On Friday I walked out my front door to the intoxicating smell of warm grass. It was one of those charmed days. I breathed in a deep draft of the fresh, vibrant, living air. A fragrant wind from the nearby hills washed over me. Spring was still a while away from full splendor, but the promise was there, of sunshine and scented blossoms and balmy days to come.

I walked to the clinic and entered through the back door. As was my usual routine, I peeked down the hall to the waiting room to get a sense of how busy the day might be. It was something of a marvel to me that often the waiting room actually held people who were there simply to provide moral support to an ill friend. Such was Watervalley. Maybe the free coffee drew them. I worried about patients hacking away in the waiting room, fearing that along with some pretty good gossip their benevolent neighbors would also pick up a virus or two.

My first patient of the day was Oni Kinser. His wife, Florence, had come with him. She was a squat, tough, fortysomething woman with a raspy voice, bushy black eyebrows, and a hard, mean face. I guessed Florence hadn't smiled in twenty years and was proud of it. She struck me as a woman who chain-smoked Marlboros and started fistfights with other moms at Little League games.

Oni was a short, portly fellow with a ruddy face and red hair. He was generally quiet with a perpetual worried look on his face. No doubt, living within backhand range of Florence had done this to him. His actual name was Oneciferous, making it understandable why he was always on the defensive and spent a lot of time trying to compensate. Ann and I followed them to the exam room. Oni remained hunched over as he walked, making pathetic grunting sounds at even the slightest motion.

Florence maintained a sour, bulldog face, her large jowls drawing her mouth into a fixed frown. She regarded Oni with a narrow-eyed scrutiny, looking for all the world like she might pop him one just for good measure. Once settled in the exam room, I asked Oni what might be the problem. Florence answered for him.

"Last night was our anniversary, so we went to the Alibi for a few beers, you know, to celebrate."

I nodded, doing my best to keep a straight face at their choice of a roadhouse as a destination date.

"Well, we got a little loopy and decided to hit the dance floor. They were playing 'Boot Scootin' Boogie.' It's kind of our song. So I made the big mistake of telling Fred Astaire here to dance like no one was watching. He took me seriously. I thought he was having a seizure."

I pressed my lips together, hard, doing my best to suppress the laugh that was threatening to erupt. Ann was doing a better job of it, standing completely poker-faced.

"Anyway, the next thing I know, he's all hunched over grabbing his back. It sure put a damper on the romance, I can tell you that."

I nodded thoughtfully, still fighting the terrible urge to cackle outright. The edges of Ann's mouth were beginning to curl upward, which wasn't helping. Thankfully, Florence had finished and I was able to examine Oni and ask him questions directly, eliminating Florence as interpreter. His injury proved to be tissue related, so I prescribed some muscle relaxers along with some medication for the pain. After the exam, Ann and I retreated to my office, where we instantly exploded behind the closed door. Admittedly, I felt a little guilty about laughing at the Kinsers' expense. Sometimes the clinic stage provided more comedy than drama.

As it turned out, all the drama occurred in the afternoon.

By two thirty we were through with all the appointments and walk-ins. The clinic stayed open until five. Typically, a few pediatric cases would show up after school let out or someone would stop by to get a prescription updated. Ann had asked to leave early, noting that she was going out that evening and had some errands to run first.

Shortly before three there was a timid knock on the door. It was Nancy, who normally had no qualms about barging in unannounced. She cautiously approached my desk and spoke in a conspiratorial whisper.

"Dr. Bradford, you have a visitor."

"Okay. And?"

"Well, it's a pharmaceutical rep and she says she knows you."

"What's her name?" Nancy handed me the card. "Michelle Herzenberg," I read. I thought for a moment. "I can't place her."

Nancy was still staring at me, frozen in a state of speechless timidity. "Nancy, what's wrong?"

"She's just, well. She's different."

"Different how? She have a third eye or something?"

"No. But she certainly has everything else."

I had no idea what Nancy was talking about and chose not to ask. It was a pharm rep. They stopped by from time to time. This was nothing unusual. "Nancy, why don't you show her in?"

She nodded and left, and within seconds, there appeared in my doorway the explanation for Nancy's trepidation.

Michelle Herzenberg was a stunning, beautiful blonde. Tall and graceful, she carried herself with an energetic assurance. Professionally dressed in a snug skirt and tall heels that accented her long legs, she had a crisp designer look about her, a kind of Madison Avenue class and style. Coupled with her long hair and sensuous facial features, she was one of those mesmerizing people who seemed to drag an invisible cape of glamour behind them. She electrified the air as she entered.

"Luke Bradford. I bet you don't remember me."

"I'd like to say we have met, but I'm afraid I can't put you in context." I had responded with a controlled confidence and not with the wide-eyed, slack-jawed wonderment that I suspect she normally received.

"I saw you at a number of the parties at Vanderbilt. I graduated from pharmacy school this past year."

"Well, there you go. That makes perfect sense. I knew I had seen you somewhere." I paused, adding hesitantly, "Sorry, though. I still don't remember meeting you."

"Oh, we were probably never introduced. But I knew who you were. Everyone knew who you were. My gosh, you were the med school phenom."

"Well, thanks. I mean, you're probably stretching the truth, but you're doing a really nice job of it. So, for heaven's sake, don't stop."

She laughed and we stood chatting for several minutes, catching up on familiar names and old haunts. Aside from being dramatically beautiful, Michelle Herzenberg had the incredible ability to look at you with total engagement. She laughed warmly and had a breathy, seductive voice that could be sweet and low, conveying an inviting, captivating charm. Even still, while it was delightful to talk with her and enjoy the full attention of such a striking woman, her magic was largely lost on me. As shallow and clichéd as it sounds, I simply wasn't fascinated by blondes.

In hindsight, I guess she sensed this. And that made her try all the harder.

I directed her to one of the tall leather chairs in front of my desk and took the other one next to her. Sales reps handed you a ton of brochures and I had learned it was easier to sit adjacent to them. She took off her coat, revealing a rather ample and blousy figure, and then sat, crossing her long, lovely legs in my direction. Nestled in the privacy created by the two wingbacks, she leaned in toward me, speaking confidentially.

"I have to ask a question. I know I heard somewhere along the way that you were going to stay at Vanderbilt and do research. How did you end up here?"

"Kind of a long story, but the short version is that Watervalley is paying off my student loans. It's a three-year gig."

"Wow. That must be tough. All I saw as I was driving to get here was cows. What kind of social life is there?"

"Actually, the cows can be quite entertaining once you get past the language barrier."

She laughed. "Well, I don't want to be too forward before we talk business, but I got in town later than I intended and thought I might spend the night at the local B and B. If you aren't busy, I thought we could grab some dinner later."

I paused. It was a flattering offer, but not one that I was

interested in accepting. "Candidly, I have tentative plans, so I probably need to take a rain check." It was an honest response. Christine and I had fallen into a routine of spending our weekend evenings together, even though we had made no specific arrangements.

Not missing a beat, Michelle smiled warmly, unfazed by my rejection. "Sure, perhaps another time." No doubt, she was confident about her capacity to attract. I suspect, in her thinking, time was on her side.

She spent the next minutes articulating details about several new drugs as well as enhancements to some existing ones. I had to admit, she knew her stuff and answered my questions thoroughly. Yet there was a certain sensuous side to her movements, a skillful use of the casual touch, a curious and tender yielding in her eyes as she spoke. Her allure was effortless, enticing, and made it easy to be drawn in.

While I was reviewing the final brochure, she rose from her chair and stood beside me to point out some specifics on the drug's possible side effects. Before I realized it, in a subtle, seductive manner, she had bent over at the waist with her long hair falling gently on my shoulder and her drooping, low-cut blouse affording an inspiring view of some of God's most wonderful creations.

That was when Christine walked in.

CHAPTER 32

The Third Degree

"Well, hello!"

Undaunted, Michelle straightened slowly and regarded Christine as an intruder. I, on the other hand, stood abruptly, a hasty move that cast a shadow of guilt over me. Before I knew it, I was doomed.

Michelle read my actions and sized up instantly that there was a clear connection between Christine and me. She changed gears fluidly, immediately walking toward Christine with a generous smile.

"Hi, I'm Michelle Herzenberg. I'm with Biotherics Pharmaceutical."

Not to be outdone, Christine answered, "Hi, Michelle. I'm Christine Chambers. I'm with Watervalley Elementary."

"So, I'm guessing you're not a patient of Dr. Bradford's?"

"Yeah, I guess that would be true."

They continued exchanging pleasantries in a diplomatic, courtly manner. I stood by doing my best to appear nonchalant while these two did a thorough sizing up of each other under the guise of gushing politeness. It was a conversation rife with all the subtle markings of one-upmanship and turf protection.

"Luke and I are old acquaintances from Vanderbilt," Michelle said. "He had quite a reputation at the med school." The message that "I knew him first" wasn't lost on Christine.

"So I've heard. You should have seen him play basketball at Mercer. He was a real sensation there as well."

I couldn't believe what I was hearing. Christine was really stretching it. Once again, just as Connie and Estelle had done, it seemed that the women in my world felt free to talk about me as if I were offstage in a soundproof booth. Part of me wanted to hold up a sign that read, "Hi, I'm the Y chromosome in the room." And while all the adoring praise was fun to hear, I plainly knew that the compliments were only a delivery system for the real points being made.

"Oh, how interesting. So, I guess you two have known each other a long time. You must be the reason no girl could ever get a date with him at Vandy? Did you follow him here from Atlanta?"

"No, I'm actually from here. Our paths have crossed over the years."

"Really, you're from this place? Hmm." There was a definite undertone of judgment in Michelle's response. Having sized up the situation, she decided it was time to retreat. But not before throwing one last volley. She turned to me, feigning a wounded tone.

"Luke Bradford, shame on you. You told me you only came here because they would pay off your loans. I can see you had lots of reasons." With this she winked at me and proceeded to gather her things. She extended her hand to me as she left.

"Thanks, Luke. I'll see you again in a month or so. Christine, good to meet you as well." But as she turned to leave, she offered me one last sly, sultry smile. Even as clueless as I was, I could still read that look: "You have no idea what you're missing."

Christine's sweet, amiable face immediately de-glossed the second Michelle was out the door. She regarded me with the sort of vacant smile that you give a child to let him know how hard he'll be spanked after the company leaves. Her tone fell a half measure short of outright reprimand.

"Well. What was that all about?"

"What was what all about?"

Christine dropped her chin in a look of disbelieving reproof. "Excuse me. Have you been in a coma for the last ten minutes?"

For some reason, Christine's stern reproach struck me as hilarious. It had all been hollow drama, nothing more. No longer able to control myself, I laughed out loud. "No, actually I have been thoroughly entertained."

Christine crossed her arms, offering a benign smile. "Oh, so you think this is funny?"

"Well, sure. What else would it be?"

Christine stared with a withering intensity.

"Okay, why is it I feel like a marshmallow over a campfire about right now?"

She smirked. "Don't try to be funny, Bradford."

Again, I laughed robustly and walked to my chair, then plopped heavily into it, relaxed and amused. With arms still folded, she followed and sat in the wingback across from me. Despite her scrutinizing tone, Christine was wearing a repressed smile. I could see that she was miffed, but her intelligent, rational side was nagging at her, struggling to justify her emotions. It was a losing battle. The miffed side was winning. She stared at me silently, apparently thinking that this tactic might yield a confession. I wasn't biting.

"So, there's not anything further you'd like to tell me about her?" she asked.

I said nothing, which for Christine seemed to say everything. Then she did something completely unexpected. There was an unassuming drop of her chin and her face softened into a low, enticing smile. I could practically see the wheels turning. Subtly, she began to exert some considerable voltage of her own. She nimbly shifted in her chair, crossing her legs so that the top one bounced lightly in a delightful, flirtatious way. By imperceptible degrees she fluidly straightened her posture and ever so seductively pulled back her shoulders, allowing for a breathtaking tightening of her blouse across her generous curves.

This wasn't fair. In a matter of seconds she was reducing me to a big blob of slobbering protoplasm. I had done nothing, but now was ready to confess to anything. Soon I would be losing all meaningful motor control. I responded while I still had breath left.

"Wow. This is adorable. I'm seeing a whole new side of you. Christine Chambers, if I didn't know better, I'd say you're acting a little jealous."

Her response was slow and assured. "Jealous? No. Curious? Sure. I mean, let's face it, she was looking at you like you were her favorite dessert."

"Oh, that's ridiculous. She's a sales rep. She looked at me like I was an ATM."

"You are so clueless, it's almost cute."

"And you are basing this on what logic?"

"Well, let's see. You're a guy. You have a pulse. Naturally, your actions are suspect."

I looked to the side, shaking my head. "That is so unfair. Look, she's just pushing her drugs. Sales reps come by all the time. They chat you up, they give you free samples, they ask you to dinner; it's all part of the routine. They're not required to be ugly."

"Oh, so she asked you to dinner?"

"She did and I refused. Surely I get a few points for that?"

Christine spoke through a low, exasperated laugh. "Luke Bradford, you're just like every other man. Sometimes even more so. She sure seemed to know a lot about you."

"Oh, come on, seriously. She said we knew each other from Vandy, but I don't remember her and told her as much. She probably boned up on a little of my history to break the ice."

"So, you're saying that my first take on her as the misguided spawn of Satan might not be completely accurate?"

"I doubt she's given me another thought."

"I doubt she has many extra to spare."

"Hey, she came, she spoke, she left. As far as I know, her intentions were well-placed."

"With the way she positioned that low-cut top right in front of your face, that wasn't the only thing that was well-placed."

This was a valid point, but I wasn't about to concede anything. "Can't say I really noticed."

Christine's eyes tightened. "So, you're telling me you were oblivious to her va-va-voom cleavage?"

It was time to put this discussion to rest. I rose from my chair, walked around the desk, and leaned against the front. I smiled warmly and spoke in a slightly teasing voice.

"Miss Chambers, surely you realize that I only have eyes for you." Mentally I was also thinking, "and your va-va-voom cleavage," but thought it best to leave that part off.

She stood, drew in nearer, and looked alluringly down as she ran her finger under the lapel of my lab coat. "So, are you trying to convince me that knighthood is still in flower?"

I brought my arms around her waist, pulling her close. "Well, I wouldn't go that far."

Her voice still carried a faint mix of affection and reprimand.

"Careful, Bradford. You're still about a half step away from being sent to the principal's office."

"Mmm, is that so? I believe I'm about a half step away from something much more pleasant."

I leaned in to kiss Christine, but she withdrew slightly, studying me with a bemused smile.

"Problem?" I asked.

"Oh, I was just thinking for a moment. Trying to figure out if you're a frog or a prince."

"If I start croaking softly at twilight, you'll have your answer."

Christine shook her head, yet all the while she smiled at me adoringly.

"Bradford, do you ever think about growing up and acting like an adult?"

"Not if it means I have to get rid of my Spider-Man pj's."

Before Christine could reply, my cell phone's blaring ring filled the room. I reached in my pocket to look at the caller. It was John Harris. I held the face of the phone toward Christine. "It's the uncle."

I put it on speakerphone. "Hello."

"Sawbones, if you can break free, come on down to the lake. I've got something I think you'll want to see."

"Really? What is it?"

"A briefcase. An extremely old one."

I told John I would be right there and hung up. Christine and I stared at each other. "Come with me," I said. "This could be really interesting."

"No, you go ahead. Just call me later and we'll figure out tonight."

"You sure?"

"Sure. I'm going to head home."

I gave her a quick kiss and departed, eager to learn more of John's discovery. The afternoon had been quite a piece of theater, much ado about nothing.

But I had missed the larger point. Christine's question about growing up had had an underlying serious intent. It was the first inquiry, a first hint of the deeper impulses of her heart and her desire to know what affections lay beneath my comic veneer. I would be foolishly slow to catch on.

CHAPTER 33
An Interesting Discovery

By the time I arrived at the lake, Sheriff Thurman was already there talking with John. Using the lowered tailgate of John's truck as a makeshift table, the two of them were examining the ancient briefcase. Their conversation stopped as I approached.

"Take a look at this, sawbones," John said.

The soft leather case looked like a prop from a Hollywood movie set. It had a classic design with heavy stitching, a tarnished brass zipper, and a nameplate where the initials "HEK" were elaborately inscribed. Other than being caked in dust, it was in excellent shape.

"Where was it found?" I asked.

"Up in the roof section of the bandstand," John replied. "When the boys were tearing the ceiling out earlier today, this plopped down. I Googled the manufacturer's name embossed on the inside. It was made by an Austrian company that went out of business in 1940. Given the vintage, we're speculating it may have belonged to our infamous murdered German."

There was no masking my excitement. "Well, what was in it?"

John and Warren exchanged uneasy glances. Warren responded.

"Unfortunately, not a thing except for a few dead insects. There was an old access panel in the ceiling about twenty feet away from where it fell. I'm guessing Oscar, or somebody, got to the panel and flung it to the far corner out of sight. Looks like it has set there for years."

"That's unbelievable," I replied. "And no one thought to look up there during the investigation all those decades ago?"

Warren shrugged. "Apparently not. It was out near the edge where the roof slopes down and was probably hidden by the ceiling joist. Someone might have looked, but it wouldn't have been easy to see. Besides, I guess everybody assumed the briefcase, along with the gun and knife, were at the bottom of the lake. And then again, I've always heard a theory that there might have been a third person involved. It's just all hard to say."

"By the way, Sheriff," I said, "whatever happened to the German's remains?"

"He's buried in Rose Hill Cemetery. I heard tell that Sheriff Lewis tried to contact the state and federal governments about what to do with him, but with no positive identification, nobody took an interest. I guess the war had everyone's hands full. So, he was buried here at Rose Hill."

My enthusiasm ebbed. In its own right, the briefcase was a fascinating discovery. But it shed no new light on what had happened and actually created new questions as to the fate of its contents. Nevertheless, Warren's mention of Sheriff Lewis prompted some questions.

"Warren, do you know about Frank Sanderson's files on the old murder mystery? You know, Lida's dad. He used to be a deputy."

"Frank was retired when I first joined the department, but he would come around occasionally and visit. I heard he had an interest in the old bandstand murder even though it was a closed case."

"Lida said something about it being a closed case, too. Why is that?"

"If memory serves, the incident was considered voluntary manslaughter. Statute of limitations in Tennessee is five years."

I went on to tell both of them about going through the old murder file box, and more specifically about Frank Sanderson's notebook and the speculation about the three men and the diamonds. Warren listened quietly, carefully taking in all that I said. In the end, he shook his head.

"There's just not much telling about some kind of conspiracy, Doc. The whole part about the diamonds is probably nothing more than Watervalley imagination. As far as the three men you mentioned, well, they all had a few bones in the closet, so to speak."

"How so?"

A wry grin spread across Warren's face, and with his large paw of a hand, he began to rub his chin. "You want the short version?"

"Sure."

"Well, when you're sheriff, you tend to hear things that aren't always common knowledge. These guys were a little before my time, but I've heard talk. Seems that Haslem Hinson had an alcohol problem, Sheriff Lewis had a gambling addiction, and Raymond Simmons—well, he just had an attitude problem."

"Attitude problem?"

"Eh, I'm not going to put a label on it, Doc. But suffice it to say that as long as he was president of the Farmers Bank, not a single black ever worked there. It's the typical story. He rose up through the ranks, but his people were pretty much white trash. They seem to be the ones with the most hardened attitudes."

I nodded.

"Still, you know, Doc, none of that points to the three of them being guilty of a crime. And you have to remember, in Watervalley one body always tells somebody. If diamonds had ever been found, we'd all know it by now."

Again I nodded. Warren was smart and, regrettably, likely correct. Even still, I couldn't help but stare at the briefcase in front of me and wonder. If it did belong to the mysterious German, then why had he come to town seventy years ago looking for something so important that he was willing to kill for it?

I stopped short of divulging any further details about Oscar Fox's lack of official ID and my theory about his actions being in self-defense. It was largely speculation. There was nothing more to be discussed. I thanked John and Warren and left for home.

The weekend passed quietly with Christine and me spending considerable time together. We seemed never to be at a loss for things to talk about, which was good given the limited amusements available. We rarely discussed the future, which suited me fine. And thankfully, nothing more was said about Michelle Herzenberg, although I felt certain she was not forgotten.

With the arrival of warmer weather, Christine and I began to take long walks on the paths near the lake and spend hours at the farm. She talked of perhaps going horseback riding, something that held no interest for me. Angus continued to invite me to help milk the cows and I invariably declined. The rural life was growing on me, but only by degrees.

The changing seasons seemed to feed my hunger for travel, my love of faraway places and new experiences. It had been a gray winter, cold and confining, warmed only by the wonderful hours I'd spent with Christine. Even still, I found myself occasionally doing random searches for flights out of Nashville to warm, sunny beaches or distant cities. I had accumulated a small amount of vacation time, but not enough to justify any major excursion. I longed to get away, but travel would have to wait until some obscure future date.

Before going to bed on Sunday evening I mulled over what Warren had said about the darker sides of the three men, trying to see how these factors might fit into the larger picture. I had little more than a broad theory, Frank Sanderson's drawing, and the one newspaper photo that actually tied them together. Once again, it seemed my investigation had reached a dead end.

CHAPTER 34
Unexpected

I was up early Monday morning for a short run. Afterward, I took care of Rhett, cleaned up, and headed over to the Depot Diner. Connie had called Sunday afternoon to beg off her normal breakfast duty, noting that she and Estelle needed to meet with the contractor to start the renovation. Her excitement had poured through the phone and I had readily assured her I could manage fine.

At the diner I ordered my usual country ham breakfast, watching warily for Sunflower Miller, who had an uncanny knack for swooping in on me whenever I ate there. Today, however, it was Lida who slid into the opposite seat when I was almost finished.

"How's the breakfast?"

I swallowed a last bite and looked at my empty plate. "Terrible. I think you should bring me another one."

Lida scrunched her nose and grinned in that sparkling way that I adored. "Thanks for forcing your way through it."

"For you, Lida, anytime." I lowered my voice and spoke confidentially. "How's your anxiety these days?"

"Since we figured out my ticker was okay, I've been doing a lot better. The medications have been a good thing too. But let me tell you my real get-well plan."

I leaned in, offering her my full attention.

"I've put the B and B up for sale on one of those Internet real estate services. I'm trying to keep it low-key, but I've had several inquiries."

"Well, okay. Good luck with that."

"Yeah. Oh, and also, now that the new bakery is in the works, I'm going to follow through with my plans to start making pastries here to keep up with the competition." She finished by giving me a quick wink and slid back out. I nodded thoughtfully. I understood the need to compete, but I hated it too. I paid my bill and walked to the clinic.

My first patient was none other than Margie Reynolds. I had been following her care ever since she had come to see me in January. She had been fortunate. The lump she'd discovered had turned out to be benign and had been removed in an outpatient procedure. When Nancy told me she was in exam room one, I was hoping Margie had not found another mass. Ann was taking her vitals as I entered.

"Marrrrgieee. How in the world are you?"

"Terrible, just terrible." She was snickering beneath her complaint. I played along.

"Now, Margie. You haven't found another lump, have you?"

"Yeah, I have. Matter of fact, I found two of them. They're the size of eggplants and are attached to my hips."

I was puzzled and my expression said as much.

"Let me translate for you. I'm getting fat."

"Well, Margie, how did this happen?"

"Okay, here's the confession. When I thought I had cancer, I figured what the heck, I'm not going to be cheated out of a lifetime of ice cream and chocolate. So I started eating like there was no tomorrow because, crud, I didn't think there would be. Now that I'm okay, I can't kick the habit. I'd eat a Wiffle ball if you put a little caramel sauce on it. So now I'm paranoid. I'm thinking I've got a thyroid issue that's giving me this bottomless appetite."

"Margie, let me look at your chart."

While I did so, she exhaled a deep sigh. "Oh crap, I hate this part. Now you're looking at how much weight I've put on since January."

I spoke without looking up from her chart. "Margie, you are more than a number on a scale."

"Luke Bradford, you can be such a sweetheart. If I didn't feel so fat, I'd kiss you right now."

I smiled and shook my head, saying nothing. I was looking at her labs from the previous visit. But my silence made Margie all the more nervous and she continued talking to fill the void.

"And, of course, now all my clothes don't fit. I'm cursed. When I was little, an evil witch cast a spell on me giving me expensive taste and a lifetime of limited funds."

I continued to study her chart, speaking vacantly. "Margie, you need to get sick more often. You crack me up."

"Sure. Have a good laugh at my expense." She looked at Ann and winked. "Here I am on the first leg of the slow descent into type two diabetes and getting snickered at by a man who's seen me naked. That just doesn't give a girl a lot of confidence, you know."

Normally I would have busted out laughing at Margie's teasing, but I was deep in thought about her thyroid and the weight gain. Then an idea struck me. I grabbed my pad and wrote a short note on it.

"Margie, I have some more questions, but first I want to do a blood draw to put this thyroid issue to rest. Ann, if you would, do a stick and have Camilla run this." I handed her the paper with the desired lab test. Ann nodded and proceeded.

"Margie, anything else different or unusual?"

"Like what, for instance?"

"Oh, any change in sleeping habits?"

"Yeah, Larry's. I'm sleeping fine, but he says my snoring no longer just annoys him—it frightens him. He said if you can't help me, we're going to an exorcist."

"Have you noticed any changes in body temperature, hot flashes, perspiration?"

"Yeah. Ever since the weather got warmer, I sweat like a pig. If it gets any worse, I'll need to wear a life jacket."

I asked her several more questions, endeavoring to reach a diagnosis. Her clever wit and big sloppy grin were nonstop. I just couldn't quit laughing. She loved it. I finally held up my hand.

"Margie, have you ever thought about doing stand-up?"

"Sure, whatever. So, what's all this mean, Doc?"

I was about to answer when Camilla returned with the results of the blood test. She handed it to me and turned to leave, but I noticed her eyes were brightly expressive and her lips pressed tightly together. I looked at the paper and nodded.

"Oh, my God," Margie exclaimed. "This looks bad. What? What is it?"

"Um, Margie. You definitely have a lump."

"What do you mean? I don't get it. Spit it out, Doc."

"Margie, dear, you're pregnant."

She responded with the lowest sound I have ever heard come out of a woman. "Noooooo!"

"Well, we ran a simple hCG serum and it came back positive. So, this little piece of paper is saying 'yessss.'"

Margie was speechless. She looked at Ann, then at me, then back at Ann. We could do little more than smile robustly at her.

She held up her finger in a statement of declaration. "You need to call Sheriff Thurman because I am going to murder Larry Reynolds. I know exactly when this happened."

"Margie, it's okay if you want to leave a few details to our imagination."

"I'm going to kill him. I am absolutely going to kill him."

"Okay, but first tell him he's going to be a father again so at least he'll die a happy man."

Margie exhaled a heavy "humph" and sat in stunned silence. Soon enough, she spoke in a low, bewildered voice.

"I'm forty-one years old. I have a child in college and one in junior high."

"At least there won't be a problem with tuition overlap."

"All I can say is, don't be surprised if you start seeing Larry Reynolds's picture on the side of milk cartons." You had to love this about Margie. Her clever wit was never far away.

I reached over and took her hand. "Margie, congratulations. You will, no doubt, continue to be an incredible mom."

By now the reality was truly sinking in. Her uproarious facade was slowly melting into a face of irrepressible joy. Margie spoke with a sense of wonder. "Oh, my goodness. I really am pregnant, aren't I?"

We talked for several more minutes. Afterward I had Camilla draw more blood to run some additional tests and Ann retrieved all the expectant-mother schedules to review with her. Before departing, I gave Margie a quick hug and congratulated her again.

There were always added risks with older pregnancies. But given where Margie's life had been only a few months ago, I could only conclude that God still had big plans for her. It was a good start to the day.

I was in my office later that afternoon when Nancy stopped by to say that Sunflower Miller was there to see me. I hesitated before telling Nancy to send her in. It was late in the day and I just wasn't sure I was up to listening to another of Sunflower's rants.

"Did she say what she wants to meet about?" I asked.

"I don't think she wants to chat."

"I don't understand."

"She's in exam room two. She's sick."

"Seriously?"

"Seriously."

"Wow. Okay. I'll be right there." This was an unexpected first and, I had to admit, rather troubling. Given Sunflower's disdain of institutional medicine, her condition must be serious. I grabbed my lab coat and stepped briskly.

As I entered, Ann had just finished getting all of Sunflower's vitals. I immediately noticed that her eyes were puffy and watery.

"Sunflower, I am not sure what to think about seeing you on this side of the clinic. Are the planets out of orbit? Tell me what's going on."

"When it rains, it pours, Doc. For some reason my eyes and nose have been running like a faucet."

I briefly examined her. "Have you been taking any antihistamines?"

"Sure have, but the relief is only temporary. It just keeps coming back."

We talked at length. Sunflower had a case of severe conjunctivitis that had been chronic for over a week. She had no history of allergies or hay fever. Her temperature was normal and there were no other symptoms. Her illness was puzzling, and as well, it was clear that it had worn her down. She seemed to have lost some of her vibrancy, as well as the spark and obstinacy that I had grown to expect. She agreed to a few tests and I prescribed some medications including an antibiotic to relieve the symptoms. She wasn't severely sick, just exasperated. For now it seemed that little more could be done other than to treat the symptoms and monitor her situation. As I turned to leave, I paused, recalling something she had said.

"Sunflower, you mentioned a moment ago something about when it rains, it pours. Are you having any other issues?"

"No. Well, yes. But not with me, with my chickens."

Chickens didn't fall under my primary practice. A veterinarian named Charlie Ingram came over from Grainger County one or two days a week, although I doubted Sunflower had ever called him. So once again I started backing toward the door, speaking lightly as I departed, "Something afoul with the home on the free range?"

"Yeah. They're all dying."

Some ancient memory clicked at this. I stopped and gave Sunflower a studied look.

"Tell me more. How many have died, Sunflower?"

She went on to tell me that in the last three weeks, ten of her best chickens had suddenly developed peculiar choking behaviors and plopped over dead. She had tried to separate them from the others whenever she saw the symptoms, but wasn't sure of the root cause.

"Have you added any new chickens lately?"

She thought for a moment. "Yeah. A friend from Kentucky gave me a couple of Indian Game chickens. They're a type of Cornish hen, but really big. They died along with the others."

I rubbed my chin and reflected on this.

"Sunflower, come to my office with me. I want to look something up."

I found my *Journal of Infectious Diseases* on the shelf beside my desk. I flipped through the pages, discovered what I was looking for, and spun the book around for Sunflower to see.

"It's called Newcastle disease. It affects chickens and causes conjunctivitis in humans. I can't be certain that's what we're dealing with here, but it sure seems suspect."

Sunflower read through the summary and began to nod her head. Her pensive and subdued appearance projected such a sad contrast to the fiery woman I had known. My heart went out to her.

"Thanks, Luke. Thanks for this and for taking care of me this afternoon." She paused for a moment and looked down, gathering her thoughts. I couldn't tell if it was solely from the infection, but her eyes seemed on the cusp of tears. Her voice was penitent. "I know I give you a hard time. But I want you to know I think you're an excellent doctor."

She offered a weak smile and began to rise from her chair. I held my hand up to stop her. "Sunflower, can you do something for me?"

"Sure, I guess."

"Tell me about you."

She caught the tenderness in my voice and slowly collapsed back into her chair.

"What do you mean?"

"How did you . . . become you?"

To my delight, an elfish smile inched across her face. Her words were bemused, reflective.

"I've always been pretty independent. I got it from my dad, I guess. By Watervalley standards, we were outsiders. Dad bought the farm and moved here in 1940. He came from Wisconsin. His people were Norwegian. In those days, Watervalley was slow to warm up to newcomers. He had friends, but I guess most people thought he was peculiar. He had a thick accent and he farmed differently. He grew different crops than the locals and had different kinds of milk cows, Brown Swiss rather than Holsteins. He was skeptical about how things were done around here and it only got worse after his best friend was killed."

I stopped her. "Hold it. Who are you talking about?"

"A man named Oscar Fox. He moved to Watervalley shortly after my dad did and opened a bakery. It's an old story and you've probably never heard about it. But back in the forties Oscar and some stranger killed each other out at the bandstand late one night. They actually found his body on the edge of our property near the lake. My dad took it hard. They had struck up a pretty strong friendship."

A name from the case file popped in my head. "Your dad, was his name Otto?"

"Yes, it was. How did you know that?"

"Actually, I know quite a bit about the Oscar Fox murder. It's been something of a curiosity to me. I read your dad's name in a copy of the police report."

Sunflower's face tightened and a trace of defensiveness entered her voice. "What did it say?"

"Nothing about your dad, as I recall. Only that he had been interviewed."

"Oh, they interviewed him all right."

"I don't understand."

"All of this happened before I was born and my dad never talked much about it. But a year or so before he died, he told me that the day after the murder the sheriff—I think Lewis was his name—came by and asked him to come down to his office to answer some questions. Daddy went, but when he got there, he was locked in a room and interrogated for several hours."

"About what?"

"About his friendship with Oscar, about what really happened that night. Oh, and get this, he kept asking Daddy about diamonds."

I was on the edge of my chair. "Diamonds?"

"Yeah. Of course Daddy had no idea what the sheriff was talking about. Anyway, after it was over, the sheriff apologized and said it was all a big misunderstanding. But he also told Daddy not to talk about what happened, because it was an ongoing investigation. I think it really shook my dad up."

"Sunflower, have you ever told anyone all this?"

"Not really. It was so long ago. By the time he told me, everyone involved was dead."

"What do you mean by everyone?"

"As Daddy was leaving the sheriff's office that night, he said there were only two other cars parked there. He never saw anyone, but he figured out who they belonged to. It was a local banker, Raymond Simmons, and the clinic doctor during that time, a guy named Hinson, I think. Daddy thought they were all in on something. Anyway, after that, Daddy never trusted the police, or banks, or doctors. I guess all that rubbed off on me."

I was speechless, fascinated by what Sunflower had told me. It was further confirmation of Frank Sanderson's conspiracy theory. As well, it was the first time diamonds had been mentioned in any context other than rumor.

In time, Sunflower looked at her watch.

"Thanks, Luke. I need to go deal with some chickens."

"Might be a good idea to call Dr. Ingram and get him involved."

Sunflower exhaled an exasperated sigh. "Yeah. I'm sure you're right. Thanks again."

I walked her to the door. Closing it, I stood and gazed around my office, still slightly stunned and wondering. Maybe, just maybe, diamonds were the key to the Oscar Fox story. A half dozen theories raced though my head. But that's where they would remain. For now, too many pieces of the puzzle were buried.

CHAPTER 35
Connie Knew

April arrived and with it came Easter Sunday along with all the glory and pageantry of the morning service and the excitement and squealing delight of the Easter egg hunt that afternoon on the church lawn.

There was an awakening to the farm life of Watervalley. By six o'clock in the morning the Farmers' Co-op was a cacophonous buzz of trucks and tow motors moving tons of seed and fertilizer. Trees were beginning to bloom into rich canopies of green and the yards of Fleming Street teemed with the fragrance of lilacs, clover, and warm grass. The farm fields were drying out and the rich black soil seemed to be waiting for the imminent planting. Spring was attaining its full glory and the days were ripe with promise and expectancy.

But not on all fronts.

The Fox home had received no offers. Its state of disrepair, and high price, necessitated by the bloated mortgage, had made for an unattractive combination. Louise refused to take any additional funds from my secret partnership, leaving foreclosure and auction her only options. Bankruptcy and a difficult future were pretty much guaranteed for her and Will. For me, the situation was a nagging frustration.

I began to take Rhett with me on my morning runs. Over the winter he'd added several pounds, and along with modifying his diet, I was determined to return him to a trimmer shape. He was not as enthusiastic. He would trot along for the first half mile or so, but eventually his heavy coat and heavier panting took their toll. He was content to plop down on someone's lawn and casually observe the world around him. Left to his own, he would be happy to stay there for hours. Eventually, I was able to cajole him on and we would walk the rest of my route.

Usually we went out to the bandstand to check the progress of the renovation, which was being accomplished at lightning speed. At just over a mile, the run from Fleming Street to the lake seemed like a perfect workout to get Rhett in shape. On Thursday of the second week of April, we started out early and reached the bandstand in record time. Our return was slower, Rhett having overextended himself and unilaterally deciding that several breaks were needed. Connie was waiting for us as we entered the front door. Rhett's energy level took a notable uptick as he dashed to find her in the kitchen.

"Hello, Mr. Rhett. My, you are looking in fine form." She rubbed both of his ears as she spoke to him. Her regard toward me was not quite so endearing.

"Good morning, Captain Stinky."

"I love you too, Connie." I walked to the counter to pour myself some coffee as she returned to the stove, wearing an amused grin.

"I've been asked to get you to do something."

I took a seat at the kitchen table. "And what would that be?"

"Carl Suggs, the principal over at the high school, wants to know if you will deliver the speech at this year's graduation."

"Gee, I don't know. Maybe. Why doesn't he ask me himself?"

"He figured you'd have a harder time saying no to me."

"Well, that's kind of sneaky. Smart, but sneaky."

"Oh, I think you could do a fine job if you put a little thought into it. Graduation is still a month away. They're just a bunch of teenagers. I'm sure you could dispense enough charm and wit to hold their attention for a few minutes."

"Why don't you do it? You were valedictorian of your class."

"And you were valedictorian of your med school class. I'd say that trumps my standing on the academic totem pole. Besides, public speaking is not my thing. I'd rather take a beating. Carl also invited you to come to the prom dance to celebrate with all the juniors and seniors. He said you could bring a date."

"That's a deal maker, there. This could be fun."

"How's that?"

"Well, dancing queen. You could be my date and show off some of those great moves John was talking about."

"Humph. Thanks for your kind offer, but I serve on the refreshments committee and won't have time to be giving any dance lessons. I think you better stick with Miss Christine for your boogie partner."

"Ahhh. Sounds like somebody's lost her groove and doesn't think she can get it back."

Connie was about to set a plate of eggs and bacon on the table but stopped and glared at me. "Just know this, Doctor. You've never seen me ride a bicycle either, but you can bet I still know how." With that, she set the plate down before me and sauntered back to the stove, certain she had made her point.

I smiled and dove in. "In any case, tell Carl that I'm fine with giving the graduation speech."

Connie brought her breakfast to the table and joined me.

"Hey," I said, "I was wondering. Did Estelle ever come up with a name for the bakery?" I knew this had been an ongoing point of contention between them, and couldn't resist pouring oil on the fire.

Connie stared at me flatly. "My, my, my. You're trying awful hard to pick a fight this morning, aren't you?"

I feigned innocence. "Just trying to make conversation, Mrs. Thompson."

"Sure you are. All that's missing from that act you're putting on is a seltzer bottle and big floppy shoes." She took a bite and studied me warily. "Anyway, it's been a struggle. She got on a literary kick for a while."

"Meaning?"

"Let's see, Grain Expectations, Pie and Prejudice, and the Bun Also Rises were the finalists in that category."

I laughed out loud. "Interesting."

"Umm-hmmm. My thoughts exactly. Then she got an epiphany that it should have a religious theme. These included Holy Cannoli, Amazin' Glazin', and the Sweet Pie and Bye."

"So what are your choices?"

"If it were up to me, I'd call it either the Flaky Baker, the Mix-up, or Retarted, if you get my drift. Anyway, the name is still a work in progress."

"I'm sure Estelle will come up with a name you can both agree on."

"She better do it soon because we've got to change the name in the tile work on the pavement outside the front door."

"So, how's the remodeling coming?"

"The work goes fine so long as I keep Estelle from having these flights of fancy."

"How so?"

"Lately she's gotten the bright idea to make sandwiches for lunch. But that requires putting things together in real time. Making cakes and pastries ahead, that she can do. Putting sandwiches together on the spot, not gonna happen. Besides, every inch of the kitchen is already dedicated. There's no more room."

I nodded thoughtfully. What Connie had said was giving me an idea, one that I would tuck away for later. I had another matter to discuss with her.

"Hey, not to change the subject, but if memory serves, you have a birthday coming up in a few weeks. A big birthday."

"Mmm-hmm. Thanks for dropping that little truth bomb. What about it?"

"We need to do a birthday celebration, of course. Speaking of which, what would you like for a birthday gift?"

"How about a particle accelerator?"

"Sure. You want that in pink?"

"No, pink's not really in my palette. Maybe we should think about something different, like forgetting all about this foolishness."

"Not gonna happen, Connie T. You don't turn sixty every day. How about a telescope? You could use it to spy on your neighbors, look at the stars, even search the heavens for intelligent life."

"Right now I'm not finding any intelligent life in this kitchen."

"Yeah, yeah. Say all you want. It's going to happen. Come on, admit it. You like the idea of a birthday party."

Connie took a sip of her coffee and spoke dispassionately. "Sure, I'm ecstatic. Pardon me while I go do a few cartwheels on the front lawn."

"Well, don't worry. I have a plan."

"Why do those words always scare me?"

She rose to take her dishes back to the sink but paused momentarily, gazing out the large rear windows at the sunlit backyard. "Going to be time to plant a garden soon."

"I'm assuming that's a rhetorical statement and not directed toward me."

Connie turned and regarded me stiffly. "Nothing wrong with getting your hands in the dirt, even for a doctor."

I was unmoved. "Nothing wrong with letting the grass grow either."

Connie shook her head. "To plant a garden is to believe in tomorrow."

"There's a nice tidbit of wisdom. Who said that, Mother Teresa?"

"No. Actually I think it was Audrey Hepburn."

"Oh, well, she was my next guess. Anyway, I don't get the whole fascination with growing a garden. John Harris has been chiding me about it too."

"At any rate, you need to be calling the Blind Boys about mowing the grass."

"The blind boys? There are blind guys who mow lawns?"

Connie regarded me with tired disdain. "No, Doctor. I'm talking about Kenny and Kevin Blind. They're brothers. By now they're probably in their early forties, but they've had a mowing service forever."

"So you're telling me there's a business called the Blind Boys Mowing Service?"

"You catch on so quickly."

I muttered under my breath, "Wow. Only in Watervalley."

"How are you and the pretty schoolteacher getting along these days?"

"We're just grand. It's spring break and she's been out of town all week visiting her grandmother in Florida. She's driving back in today."

Connie spoke to the general air. "'In the spring a young man's fancy lightly turns to thoughts of love.'" She finished with a low, wheezy chuckle.

"Nice. Tennyson, huh? Seems like he's the same guy who wrote, 'Tears, idle tears, I know not what they mean.'"

Connie exhaled a low hum. "Mmm-mmm, Luke Bradford. What is wrong with you, boy? There's not a finer, more beautiful young woman to be found than Christine Chambers. To be so smart, you sure are a slow learner."

Despite this open challenge, I defaulted to my normal evasive tactics when my feelings were the topic of conversation. I responded with a dramatic flourish. "'Fools rush in where angels fear to tread.'"

Connie glared at me above her glasses. "You can quote Alexander Pope all you want to. But remind yourself of this: all you're doing is taking advice from another man."

Retort seemed pointless. I rose and cleared my dishes from the table. "Connie, I would love to stay and explore the deeper aspects of this incredible circular logic of yours, but I must go cure the sick, heal the maimed, and care for the otherwise infirm."

I headed up the kitchen stairs that led to the second floor. By about the third step Connie's clear, imploring voice stopped me.

"Luke."

She was staring at me with a changed, contemplative face. I knew that look. She had something important to say. But instead, she pursed her lips and shook her head lightly, signaling that she had thought better of it. Her eyes softened and she spoke with simple resolve.

"You've got a good, caring heart, Luke Bradford; a kind, loving heart. Don't be afraid to let it see the light of day. You're a lot stronger than you think."

As I climbed the steps, I was again reminded that Connie Thompson was the smartest person I had ever known.

CHAPTER 36
An Old Secret

"Why don't we go on a picnic? I'll fry up some chicken. I still owe you a meal from the basketball game in the barn, you know." Christine's voice poured buoyantly through the phone.

It was Friday morning and I was taking the day off, since it was Christine's last day of spring break. Mid-April had been cosmically beautiful in Watervalley, a perfect blend of warm sun, exploding color, and rich, earthy fragrances. Around nine o'clock I had called Christine to make plans for the day.

"Seems like I remember that bet came with a condition about wearing a saucy French chambermaid outfit."

"Are you familiar with the phrase 'when pigs fly'?"

"I'm going to take that as a no."

"Just listen to you, handsome *and* smart. How did I get so lucky?"

"Brown eyes, I haven't seen you in a week. You could wear a Hefty bag, and make me happy."

"So, absence *does* make the heart grow fonder?"

"By the way, did I get that right? Your eyes are brown, aren't they?"

"Stop while you're ahead, Bradford."

"Anyway, a picnic sounds wonderful. Where do you want to go?"

"How about out beside the lake?"

"I guess we could, but something about the sound of power saws and nail guns sort of takes the enchantment right out of the moment."

"No, silly. I meant Moon Lake. You still have a key, don't you?"

"That I do. Good idea. How does one o'clock sound?"

"See you then."

As I hung up the phone, I became deeply aware of how much I had missed her—the light of her smile, the sound of her voice, and simply having someone to talk with about the events of the day. One o'clock couldn't arrive soon enough.

It was unseasonably warm, reaching into the low eighties by midday. Christine met me at her door with a lingering, delightful kiss. Her time in Florida had given her a deep, rich tan. With her olive complexion and dark hair, her beauty now bordered on the exotic. She was breathtaking.

The drive out to Moon Lake was a celebration of laughter and excitement. It was a charmed day and the countryside was filled with the sensuous smells of spring, made all the more radiant by the freshly scrubbed air and the brilliant sun.

We spread a large blanket near the water's edge and lazily ate and talked, lulled by the fragrant smell of the untamed grass and the delicate, shimmering light on the water. In time we finished, stopping before we completely stuffed ourselves. I was sitting with my arms draped around my knees, facing down the length of the lake. Christine shifted to sit behind me, pressing her back to mine, looking in the opposite direction. We sat in silence, letting the warm, sleepy afternoon breeze float idly by.

Finally, I said, "By the way, I have been asked to give the commencement speech at the high school graduation."

"Really? And what choice bits of worldly wisdom are you planning on sharing?"

"Oh, the usual platitudes . . . don't poke the bear, it's a small world after all, smoke 'em if you got 'em."

"That should inspire them."

"Yeah, I'm a little nervous about it actually. Truth is, I haven't quite figured out exactly what to say."

"There's plenty of time. You'll come up with something."

"Hey, there's an added bonus."

"What's that?"

"We've been asked to attend the prom dance. Or at least, I was asked and was told I can bring a date. You're pretty close to the top of the list."

"Sounds okay. But I'm going to wait and see who else offers before I give you a definite answer."

"I expected no less."

Christine rolled her head back, resting it on my shoulder. I spoke again. "So, tell me about your senior prom. I bet you were prom queen, weren't you?"

"Not even close."

"Really?"

"No, and that was fine by me."

"So, who did you go with?"

"Went without a date."

"Okay, were you a leper for several years and forgot to tell me about it?"

"Noooo. Several fellows asked, but I turned them down. They

were all sweet guys, but they were just friends, not anyone special. I thought it would be more fun to dance with all of them."

"And how did that work out?"

"It was fun. Kind of strange driving home alone when it was over, though."

I closed my eyes, drinking deeply of the drowsy feel of the day. After a while, Christine spoke again. "Luke?"

"Hmmm."

"Will you take me to the prom?" The question floated in the air, full of tenderness and yearning.

"Sure. How do I know you won't stand me up, though?"

Her voice was delicate, almost fragile, and I could sense the affection in her words. "Because *you are* special."

As she spoke, I could feel her back melt against mine, subtly pushing against me to somehow draw in closer. The breeze stilled and a lingering hush fell over the open fields. It seemed a perfect moment to sit and delight in the quiet world around us. But I would soon realize that I was mistaken. When Christine spoke again, her teasing voice had a faintly wounded quality.

"Okay, Bradford. You could at least try to do half of the work of this conversation."

"Oh, sorry. I didn't realize I was spoiling the magic."

Foolishly, I let a tinge of sarcasm creep into my tone. Christine took it the wrong way and a veil came between us, ending the conversation. I felt her back stiffen and a knotty silence ensued. I needed to respond, to say something to reassure her, to convince her, to fill in the void. But the moment seemed already lost, the damage done.

I stood, reached down, and pulled her up, all the while looking deep into her sensitive face. What had she wanted? What should I have said? It seemed insane. We knew each other so well, yet here we stood in this clumsy, awkward moment. Not knowing what else to do, I blurted out a question.

"Want to take a walk around the lake?"

Christine's tone was resigned, her eyes patient and understanding. "Sure."

We circled the lake and talked for the next hour. But the air between us seemed thick with the clutter and confusion of uncertainty and bruised emotions. To make matters worse, dark clouds had built up in the west and we were caught on the far side of the lake in a nearly instantaneous downpour. The large drops pelted us, and by the time we gathered our things and reached the car, we were soaked.

The drive back to Christine's passed largely in silence. Once there, we dashed toward the front door under an absolute waterfall. Thankfully, the onslaught took some of the edge off the tension between us and we stood in her entrance hall flipping water from our hands and gasping for air. Drenched and pathetic, we exploded in spontaneous laughter. It seemed we both were hungry for an excuse to put the unspoken awkwardness of the past hour behind us.

"Let me go upstairs and change. I'll try to find something dry for you to put on," she said.

"Sure, I'll probably be fine, though."

Christine ascended the steps and I was left holding the dripping picnic basket. I kicked off my shoes and headed toward the kitchen to put it away. But as I entered, I came upon her grandmother sitting at the kitchen table drinking a glass of tea and reading a magazine. Instantly, I had a sick feeling in my stomach. She stared at me with strained curiosity. "It's Luke, isn't it? Your name, that is."

"Yes, Mrs. Chambers, Luke Bradford."

She continued to focus on me, her mind distant, searching. "You're soaked."

"We were having a picnic. The rain caught us."

I walked across the room and set the basket on the counter. She took a sip of tea, her eyes still on me. The silence was uncomfortable, but infinitely better than her threatening disdain of our previous encounters. She seemed harmless, approachable. I grabbed a glass from the cabinet, filled it with water from the fridge dispenser, and came and sat across from her. Admittedly, I was curious, wondering if this was actually a moment of lucidity. I couldn't be sure.

"You were the one talking about Oscar Fox a couple of months ago, weren't you?"

At first, the question threw me. "Yes, we were talking about him at Sunday lunch a little while back."

"Mmm. I remember now. I'm glad I saw you. There's something I've been wanting to tell you."

My answer was hesitant. "Sure."

"I want to tell you a secret. Oscar Fox was a good friend to my dad and my dad's brother, Mutt. Mutt died in a car wreck in 1945, or maybe '46." She paused for a moment, her mind on a short detour.

"Anyway, Mutt was a real handyman and did a lot of the trim and finish work at the bakery. He was the one who did the tile work in front of the entrance door."

I wasn't sure where this was going. "Looks like he did excellent work. It's still there today."

"When I was a little girl, Mutt told me something, but he said I had to promise never to tell anyone. I forgot about it for years, but I remembered again after you mentioned Oscar Fox."

I listened closely, caught up in this surreal conversation.

"Mutt said that when he was pouring the concrete before laying the tile, Oscar came to him with a metal box and told him he wanted it buried there. Oscar said it was a kind of time capsule, something for good luck. He made Mutt promise not to tell anybody. But I was Mutt's favorite, so he told me. Maybe I shouldn't be telling you. But it was a long time ago. Doesn't seem to matter anymore."

A thousand thoughts poured through my head, a thousand possibilities of what the box might contain. I thanked Mrs. Chambers and excused myself. Christine was coming down the stairs as I was passing through the entrance hall. She read the excitement on my face.

"Your grandmother and I just had the most, well, unusual conversation. She told me something incredible."

"Really? What on earth did she say?"

I briefly related the exchange, then told Christine I needed to go but that I would call her later. She nodded sweetly.

By nine the next morning Connie, Estelle, and I were at the old bakery with the contractor. He had scheduled some men to work that morning and was glad to jackhammer out the tile work and concrete ahead of schedule. We stood by anxiously as the work began.

The tile came up easily enough, but the concrete was less forgiving. Soon, however, small cracks began to appear. These gave way to bigger chunks that were methodically removed. They revealed nothing. But it was a large area. The hammering continued.

Finally, about two feet out from the door, a large chunk broke off and the corner of a heavy metal box was exposed. We all strained to get a view of it, barely able to contain our excitement. It took several more minutes to break away the surrounding concrete, but finally, with the help of a pickax, the large box was pried from the ground. It was approximately fifteen inches square and about four inches deep. I took it inside and set it on a cleared table.

"Estelle, technically, this belongs to you," I said.

"Oh, heavens no, sugar. This is your thing. You have at it."

I carefully flipped back the two metal hasps and lifted the lid.

CHAPTER 37
Time Capsule

The first document we found was a birth certificate written in German. It should have been no surprise to me that Connie could read that language well enough to interpret.

"The name on this is Oscar Wilhelm Fuchs, born in Wiesbaden, Germany, on November 17, 1913." She grinned. "Well, isn't that clever. *Fuchs* is German for 'fox.' Looks like Oscar Americanized his name."

"So he really was German?" I exclaimed.

"Apparently so."

"But how could he speak English so well that no one picked up on an accent?"

"Maybe the rest of this will tell us."

We dug further.

I found an old black-and-white picture of Oscar standing with a woman in front of a bakery. All the signs were in German and an inscription was penciled on the back.

Connie interpreted. "My mother's shop, Wiesbaden, 1923."

"This picture was taken when Oscar was nine," I added. "His

mother must have owned a bakeshop and that's where Oscar learned the business."

"Listen to this," said Connie. She had been reading a letter to Oscar from his father dated March 12, 1924. The envelope had a Wiesbaden address but had been sent from New York. "My German is a little sketchy, but it appears that Oscar's parents had gotten divorced and his father had moved to America. The letter discusses arrangements for Oscar to come visit him in New York."

We had spread the documents across the table and I was next drawn to one written in English. "And look here. This is a diploma from Dartmouth College, dated 1935. Oscar graduated with a degree in finance."

Connie and Estelle found other documents and mementos from Oscar's youth, including a receipt for a transatlantic passage on the liner *Berengaria*, report cards from his years in *Mittelschule*, and ticket stubs from New York Yankees baseball games. From what we gathered, it appeared that Oscar went to middle and secondary school in Germany but spent his summers in New York with his father. Ultimately, he attended college in America; among other things, we found pictures of him on the Dartmouth track team and programs to plays with him listed in the cast.

I stared at Connie and Estelle in amazement. "You know what this is telling us? Growing up, Oscar Fox led a dual life. That's how he learned to speak English so fluently. He wanted to fit in. Looks like at Dartmouth he had a heavy interest in drama. And why wouldn't he? He'd probably been acting all his life."

The business papers we found told of Oscar's career. He had worked for the Lamerslint-Jorg Diamond Company out of Frankfurt, Germany. He was their North American sales rep with company offices based out of New York. Oscar was a German citizen, working in America on a visa. Some of the final documents we found told the most interesting part of his story.

"My, my, my," exclaimed Estelle as she was reading through a typed list of names. "Looks like Oscar did some time at Montreat."

"What's Montreat?" I inquired.

"The Presbyterian Assembly Grounds. You know, in North Carolina."

"I don't think I understand."

"Well, when I was at Vanderbilt, a girlfriend of mine taught in the history department. She was the cutest thing and always wore the most wonderful shoes."

Connie abruptly interrupted. "Montreat, sweetie, Montreat. Focus now."

"Anyway, she loved to talk about twentieth-century American history. When the U.S. entered the war in 1941, German businessmen and diplomats were rounded up and interned for deportation. Many of them were held at the Montreat assembly grounds. This document is a housing assignment. It looks like Oscar was sent there and later, somehow, escaped."

The three of us stood quietly, trying to fit together the pieces. Connie broke the silence. "If he spoke English without an accent, I guess it would be pretty easy for him to pose as an everyday person."

"Looks like that's what he did when he came here," I said.

We all nodded in agreement and spent the next half hour poring over the other documents, including a few letters, some odd photos, and a family Bible.

All the while, I was thinking about Oscar and the incredible journey his life had taken. He had arrived here on the train in flight from being incarcerated and almost deported. I imagined that Oscar probably never intended to live permanently in Watervalley. But somewhere along the way he fell in love with Elise Chastain and decided to stay and build a new life. It was easy to surmise that Oscar must have had some money with him, whether in cash or in diamonds, as had been so widely rumored. I remembered Frank Sanderson's notes stating that Oscar made frequent trips to Nashville. Perhaps he had a safety-deposit box there where he kept his secret finances. It was impossible to know. That much of his story was buried in the dust and forgotten memories of decades past.

"My, my, my," exclaimed Connie. "All these years and this has been right under our feet."

I told them about what I had read in Frank Sanderson's report, about the missing autopsy report on Oscar Fox and my conjecture that he had actually been the one to act in self-defense.

Connie placed her hand on the stack of documents. "Estelle, honey. I know we own this place, but these documents belong to Louise Fox."

"Sweetie, I couldn't agree more," Estelle replied. "But don't you think the sheriff is going to want to see them?"

"I doubt it," I injected.

Connie looked puzzled. "Really? Why not?"

"He's probably curious like all of us. But I'm pretty sure he'll say it's not a police matter. We talked about it after the briefcase was found at the bandstand. The statute of limitations has run out on the case. He'd probably say this is no different than if we came across Oscar's high school annual. It's interesting to know the truth about Oscar's past, but it really doesn't change anything."

They both nodded their understanding. Then Connie added,

"The local newspaper is going to want to know about all this, Luke. I'm not sure Oscar being a German is going to help his reputation."

"You may be right. But I agree with you two. This box and its contents belong to Louise Fox. What she tells the newspaper is her business."

We talked for several more minutes and decided that I would take the box with me to give to Louise. I would discuss everything with her and let her decide whom else to tell. Even as we all departed, we stared at each other wide-eyed. It had been an unbelievable discovery.

As I drove home, I called Christine to tell her everything. She too was fascinated. I apologized for our disrupted time together the previous afternoon. She dismissed it as unimportant, but something in her voice told me otherwise. We made plans for the evening, but before she hung up, she had a question for me.

"Have you talked to my uncle recently?"

"Come to think of it, no. Is something wrong?"

"Momma has been trying to call him for the last several days, but he doesn't answer his cell phone or his answering machine. Uncle John can be kind of a loner, but this is odd."

"I'll take a drive up later this afternoon and check on him. He'd probably like to hear about this Oscar Fox story anyway."

There could be any number of reasons why no one had heard from John. Still, his lack of response was unsettling.

I spent the next hour with Louise and Will, telling them the whole story. They were captivated, especially Will, and they looked through the documents with great absorption. The discoveries seemed to lighten their spirits, but I knew in reality it was a distraction. It did little to alleviate their desperate financial situation.

To my surprise, Louise politely asked me to keep everything at my house for now, not wanting the attention she thought it would bring. I agreed and carried it back with me.

I called Sheriff Thurman on his cell phone to tell him of the box. His response confirmed my earlier suspicions.

"Doc, as interesting as all this is, it's really not a police matter."

"What about the newspaper? Should Louise contact Luther Whitmore?"

"Louise can tell him as much or as little as she wants. It's her business. But realize this, Doc. This is Saturday, and the next edition of the paper comes out Tuesday. Everybody in town will know about it long before that. The main thing the paper does is separate the fact from the rumors. Luther is an ornery jackass, but he does have a penchant for printing the truth. That may have some benefit."

I thanked him and hung up, unsure of what to advise Louise. I decided to stew on it. Moments later, I headed up to the hills.

CHAPTER 38
Every Branch That Bears Fruit

I arrived at John's house shortly before four o'clock and there was no answer to my repeated knocks on the door. A peek in the garage window revealed that all of his vehicles were there. This didn't bode well and a small voice of concern began to nag at me, suggesting various explanations, none of them good. I walked around back and shouted his name but got no response. I could think of only one other possibility.

I found John in the apple orchard that spread across the sloping hillside down from the high landing of the house and yard. He was sitting on the ground next to his ladder, staring absently into the distance. His demeanor and posture were the definition of total exhaustion, a consuming surrender of mind, body, and spirit.

I called out to him as I approached. He heard my voice, but only glanced sideways at me—no more than if I were a passing bird whose motion happened to catch his eye. I walked up and sat down next to him. I was well accustomed to John's reflective and brooding nature. But that was normally precipitated by long dives into a Scotch bottle. Different forces were at work here. A long silence ensued. In time, he spoke without ever changing his focused gaze into the far distance.

"I've been pruning trees nonstop for days. Pruning and pruning and pruning. Now I don't think I can remember my life before pruning. I pruned for so long that I began talking to myself. Eventually, I got tired of listening. So I started to talk to God about pruning, thinking he wouldn't get tired of hearing about it. But I was wrong. After a while he said he had a meeting and would get back with me. A few hours ago, I found myself randomly clipping branches. I came out of a trance and realized I was pruning the oak tree in the corner of the grove."

This was something of a surreal moment for me, producing both amusement and concern. For some reason, John had driven himself to the edge of his endurance. What I was seeing was the last sparks of his clever wit, struggling to find mastery over his defeated state.

In time he looked over at me and extended his hand. "Help me up, sawbones."

I pulled him to his feet, but he stood awkwardly, hunched over from the stiffness in his back.

"Come on, Johnny Appleseed," I said. "Let's get you back to the house."

He exhaled with a low resolve. "Lead the way."

We walked back up the steep rise with John making occasional comments about the orchard and the casualties of the previous winter. In the kitchen he retrieved a couple of waters and we retreated back outside to the Adirondack chairs. Once seated, John seemed to regain some of his vigor. I told him about the morning's discoveries. He listened patiently, and when I finished, he turned and looked at me for a studied moment.

"Sawbones, that is a hell of a story."

I went on to tell him about the old case file and my belief that Oscar Fox was acting in self-defense. I outlined my conspiracy theory.

When I finished, John said, "I doubt you'll ever be able to prove anything about the conspiracy trio and any diamonds. Does make you wonder, though. If Oscar Fox—or Fuchs, as it were—had a stash of diamonds, seems like they would have been discovered by now."

I nodded in agreement. There seemed to be little more to understand about the matter.

"By the way, your relatives have been trying to get in touch with you for a few days," I said.

"Yeah, I know. I saw the calls."

"What gives, Professor? That's a little unsociable, don't you think?"

"Ah, I've just had a lot on my mind lately, wanted time to think. Tell them I'm fine."

"By all means, allow me to rudely pry into your personal life. What's eating you?"

John grinned. "You want a beer?"

"No, I'm good."

"Be right back." He ambled up to the house, but when he returned, it was with a Scotch bottle and a glass. He was notably silent. For much of our friendship, John had been remote and complicated, resolute in his opinions. But this was different. He was struggling, baffled and uncertain.

"Well, John, looks like you and hooch are still on good terms."

"Sawbones, I like you. I really do. But if all you're going to do is give me a lecture about drinking, then you might want to do the hokey pokey and turn your ass around."

I laughed. "Oh, well, don't mind me, John. No need to

approach your problems with maturity when alcohol is so readily available." He grunted an amused laugh. I spoke again. "The 'what's eating you' question still stands."

Slowly, a derisive smile inched across John's face. "How do you do it, sawbones?"

"Do . . . what?"

"Get along with everybody so well."

"I generally tend to like people, that's all. Why do you ask?"

John exhaled a deep sigh. "In case you haven't noticed, I don't have the all-embracing affection for my fellow humans that you seem to come by so naturally. My talents are much better suited for pissing people off."

"Anyone in particular?"

"Yeah, a certain nurse."

"Oh." John and Ann had been seeing each other regularly, but I knew few details beyond that. "Any problem in particular?"

"Yeah, she thinks I drink too much. Who knew?"

John was poking fun at himself. Even still, his frustration was real. "So, I take it you like her. Otherwise, this wouldn't be a problem."

John rubbed his chin and smiled. "I do like her. And I didn't think I would like anybody after Molly. Ann's cute, smart, has a lot of spunk. She's not the problem."

"Then what is the problem?"

John's words came slowly. "I'm the problem. For the past couple of years I've been trying to box with God. But I finally figured out my arms aren't long enough. Even though I've always harbored a certain resentment toward the Church, I guess the old instructions from pew and altar are still with me. I think I'm just tired of trying to make all the rules. Now I just want to live by them, be at peace."

He took a sip of his drink. "On the surface, it would seem that all things are coming together. The bandstand's being renovated, fulfilling Molly's last dream. The in-laws and I are back on good terms. Now Ann comes along. I don't know her extremely well, but what I do know I like."

I spoke cautiously. "So, what's below the surface?"

"I've lived for the longest time with my anger and grief. I've gotten comfortable with them, understood them. But now I realize that that part of me needs pruning. I never expected that somehow everything would eventually be redeemed and made whole again. I guess I've just needed a few days to come to terms with that, to figure out how to change."

"Change how?"

"How? Stop drinking, that's how. At least, the hard stuff anyway."

I scrutinized John's glass and bottle, a gesture that did not go unnoticed.

"It's not what you think."

"How so?"

"It's tea. Laugh all you want, I like it better if I keep it in a Scotch bottle. Here, smell it."

I laughed and refused. "Well, isn't that just a cute little parlor trick?"

John's mood lightened. "Yeah, isn't it, though? I still miss the Scotch a little, but I try to focus on the upsides."

"Which are?"

"For starters, being more of a teetotaler ought to be good for some kind of heavenly upgrade. Besides, with all this good behavior, I might just get lucky."

"Okay. One I doubt; the other I don't want to know about."

John laughed, proud of his ability to cajole me.

After a long silence I turned to him. "John, you need to know something. You're a good man and a good friend. You've had your share of pain, and pain takes time to process. But what you're doing with the bandstand, what you did for Connie at the bank, and all those years of service to the town, those are some pretty selfless things. And I suspect that's only a fraction of what you're capable of. So, Scotch or no Scotch, you're still my friend and someone I greatly admire. But if you are coming to terms with your drinking, I can only say I'm happy for you."

John glanced sideways toward me and rubbed his chin. His voice was contemplative. "Yeah, well, thanks, sawbones." His gaze tightened. "As far as the bank situation goes, there's only one remaining item on the checklist."

"Meaning?"

"Simmons. He's going to be fired and I'd say by now he knows it."

"Have you told Connie?"

"Yes. But I'm taking the lead on it. Exacting a little justice in that situation has been long overdue."

I nodded. "Well, so be it."

I rose from my chair. "Okay, fellow. Time to go. I have promises to keep. I'll report to your adoring fans that you are alive and well."

John walked with me back to my car. "Thanks for coming up, Luke. Pretty fascinating stuff about the big Oscar Fox discovery."

"Yeah, it's quite a story. I met with Louise and Will this afternoon and told them all about it. I think it was a nice diversion for them. Louise asked me to hold on to the box for now. They're getting the house ready for auction. It's a pretty grim situation."

John nodded thoughtfully, adding nothing further on the topic. Then he said, "You know, I almost mentioned this before, but years ago, my dad told me that Oscar Fox would occasionally mail packages overseas to Switzerland. He remembered because he always had to figure out postage and it was difficult during the war to know if parcels would get through. People mailed things to the front all the time, but he always thought it was odd to mail packages to Switzerland."

I nodded, finding this curious but not sure if it meant anything. The next day, I would have my answer.

CHAPTER 39

A Good Man's Story

I attended church the next morning, sitting in the back as had become my norm. After the service, several people approached me to inquire discreetly about "a box that had been discovered down at the old bakery." I suspected they already knew the details but wanted to hear them from me. Word had traveled fast. I politely avoided comment and beat a hasty retreat to my car.

After arriving home, I changed clothes and made a sandwich for lunch and then took Rhett out to the backyard for a long-over-due session of retrieving the tennis ball. There seemed to be no end to his excitement as I continually heaved the ball to the far corners of the yard from where he would dutifully bring it back. It was a drowsy, splendid spring afternoon. As I mindlessly threw the ball, along with a little accumulated slobber, I began rolling over and over in my mind what I would say for the commencement speech.

I wanted to talk about the larger world, about the possibilities, the opportunities, the challenges, that lay beyond these familiar hills. Watervalley had its charms and its strengths, and while I was generally comfortable with the reality that my life was here for a season, I began to be keenly reminded that I saw my future unfolding elsewhere. I had grown content with the path in front of me, but the mental exercise of preparing the graduation speech confirmed my conviction that I still had larger plans and bigger goals. I was struggling with how to translate my own grand vision, my own knowledge of a broader life, to these students without making Watervalley seem small and unimportant. I had reached an impasse. It seemed that secretly my hunger for journeys still haunted me.

In time Rhett began to plop down in the cool grass sooner and sooner after retrieving the ball, and farther and farther away from me. He would lie there and chew on the ball, panting with a rhythmic motion that involved his entire body. Ultimately, I had to yield and walk over to him. Playtime was over.

Still, it amazed me how he alertly followed me all the way up the back steps and through the back door, never losing hope that I'd have a change of heart and heave the ball skyward one last time. Once inside he immediately went to his water bowl and dropped to his belly, cradling the bowl between his two front paws and immersing his big sloppy face into it. After what seemed like minutes of unashamed slurping, he again stared at me in quiet anticipation, with tongue dangling and body rocking in sync with his hyperactive breathing.

A moment later, there was a rap on the front door. Rhett's head lifted in focused curiosity and from his actions I could tell that the visitor was not someone he knew. He followed me to the door, vigilant in determining my reaction to the caller. I opened the door to a well-known face. It was Ann Patterson.

"Hey, did I catch you at a bad time?" she asked.

"No, not at all. Come in."

As I showed her to the living room I couldn't help but notice that she seemed apprehensive and unsure of herself. As well, despite her generally cheerful nature, her face had settled into a look of anxious unease.

I did my best to offer her an accommodating smile. "Ann, what's up? What can I do for you?"

"I need to ask you about something."

"Sure."

"I talked with John last night and he told me about the big discovery yesterday."

It took me a moment to process her words. Given the unexpectedness of this visit, my mind had been racing across the possible reasons for her presence. Oscar Fox hadn't figured in the mix.

"Um, yes, yes. It was an incredible find, actually."

"John said you mentioned that there was a family Bible among the papers. Is that true?"

"Yes."

She nodded. "Could I possibly look at it?"

Surprised, I didn't answer immediately. My hesitation distressed her.

"Please."

"Oh, sure, sure."

She followed me into the kitchen, where I had left the box on the table. I carefully opened it and retrieved the modest-sized Bible and handed it to her. She laid it on the table and turned to the genealogy page, where Oscar Fox's lineage had been inscribed in elegant cursive handwriting. Slowly she ran her fingers over the names, stopping on Oscar's mother. Her maiden name was Gretchen Esther Goldstein. Ann exhaled a heavy sigh and then looked at me with a sweet face of complete, contented joy.

"It was Oscar, after all."

"I don't understand."

"Oscar's mother was my grandmother's oldest sister. There were eight children in their family. My grandmother, Miriam, was the youngest. She and Gretchen were separated by sixteen years. They were Jews. Oscar's father, Dieter Fuchs, was not. When the war broke out, my mother was only seven years old and she and my grandmother went into hiding. Some of my cousins had made it to Switzerland and from there they worked to get the extended family out of Germany, mostly through bribes. That's how my mother and grandmother got out. I had always been told that we had a wealthy cousin in America who would mail cookies to Switzerland."

"I'm not sure I understand. Cookies?"

"Yes. The cookies had diamonds baked into them. They were used to pay off German officials. Altogether, Oscar helped fourteen of my relatives escape Germany and Austria. After the war my mother came to Pennsylvania, married a farmer, and they had me. I wouldn't be here if it wasn't for Oscar Fox."

I was stunned beyond words. Questions poured through my head. I blurted out one of the least important ones.

"So, you're Jewish?"

"Not really. I'm proud of my heritage, but I grew up Lutheran."

"Well, I just . . . I guess I'm just trying to fit everything together here. So you're saying that Oscar Fox, or Fuchs, sent diamonds hidden in cookies to Switzerland to help get your mom and your Jewish relatives out of Germany?"

"And Austria."

"And Austria."

"Yes." She pointed to the Bible. "This is who he really was and that is what he really did." Ann's consuming smile continued and she nodded. She gazed at the Bible before her and was beaming with an almost tearful happiness.

"Holy crap." It was an astounding revelation. But I still had questions. "But why didn't you tell me this before?"

Ann shrugged. "First of all, the details of the story have always been sketchy. The name Watervalley had been passed down only by word of mouth. I had never seen it written on anything. My cousins never knew what happened to Oscar, just that the letters and packages stopped coming. He had a post office box in Nashville where they were supposed to send any correspondence. Never to Watervalley. At any rate, you can't blame a girl for hesitating to claim kinship to Watervalley's infamous murderer."

It was all starting to come together. Oscar's new identity, the packages to Switzerland, his opening of the bakery, and the rumors about diamonds now all fit into a larger narrative. Yet, as I stood there, another incident from recent memory came to mind.

"When did you first suspect Oscar Fox was Oscar Fuchs?"

"Actually, it was when I first came to town. You might remember I came a day early. The first thing I did when I got here was look through the archives at the county library. Oscar had never put his name on the packages and signed the letters with his first name only. I found the name Oscar Fox in the records and figured he used the English spelling of the word. That's how I found out where Oscar was buried."

"So you're the one who put the Star of David on his grave marker."

Ann answered sheepishly. "Oh, you found that? I figured no one would ever visit his grave. I didn't know for sure, of course. I guess I just wanted it to be him. But, yes. The star belonged to my mother. I put it there in honor of him and what he did for her."

"Ann, this is a big deal. Don't you see? For decades Oscar Fox has been cast as a murderer. In reality, he was the exact opposite. He was a profoundly selfless man."

"True. But you do have to concede that he might have been a thief."

"How so?"

"Whatever diamonds he possessed couldn't have belonged to him."

"Well, there you may have a point. But still, look at his choices. He was on the run and couldn't get out of the country. I'm only speculating, but it sounds like he didn't want to be deported back to Germany, especially since he saw a way of helping his Jewish relatives with the diamonds by staying in this country. He probably came to Watervalley to lie low before moving on. But something happened and he stayed."

"What do you think changed his mind?"

"I'm guessing he fell in love."

Ann smiled. There was a subtle twinkle in her eye and she offered an amused nod. "Yeah, they say that happens."

I smiled in return. "Anyway, looks like he tried to do all he could to help those around him and his larger family, to make the most of where he found himself. It's a shame his life ended so tragically. I don't guess we'll ever know the identity of the man Oscar killed, or exactly how he and his associates got their hands on the information that led them to Watervalley."

"I might know something about that. At least, I have a theory. The diamond company Oscar worked for, Lamerslint-Jorg, was owned by some Jewish cousins of mine. That's how Oscar came to work for them as their North American sales representative. The Nazis took over the company early in the war, like they did most Jewish-owned companies. That might explain why Oscar felt justified in keeping the diamonds. And it doesn't take much to understand why he didn't want to be deported back to Germany."

"And if that's correct, then he really didn't steal them. He simply used them to help their rightful owners. I looked it up and Lamerslint-Jorg went defunct at the end of the war."

"Along with the Nazis," Ann added.

"So, the German guy. What's your theory?"

"Lamerslint-Jorg was owned by the Nazis. No doubt, they had agents hidden across America during the war. So, it seems logical that he was a German agent of some kind, sent to recover the diamonds."

"Which would explain why no one ever claimed knowledge of him."

"It makes sense."

"Yes, it does." I thought about it for a moment. "You know what else? It also explains why the telegram found on him was over a private Teletype machine. Seems logical that a German agent or spy wouldn't be using Western Union to transmit messages."

She shook her head. "Still, I don't know how the Nazis traced Oscar to Watervalley. That part's probably lost to history."

I nodded in agreement. For the longest time, we stared at each other in amazement. "This is truly incredible. You know that this story needs to be told."

Her smile faltered. "I think I'll let you tell it."

I didn't understand her hesitation. "You know, Louise Fox feels the same way. Why is that? It's your family's story."

"You're right. But I guess Louise is like me and doesn't care for the spotlight."

I laughed. "Well, neither do I, but someone needs to tell this story."

"You're the one who's brought all of this to light. It's yours, Luke. It's your story to tell."

"I'll speak to Louise again and see if she changes her mind. It just seems to be the right thing to do to set the record straight about who Oscar really was."

Ann lingered for another half hour, paging through the documents and taking several pictures with her cell phone. She was awash in a bemused euphoria, delighted to have finally found an answer to a lifelong question.

As she was leaving, I couldn't help but ask, "So, you and John have been getting along okay?"

She gave me a sly smile, her face radiant at the mention of his name. With her delicate features, petite figure, and sparkling eyes, I could see why John was taken with her.

"It's been a little difficult to keep the bit in his mouth, but he's coming along."

"Well, keep it up, Ann. I suspect you're good medicine for him."

"Hmm, John's got potential. He's intelligent, nice looking, and with that house and everything, you have to admit, he's done okay for himself financially." She paused and gave me a conspiratorial wink. "Don't forget, I'm still half-Jewish. Momma would approve."

I laughed and bid her good-bye, shutting the door behind her, and turned to find Rhett beside me with the tennis ball in his mouth. It had been a remarkable afternoon. But clearly he believed I should rethink my priorities.

In the days to come, he wouldn't be the only one.

CHAPTER 40
The Stars Align

With Louise's approval Luther Whitmore ran a special edition devoted to Oscar Fox, telling the details of his story and his secret mission to save his Jewish relatives from Nazi Germany. As well, considerable space was allocated to my theory that he had acted in self-defense. The result was a massive vindication of Oscar Fox's legacy in the minds of Watervalley's citizens. In a few short days he went from the notorious shadows of folklore to the status of local hero. There was even talk of placing a historic marker in front of the old bakery to commemorate him. He was the subject of gossip across the valley for weeks, and everywhere I went, people would stop me on the sidewalk, or in the grocery store, or while I was pumping gas and expound at length on the matter.

Diamonds were still a lively topic of speculation, but the common consensus was that if any still existed, they were lost forever, appropriately putting that old rumor to bed. Additionally, I made no further mention of a possible conspiracy surrounding the three men from decades ago. I had my suspicions, but ultimately, despite what Sunflower had told me about her dad, what Sheriff Thurman had said still rang true: it was just conjecture.

In a small way the vindication of Oscar's name lifted the morale of his descendants. Louise seemed to be emboldened by the improvement of Oscar's reputation and was taking on her new challenges with commendable courage and dignity. She had put the temptations of alcohol behind her, had accepted Estelle's offer to work at the bakery once it opened, and had begun the arduous process of boxing up their belongings in light of the inevitable bank foreclosure. I admired her. Even still, she was a single mom facing years of tight finances and little hope of ever getting ahead. One of the families from church had an above-garage apartment they were willing to lease to her at a modest rate. Several of the guys from church along with myself had agreed to help her move when the time came. There seemed little else I could do.

May arrived, and along with the continued excitement of the Oscar Fox story and the daily demands of the clinic, the pace of my life shifted into high gear. Connie's birthday was coming soon and despite her protestations I had arranged a small party at my house. Meanwhile, the bandstand was nearing completion and the grand opening for the bakery was only a few weeks away. Christine and I were still enjoying some delightful hours together, but with the imminent close of the school year, her nights and weekends were busy as well, limiting our opportunities to see each other. The lack of shared time only intensified my thoughts of her and I found myself missing her with an all-consuming passion.

Happily, I did manage to facilitate the answer to one small problem. I had come up with a way to resolve the nagging competition between Lida and Estelle. Bringing the two of them together in my office, I proposed a partnership in which Estelle could provide Lida with pastries and cakes for display to sell down at the diner and Lida could make gourmet sandwiches and wraps that could be prepackaged and sold over at the bakery. With a little coaxing, they both agreed to this exchange. I also proposed that since I had brokered this deal, I should get free samples for the balance of the year. This, they refused to do, sharing a conspiratorial giggle between them.

On the way out the door, however, Lida pulled me aside to tell me some good news.

"Doc, keep it under your hat, but I've got a contract on the B and B."

"Well, good deal. Somebody local buy it?"

"Not even close. Get this. A man out of Charleston, South Carolina, is buying it. I got a call last week from his Realtor, a Melanie Middleton. We talked for thirty minutes. She was adorable. She said she knew it was a little nuts but her client was willing to make an offer and put down a deposit based on nothing more than the Web site description and pictures."

"That's pretty unusual. She tell you anything about this guy?"

"Only a little. He's late thirties, recently widowed, and I think she said he has twin daughters. Not sure about their age. Eight or nine, I think."

"Interesting. I guess you never know."

"Of course, the deal is subject to an on-site inspection, so I'm not counting my chickens yet. But maybe when he comes, I can get the spooks to behave for one night and not scare him off."

"Spooks? What are you talking about, Lida?"

My puzzled face told her that I was clueless. She remained in a light humor but paused and sharpened her gaze at me. "You never have spent a night there, have you, Doc?"

"Can't say I have."

Lida nodded, weighing my response for a moment. Then she

shrugged, making a noticeable effort to downplay her previous comment. "Eh, well, it's like most old mansions. Things creak and moan and go bump in the night. It only adds to the charm. Anyway, the Realtor sounded pretty confident over the phone that her client was dead set on the place, said he thought it was just what his life needed."

"Well, I hope it works out."

"Me too. I've got a grandbaby coming and a huge responsibility to spoil that child rotten."

I laughed, bid Lida good-bye, and walked back toward my desk. I was happy for her and glad that things seemed to be working out. For a moment, I stood and looked out the huge windows of my office at the incredible May day before me. Perhaps Connie was right. Something about spring did stir the heart.

I had made some progress on the commencement address, managing to jot down a few thoughts that could be pieced together into a respectable message. But before that was to happen, there was the prom dance. And as I stood there absorbing the intoxicating beauty of the day, small sparks of anticipation and excitement were filling my thoughts. Admittedly, as much as I struggled with the idea of the graduation speech, I was almost giddy about going to the dance.

During my brief tenure in Watervalley I had come to know most of the high school seniors. Some had been patients of mine; others I knew from attending their basketball and soccer games. I enjoyed a certain celebrity status with them, and candidly, I loved it. It seemed I was at that right age, old enough to be seen as cool and too young to be seen as a parent. So, since the town offered so few opportunities to cut loose, I was as caught up as anyone with expectation about the dance.

Prom was only a few days away, the first Saturday in May.

Somehow, with our hectic schedules, Christine and I had not seen each other for more than five minutes in over a week and admittedly my heart was feeling the strain. More than in any other relationship I had been in, she owned my thoughts. My emotions were carrying me beyond the safe boundaries of the familiar. In the quiet hours I harbored a desperate yearning to be with her, to hear her voice, to hold her. I was convinced she felt the same.

It seemed our conversations had become laced with an underlying tension from the delicate hunger between us. And now the prom dance, with its alluring air of release and celebration, held all the potential for chemistry and combustion. I suspected that each of us had secretly nurtured idle daydreams of what was possible between us; had delighted in sumptuous thoughts of what would befall if our unspoken wishes were to find a voice. Measure by measure, as Saturday approached, my imagination began to flirt boldly with this furtive and consuming desire.

Late Friday afternoon, however, Nancy buzzed me in my office to say I had a phone call from Will Fox.

"Will, what's up, big guy? You okay?"

"Sure. I'm fine. Excellent, actually."

I laughed to myself. No child other than Will Fox would talk in such a superlative way. "Good to know. What's on your mind?"

"When you're done with work today, come over to Chick's. We've got something to show you."

"Oooh, this sounds promising. Wouldn't have anything to do with a sports car, would it?"

"It might. When can you get here?"

"I'm on my way."

When I arrived, the Austin-Healey was parked out front with the top down, shining brilliantly with a brand-new powder blue paint job. It had been completely restored with new cream-colored leather upholstery and a lustrous wood dash. It was a thing of beauty.

I walked around it in amazement. "Chick, you and Will have outdone yourselves. It looks fabulous."

Chick grinned from ear to ear. "The best part, Doc, is that she purrs like a kitten. Completely rebuilt the engine. My man Will here did a lot of the finished work."

I smiled at him. "You did a great job, Will. Looks perfect."

He seemed quite pleased with himself. "So, you going to go show it to Miss Chambers?"

I thought about this. "You know, Will, she and I have a date tomorrow night. I think I might make the fact that it's finally ready a surprise. You think you can keep quiet about it?"

"Sure. I imagine you need all the help you can get to keep her interested."

"Okay, I'm feeling pretty good right now, so I'm going to overlook that comment."

Chick cackled. It was great to see Will happy. I settled up with Chick and drove my new wheels home, leaving the Corolla to be picked up later. I pulled the Austin-Healey onto the grass behind the house and admired it in the cool of the May evening. It was a dream car, perfect for a special night. It seemed the stars were aligning.

CHAPTER 41
The Prom

On prom night, I arrived at Christine's house a little before seven. I had opted to forgo renting a tux and wore my dark dress suit. I waited in the entry hall, making small talk with her mother. As always, Madeline Chambers was a delight to speak with. But in time she asked to excuse herself and departed to the kitchen. After a few minutes, Christine made her appearance, descending the stairs and smiling luxuriously. To no surprise, she was stunning.

She was wearing a sleeveless black cocktail dress that fit seductively around her, accentuating her brimming curves. Her long legs moved in a fluid, sensuous motion with each downward step and her dark hair fell thickly around the soft lines of her face. There would be no mistaking her for a gushing teenager. She was a woman, fully bloomed: captivating, self-assured, beautiful.

"Wow. Can you just stand there and let me stare at you for an hour or so?"

"Oh, stop it." She spoke in a low voice of reproach, but her animated smile betrayed her delight.

"I should have asked John if I could borrow the Mercedes. Seems a little shabby for you to show up in the Corolla."

"It's no big deal, Luke. We're acting as chaperones to a high school prom, not walking the runway for a movie premiere."

"Okay, I'm not being fair here. I actually have a little surprise for you."

We stepped onto the porch in full view of the Austin-Healey.

"Oh, my gosh! It's gorgeous!"

"Chick finished it yesterday, just in time to take a pretty girl to the dance."

"Wow, Luke. It is simply beautiful. A guy could sweep a girl off her feet with a car like this."

"Well, that's certainly my plan."

"Oh, hush. Let's go."

I opened her door for her and she slid nimbly into the passenger seat. Then I quickly pulled the soft-top forward, latched it, and got in.

"You look a little too perfect," I said. "I'm not sure the windblown look would improve on that."

Christine smiled, adoring the interior of the old roadster. We headed out Shiloh Road, where the dance was being held in the high school gymnasium. Along the way, I couldn't seem to stop gazing over at her. This didn't go unnoticed.

"What?"

I chuckled. "You, that's what. You look unbelievable. I don't think I've seen you dressed to the nines like this."

"Well, it's not every day a girl gets to relive a little prom magic."

Just as Christine finished, my phone dinged a text message. She picked it up from the console between us.

"What's it say?" I asked.

" 'Great to see you again. Enjoy the dance tonight. Sounds like fun. Almost wish I were going. Ha!' "

"Oh, that's what's her name, the sales rep. She came by yesterday."

"Michelle Herzenberg? How come Miss 'what's her name' is in your phone?"

"Because I put her there. There are at least half a dozen sales reps in my phone. I put them in there so I know who's calling or texting me."

"What's this earlier text message from her about dinner last night?"

"Hey, that's a little bit prying, isn't it?"

Christine playfully invoked her schoolteacher voice. "Answer the question, Bradford."

I gave her a furrowed look. "Well, if you must know, the message is self-explanatory. She came by late yesterday afternoon and wanted to know if I could join her for dinner."

"Humph. Dinner, my foot. She probably wanted to have you for dessert. Does this girl not have a life?"

I laughed. "You're killing me here, Chambers. Who cares? Right now I'm driving a fabulous car and sitting next to the most beautiful woman in the cosmos. That's all I want to think about."

Christine looked down and smiled. "Okay, Bradford, pretty good comeback. I might dance with you after all."

I reached over to hold her hand. She gently and immediately gloved hers around mine. The months had molded us together, blended us into a second nature of understanding where even the slightest nuance or gesture was grasped without words. Still, my cautious heart had kept me from expressing the depth of my feelings. I found myself at a loss to say the things that I suspected Christine would like to hear.

But my devotion had been unmistakable and I had resolved that my affection was simply understood. Furthermore, words were not the only means of expression. As we drove on in silence, the soft, surrendering touch of her hands pulled my imagination deeper into the possibilities of the night.

The gym had been fabulously decorated with banners, paper ribbons, and low lights. The basketball court had been transformed into a glittering dance floor packed with energy and magic. Walking in with Christine on my arm felt like being a rock star. I was spontaneously greeted by the engaging shouts of the riotous teenagers, who seemed well charged for any excuse for revelry. The air was filled with electricity, laughter, celebration.

We found Connie and Estelle behind the refreshment counter. Despite their service roles for the evening, they both were attired in dazzling cocktail dresses, clearly communicating that they were open to some festive spontaneity. A DJ was spinning records before the band came on and both sisters were lightly bouncing to the pounding beat.

"My, my, my," I yelled above the noise. "Check out these two fine-looking ladies."

Estelle playfully responded, "You're looking pretty fine yourself, Dr. B. Nice suit." Showing much less restraint than her sister, she continued to rhythmically dip and shake her shoulders to the music, lifting her hands for added expression.

"I like that dress, Estelle."

Estelle continued to step lightly and sway, speaking with an aloof, confident certainty. "You like what's in it, too."

Christine put a hand over her mouth and we both choked back our laughter at Estelle's unabashed declaration. Connie rolled her eyes.

"Estelle, what can I say? You read my mind."

She continued her preoccupation with the music, turning her head from side to side, and answered casually, "It's okay, sweetie. You go ahead and have a good time with Miss Christine there. But you come back and see me for a dance if you want to get a little sweet chocolate in your diet."

Christine and I could barely control ourselves from bursting. The fun was just beginning.

The band was a group of locals called the Joint Chiefs, who apparently had known some modest success years ago. I recognized most of them, including the lead singer, Barry Satterfield. They started out by trying to play some recent hits but struggled with them. The kids seemed uninspired, which left the dance floor barely occupied. Many began to drift out the large double doors to the parking lot. Then the band huddled for a moment. Barry made a short announcement.

"Okay, everybody. We're going to try something a little different."

With that, he cranked out the opening licks to "Satisfaction" by the Rolling Stones. His pick hand hit the strings in a succession of crashing, blaring notes. It was an explosion of sound. Instantly the teenagers were leaving the bleachers and crowding the dance floor. They began pouring in from outside, almost running to catch an open space.

The next hours were filled with a long list of classic rock songs. The Joint Chiefs weren't just good; they were incredibly good. And the kids danced. They danced joyously, wondrously celebrating the moment, unhindered by any cares of the challenging and uncertain world beyond high school.

The grand moment of the evening occurred when all the teenagers lined up for the runway dance. While the music blared, each couple split into one of two rows that faced each other. This formed a long, ten-foot-wide central runway that extended the length of the gym. The head couple would dance their way down while everyone slowly sidestepped toward the head of the line.

Couple by couple the teenagers took their turn. Some displayed incredible rhythm and skill; others, not so much. All were having the absolute time of their lives. Christine and I were one of the later couples to dance our way down the middle. We were met with a grand round of whoops and applause. Eventually even the principal, Carl Suggs, and his wife, Shirley, joined in and stiffly stepped their way down the line.

But the biggest explosion of cheers came last. It began as a wave of deafening sound that started at the far end and rippled in our direction. Under the shadows and flash of the strobing lights, at first I couldn't make out who was causing such an earthquake of shouts and whistles. Somewhere about half-court, the two shapes came clearly into view. It was Connie and Estelle.

The two plus-size sisters were moving in a fluid choreography that left me staring in slack-jawed wonder. With their faces locked in a fixed intensity, they were oblivious to the roar of the crowd. Each movement, each hand motion, each twist and dip, were in perfect sync. They were stepping and sliding in unison to the thunderous beat of the music. John Harris hadn't been kidding. Connie Thompson could dance. When the music stopped, she and Estelle went back to serving refreshments. I would never be able to look at them the same way again.

Long into the night Christine and I danced, but we were often pulled away from each other: she by single boys who had mustered up their courage or who were responding to a dare; me by odd pairs of girls who wanted me to join in some coordinated dance step.

For some time we caught only fleeting glimpses of each other against the throb and roar of the music and the spinning lights. And yet, in the lost, dizzying moments, amidst the insanity of the shouts and laughter, something in the night's enchantment was drawing us to each other. The air swelled with a sense of liberation and the music pounded a reverberating message to stop and revel in the moment, that life was here and now, and that tomorrow was not guaranteed. Almost unknowingly we were being pulled into the contagious euphoria, the intoxicating spell of release and celebration. My desire for her burned within me.

The music continued, the magic grew, and we danced. And somewhere in the depth of the night, from across the room our eyes met for a willful, telling moment. All the sound and motion fell away. Christine was staring at me with a face full of sensuous promise. There, against the crush and noise, we shared an unmistakable knowing look, a spontaneous agreement, a mutual willingness to abandon ourselves to our deep attraction to each other.

It seemed the open doors were calling us to leave the roar and confusion of the dance behind and come out into the starlight. I went to her, took her by the hand, and led her out, away from the blare of the music and into the far shadows of the parking lot. We were alone, breathless, delirious.

I leaned against the car and pulled Christine close. She draped her arms around my neck and pressed the full length of her pliant and sensuous body in to me. No words passed between us. There were only our pounding and longing hearts. In that moment, the universe was ours.

Her skin was warm and fragrant and she breathed softly through moist and lightly parted lips. There was no clumsy awkwardness here, no confusion, no second-guessing our singular intent. There was only the two of us, pulled together under this starlit night, sharing an unvoiced, deep and tender desire. I pressed my hand against the small of her back, molding us together. We kissed again and again. I could sense the subtle rise and fall of her chest as her breath shortened. She put her hand to my face, searched my eyes, and spoke in a low, sweet whisper filled with certainty and promise.

"Let's get away from here."

Then the blare of my phone pierced the night. "Oh, hell!"

I wanted to ignore it, to throw the blasted thing into some black corner of the parking lot. But the doctor in me won out. I had to respond. I stepped away to answer it. I couldn't believe what I was hearing and from whom I was hearing it. It was a trauma, a medical emergency. I hung up and returned to Christine, speaking in a disgusted voice. "It's an emergency. I have to go. Not sure when I'll be back. Think you can possibly get a ride home?"

Christine spoke in a low, dejected voice. "Sure. I imagine Connie can take me."

"I'll call you later."

I hopped in the Austin-Healey and headed toward town to Estelle's bakery, where the caller, Randall Simmons, was expecting me.

CHAPTER 42
Sins of the Fathers

Randall's voice had sounded raspy and desperate. Clearly in agony, he had pleaded with me to come immediately, gasping between words to catch his breath. Then he begged me to please not tell a soul where he was and come by myself. I sped toward town, angry and bewildered. He was at the bakery, where he had no right to be. Something was grandly wrong.

Downtown Watervalley was asleep under the gray and silent shadows left by random streetlights. It seemed a ghostly, sterile world compared to the roar and passion of the one I had just left. I parked in front of the bakery, grabbed my emergency medical bag, and found the front door unlocked.

I called out firmly, "Hello."

"Back here." Randall's voice cracked with anguish.

Unable to find a light switch, I used my phone as a flashlight. I found him sitting on the tile floor of the kitchen. There was a significant pool of blood around his leg and his face was as white as a sheet. There was also blood on his hands and he was panting with rapid rises of his chest, struggling to catch his breath. He was in near shock. As I approached him, he was tightly holding a large flashlight.

"Thank you. Thank you for coming, Dr. Bradford. I'm hurt and I think I've lost a lot of blood."

A dozen questions ran through my head. Why was he here? What had he been doing? How had he hurt himself? In my anger I wanted immediate answers. But that would have to wait. "Randall, take some deep, slow breaths. Let me have your flashlight."

A quick examination of his leg told the ugly story. A ragged shaft of wood approximately the size of a pencil had pierced the calf of his right leg. The amount of blood soaking his pants and the surrounding floor suggested it may have nicked or severed the posterior tibial artery. I could call the EMTs and have them drive Randall to the hospital in neighboring Gunther County, but that would involve an hour's delay. The wound wasn't necessarily life threatening, but it needed immediate attention.

"Randall, you're going to be all right, but I need to deal with this injury right now. Sit tight, I am going to turn on some lights."

Using the flashlight, I moved toward the back door and almost stepped into a two-foot square hole in the floor. Beside it lay a piece of heavy plywood that no doubt had been used to cover it. The plywood had been pushed aside. The back light switches didn't work. I found the fuse box and was eventually able to turn on the kitchen lights.

Randall lay on the floor in a pitiful heap, far from the arrogant banker I had previously known. I had him turn on his side and away from the pool of blood. Using scissors from my medical kit, I cut away his pant leg. The wound was still oozing blood but not profusely. This was a good sign. As I grabbed what I needed from my medical bag, curiosity overtook me. Moving rapidly, I remained intently focused on the task at hand. I spoke sternly.

"How did this happen?"

"I accidentally stepped through the hole in the floor and my leg caught that piece of wood."

I pursed my lips hard and nodded while drawing lidocaine into a hypodermic to numb the wound. My words were fueled by my aggravation. I instructed him in a low, cool voice. "Randall, here's what's going to happen. You're going to lie still until I say move. I'm going to stop the bleeding, remove the wood, and sew you up. Then you're going to tell me exactly what you were doing here in the middle of the night."

He responded with frightened, quick bobs of his head. "Thank you. Thank you, Dr. Bradford."

I cleaned the wound with sterile laps and saline and injected the lidocaine. He winced at the sting of the syringe. The wood shaft was embedded only about a half inch below the back of his leg and ran parallel about three inches through the calf muscle before reemerging. It was too jagged to pull out. I would have to lacerate the leg to remove it. Fortunately, the bakery's hot water heater was functional. I scrubbed up as best I could, set up a sterile field, and went to work. Within half an hour, I had him sewn up. He would have an ugly scar, but he was lucky. I could detect no significant arterial, tendon, or nerve damage. At worst he would have some minor pain and a limp for a few days.

I wrapped his leg with gauze and told Randall he could turn over but to keep his leg extended. He did so and pushed himself across the floor, resting his back against a nearby wall. I stowed my things in my bag and found some rags. After scouring them in hot water, I wiped the blood from the floor. I did it for Estelle and Connie. A pool of blood was not something I wanted them to walk in and see.

Randall's head sagged to one side. He seemed a defeated man.

I grabbed a small chair and set it in front of him. Taking a seat, I spoke in a less-than-accommodating voice.

"All right, Randall. Talk."

He glanced up at me, nodding in resignation. "What would you like to know?"

"Everything. I think the questions are pretty obvious."

He exhaled, and spoke in a low, penitent voice. "I'm a ruined man. John Harris is going to have me fired next week. And I just thought if I could find them, find where they were stashed, I would be okay."

"Find what?"

"The diamonds."

"What makes you think there are diamonds here?"

"Because of what my dad told me."

A tingling sensation fluttered up the back of my neck. "And what did he tell you?"

Randall held up his hand, a gesture to give him a moment. He closed his eyes for a second, seemingly to gather his strength. Then the words began to pour out of him, as if he was speaking a confession from which he had long desired to unburden himself.

"My father was not a good man. His people were poor and pretty backward, so he scraped by and got an education in finance because he loved money and he wanted to show all his dirt-poor relatives that he wasn't like them. When Oscar Fox came to town and started to spend a lot, my dad took notice. He said Oscar never seemed to have much on deposit but always had a lot of cash. He noticed that Oscar had a safety-deposit box at the bank that he visited often. The box was in Oscar's name, not his wife's. Dad was a vice president at that time, and one day, he did something he shouldn't have. After hours late one night, he got a key and looked in Oscar's box. He found diamonds there, hundreds of them. Oscar made frequent trips to Nashville. Apparently, someone there bought them from him for cash."

"So, your dad broke the law."

"Yeah, he broke the law. Like I said, he was not a good man."

"Go on."

"The day the German arrived in town, Oscar came to the bank in a big hurry, carrying a metal container. He went to the vault, opened his safety-deposit box, and left soon afterward. Dad was convinced he took the diamonds and hid them here. He was also convinced that Elise Fox knew nothing about them. Years later, when he became bank president, he put a lot of pressure on Elise to sell the bakery. As soon as she did, he searched it thoroughly. He was the one who cut the holes in the walls and floors, thinking the diamonds were hidden there. But he never found them. Eventually, he gave up. But he was still convinced that there were diamonds somewhere."

"Why wouldn't Oscar have hidden them at his house?"

"Because they checked there."

"Who are 'they'?"

"My dad had a couple of drinking buddies he was pretty tight with in those days. The sheriff, Crawford Lewis, and the town doctor, Haslem Hinson. Lewis called my dad the night of the murder. The three of them decided to make it look like Oscar Fox had killed the German in cold blood. They figured whoever the guy was, he had come to town for the diamonds. It was sort of a half-baked plan, but they thought if Oscar could be rumored to be tied up with some German spy, it would be a good cover to search for the diamonds. That night Hinson gave Elise Fox a sedative and kept her down at the clinic while the sheriff and my dad searched the house. They found nothing. The diamonds had vanished. They thought for the longest time that the guy who lived by the lake had them."

"Otto Miller, Sunflower's father?"

"Yeah. They gave him a pretty hard time of it. But ultimately, they were convinced he knew nothing. Hinson and Lewis eventually died. Neither of them had any children, so the story died with them."

Randall paused for a moment, catching his breath. "You need to know something, Dr. Bradford. I didn't know any of this when I was growing up. My dad told me all of it a week before he died. He told me never to let the bank sell the bakery. I asked him why and that's when the whole story came out. That was fifteen years ago and I hated my dad when he told me. I wanted nothing to do with the bakery. But time does funny things to you. You forget the bad stuff about your parents; you gloss over them and construct a memory that's more workable, more acceptable. That's why I . . ." He paused for a moment. "That's why I didn't want to sell the bakery at the board meeting a few months ago, even though I hated my father for what he'd done. I couldn't shake his voice in my head telling me not to sell. Stupid, I guess. Now I've let his twisted business become my undoing as well."

I absorbed all that Randall had told me. It seemed that the knowledge that John Harris had both the means and the determination to have him sacked had eaten at Randall like a cancer during the past months. This was a humbled and desperate man. So desperate that he had succumbed to the reckless idea of sneaking into the bakery and resuming the search his father had abandoned. Though he remained a pathetic figure, I still found it difficult to pity him.

Then another question occurred to me. "Tell me something else, Randall. What happened when Connie Thompson's mother was fired from working here? Your dad have anything to do with that?"

A pained grin inched across his face and he spoke with mild sarcasm. "Among his other virtues, my dad was a racist. He was very low-key about it, but I knew it. My dad was one-eighth black and was always embarrassed about it."

He paused, speaking reflectively. "You know, when you're young, you take everything your parents think and double it. I picked on Connie when I was a kid. I'm not proud of it, but it's true. I'm not going to sit here and lie and tell you I've ever really liked her. But I have a lot of respect for her. What John Harris said in the board meeting was true. Connie saved the bank, and the community along with it."

There was a long silence between us. Randall looked up at me, speaking in a voice of defeat and resolve.

"So, Doctor, what happens now? I guess you're going to have to tell the sheriff and the Pillow sisters about all this."

I thought for a minute. "I'm not telling anyone anything—at least, not yet. But you may have some things that need to be said."

I explained to Randall what was on my mind. He agreed. I helped him to my car and drove him home.

Sometime after two o'clock in the morning I turned the key in my front door. Rhett greeted me with sleepy enthusiasm. I let him out into the backyard and stood under the stars while he took care of his business. Regrettably, it was far too late to call Christine. I wasn't sure what to tell her in any case. Randall's confession was not something I could speak about for the time being.

My head and my heart were spinning. Equal measures of wonder, bewilderment, and aching passion were vying for my attention, flooding my thoughts despite my exhaustion. I collapsed into bed, comforted only by the opiate of sleep.

CHAPTER 43
Birthday

Sunday morning I slept in. The eleven o'clock church bells woke me from a deep slumber and I sat straight up in bed in a panicked state. In two hours the guests invited to Connie's birthday party would be arriving and I had a lot to do to prepare. I took care of Rhett, showered, and scurried around making sure all was ready for the small gathering. The only interruption in the flow came shortly after noon when there was a knock on the door. It was Louise Fox.

"Hello, Dr. Bradford. I hope I'm not interrupting, but I wanted to give you this." She held out an old envelope. "We're trying to get everything packed up and I ran across it in a box of things that had belonged to my husband's grandmother Elise Fox. It's addressed to Connie's mother, and, well, I just thought Connie might like to have it."

It was a letter dated 1968 that had been returned to sender. I remembered Connie mentioning that Elise Fox had written to her mother shortly before Maylene Pillow died of cancer. But Maylene had refused to read it. I took the envelope.

"Thanks, I'll see that Connie gets it."

Louise turned to leave. She was a good woman and I admired her thoughtfulness. I wished things could be different for them. I stuck the letter in a basket on the desk where I kept the bills. It would have to wait till later. Time was running short.

The party turned out to be a riotous affair. A delightful collection of friends, including the mayor, Walt Hickman, Chick McKissick, Nancy Orman, John, and several others, came together for a robust couple of hours to celebrate Connie's sixty years. All four of Connie's children called during the party to wish her happy birthday. They all lived in distant cities and at her insistence had not come since they were all scheduled to gather for a family reunion in another month. Estelle had outdone herself making a cake that could have fed half the county. She also reminded everyone that the grand opening of the bakery would be held the following Saturday, less than a week away.

"Everybody, be sure to come," Estelle said. "There'll be lots of fun things to taste and free gâteaux."

This comment piqued Chick's interest. "What's a gâteau, Miss Estelle?"

Connie answered for her. "It's a cupcake, but roughly translated, it's French for 'I'm charging a dollar extra.'"

Chick cackled, and not to be outdone, he quickly typed something into his cell phone. "Well, next time you come for an oil change, I'll have to charge you for a"—he read the translation off his phone—"'*changement d'huile.*'"

Everyone laughed and toasted and told favorite stories. While Connie did her best to appear unmoved by all the fuss and attention, her irrepressible smile kept bubbling up. John endeavored to tease and cajole her, but her sharp retorts stopped him from getting the best of her.

We all had a grand time. But my enjoyment was tempered by a burning concern. Christine had not come. I suspected she was furious with me, and deservedly so. I needed to call her and make amends.

Still, I was surprised she would be inconsiderate to Connie, given that the gathering was really about her. I learned otherwise once all the guests had departed. Estelle had to run home because she had forgotten her blood sugar medicine, leaving only Connie and me to gather up the party remains and finish up in the kitchen.

I said, "Sorry about Christine. I'm not sure why she didn't make it."

Connie gave me a surprised stare. "You don't know? Why, she called me earlier to apologize for not coming. Madeline was taking Grandmother Chambers back to the airport in Nashville this morning and asked Christine to come along. I thought you knew."

"No, I didn't. But I'm glad she called you. It just didn't seem like her not to show."

I tried to act as if the incident meant nothing, but I was sure Connie wasn't convinced. In reality, neither was I. I had left Christine to fend for herself at the dance in a lousy way. Medical emergencies took precedence, but I hadn't called and explained afterward. Part of the prom evening had been a dream, a near culmination of long-repressed feelings, a release of deep and tender desire. Yet it had ended in such a bizarre ordeal, an odd mix of disgust and revelation.

I needed to tell Connie, to speak of what I had learned. But the last two hours had been such happy ones that I thought it best not to ruin the moment. Even still, I knew that Connie was reading my thoughts; she knew that something was bothering me and struggling to find a voice.

A knock on the door made the decision for me. I left Connie

in the kitchen and answered it. Before me stood Randall Simmons. He spoke penitently.

"Dr. Bradford, I noticed Connie's car in the driveway. I was wondering if I might have a moment to speak to her."

A voice behind me spoke firmly and coolly. "Show Mr. Simmons to the living room, Luke. I'll be right there." Connie was standing in the hallway, stoic defiance etched on her face. She read my questioning look and nodded lightly. I did as she said.

Randall hobbled over to one of the large wingback chairs and plopped down in it. He was doing what I had told him the previous night he should do: confess and apologize to Connie. But on the heels of her birthday party, it seemed like rotten timing. Nevertheless, here he was. Truth, it seemed, followed its own clock.

Connie entered and sat on the couch across from him.

"I'm going to take Rhett out back and let you two talk," I said.

In the backyard I tossed the tennis ball to Rhett, wondering what awkward conversation was taking place in my living room. After about thirty minutes, I heard a car start up in the driveway and walked to the yard's edge to see Randall leaving.

As I entered through the back door, I found Connie washing dishes at the kitchen sink. She didn't look up at me but only stared at the plates and cups moving from her hands to the drying rack. Her lips were puckered and pressed hard together in a mixture of bitterness and resolve, forcing her to inhale and exhale through her nose in deep, sullen breaths.

I moved close to her and casually leaned against the kitchen counter beside her, tilting my head sideways toward her as if to pry her gaze toward me. Without looking up, she continued to stubbornly and methodically wash the dishes and place them to one side. She was occupying herself, seemingly avoiding the tempest of emotions knotting within her. Eventually, despite her stern countenance, large tears began to roll down her face, falling from the edge of her cheeks and into the dishwater. She made no effort to wipe them away.

Perhaps I should have spoken, but it seemed best to stand silently and reassure her with my presence. Welling up within her was all the grief, all the loss, all the accumulated years of petty injustices. And somewhere in the naked pain of her tears I saw a glimpse of Connie Thompson from decades ago: a vulnerable and excluded little girl, desperate to understand the unfairness and prejudice of the world around her.

Finally, she broke the silence. Remaining focused on the dishes, she lifted her quivering chin, and quoted Scripture in a low, determined voice. " 'I am not my own but bought with a price.' "

She stepped back, placed her hands on the edge of the sink counter, and leaned forward with her head down. I instinctively moved toward her and gathered her up in an enveloping embrace. She buried her face in my shoulder and wept, pouring out her heart like water from a vase. Her deep sobs washed over me, filling the room.

I shamefully realized that my thoughts of Connie's early years had been minted in my imagination, where I'd naively filled in unknown chapters of her life. I'd imagined those years as sweet, wholesome, protected. Instead, cruel and unjust acts had placed their stain upon her. Yet she had found the courage to rise above them. I saw with burning clarity that her tough exterior was only a facade to protect her tender and generous heart.

In time, she patted me on the back and stepped away, grabbing a paper napkin to dry her face.

"So, I guess he told you everything," I said.

"Yes. Yes, he did."

"I'm sorry. I didn't realize he would come to tell you today."

"No, no. It's fine." She continued to gather herself, occasionally offering a fleeting smile in that odd way people do after a good cry.

"Connie, can I get anything for you?"

She thought for a moment. "Yeah. You know what? I think I'd like to have a beer."

My wide-eyed and amused face communicated my surprise. "Fair enough. Think I might join you."

I grabbed two bottles from the fridge and we sat at the kitchen table. Connie took a long swallow.

"Ohhh, that's good. I haven't had one of these in a long time."

"You do realize how badly I want to get my camera right now, don't you?"

"Not unless you're planning on taking a before and after picture of your broken arm."

"Yeah, that's kind of what I figured." I took a drink of my beer and we sat in silence.

"So, what happens now?" I asked. "You think you and Estelle will press charges?"

Connie shrugged. "For what? Randall didn't do anything but hurt himself."

"I guess you're right. Still, it was a pretty desperate thing to do. Looks like John's making good on his promise to can Randall is what drove him to it."

"We talked about that."

"Really?"

"Umm-hmm. He asked me to forgive him."

"What did you tell him?"

"I told him I would think about it. But I'll probably let him stay on."

"You're kidding. Why?"

"Because it may be the right thing to do."

"But, Connie, his family has been the cause of a lot of misery for you."

"I know. I just need to think about it."

A long silence ensued and I could only sit and stare incredulously. Connie finished her beer and began to talk, opening up about her life, unburdening the weight of cares that she had carried for so many years. I listened in silent fascination.

"Sometimes being me is not a rewarding experience. I know it sounds silly, but when I was a little girl, for the longest time I thought my name was Constant Grace, not Constance Grace. I thought Momma expected me to always be good, to always do the right thing, to act in every waking moment in obedience to God's will. So I did, and truth be known, a lot of times I didn't like it and I was actually pretty angry about it. But over time, I began to see that if I would just be a little patient, things had a way of working out. Not always as I wanted, but enough for me to believe it was true. And lo and behold, on my birthday here comes Randall Simmons, apologizing for the sins of his family, restoring the years the locusts have eaten."

Her words made me remember the letter. I held up a finger to Connie, signaling her to pause for a moment while I retrieved it.

"Louise brought this by earlier. She said she found it among Elise Fox's things, while packing up to move."

Connie examined it and immediately realized what it was. She looked at me with a curious face. "I'd like to open this."

"I think you should."

She nodded, tore open the seal with her finger, and unfolded the small note. As she silently read the words, a soft smile spread across her face. She finished and held the letter to her chest, closing her eyes for a brief moment. In time she opened them and held the letter before her.

"I want to read this to you."

"Sure."

> Dear Maylene,
>
> I know that you are not doing well and I wanted to tell you some things that are important to me. For years Raymond Simmons pressured me to sell the bakery, but I refused. He knew that it was your hard work and friendship that kept the bakery and me going. I fell into some financial hard times and he forced me to fire you. I'm sorry. I didn't have the strength to stand up to him.
>
> I have always lived under the shadow of my husband's death. I know Oscar had many secrets, but his love for me was not one of them. He loved me deeply and I miss him every day. Everyone thinks there were diamonds hidden at the store, but that simply wasn't true. Trust me, if there were, we would have found them.
>
> The only diamond at the bakery was you, Maylene. You are a unique and wonderful and godly woman and I am thankful for the years of laughter and friendship we shared. I will always love you. Please know that.
>
> Sincerely,
> Elise Fox

Connie's face beamed with a sweet and grateful pride. "This is the best birthday gift of all."

I smiled and squeezed her hand. "It's amazing, isn't it? All the things that have transpired because one man came to Watervalley and decided to stay."

Connie shook her head. "I don't blame Oscar Fox. I don't guess he planned on falling in love with Elise, but it happened and it changed the course of his life. So he stayed and did everything he could to help those around him. And with the diamonds, he was just trying to undo some of the evil he saw happening in this world. He was a good man who was trying to do the right thing."

She paused and pressed my hand in return. "Years from now, Luke, people will talk about you in much the same way."

"I don't understand."

"They'll talk about all the good you've done, about all the people you've helped, all the sickness you've cured. Seems like Oscar's life and yours share a lot of parallels. Both of you have made each day count for something positive in people's lives."

Her words overwhelmed me. I sat silently.

"Thank you for encouraging Randall Simmons to come talk to me. I've got some healing to do and that's going to take some time. But I'd rather see him a changed man and us living in peace than him fired and hatred growing between us."

I shrugged and smiled wryly at her. "How do you do that?"

Her response was reflective, gentle. "How do I do what?"

"How do you so easily forgive those past cruelties?"

Connie looked down for a moment and sighed. "It's hard. Sometimes it's terribly hard. Truthfully, I'd like to punch Randall in the nose. But he seems to be trying. If I don't forgive him, then I have to carry that hatred around."

"So you think this is what you need to do?"

"It is. I don't feel like forgiving him, but it's the right thing."

"How so?"

"Because I know my name is written in the palm of His hand."

Connie Thompson was beyond me. Her depth of wisdom and her capacity to love and forgive came from a well of strength I could not begin to comprehend. And yet, all that she had said rang true. Now it seemed the inequities and injustices of her life were finding redemption.

In time, she rose to go.

"Thank you, Luke, for everything."

"By the way, would this be a good time to ask you about that unbelievable dance routine I witnessed you and Estelle doing last night?"

Connie regarded me flatly. "No. Don't think it would."

"Oh, now, that's not fair. Inquiring minds need to know."

Connie's old self had returned. She lifted her chin and regarded me through the bottom of her gold inlay glasses, speaking a voice of low reprimand. "What happens at the prom stays at the prom, Dr. Bradford."

I smiled and nodded, knowing that further queries were useless.

"So, the grand opening is this weekend?"

"Yes. We're both pretty nervous about it. We're afraid no one's going to show up. It's silly, I guess. But a gourmet bakery is a bit radical for Watervalley."

"I think folks are going to love it. Pastries, artisan breads, barista coffee . . . I can't wait."

"I hope you're right."

"Hey, what name did you decide on?"

Connie closed her eyes and shook her head. It was clear this was an exasperating topic for her. "You'll have to wait for it. It's a big surprise. The sign has been covered up and will be unveiled Saturday."

I smiled. "All sounds good to me."

Connie nodded. I walked her to the door, where she gave me a long hug. She was about to leave, but then she turned toward me, and as was her way, she spoke in a kind but instructive voice.

"You know, Luke, I wasn't kidding when I said that Oscar Fox and you have followed similar paths."

"How so?"

"Just like him, you came to town without any intention of staying. I don't guess you planned on falling in love either. But these things happen."

I only stood and glanced down, not wanting to meet Connie's tender but penetrating gaze. No doubt, this was her way of telling me something I hadn't told myself. I let silence be my answer.

Her voice of mild reprimand continued. "Anyway, go call that pretty girlfriend of yours and fix whatever it is you're not telling me about."

I grinned. "See you tomorrow."

"Humph," was all Connie offered before walking to her car.

As I shut the door behind her, I knew she was right. My head and heart were burning to talk with Christine. As it turned out, they would have to smolder for several days.

CHAPTER 44
Finding the Words

I probably should have figured something was wrong when Christine didn't return my call on Sunday. It didn't occur to me until Tuesday morning that she didn't want to talk, or at least, at a minimum, she wanted a cooling-off period.

At first I was panicked. A dozen scenarios ran through my mind. I replayed Saturday night over and over in my head, remembering every word, every gesture, desperately wanting to comprehend what had driven her to be this angry and hurt. As the hours passed, my early frenzy gave way to an irritated frustration. She was being childish if not outright rude. Fine. If she didn't want to talk, then we wouldn't talk. I would give her the space she wanted. I had left her several messages, so the ball was in her court. Besides, Friday was graduation and my speech was sorely lacking. I needed time and space to think about what I wanted to say. But even in this I was greatly conflicted.

I adored the people of Watervalley and had grown to appreciate their rural life. But I had known a larger existence. There was a broader world out there and it wasn't all bad. I considered ignoring the advantages it offered, but I felt a great sense of personal responsibility to speak honestly. Somehow I had to find a way to tell them about a world that might make theirs seem petty and small and backward. I should never have agreed to the task.

Wednesday passed into Thursday and still no word from Christine. Left to my own, I filled the empty days with a low-boiling anger and a general disdain. Ann and the staff had taken notice and seemed to be tiptoeing around me at the clinic, leaving me to brood in my office when patients were not waiting to be seen. I made a point of avoiding Connie, not wanting to be called to account regarding the affairs of my heart. Even Rhett seemed to shy away from me, cautiously lying across the room and eyeing me with wary curiosity.

I arrived home Thursday afternoon to an empty, silent house. After changing clothes, I took a moment to stare at my phone. Secretly, I was hoping that somehow I had missed a call from Christine. But I hadn't. I went back downstairs to grab a beer. But as I shut the refrigerator, there was a knock on the front door.

My heart leaped. Rhett sensed this and wagged his tail intensely as he followed me down the hall. It seemed I couldn't get to the door fast enough, and upon opening it, despite all the thoughts that had been pouring through my head over the last several days, I was struck mute by the sight of Christine standing before me, as lustrous and beautiful as ever. She smiled cautiously, sweetly.

"Hi."

"Hi."

"Can I come in?"

"Sure." The mere sight of her, the pressing delight of simply being near her again, brought a smile to my face. Forgotten was all the frustration, all the invective that had been swirling in my head since the start of the week. Even still, I wasn't about to show my hand, to offer anything. For the moment, I would play a game of wait and see.

Christine noticed the beer I was holding. "Mind if I grab something to drink?"

"No, help yourself." I followed her to the kitchen, where she retrieved a water bottle from the fridge and then patted Rhett on the head. The air between us was stiff, awkward.

"How have you been?" she asked.

"Okay. Busy. The clinic's been a little crazy this week. But not too bad. How's school?"

"Same. Busy. Got the year wrapped up, which is always sad and happy at the same time."

I nodded, content to let her carry the conversation.

She looked away and saw my laptop on the kitchen table. "So, how's the graduation speech coming along?"

"Not that great." I had responded slowly. What was she doing? She didn't return my phone call for a week and now she came by only to make small talk? My amiable veneer was beginning to wear.

"Oh? Why not so great?"

Her words were nonemoting, polite. My chafed feelings began to bleed through my words.

"I'm at a loss, you see. I'm at a loss for what to tell them. Watervalley is what it is, and that's been fine. But there's a larger world out there. And as big of a shock as it might be, there are actually people living happy, interesting, fulfilled lives beyond the county line."

"I think they know that."

"Do they?"

"Of course they do. They're not lepers living in isolation."

"Well, I'm not so sure. Sometimes I think what living here teaches you is to have a healthy fear of any place with more than three stoplights."

"That's absurd."

"Is it?"

"Of course it is. I don't understand, Luke. What's brought all this on?"

"Well, I think that's a little self-explanatory, isn't it? Look, Christine, there's a whole world out there beyond the hills. I know it and you know it. So maybe, just maybe, I'm having a bit of a hard time trying to figure out how to tell them that there's more to life than just shit-kicking manure around the farm."

"I don't think this is about them."

"What do you mean?"

"I think this is about you."

"Oh, don't do that."

"Do what?"

"Don't, you know, turn into Madam Freud all of a sudden."

"Fine. It's just that you seem upset because some of them may be happy here, because some of them are okay with living modest, simple lives, while you actually think it's beneath them."

"That's not true."

"Isn't it, though? I mean, you're discounting the things that they know and love when you haven't tried them yourself."

That did it. Something in me snapped. My voice grew stern, forced, pushed to anger. I released in one infuriated outburst the whole packed weight of my confusion, my burning aggravation.

"Oh, I get it. This is all about me and life on the farm, isn't it? Is that what the silent treatment has been about all this week? Ha, and here I was thinking it was all about me leaving so suddenly Saturday night. Look, I don't want to milk cows, I don't want to ride a horse, and I don't want to grow a blasted garden. I just want to be a doctor. I want to do what I promised I'd do. Be here for three years, and then after that, I guess I'll just see."

Christine stared at me for the longest time, enduring my strident and abusive words, absorbing them like a seasoned boxer taking punches. She stood with a fragile and sensitive face, waiting for me to exhaust myself, to spill out all of the festering frustration.

Finally, she spoke with a mixture of hurt and resolve. "So, I guess those three words pretty well sum it up, don't they?"

"What three words? 'For three years'? Well, yeah, I guess they do."

"No, Luke. Not those three words."

"What, then?"

" 'I'll just see.' You said 'I'll just see.' Not 'we'll just see.' "

"Well . . . okay, fine, but . . . you're splitting hairs."

"No, it's okay. I just . . . It's just that I've been thinking about things differently. I guess . . . I guess I've made some assumptions that I shouldn't have."

She paused, folded her arms, and looked down at the floor. Then she nodded in resignation and exhaled a deep breath. A frail smile trembled on her lips.

"You're right, I haven't called you back this week and I'm sorry about that. I know all about what happened with Randall Simmons Saturday night. That's not it. And it's not about you and farm life. I just needed time to think. You see, I'm a foolish girl, Luke. I can't hide my feelings . . . don't want to hide my feelings. I knew that first day I saw you standing in my doorway at school that I would fall in love with you. That's why . . . that's why for the longest time I wouldn't go out with you. Because I thought you probably hated this place, and I don't. I love Watervalley. Despite its faults, and failings, and stupidity, I still love it, almost as much as I love you. If you moved away tomorrow, if we never saw each other again, neither love would change. It would break my heart, but it wouldn't change my love for this place, and it wouldn't change my love for you. Watervalley will always be home. But staying here or not staying here is not a deal breaker. I just thought it was a decision that, in time, we would make together. I was wrong."

I tried to absorb everything she said. But it was all too much. There were too many emotions at play in this conversation. Anger and hurt from her weeklong silence, frustration and anxiety over this damnable speech, and now Christine's talk of love. It wasn't the right time, the right place, the right moment to discuss these things.

I stared blankly into her face, so sweet and soft and fragile, like I was looking at the petals of a delicate flower. I wanted to pour the words of my heart into her silence, to empty the full measure of my affection and passion. But I couldn't. I couldn't find the words. I could only stand before her like a foolish mute, able to do little more than exercise my talent for concealment.

After several long, silent moments, Christine pursed her lips into an accepting smile and nodded. She turned and walked to the entrance hall and out the front door. I wanted to speak, to somehow change everything. But it was not to be. She was gone. My cautious and protective heart had once again been the author of an inexpressible loneliness.

I had no one to blame but myself. My world had slid sideways. I walked to the fridge to retrieve another beer. It wouldn't be my last of the night.

CHAPTER 45

The Graduation Speech

Friday morning I woke up to a brilliant sun pouring through my bedroom window. I took Rhett downstairs and out to the backyard. The world before me was fully bloomed. The thick grass and densely canopied trees were wrapped in a calming, soft haze. The air was sweet and balmy and a delicate breeze stirred occasionally, pulling at the heads of the newly arrived daisies. A light dew remained. Even still, the expanding warmth of the early morning foretold that the hot-breathed days of summer would be soon upon us.

Despite the splendid day, my world had a strange feel to it, an odd combination of foreboding and expectancy. And why wouldn't it? I was unsettled in both head and heart, wrestling with my own thoughts, my own desires. Yet in a couple of hours I was expected to stand before a gathering of Watervalley seniors who stood at the pinnacle of hope for their lives and somehow offer them words of insight, wisdom, and assurance. I was profoundly unfit and unprepared for the part.

Shortly after nine thirty I arrived at Watervalley Lake, where row upon row of white chairs had been neatly lined up on the flat grassy area near the entrance to the newly finished bandstand. The first three rows had been cordoned off for the Watervalley High seniors, all forty-two of them. Additional chairs had been placed behind and along the sides. Altogether, over four hundred family and friends would be seated and waiting for the processional. A place like Watervalley had few ceremonies during the year, so events like a graduation served as a good excuse for a large community turnout.

In the front a low stage had been built, draped in the gold and purple banners of the school's colors. A row of chairs lined the back of the platform and a small podium stood front and center. The bandstand, now glistening white in the perfect May sun, had also been richly decorated for the reception to follow the ceremony. Conversations from the gathering crowd were lively and the clamor of preparations could be heard echoing out across the lake as several moms on the bandstand set out refreshments.

I found the principal, Carl Suggs, who greeted me cordially and showed me to my chair behind the podium. I spoke politely to those around me, sat down, and awaited the processional of the seniors, who were gathered under a tree in the far distance. As nonchalantly as possible, I surveyed the crowd and, to my delight, found Christine smiling warmly at me. The light seemed to shimmer off of her. She was radiant, beautiful, and she gazed at me without reservation. I smiled and glanced down, pretending to review my notes.

Eventually, I looked up and noticed Connie taking the seat beside Christine. This shouldn't have surprised me. They were friends. But I couldn't help wondering about the level of intimacy and disclosure between them. I was burdened with regret over my outburst from the day before and now was hounded with embarrassed contrition that Connie might know. This served only to further fuel my uncertainty, my nervousness.

Yet as I sat there and thought about the two of them, a simple reality washed over me. These two women loved me. Less than a year ago I had come to them a stranger. Now all I knew from both of them was pure affection and devotion.

It was a crushing realization.

I needed to concentrate, focus on the words I was about to say. But a wealth of feelings poured over me, paralyzing me. It seemed that my time at the podium was now destined to be a disaster.

The processional music started, abruptly waking me from the fog of my confused state. The seniors filed in. Some were striding anxiously; others were plodding along; all were wearing irrepressible smiles. They were seated and Principal Suggs gave a few opening remarks. This was followed by an invocation and the singing of the school alma mater. I had a few last moments to think.

I found myself looking around, absorbing all that I could see and feel: the perfect blue of the sky, the warmth of the sun, and the soft breeze that drifted in from the lake. A spontaneous excitement, a collective pride, permeated the air. Before me lay an ocean of smiles, of beaming, adoring faces. And as always, the people of Watervalley humbled me. Despite their uncomplicated outlook and their unadorned ways, they had become my people, my friends, my community.

As the students and faculty and parents sang allegiance to their school and their small town, it seemed in that moment, under the sunlight of this perfect day, that we had all been gathered into one shared life. In that instant, time stood still.

I was reminded again that my presence here was part of a larger story. In the faces of the students before me I saw the light of hope and in their parents' eyes shone the joy of expectation.

But most importantly, I saw in the eyes of Christine a pure and selfless love . . . strong, audacious, unapologetic. My guarded and protected heart could not comprehend it, could never allow itself to be so open, so genuine, so vulnerable. Yet I knew in that breath that I saw in her gaze a potential for happiness beyond the farthest reaches of my dreams.

I shuddered to think that I could be so incredibly fortunate, to breathe in such air, to experience such a day, to know such a feeling that defied the brokenness of this life. For years I had silenced my emotions, seeking some perfect time and place for them to safely find a voice. But I was wrong. This was as close to pure happiness as anyone ever got.

I had been struggling with what to say to the graduating seniors because I had foolishly assumed that idiot chance had thrust their way of life upon them and had limited their choices. But I was wrong. What I had failed to see was that time, and chance, and difficulties, happen in all lives, including mine. I had wanted to be prescriptive, to give them the cure to life's challenges. But I had no such answers, nor did I need them. I only needed to assure them of what they already knew.

Principal Suggs had called my name a second time. I abruptly realized that I had been sitting oblivious to the progress of the ceremony, lost in the past minutes' revelation. The entire gathering was absolutely silent, waiting for me to stand and speak.

Quickly, I rose and shook the principal's hand, thanking him. I moved to the podium, spread my papers, and took a deep breath. For several long seconds I stood speechless, able to do nothing more than stare at Christine from across the crowd. Finally, Principal Suggs cleared his throat and I realized that the long silence had grown awkward. I looked toward him and gave him a shallow nod. I finally knew what I wanted to say.

But first, I wanted to have a little fun.

"Thank you, Principal Suggs."

I gazed buoyantly at the crowd before me. "Graduating seniors, distinguished faculty, school administrators, students, parents, family, and all you old people who just come to these things, welcome!" The crowd rippled with laughter.

"I am delighted to be here and amazed at you graduates sitting before me. Just look at you. You're all grown-up, confident eighteen-year-olds. And to think, I knew many of you all the way back when you were just shy, budding seventeen-and-a-half-year-olds.

"The other thing that amazes me about all of you is that after four years at Watervalley High School, none of you know the words to the second verse of the school's alma mater. Admit it. I watched you. All of you mumbled right through it."

The graduates laughed, exchanging nodding glances among themselves.

"Before I get started, it's important that all of you know something. Though you see me as a doctor with several degrees and various accomplishments, there was a time when I sat exactly where each of you is sitting. No, really. I came over here early this morning and sat in every chair, all forty-two of them. It was fun. I took selfies from each one. Oh, also, I think I absentmindedly stuck my gum under one of them, so if you get bored and start feeling around . . . well, just be careful." The students cackled. Clearly they were content to spend the entire time laughing rather than listening to a handful of clichéd truths.

"I want each of you to know that a couple of months ago when I received the invitation to make this speech and attend the prom, I was greatly honored and set aside a considerable amount of time and went to some effort to prepare. Of course, I'm talking about the prom and not this speech. I started working on that last night. After twenty agonizing minutes, I couldn't come up with anything so, as a short diversion, I got into an online game of Assassin's Creed with a guy out of Wisconsin who kicked my tail for several hours. Fortunately, he was only nine years old and eventually his mother made him go to bed."

This comment brought about some confused looks from a few of the older adults, but the senior high class laughed outrageously, ending with a short applause.

"So, as I started preparing my speech this morning, I have to confess that I was pretty conflicted. There are several messages I would like to share and it is difficult to pick which one. So what the heck, I'm going to give them all to you. Not to worry, though. I should be done in three or four hours."

This brought a roar of laughter from the parents. Even they got that one. Now I began to shuffle my papers, pausing for effect.

"Well, this is fun. But I think it would be good to say a few things of substance to you before I end. So, here it is. I'd love to stand before you today and be the pied piper of possibility, to offer you lofty thoughts about reaching for the stars but keeping your feet on the ground, to tell you your life is an open book and you are completely empowered to write whatever you want on the pages. But I would do so knowing that, sadly, those things, at least in part, are lies.

"Furthermore, if I was to do that, I would be insulting each of you, wouldn't I? I would be assuming that you have learned nothing about life over the last eighteen years. I think we all know the world can be difficult, and unfair, and, worst of all, sometimes uninteresting.

"So, fact. If you haven't been paying attention for the past several years, then you have limited your possibilities. Since many of you have been applying to college, I imagine you've already figured that out. Fact. If you have been going through the motions, sleepwalking, if you will, through any or all aspects of your life—whether it be your academic, your social, your athletic, or yes, even your spiritual life—odds are you are likely to do the same in the years ahead, and it will take a conscious effort to change course."

I paused for a moment and looked to the side. Then I looked directly at Christine, whose smile had never faltered, and at Connie, beside her, whose face beamed with pride.

"You see I know this because . . . well, because I have sleepwalked through certain parts of my life. I have failed to see the strength and courage of those around me. I have failed to understand the selfless hearts of those who have loved me. And I have failed to appreciate the good and beautiful things in my life. Sometimes, even when those things and those people were right in front of me.

"So my comments to you today are not so much about attaining your hopes and dreams, but about how you live your life. It seems our souls are restless and we are easily enamored with the glamorous, with the new and different, and with the promised adventure and glow of distant lights. These things have their place. And yet it is the modest, happy life—the life that each day is filled with love, and significance, and simple enjoyment—that in our heart of hearts each of us seeks.

"So, with that understanding, here is my advice. Chart your course, set your goals, and be about the business of attaining them while keeping one simple thing in mind. Life will, and invariably does, change your plans. And know that the disappointments, the setbacks, the unintended redirections, can become catalysts for reinvention. For it is how we adapt and how we persevere that defines our lives.

"And sure, have dreams that are big. But I would also encourage you to have dreams that are small. Have big hopes, but have little hopes too. Take pride in big accomplishments, but take delight in small ones also. Practice tolerance, kindness, and patience. Because the world out there will rarely reward you for these things in the short term, but it will revere you for them in the long run. And every day, every single day, take time to try and understand what your creator is doing with your life."

I paused for a brief second and chuckled lowly. "And if you don't think you have a creator, spend some time each day trying to figure out what makes you so sure." This brought an array of smiles from the teenagers.

"You see, I have come to realize that in this life, all things have their time and are gone. During our short years here we attain only a few glimpses of what perfection can be, of what heaven can hold; and those glimpses are what give us hope, give us courage, and remind us to hold tight to all that is good and true and enduring.

"I want to close by telling you something about myself. As many of you know, I grew up in a large city, went to college in a large city, learned my mad dancing skills you all saw at prom in a large city. And while I know that some of you may look to the distant horizons with great envy, I would submit to you that growing up there did not give me many of the advantages that you have had by growing up here in Watervalley.

"Life in the city did not teach me to appreciate slow winter days, or the change of the seasons, or the sweet, laughing sound a brook makes in springtime. It did not teach me to appreciate the multitude of colors that can be found in a sunset, the beauty of frost on an open field, or the good honest smell of a hay barn. It did not teach me the blessing of having a good neighbor, the joy of knowing that everyone I pass on the street knows my name, or the contentment of recognizing that there is a place where your roots are so deep, the storms of life cannot blow you away. It did not teach me a thousand things that have been second nature to each of you all your lives. Things that in their own way are beautiful, strong, and eternal. The earth endures, and living in Watervalley has taught you this. Living here has taught you to be close to the soil, to cherish friends, and community, and faith, and to know there is a place you can always call home. Never underestimate the value of your experiences here.

"Therefore, Watervalley High seniors, go. Go and live your lives, pursue your dreams, and follow your passions: whether they lie here or thousands of miles away. And know that your days in this small community, in this wide valley, among these familiar hills, have well prepared you to live a happy, fulfilled life. Good luck and God bless."

I finished to a thunderous standing ovation, one that I wasn't at all convinced I deserved. Nevertheless, I enjoyed the moment. Diplomas were awarded and the ceremony closed. Afterward, I received an endless array of handshakes and thanks. All the while, I was searching for Christine. But she was not to be found.

Eventually I saw Connie, who smiled at me in her stern way and spoke in a deadpan voice. "Nice speech, Doctor. I never knew you could be so funny. Maybe you should host a talk show."

"Thanks, I'll keep that in mind. Hey, you haven't seen where Christine went, have you? I saw you two sitting together."

"She went home."

"Oh, okay." I did my best to answer casually, still unsure if Connie knew about our falling-out.

"I think she was going to go riding on one of her horses." Her response was aloof, detached.

"Well, certainly a pretty day for that."

Connie stared at me flatly, offering me the opportunity to tell more. But I chose not to. Finally, resigned that her game of silence would yield nothing further, she added, "So, Doctor. There's still plenty of this fine, beautiful day in front of you. Whatcha going to do with yourself now?"

I stared out across the lake and up into the warm blue sky. Then, I gave her an answer that I don't think she was expecting.

"Connie, I think I'm going to go milk some cows."

CHAPTER 46
The Words

I drove home, changed into some blue jeans and boots, and drove the Corolla out to Christine's, thinking it was a better fit for the mud and manure of the farm than the Austin-Healey. I arrived shortly before two o'clock, parked beside the house, and immediately hiked the short distance to the dairy barn. Christine was nowhere to be seen.

I found Angus Pilkington in the concrete pit of the milk parlor, where he had just begun the afternoon milking. We shook hands and he seemed elated to see me.

"Dr. Bradford! What a grand thing! So, you've finally decided to give it a try?"

"Yup, Angus. Here I am. Put me in, coach."

We talked for another minute and Angus repeatedly expressed his delight that I had joined him. He found me a long rubber apron and gave me a short tutorial on how to prep the udders and attach the electric milker. The cows entered on either side of the pit and were fed while they were being milked. The four electric milkers hung in the middle and were alternated between each side.

It was a rancorous and noisy affair.

The cows bayed on a regular basis, the radio blasted country music, and the suction of the milk machines made a loud and constant *tonk-tish, tonk-tish* sound. Several of the cows turned from their feed troughs and tried to catch a glimpse of the newcomer. At Angus's instruction, I spoke to them in a soothing, steady voice to keep them relaxed and calm. Curiously, that's what kept the milk flowing.

Pretty soon I got the hang of using the milking apparatus and Angus showed me how to strip out the last of the milk by hand when that was called for. He talked nonstop, laughing and joking and telling me in great detail about each cow's history along with hilarious milking stories he'd accumulated over the years. I was having a great time.

Roughly two hours passed and the last of the herd had been brought into the parlor. I was sharing an endearing conversation with one of the older Holsteins when there was a light tap on my shoulder. I turned around to find Angus grinning from ear to ear and pointing to the landing at the end of the pit. There stood Christine with a delighted expression of shock and wonder.

"I think someone's looking for you," Angus said.

Christine and I exchanged smiles. She was wearing riding boots and pants and a white T-shirt.

"Time to turn in your apron, Doctor. I've got it from here."

Angus shook my hand vigorously and walked me to the front where Christine was standing, still regarding me with astonishment.

"Well, I was wondering where you were," she said. "I saw your car parked at the house and have been looking everywhere for the last half hour."

Angus slapped me on the back and responded enthusiastically,

"He helped me milk the whole herd and did just grand. The cows took an immediate liking to him. He's got the magic touch with them, I tell you, a real natural with the lady parts."

His comment was innocently intended, but I could tell that Christine and I conjured a different meaning from it. I proudly lifted my chin and nodded in agreement. She cut her eyes at me and suppressed an explosive laugh. I thanked Angus again and Christine and I walked outside into the afternoon sun. She had tied her horse to a nearby fence post.

Sunlight reflected off her dark hair, and as always, she was radiantly beautiful. I smiled affectionately. She spoke with fondness and uncertainty.

"So, you're milking cows?"

I folded my arms and continued to smile at her, awash in an unquenchable joy at seeing her again. "Yes. Yes, I am."

Christine nodded and looked away, tucking a lock of hair behind her ear. "I see."

She was nervous, off-balance, but her eyes kept returning to my fixed and adoring gaze. She seemed to be gathering herself, trying to read my thoughts.

She spoke cautiously. "So, is this your way of doing penance?"

Having asked this question, she searched my face, not wanting to miss the slightest nuance in my answer.

"No," I said firmly. I paused and looked into the deep well of her dark eyes. "This is my way of telling you that I'm in love with you. It's my way of telling you that you are the most beautiful, most fascinating woman I have ever known. It's my way of telling you that I don't know what will happen when my three years here are up. But it doesn't matter. Because in three years, and for years beyond that, I will still be in love with you."

Christine said nothing. She simply stepped toward me and

pressed her cheek against my chest, wrapping her arms around me in an embrace full of affection, belonging, release. I held her for the longest time and it seemed that she was content to stay right there, listening quietly to the beat of my heart, which now so unfailingly belonged to her.

I brought my hand lightly to the side of her face, lifting it toward mine. "I'm sorry. I should have told you this long before now."

She nodded and closed her eyes. We kissed, long and luxuriously. Again she pressed her cheek to my shoulder and held me tightly. I continued to gently cradle her face in my hand. It was a perfect and tender moment.

That was, until Christine spoke in a low, matter-of-fact voice.

"Bradford, as wonderful as all this is, your hand really smells like cow."

We immediately stepped apart and I stared blankly at my hand. Then we both erupted into foolish laughter.

"I'm sorry. Your hand was right there beside my nose and I just couldn't stop thinking about it."

For me, however, the temptation was too great. I stepped toward her with both hands extended and spoke in a haughty voice of teasing sarcasm. "Oh, no, no, no. Darling, please, let me hold your lovely face, just for, you know, an hour or two."

Christine continued to cackle and pushed me away. "Bradford, that is not fair."

I lifted my arms in surrender and smiled at her warmly. "Okay, Chambers. You can't have it both ways. Love me, love my cow smell."

Christine continued to laugh but regarded me artfully, not wanting to yield to my playful ultimatum. Then she stepped toward me, gave me a taunting smile, and looped her hands around my neck, standing at arm's length. For a few moments, she said nothing, but offered only an enticing, devilish grin.

And in the span of those brief seconds, I wondered.

I wondered if she knew how incredibly seductive and electrifying she was when she did these things. Her warm, alluring smile, the light touch of her hands, and the subtle message in her willfully raised arms . . . a gesture that left her generous and sensuous curves unshielded and inviting . . . all stirred within me a maddening desire. She was so intelligent and intuitive. She had to know her effect on me.

Or did she? Was this instead simply a spontaneous and innocent expression of affection, with no awareness of the incredible primal emotions she aroused? I had to laugh at myself. I knew I loved her passionately. But there was so much about her that I didn't understand. It seemed that part of love's mystery was the unexplainable delight of knowing that she could and would always fascinate me.

Her voice brought me back. "How about this? Love you, love you with a bath."

The sparkle in her eyes was intoxicating. "Well, since you asked so nicely . . . what say you walk me to my car?"

Christine untied the reins and led her horse as we walked back to the house. The huge animal seemed pleased to be free of a rider and to walk leisurely. She and I held hands but talked little as we made our way down the farm road. She seemed wonderfully happy. Nothing more was necessary.

We arrived at my car and Christine tied the horse's reins to one of the porch railings.

"He's a beautiful animal by the way."

"Thanks," she responded. "His name is Casper. He's a three-year-old stallion. A little rambunctious still, but a real sweetheart once you get to know him."

"I'll take your word on that."

"You want to ride him?"

I responded cautiously. "Wow, I don't know. First milking cows and now this. That's kind of pushing the envelope on the whole farm immersion thing. Not sure riding a horse is in my comfort zone."

Christine was undaunted. "Well, the way Mr. Pilkington talked, you're a natural with animals. Why don't you give it a try?"

"Why do I feel like Casper is not the only one with a bit in his mouth?"

"Oh, come on. You might really enjoy it."

I shrugged and responded half under my breath, "Sure. Nothing says I love you like riding a horse."

Christine smiled and began to untie the reins.

"You mount on the left side, don't you?"

"That's correct."

I was standing on the horse's right, so I proceeded to walk around his tail. But I must have passed too close for comfort for Casper. Because as I rounded his rump, he kicked backward with his left leg and caught me squarely on my shinbone.

"Ooow! Holy crap, that hurts!"

Christine retied the reins and was immediately by my side. "Luke, I'm so sorry. I'm so sorry."

The pain was so excruciating that I literally had to stop and catch my breath.

"He's never kicked anyone. I don't know what happened."

"Here, just let me go sit." I hobbled over to the porch steps and plopped down. As I sat, cringing in pain, I noticed in the distance that a truck was turning in from the highway and proceeding up Christine's driveway. The throbbing pain was shooting up my leg. Instinctively, I knew the bone wasn't broken, but the sharpness of the injury was excruciating.

Christine sat beside me awash with apologies. Spontaneous tears involuntarily formed in my eyes due to the sting and suddenness. I rocked slightly, waiting for the severity of the agony to subside.

By now the truck had pulled to a stop and none other than John Harris emerged. He walked toward us and began to climb the steps. But when he saw my red and grimacing face, he paused to assess the situation and offer some choice words of comfort. "Huh. See, sport. I told you this one would have you crying like a little girl."

CHAPTER 47
The Garden

The next morning I was out of bed and finishing my coffee by six o'clock. Other than a nasty bruise, my leg was fine and I didn't want it to stop me from my plans. It was Saturday, and the ribbon cutting for the grand opening of the bakery would be held promptly at ten. But I had something to do before then. I was going to plant a garden.

Perhaps I was still riding a wave of exhilaration from all that had happened in the last twenty-four hours, but I had decided to take John and Connie's advice and try my hand at raising a few vegetables. I had arranged to have a tiller delivered from the Farmers' Co-op so I could break up a patch of ground in the backyard. After leaving Christine's the previous afternoon, I had stopped at the Co-op and picked up some seeds and fertilizer along with half an hour's worth of unwanted but well-intended advice.

At six thirty the Co-op delivery truck pulled into the driveway. It was Lester from the loading dock. Together we used a motorized tailgate to lower the tiller to the ground. I have to admit it was one of the more surreal experiences of my life to hear Lester articulate insightful and highly useful information regarding the proper use of the machine, employing three- and even four-syllable words. The day was rife with marvels.

After he departed, I rolled the tiller to a sunny section of the backyard where the grass was thin. I put on gloves, but for some reason, before pulling the start cord, I stood and leaned against the handles and absorbed my surroundings. The wind stirred the leaves of the nearby trees and the early morning sun shone brilliantly. Yet for a brief second I thought I heard the distant murmur of a sweet, familiar hymn, borne on the breeze.

"Well, sounds like the angels are having a good day."

I shook my head and laughed at myself. Only a place like Watervalley could make me say such a thing, or listen for voices in the chasing wind.

I pulled the start cord and the tiller motor roared to life. Bracing myself, I engaged the rotors and began breaking up the lawn before me. It was a slow grind, but productive. The tines dug deep into the black dirt, mincing the clods into a fine, workable soil.

The machine jostled and tossed me and I chugged along sluggishly. Occasionally I would stop and cast aside the clumps of grass that had been broken free. But in time the dark earth began to yield to the pounding of the tines, and admittedly, I found the work deeply satisfying. Until I had traveled about twenty feet.

Suddenly, the tiller rotors began to bang and clank and kick up wildly. I disengaged the tines and shut off the engine. Bending low to the ground, I began to brush the dirt away to find out what had made the tiller shudder so violently, thinking I had hit a large rock.

But instead of a rock it was a metal container.

The size of a large shoe box, it was made of heavy steel and had been buried about six inches under the soil. Two large clasps held the hinged lid and base snugly together. I managed to wedge it out from where it had been caked in the ground. After removing my gloves, I released the rusty clasps and lifted the lid. My heart jumped at what lay before me.

The box contained a rusted pocketknife and a small, equally rusted revolver. I carefully set these aside. Underneath I found deteriorated documents and a leather wallet which was still loosely intact by the tethers of old stitching. I peeled it open and found some illegible and ruined pieces of paper, smudged and glued together from time and moisture, along with the remnants of some dollar bills. Below that was a rotted cloth bag.

My pulse began to race as the reality of what I was looking at hit me full force. The gun, the knife, and the wallet: all of these had been missing from the Oscar Fox crime scene. I carefully pulled at the cloth sack. Weakened from years in the moist earth, it fell apart instantly. And there before me, glistening beautifully and brilliantly in the morning sun, lay a large cache of diamonds.

Stunned, I could do little more than sit in the soft grass. I was endeavoring to understand, to connect the dots. The story as it must have played out began to unfold in my imagination.

The first thing I did when I could finally move was call Warren Thurman, the sheriff.

Within the hour he and I were seated at my kitchen table, both of us still in a state of wonder. We reasoned that all those years ago, Oscar Fox had somehow made it home from the crime scene with these items and cleverly buried them along with the diamonds in the backyard of his neighbor, Lovett Mayfield.

It was ingenious. No doubt, Lovett had already broken up his garden area, making it easy for Oscar to bury the box with his hands. Oscar knew that an investigation would call for a thorough search of his own home and property. A freshly dug hole in his own yard would be easily noticed. No one would think to look in Lovett Mayfield's garden. Apparently, the box had been buried on the back fringe of the plowed area and had never been discovered. For some reason, Oscar was returning to the crime scene when he died. Yet everyone assumed he had been fleeing it. I recalled that he had run track at Dartmouth and had likely covered the mile distance to his house and back out to the bandstand in such a short time that no one would have guessed he had been home.

All told, we counted over two hundred cut diamonds in various shapes and sizes. Warren and I could only shake our heads, staring at each other in astonishment.

Finally he said, "I guess Oscar wanted to hide anything that connected him to his past. He probably thought that if people figured out the other guy was German, it would raise questions about his own identity."

"So, Warren. What happens now?" I asked.

In his slow, easy way Warren smiled at me. "Doc, I'm glad you called me and brought me into the loop on this. But here's how I see things. The papers from the wallet are all but destroyed, so I guess we'll never know who the German fellow was. I wouldn't be surprised if his identification was fake anyway. These diamonds aren't a police matter. Beyond a doubt, they belonged to Oscar Fox, and like we've talked about before, the statute of limitations on anything involving him has long since passed. Now admittedly, the town of Watervalley does own this property and is merely loaning it to you during your time here. But no one in his right mind can seriously believe that the town has any rightful claim to the diamonds."

"Then who does own them?"

"Seems simple enough to me. They belong to Oscar's family, to Louise and Will."

"What about the company Oscar worked for? Wouldn't they have some claim to them?"

Warren shrugged. "You tell me, Doc. From what I understand, the company went defunct and the diamonds all belonged to Oscar's relatives in the first place, that is, before the Nazis took over their business. I say they go to Louise. If she finds other family members with a claim, what she does about it is up to her."

I was elated. "Can we give them to her now?"

Again, Warren shrugged. "Don't see any reason why not."

I doubt I could ever describe the look of shock and elation on the faces of Louise and Will Fox as Warren and I explained the situation to them. We four sat in the Fox living room as I unfolded the cloth in which I had placed the diamonds. Tears of joy and deliverance filled Louise's eyes and began to fall down her face. Although more quiet, Will was equally excited, hugging his mother repeatedly. She was so beside herself with exclamations of amazement and delight, I thought I might need to give her a sedative. But soon enough she regained control of herself and offered Warren and me an endless stream of earnest thanks.

Warren said, "Listen, as a formality I'm going to let the mayor know about this. But past that, Luke, I'm going to let you and Louise decide who else should hear the story."

Louise responded immediately, "I'll be glad to let Dr. Bradford tell it to whomever he likes."

I smiled at them both. "I'll tell Connie. That way, by my calculations, everyone in the town of Watervalley and all the way up to the international space station will have the news by Monday."

A minute later, Warren rose, bid good-bye, and made his departure. I lingered for a moment longer, then stood to do the same.

Louise gave me a long hug. "Thank you so much for all you've done for Will and me."

"I'm happy for the both of you, Louise. Maybe this can turn things around for you. No doubt, you can pay off the mortgage and maybe set some college money aside for Will." I reached over and briskly rubbed his head.

"Our lives won't be the same," she confirmed, then looked at her watch. "Oh, my goodness! Look at the time. The grand opening is in less than an hour and I need to be there in the next ten minutes. I can't be late for my first day on the job."

I smiled broadly. "I'm sure Connie and Estelle will understand, given the circumstances. Just send Will over to my house later and he can ride with me."

"Are you certain that's okay?"

"More than okay. I've been promising him a ride in the Austin-Healey anyway."

Louise clasped my hand in hers. "Thank you, again."

I departed her front door practically walking on air. The sun, the sky, the wind, and the trees engulfed my senses and I soaked them all in. Lightly humming a familiar tune, I made my way to the backyard and started up the tiller once again.

At nine thirty there was a knock on my front door. I had just cleaned up and dressed and was pouring a glass of iced tea.

"Come in!" I shouted from the kitchen.

Will strolled in, his curiosity-filled eyes absorbing everything. Rhett wagged his tail in excited expectation of a few pats on the head. Will was happy to oblige.

"Hey, Will, want something to drink?" I asked.

"No. I'm good."

"You know, I've got a question. That comic book you were writing, Captain Blue Jeans—did you ever finish it?"

"Nah. I'm dragging it out."

"Dragging it out? I don't understand."

"It's just a way to spend a little one-on-one with Wendy Wilson since she was doing all the artwork. I kind of like her."

"Well, Will Fox. Aren't you the clever Casanova? So, tell me more."

Will assumed a confidential tone, speaking in a manner that made me think he was passing along classified information critical to national security. "We're just good friends. She's one of the few girls around that actually has a brain. But we're keeping everything on the down low. Around here, people talk."

I offered a ponderous nod, but I was cracking up inside. "Probably a smart idea." I paused for a long moment, then added, "So, have you kissed her?" I couldn't resist giving some of his own medicine back.

He cut his eyes at me and spoke with as much hauteur as a twelve-year-old could muster. "In the words of the twenty-first-century philosopher Luke Bradford, 'That's none of your business.'"

I laughed out loud. "Come on, big man. Let's get going."

We buckled ourselves into the Austin-Healey and I took a short detour out toward the lake to let Will experience the feel of the open convertible. He smiled nonstop on the way there, but as we pulled into the bandstand's parking lot, it occurred to me that this place had history for Will and coming here might have been a poor choice. To my surprise, however, he asked me to stop the car.

We sat for a minute as he carefully studied the new bandstand. After a few moments, he said, "You know, Dr. Bradford, it's a funny thing. I've always lived with a bad feeling about my last name because of all the old stories. You hear things, people let things slip, and it leaves you wondering if your family's past is always going to be this weight you have to carry around."

He paused and looked at me. "Now I'm wondering if I can live up to my family's past."

I nodded and thought about his words, about my own father and his choice to remain a small-town doctor despite the much grander opportunities that came his way.

"Well, Will. If I have learned anything from the legacy of your great-grandfather, it is that life is short and precious and that you have to make the most of each shining hour." We sat just steps away from where Oscar had taken his last breath. And yet an abiding peace floated in the soft spring air, a sense of completion. It seemed that all the good that Oscar had intended had permeated the years and finally surfaced in the fullness of time. I spoke again.

"Hold your head high, Will. You come from good people."

He nodded thoughtfully and we sat in silence for another minute. Finally, he turned to me with a face of quiet resolve. "Thanks, Dr. Bradford. Thanks for bringing me here."

I smiled and reached over, tousling his hair. "You bet."

I turned the Austin-Healey around and headed toward town. It was time to celebrate.

CHAPTER 48
Celebration

We arrived at the bakery ten minutes before the ribbon-cutting ceremony. Downtown Watervalley seemed to be dressed for some great occasion and Connie's fears that no one would come to the grand opening couldn't have been more misplaced. It seemed that everyone in the valley had shown up.

The bakery side of Courthouse Square had been cordoned off and the sidewalk, street, and courthouse lawn were packed with throngs of people, some of them tapping their feet to a lively bluegrass band. I parked and before wading into the boisterous crowd, I joked to Will, "They don't teach you this in Anatomy and Physiology, but one thing's for sure. Everybody has a sweet tooth."

Will headed off toward some classmates and I found Christine talking with John. Smiles were everywhere and I quickly became caught up in the general delight and anticipation.

The ribbon cutting and sign unveiling were only moments away when Louise Fox approached the three of us with a panicked look on her face.

"Connie wanted me to ask if you three can help. The crowd is five times what we anticipated and we could use a few extra hands."

John, Christine, and I responded simultaneously, "Sure."

Louise led us through the crowd to where customers were lined up, waiting for the ceremony to start and for the front doors to open. We slipped inside, past display cases loaded with light-as-air pastries and breads, and into the hot kitchen, where we found Connie and Estelle in a fluster of activity. But they weren't alone. Dressed in a white apron was Lida Wilkins. Apparently she had come by two hours earlier to wish them luck and realized that they desperately needed help.

She wiped her forehead as we entered and winked at me. "Hot dog, the cavalry has arrived!"

"Lida Wilkins, just look at you," I exclaimed. "Aren't you a saint?"

"Saint, my foot," she replied. "If it gets any hotter in here, the two sisters and I are going to change our names to Shadrach, Meshach, and Abednego." She grinned, scrunching her nose in that delightful way of hers.

Connie explained the situation. "By the looks of the crowd, we are way low on the number of free cupcakes we've made."

"Gâteaux!" blurted out Estelle as she darted by carrying a huge bowl of frosting.

"Whatever! Anyway, we're making a bunch more but need help getting them decorated and arranged out front."

Lida joined in. "Connie, you and Estelle scat and go do the ribbon cutting. I'll direct traffic back here. We've got this. You two go have your Kodak moment."

The two sisters thanked Lida profusely and then shed their aprons and headed out front. Lida took control.

"Okay, team, we've got about fifteen or twenty minutes before the floodgates open."

She gave assignments to the three of us. At first, we were out of sync, but soon we fell into a working rhythm. Flour and frosting was everywhere, but it was great fun. During the thick of it, Louise came over and spoke in a low voice. "Why don't you tell them the big news?"

Christine and Lida overheard her, and sent me looks full of curiosity.

"Are you sure?" I asked.

Louise nodded excitedly. "I'd like you to do it."

By now, even John had caught on that something was astir. Everyone paused in what they were doing and looked at me.

"Well, everyone, this morning while I was tilling up a garden, I found a metal box containing a cache of diamonds in my backyard."

We lost several minutes of production time while everyone listened with astonishment to the story of the discovery. Lida and Christine both hugged Louise, who tearfully thanked them. She no longer was the pale wisp of a woman I had known, but seemed to find great delight in her new role at the bakery. Eventually, we returned to the tasks at hand.

John and I had frosting duty and he took the opportunity to chide me on a different subject. "So, sport. I heard you were milking cows yesterday. Don't tell me you're going native on us."

"Ha! Seems like I'm not the first guy in this duo to milk cows because of a pretty brunette."

John laughed. "Touché."

"And for your information, I had just been kicked in the leg by the horse when you arrived yesterday. It hurt, big-time. That's what the tears were about."

John feigned looking around to make sure Christine was out of earshot. "Yeah, I'm betting another little filly has kicked you elsewhere." He tapped on my chest with his index finger.

I laughed. "Well, John, politically incorrect female references aside, I wouldn't deny that insight for one minute." He smiled and returned his attention to the scores of cooling cupcakes.

In time the doors opened and Connie asked me if I would attend the cash register while she and Estelle waited on customers, wrapping up one delicious treat after another. Running the register turned out to be a wonderful job. I got to talk to everybody.

One of the first in line was Margie Reynolds.

"How's the pregnancy coming these days, Margie?" I asked.

"Oh, just peachy, Doc. Among all my other gifts I now realize I have the gift of consumption. I've consumed my body weight in cupcakes. If I eat one more thing, I'll be visible from space."

"I think you're being a little hard on yourself."

"Are you kidding? Right now I could snort powdered sugar through a garden hose." She winked at me as I returned her change. "And, by the way, the pregnancy is going great. I'll see you next week."

The next few hours were filled with an endless stream of familiar faces. Maylen Cook, Reverend Joe Dawson, Nancy Orman, Chick McKissick, Madeline, the sheriff, and the mayor along with seemingly hundreds of others made their way through. Even Sunflower Miller showed up and bought some artisan bread.

She was back to full health and full of herself, as opinionated as ever. "I can't say I completely endorse this diabetes factory," she commented.

I smiled, seeing right through her facade of indignation.

"Sunflower, you have the most beautiful skin. How do you keep it looking so fresh and youthful?"

I had caught her off guard. She looked at me for a brief moment of delight and vulnerability. Then, just that quickly, she regained herself.

"Forget it, Doctor. It's genetic and unattainable."

But it was too late, and my knowing smirk told as much. As she gathered up her package, she smiled at me cunningly with all the weight of her stunning Norwegian good looks and whispered, "You're going to pay for that."

By one thirty the steady line had ended, but dozens of folks still lingered, crowding the store and the sidewalk, talking, laughing, and just generally gossiping. Apparently, the story of the diamonds hadn't spread yet. But it was only a matter of time. John and Christine had been relieved of kitchen duty and Ann had arrived as well. Louise came to take over at the register, but before I stepped away, she pressed an envelope in my hand.

"You can open this later. It's just a quick thank-you."

"Well, Louise, that's certainly not necessary."

I wanted to say more, but a line of customers had formed again at the cash register. I stuffed the envelope in my back pocket and joined John, Ann, and Christine at one of the small tables. Just as I sat down, however, a sudden hush came over the crowd. I noticed everyone staring toward the front door.

Standing two steps in from the entry was Randall Simmons wearing a face of quiet contrition. Though it had never been on the front page, no doubt everyone in this crowded room was aware of the strife that had come between Connie and him. She was standing behind the counter, and at first, she froze. John began to rise from the table, but I reached over and gestured him to wait a moment.

Randall was looking at the floor, petrified as well, seemingly regretting he had come and at a loss regarding what to do next. Connie pursed her lips and grabbed a cupcake, then stepped out from behind the counter. Amid the silence she walked straight up to Randall and stopped in front of him as he looked up to meet her gaze.

Connie raised her chin and regarded him through the lower half of her glasses. She spoke with diplomatic reserve. "Hello, Randall. This is one of our specialty cupcakes. Here, try it."

He nodded, took it from her hand, and bit off a healthy bite.

"It's a special recipe," Connie explained. "You can barely taste the arsenic."

Randall halted in midchew.

Connie looked at him innocently. "Go ahead, eat up now."

He still didn't move and, instead, remained anxiously fixated on her.

Releasing a sly giggle, Connie reached over and took the cupcake from him, peeled back part of the paper, and took a large bite. "Umm," she exclaimed. "Pretty darn good, isn't it?"

Randall began to nod slowly, swallowing the bite he had in his mouth. "Very good, actually." He politely took the cupcake from Connie, took another bite, and handed it back to her. She finished it and the two of them shared guarded but accommodating smiles.

"Come on, Randall. I'll show you what else we've got that you might like."

Discussions picked up again as she led him to a display counter and within moments the cacophony of a dozen conversations had resumed.

John continued to scrutinize Randall and spoke with shrewd calculation. "Well, I'd say that about right now, over at Rose Hill Cemetery, Raymond Simmons is beginning to slowly rotate."

We talked and laughed for another hour, enjoying all the delight and celebration. The opening had been a grand success. John and Ann rose to leave, saying that they were going to open a bottle of wine down at the bandstand.

"Have fun, kids," I said. "Don't go skinny-dipping."

John turned back and spoke flatly. "At our age, sport, we don't skinny-dip. It's more like chunky dunk." Ann swatted him in the stomach.

"Leave, now. Both of you."

Christine and I watched them depart.

"My uncle John brought me here. So you're my ride," she said.

"I'm good with that. Give me a moment, though. I want to go speak to Connie before we go."

"Sure."

I found Connie outside the back door, sitting by herself and taking a break in one of two folding chairs. She sat with her arms crossed and her legs extended like a boxer resting in a corner. She was staring blankly at the wall across the alley.

"Hey, you okay?" I asked softly.

Her gaze never wavered. "Sure. I haven't had this much fun since the last time I played Twister."

I sat beside her in the other chair. "You look tired."

"Sweetie, I'm exhausted. I'm not sure why, but I've been dreading this day. Now I wonder what in the world I was thinking. It's gone fabulously."

"Estelle seems happy."

"Are you kidding? Right now she thinks she's the queen of culinary. The only thing she forgot today was to bring her tiara."

"I guess you can't tease her anymore about the bakery being a bad idea."

"Yeah, the first step off that high horse is going to be a doozy."

I laughed. "You might free-fall a little, but I'm sure you'll stick your landing."

She chuckled lightly and a long silence ensued.

"So, are you at peace with Randall now that the two of you have broken cupcake together?"

Connie's cheerful face dissolved into a sour frown of resignation. "Yeah. I guess so. I still just wanted to punch him in the nose."

"Understood."

"But I couldn't. It was one of Momma's rules. She always said you have to act your way into feeling right because you'll never feel your way into acting right."

"Meaning . . . do the right thing and in time you'll feel better about it."

"Yeah."

I nodded silently. Another long minute passed.

"You know, Luke, I think I've always jinxed myself."

"How so?"

"When I was a little girl, I thought that if I ever did even one teeny tiny little thing wrong, God would punish me, big-time. And because of that one mistake, I would end up as a strange old woman with gin on my breath, bad teeth, and weird, spiky hair. I'd wander around downtown, mumbling to myself and wearing layers of smelly clothes and an old pair of men's basketball shoes. And I'd carry this big plastic trash bag of aluminum cans and spend all my time feeding pigeons and rummaging through Dumpsters."

She paused. Then, with an enlightened look on her face, she added, "And you know, sometimes I think I'd like to give it a try."

We both laughed for a solid minute. I finally rose to my feet, bent over, and kissed her on the forehead.

"I think your mother still lives in the stones of this place."

She took my hand, enclosed it in both of hers, and looked up at me, smiling warmly. "Thank you, sweetheart. I think you're right."

After a pause, she spoke again. "Going out with Christine tonight?"

"That's my plan."

"Well, have fun."

"Thanks, see you."

"Luke." She paused. With her chin lowered, she regarded me sharply over the top of her glasses. "Not too much fun. You understand?"

I let out a low laugh. "Yes, ma'am."

I found Christine at the table talking to Will. As I approached, he spoke with a sly grin. "She says you're a lousy kisser."

Christine regarded both of us with a curious and startled face, clearly having said no such thing.

"Nice try, buddy. Go fish." He and I exchanged crafty smiles and I went on the offensive. "Are you familiar with the phrase 'People who live in glass houses'?"

Will heard me but was distracted by the arrival of Hoot Wilson coming through the entry. His daughter, Wendy, was with him.

"Yeah, we'll talk about it later. I gotta go."

"What was that all about?" Christine inquired casually.

"Eh, guy talk. Nothing important. You ready?"

Together, we walked out onto the sidewalk.

"So, brown eyes. What do you want to do on this fine warm evening?"

Christine's voice was lighthearted, animated. "Why don't we get a pizza and a blanket and go out to Moon Lake and watch the sunset? I love it out there."

"Sure. I'm game for an evening of takeout and make-out."

Christine rolled her eyes and smiled warily. "Bradford, you are soooo predictable. That's not exactly what I meant."

Undaunted, I quickly responded, "Predictable, huh? Maybe it's because you are soooo beautiful. And I do mean that!"

"Just listen to you! You're doing so much better at finding the right thing to say. I am so proud of you."

"Okay, first of all, I am going to ignore the fact that you said that in your schoolteacher voice and are clearly trying to use your behavior modification tactics on me. Second, I'll have you know, Miss Chambers, that I know plenty of words, and candidly, well, you ain't seen nothing yet."

Christine lowered her chin. Playfully, she placed her fingers over my lips. Then she lifted one of her eyebrows, smiled that wonderful, taunting, seductive smile, and whispered three simple words ever so slowly and deliciously into my ear.

"Neither have you!"

She turned and walked toward the Austin-Healey, but I stood motionless, giving myself a moment to regain the power of speech. I was in way over my head with her, and I knew it. Something told me that she knew it too.

I began to follow her but stopped at the street to turn back and admire the marvelous details of the newly finished bakery. It was only then that I realized that I had yet to see the now unveiled sign.

"Well, how about that?" I said.

Something about the name was magically perfect, capturing what living in Watervalley was all about. I smiled deeply, turned, and stepped away. Glowing behind me in the soft light of that wonderful May afternoon was the neon sign of the town's new bakery: THE SWEETLIFE.

POSTLUDE

*T*oward midnight, Luke stood in the dark of his backyard, admiring the splendor of the vast and luminous universe above him. He hadn't wanted the day to end. He breathed in deeply of the moist, fragrant air and his thoughts drifted to that moment in his office months ago.

The autopsy report had been nothing more than a yellowed piece of paper from an ancient folder, long forgotten and hidden for years in a dusty filing cabinet. At the time it had seemed insignificant. But now, looking back, he realized how that one piece of paper had connected so many lives; had linked them over time and distance with an invisible thread, stepping indifferently across the boundaries of race, education, fortune, and faith.

Standing in the silent moonlight, Luke thought of Oscar Fox, of how decades ago he had come to Watervalley, started a new life, and come so close to realizing his dream. Luke thought of Oscar's noble kindness, of the incredible love he must have felt for Elise, and how one moment had changed all of that. He wondered if Oscar's last *thoughts were of her, wondered if in those last desperate minutes Oscar saw a lifetime of promised happiness slipping away.*

Luke thought of his own dreams. And there, under the grand canopy of stars, an indefinable serenity washed over him, a contented awareness of the richness of his life being played out within the shouldering hills of this small valley.

He looked up, starring briefly into the infinite, voiceless heavens, and slid his hands into his back pockets. He pulled out an envelope and realized it was the one Louise Fox had given him earlier in the day. He held it up toward the distant porch light and used his thumb to break the seal. Inside he found a letter. When he unfolded it, he also discovered a small, tightly sealed plastic bag. Written in elegant script on the letter were the words, "THANK YOU," and inside the bag was one large, shimmering diamond, radiant even in the faint moonlight.

Luke shook his head. It was an incredible gesture, a gift that was completely unnecessary and over-the-top. Even still, he suspected that Louise would not hear of accepting it back.

He held the small bag high above him and studied the diamond against the backdrop of distant stars. And as he did, a powerful thought came to him, capturing him with a euphoric, exhilarating idea.

He returned everything to the envelope and placed it back in his pocket. Again, he inhaled deeply, drawing in the warm, fresh, intoxicating aromas of the night, the splendid air of Eden. His thoughts were sublimely occupied, filled with tender musings. Unhurriedly, he began to make his way through the dewy grass toward the distant porch light.

All the while, his mind was consumed with a single word . . . Christine, Christine, Christine.

ACKNOWLEDGMENTS

For me, writing is a family affair, meaning . . . I couldn't pull it off without their support. Heartfelt thanks go to my wife, Dawn, who brings a wonderful balance to some of my zany ideas for plot and story, and who graciously endures my frustration when she doesn't absolutely love my first drafts. As well, huge thanks go to my son, Austin, who brilliantly created, ex nihilo, the watervalleybooks.com Web site and who continues to be the brains and organizer of the business side of writing books.

Also, sincere thanks for all their support go out to dear friends from the old Columbia, Belmont, and Vandy gangs, including Marsha, Jeri Ann, Cindy, Phyllis, Vicki, Kim, Terri, Teresa, Pam, Jane, Amy, and Melissa. You guys are more wonderful than you know.

A special thank-you to Joe Evans for his continued enthusiasm and mentoring is also in order. And to Jim Ross for his ever-steady encouragement.

As always, thanks to my agent, Susan Gleason, for guiding me through another project.

And finally, a huge thanks to my most excellent editor, Ellen Edwards, who once again has patiently and meticulously helped me craft a wonderful story. You're the best!

Photo by Amanda Hagler

After growing up on a farm in rural Tennessee, **Jeff High** attained degrees in literature and nursing. He is the three-time winner, in fiction and poetry, of an annual writing contest held by Vanderbilt Medical Center. He lived in Nashville for many years, and throughout the country as a travel nurse, before returning to his original hometown, near where he now works as an operating room RN in open-heart surgery.

CONNECT ONLINE

watervalleybooks.com
facebook.com/watervalleybooks

EACH SHINING HOUR

A NOVEL OF WATERVALLEY

JEFF HIGH

A CONVERSATION WITH
JEFF HIGH

Q. Each Shining Hour *is your second novel. How did your experience of writing it compare to writing your first book,* More Things in Heaven and Earth?

A. *More Things in Heaven and Earth* was written over a period of several years, and I experimented with several different writing styles before settling on the first-person mode. So with *Each Shining Hour*, I had a working framework from which to build the story. I think this allowed me to place a greater focus on the twists and turns of the plot.

Q. At the heart of Each Shining Hour *lies a double homicide—the only murder in the history of your fictional community, Watervalley, Tennessee. What inspired you to center your story around a murder?*

A. Murder is still the ultimate misdeed. I grew up in the sixties on a large farm in a sleepy rural community. Few murders occurred. But when they did, they consumed us because they were so foreign to the life we knew. Serious crime spoke of discord and brought doubt into how we saw our lives. By small degrees, it forced us to redefine our understanding of our small world. Thus, a murder in a small community resonated with me from all those years ago as a defining moment that changed everything.

Q. I love your strong, forthright female characters—Estelle Pillow, Lida Wilkins, Ann Patterson, and, of course, Connie Thompson. You've told me that you believe such women form the backbone of small Southern communities. Can you explain what you mean?

A. I can't speak for other parts of the country, but women in the South have many diverse expectations placed upon them. They are expected to be devoted wives and mothers; be committed to either church or community work, or both; hold down jobs outside the home; and, whenever possible, look like a million bucks. Just go to an SEC football game and see how the women are dressed. I have known many women who have led selfless, hardworking lives with an unimaginable devotion to their families and communities. They are the glue of Southern life.

Q. Much of this novel seems to be about how events in the past continue to exert an influence on the present. In your experience, is that especially true of small towns, where people tend to stay put from one generation to another?

A. Absolutely. Significant events, especially tragic ones, become part of the shared history of people in a small community. As the years pass, references to those events become part of the common vernacular, an unspoken understanding that transcends economic status, or race, or education. And these events—whether a murder, a flood, the death of a local soldier in combat, or even the loss of a major high school football game—have a ripple effect on people for years to come.

Q. Luke Bradford notices that Christine Chambers, who has recently returned to Watervalley from Atlanta, has an "urban polish." He, and everyone else in town, can tell right away that she's lived in a city. How the heck do they know?

A. It may come as a surprise to some, but the urban South is high on style. How your hair is cut, how you speak, what you wear—they matter. We are social creatures, and these subtle influences permeate our choices if we are part of a larger city for any length of time. It is not an issue of vanity or shallowness; it is the reality of our nature. Typically, small towns, especially remote ones, simply don't have the same multitude of choices and influences. Dress and language tend to be more homogenized and generic. So, when you meet someone from an urban environment . . . you can tell.

Q. One of my favorite things about Luke is that he's such a dreamer. He daydreams in his backyard, looking at the stars. He daydreams while jogging along Summerfield Road, thinking about Christine Chambers. He daydreams in his office between seeing patients. Is daydreaming still alive and well in the South, or is it in danger of disappearing, like so many "old-fashioned" activities that require time and leisure? (I could go on and on about how nobody whistles anymore!)

A. I think it is alive and well in the South. . . but typically starts with the statement "After I win the lottery, I'm going to . . ." That being said, without a doubt the pace of rural small-town life is slower and lends itself to reflection. In the twilight hours we work in our gardens, we talk to our next-door neighbors, we hear the sounds of the Little League game being played in the park across the way, and we dream about going to the beach. As well, Luke is an idealist . . . always dreaming about what life could be. In *Each Shining Hour*, this begins to change. He begins to evolve his understanding about perceived perfection and living in the moment.

Q. In this book you introduce travel nurse Ann Patterson. You once worked as a travel nurse. Being from the North, I'm not familiar with the concept. Can you explain it? Do certain regions of the country rely more heavily on travel nurses than others?

A. Actually, travel nursing is common all across the country. Typically, the jobs occur in thirteen-week assignments and are for an RN specialty. For a while, I traveled as a cardiac operating room nurse. Remote assignments like the one Ann Patterson takes in Watervalley are less prevalent. However, travel nursing is a great way to experience different parts of the country and become immersed in the local culture for a short period. I loved it. And I can't help but mention that once, on an assignment in Oregon, several people mentioned that they loved the way I talked. I told them I was from the South. This was invariably met with "No joke." How did they know?

Q. Another aspect of this book I noticed, and enjoyed, is that even dead people are not really dead to those who loved them. Connie's mother, Maylene; John's wife, Molly; Christine's father, Albert were all strong influences in their lives, and continue to inspire their choices and attitudes. This strikes me as so true to life. Care to comment?

A. This is unquestionably true. People in our past who loved us, and whom we truly loved, continue to speak to us, guiding our choices and our expectations of ourselves. The richness of our experiences with them lends richness, meaning, and order to our daily lives. This is also true of those we have lost and didn't get an opportunity to love enough. We are haunted in both positive and sometimes sorrowful ways by those who are no longer with us.

Q. The theme of redemption also runs through the novel. Was that intentional?

A. Very much so. I guess this is a rich part of my world and life view. Some might consider it naive, but I tend to think that in the fullness of time, things tend to work out in ways that are positive and redemptive. They don't always happen on our time schedule, or even in our lifetimes. But regardless of one's personal beliefs, the human condition seems to be such that we eventually find resolution for injustice. All too often we simply don't have the patience or the imagination to look for it and see it.

Q. I love the Watervalley characters, but you also provide vivid descriptions of the landscape and town: the winter-barren farm fields; a late-night bonfire at Moon Lake; the creepy overgrown cemetery where Luke and Christine find Oscar Fox's grave marker; and the town square jumping with people and lively with music during the Runs with Scissors race. Such scenes have stayed with me long after I finished the book. Are such places as real for you as they are for us readers?

A. Yes, and it may be either a blessing or a curse of my writing style, but I have a tremendous sense of place when I write. It is critically important to me that the reader be transported by the texture, the smells, the color, the light, the excitement, and even the awkwardness of what the characters are experiencing. But these sensations have to be conveyed with an economy of words or the story begins to drag. Admittedly, sometimes I get carried away with these narrative descriptions. Maybe at heart I'm just a frustrated (or not very good) poet looking for that perfect collection of words to capture a scene.

Q. Your novels poke gentle fun at human foibles, including Luke's. I particularly love when Mattie Chambers threatens Luke, and when Lester Caruthers is described as needing "special pills" for LOA (lack of ambition). Do such ideas come from a lifetime's observations? Do you carry a notebook around and take notes about what you see and hear?

A. Not exactly . . . but there is some truth to your suggestion. I hear funny things every day, and it has become a habit to write them down. I have pages and pages of notes, and often in the course of writing, I will refer back to them to see if something fits a certain character or scene. I never use most of them, but somehow writing them down helps me; the act empowers me to translate a certain mood or conversation onto the page.

Q. Life in Watervalley feels timeless. I can imagine much of the action taking place in any decade of the later twentieth century. Is that a deliberate choice, or has it come naturally?

A. It is very much intentional, even though the stories are set in modern day. Admittedly there is a certain "halo effect" to the people and the life of Watervalley. As I have mentioned before, I tend to be a "glass half full" kind of guy. Thus, I enjoy the challenge of writing stories that ultimately are funny, thought provoking, and life affirming. There's plenty of depravity and loss, even in a small town and even in my own life, that I could write about. And someday, maybe I will write one of those stories. But for now I only want to write novels that seek to illuminate those things that are good and bright and positive about small-town Southern life.

Q. The book's title comes from the Isaac Watts poem "How Doth the Little Busy Bee," a poem that might seem quaint to some readers. Can you explain your choice?

A. The poem is about living in the moment and making the most of each day. In the novel, this simple but challenging idea plays heavily in Luke Bradford's life. As noted above, he is a daydreamer . . . always thinking about what could or might be. But as his experiences unfold, he grows to understand the importance, the necessity, and the beauty of embracing each day . . . to make the most of each shining hour. By way of confession, the only thing wrong with the title is that I did not come up with it. My crafty editor, Ellen Edwards, suggested it after reading the story concept. It only took a second for me to realize it was a perfect fit. Darn it.

Curiously, Isaac Watts is best known as a hymn writer and wrote the popular Christmas carol "Joy to the World."

Q. What's next for Watervalley?

A. The next novel, *They Also Serve* (a tentative title, my editor reminds me), continues the romance of Luke and Christine Chambers but with some unexpected turns. When Christine comes across the journal she kept as a teenager, she can't help comparing Luke to the idealized future love she dreamed about in those early years. As well, Luke becomes embroiled in issues surrounding the small Mennonite community nearby and the town's military veterans, through which he sees some new sides of Watervalley. He also finds himself caught up in the trials and troubles of a new veterinarian as she struggles to win acceptance from the local farmers. John, Connie, and Estelle are still in the thick of everything happening in Luke's life . . . whether he wants them there or not.

Ultimately, Luke finds himself at the center of decades-old conflicts and resentments that threaten to permanently scar the Watervalley life he has come to love. At the same time, his relationship with Christine comes to an unexpected crisis point. Collectively, these adversities force Luke to make some tough decisions . . . about love, ambition, and the role he should play in the lives of those around him. He must define the terms by which he will live the rest of his life.

QUESTIONS
FOR DISCUSSION

1. What did you enjoy most about *Each Shining Hour*? What do you think you'll remember best about it?

2. Talk about what in the book made you laugh. Did anything make you cry?

3. Who is your favorite character, and why?

4. Several characters find redemption in this book or are on the way to finding it. Who are they, and how do they discover it?

5. How does life in Watervalley differ from where you live? How is it similar?

6. Discuss Luke's courtship of Christine Chambers. What do you like about it? In what ways is theirs a modern relationship and in what ways is it old-fashioned?

7. Discuss Connie Thompson's relationship with Luke; her sister, Estelle; John Harris; and Randall Simmons. What do we learn about her in this book that fills in some of her background? Is her

trepidation at the bank inconsistent with the strength she shows at other times?

8. Luke is bequeathed a vintage Austin-Healey. Have you ever received something valuable through an inheritance or bequest? What was it? What effect did it have on your life?

9. Oscar Fox's reputation was unfairly maligned for decades because of ignorance and misunderstanding. Discuss how that affected his descendants and other people in town, and how their lives might change once the truth is revealed. Discuss those who worked to bring the truth to light and what forces opposed their efforts.

10. What appeals to you about life in Watervalley? Can those qualities be replicated in your own community? Why or why not?

11. What do you think will happen in the next book? What do you want to happen?

AVAILABLE IN OCTOBER 2015

If you enjoy spending time in Watervalley,
you'll want to return for another visit.

DON'T MISS BOOK THREE OF
JEFF HIGH'S SERIES SET IN SMALL-TOWN
WATERVALLEY, TENNESSEE. . . .

As Luke Bradford's courtship of Christine Chambers continues along a bumpy path, he also gains insights into how the service of loyal townspeople holds the town together . . . and what happens when their sacrifices are forgotten.

Available from New American Library
wherever books and e-books are sold.